What It Could Be

BOOK 4 IN THE OFF ICE SERIES

GRAYCE RIAN

Book Cover Design by Kateryna Meleshchuk

Editing by Ciara Lewis

Song Lyrics by Alyssa Brigiotta

Dedication

To those who fight invisible battles:
You matter.
You are loved.
I'm so glad that you exist.

Content Note

Dear readers, this book was very heavy for me to write. It resurfaced a lot of emotions of past struggles and losses I've experienced. While writing this book felt cathartic for me, it does contain mature themes and potentially triggering content.

Please consider reviewing the following content warnings before continuing: religious depictions, descriptions of loss of a parent and friend (off-page), grief, depression, and on-page description of miscarriage, cancer diagnosis and treatment, infertility treatments and permanent infertility, hysterectomy, surrogacy, blackmail, revenge pornography, attempted violence, and on-page suicidal ideation. Despite being a romance novel with a happy ever after, readers should be aware of these themes.

CONTENTS

Playlist

Feels Like Home – Chantal Kreviazuk
You Say – Lauren Daigle
The Night We Met – Lord Huron
Pretty Little Poison – Warren Zeiders
Memory I Don't Mess With – Lee Brice
scared of my guitar – Olivia Rodrigo
Just To See You Smile – Tim McGraw
Are You Gonna Kiss Me Or Not – Thompson Square
Holy Smokes – Bailey Zimmerman
cardigan – Taylor Swift
Everytime - BBC Radio – Lewis Capaldi
Someone In This Room – Jessie Murph, Bailey Zimmerman
Landslide – The Chicks
Dangerous Woman – Ariana Grande
Falling Like The Stars – James Arthur
The One That Got Away – Brielle Von Hugel
Indigo (feat. Avery Anna) – Sam Barber
River - Acoustic – Myles Smith
Look After You – The Fray
Fight Like Hell - Piano Version – Warren Zeiders
It's All Coming Back to Me Now – Celine Dion
Love The Hell Out Of You – Lewis Capaldi
Soon You'll Get Better – Taylor Swift
Wouldn't It Be Nice – Kate McGill
Young And Beautiful - Lana Del Rey
That Part – Lauren Spencer Smith

ONCE - Wedding Version – David J

Worst Way – Riley Green

Overcome – Skott

Head Above Water – Avril Lavigne

Bigger Than The Whole Sky – Taylor Swift

While You're At It – Jessie Murph

Need You Now – Lady A

Just Another Day In Paradise – Phil Vassar

Holding On – Bailey Zimmerman

Remedy – Adele

Midnight Rain – Taylor Swift

Lost Without You – Freya Ridings

Poison & Wine – The Civil Wars

Don't Mind If I Do – Riley Green, Ella Langley

Religiously – Bailey Zimmerman

Without You – Warren Zeiders

I'm Never Getting Over You – Gone West

Yours For The Breaking – Bailey Zimmerman

see you later (ten years) – Jenna Raine

Chasing Cars – Tommee Profitt, Fleurie

Oceans (Where My Feet May Fail) – Hillsong UNITED, TAYA

I Will Wait – Candlelight Version – Matt Johnson, Amber Leigh Irish

Rainbow – Kacey Musgraves

I Get to Love You – Ruelle

Prologue

JACKSON

The opening chords of "Feels Like Home" by Chantal Kreviazuk play, which is the first dance song Bennett told me he and Scarlett had picked out, but what I wasn't anticipating was the voice that begins singing the lyrics.

I'm standing at the bar with my back to the stage, but I don't need to look to know who is singing right now.

No, not as her melodic tone floods my system and wraps around me like a warm embrace—a voice I'd know anywhere, anytime, because it's the voice that haunts me in my dreams.

Chills unwillingly work their way down my spine as the beautiful tone sinks into my very being.

But this can't be right. I must be imagining things as I've often done over the past decade. *She* can't be here. Not in Paris. Not at my big brother's wedding. She'd never do that.

She wouldn't, would she?

Turning around as if in slow motion, I'm shocked to find her on stage beneath one of the spotlights playing the piano and singing with her eyes closed, lost in the lyrics that are currently cutting me with each line she sings.

I block out everything happening around me, my sole focus tunneled in on the woman with raven hair that spirals down her back, nearly touching the piano bench she's sitting on.

This isn't right. This can't be happening. Not after all this time. Not here like this.

And then reality smacks me in the face like an uppercut to the jaw, causing my world to come to a standstill. She opens her eyes and turns her head to the side to smile at the happy couple dancing on the dance floor only for her face to go ghostly white as she takes in the groom, or rather, as she realizes *who* the groom is.

Without missing a beat, she turns her focus on the ivory keys beneath her fingers as she sings the last lines of the song.

Rushing past everyone, shoving a wide-eyed Griffin and Carson out of my way, I cross the dance floor, hardly comprehending the fact that my brother is dipping his bride as the song comes to a close.

The singer stands abruptly and tries to rush offstage but I'm there before either of us can realize what's happening.

My chest is heaving as I try to grapple the waves of emotions crashing into me.

What the actual fuck is *she* doing *here*? This has to be some sick joke, or maybe a revenge plot by Bennett for all of the crazy shit I've put him through over the years. But if it is, my brother's gone too far this time.

I look into her deep brown eyes that once looked at me with reverence as if I was her sole salvation. Those same mahogany eyes that stared back at me full of tears as the only girl I've ever loved broke me—broke *us*—without a moment's pause so she could pursue her dreams. Without me.

Taevin Gray left me and became a household name—a country star so bright that she now sells out stadiums in order to fit the large crowds of her adoring fans.

And even standing here before her a decade later, I can't help but fight the feelings resurfacing. My pathetic heart is at war with my head, screaming for me to walk away just like she did.

Like she tried to do once more just now.

Run. I should run. I need to run.

But I don't have more than a moment to attempt an escape because not even seconds after our gazes lock, Taevin pales further and her eyes roll to the back of her head.

"Tae!" I shout as I move to catch her before her head hits the ground. Her limp weight feels like nothing in my arms, causing a sharp chill of fear to run down my spine.

I search the faces surrounding us, begging for someone to help. One of the wedding guests calls out she's a doctor and comes rushing up to us, ordering me to set her down and move back so she can examine her.

Shoving people aside, a man who claims he came with her as her date kneels down beside her. I make my way over to the guy who looks oddly familiar, though I can't place him.

"What's the matter with her? What'd she take?" I ask, pulling him up by the lapels of his suit jacket.

He looks taken aback by my accusing tone. "Take? What are you talking about? She doesn't use." He pauses to scoff, somehow looking down his nose at me though he's several inches shorter than me. "She's not an addict. You of all people should know how the media can twist a story to fit their narrative. And you've played right into their hands." He shakes his head at me. "Such a disappointment, Jackson."

My eyes narrow at him in confusion and anger. "Who the hell are you and how do you know who I am?"

"I'm Kyle Blackwood, Tae's manager and one of her closest *friends*." I don't miss the emphasis he puts on their label as friends, but it doesn't mean I have to like the guy.

There's commotion behind us as the Paris paramedics arrive and begin transferring Taevin onto a stretcher.

Pushing my way past those surrounding her, I shout, "Step aside so I can get in the ambulance with her."

"No, I'll go," Kyle has the nerve to tell me.

"Over my dead fucking body," I growl out in a lethal tone that says I'm not fucking around.

He lets out a deep sigh. "Just stop making a scene, Jackson. I can't let you go, she'd never forgive me."

I get in his face to show him how serious I am. "I said step aside."

He crosses his arms, looking as if he'll refuse to let me by him. "I can't. And *you* can't."

"The fuck I can't. Step aside and let me be with my wife!"

"Your what?" Kyle's eyes nearly bulge out of his head, and it'd be funny if I wasn't ready to kill the fucker for standing in my way. Guess he isn't as close with Taevin as he thought.

Murmurs echo behind me at my declaration, and I hear my younger sister, Walker's voice ring out above the rest.

"Jax, did you just refer to Tae as your wife?" she asks incredulously.

Fuck. This is not how I wanted this to go.

But I don't have time to waste worrying about anything other than getting to Taevin right now.

"Move or I swear to god I'll hurt everyone standing in my way," I bite out in a chilling tone.

Bodies move out of my way, and I make it out of the back of the reception venue to where the paramedics are loading Taevin into the back of the ambulance. Taking my phone out of my pocket, I use a translating app to inform them I'm her husband.

Next thing I know, I'm sitting in the back of an ambulance, holding on to her limp hand, and praying, for the first time in over a decade, she's okay as we race through the streets in a foreign country.

"Please be okay, Thorn," I beg aloud while silently pleading.

Come back to me, baby. Stay so you can cut me all over again.

Breaking News

Country star Taevin Gray collapses at the wedding of NHL star Bennett Wilson

Country music's bad girl Taevin Gray reportedly collapsed after performing the first dance song at NHL star Bennett Wilson's wedding in Paris earlier this evening.

By LARA BRADLEY

Taevin Gray suffered what is being reported as a medical emergency.

The country music star, 28, was in Paris, France to perform at the wedding of NHL star Bennett Wilson to his bride, the new team owner of the Minnesota Wolverines, Scarlett Carlisle.

According to sources at the wedding, Gray was finishing the final lines of the happy couple's first dance song when she fled offstage and collapsed only moments later.

Gray was then rushed to the hospital via ambulance. Early reports on Gray's current medical status are still unclear at this time.

Country Know Now has reached out to Gray's reps for comment, but have not yet heard back.

To stay up to date on all the latest country celebrity news, subscribe below.

1

Taevin

Then

Ten Years Ago

Music has always been my preferred escape mechanism—the one thing that brings me peace no matter what I'm going through.

My fingers fly over the ivories of our church's new parlor grand piano, and I can't stop the carefree smile that takes over my face as the choir finishes singing alongside me. After weeks of practicing our arrangement of Lauren Daigle's "You Say," we did it. Overwhelming satisfaction hits me as pride warms my chest, and I take a moment to bask in this moment.

Opening my eyes, I stand from the piano to take my seat in the first pew where I've sat every Sunday for as long as my father's been the pastor of our church. Only my steps falter when my gaze lands on the new family that joined our church last month, or rather on their son, who sits between his mother and his sister in the pew behind mine. His broad shoulders and chest fill out his navy suit unlike any other boy my age attending our church or my school. When my eyes travel up the expanse of his chest, past where a tie hugs his corded neck, over his beautifully chiseled jaw, I'm shocked to find his sage green gaze fixed on me.

My stomach dips and my chest tightens involuntarily as a lopsided, boyish grin appears on his face; the sight has me fighting to regain my composure. Relief floods me as I turn my back to him and take my seat, though it's a fleeting reprieve because the hairs on the back of my neck rise when I feel his stare still on me.

I'm thankful I chose to wear my hair down today, my long black locks covering the flush creeping up my neck and heating the tips of my ears. His gaze feels like a warm caress burning my skin, which is a foreign feeling to me. It feels wrong—forbidden—the way my body has reacted each time I've seen him these past four Sundays.

His name, according to my father, is Jackson Wilson. I have yet to speak a word to him; I was too shy to introduce myself when he and his family thanked my father after the first service they attended.

But today, it seems I have no choice as we go around to express peace to those in the congregation surrounding us. Jackson doesn't give me the option to avoid him, as I had successfully done the past month. No, today his towering frame approaches me with an outstretched hand and that lopsided grin that has butterflies swirling to life inside my stomach.

"Peace be with you, Miss Gray," he rasps in a smooth baritone as I place my hand in his.

I gasp as our hands connect and chills erupt up my arm, leaving goosebumps in their wake. Forget butterflies, there is a full flock of songbirds flapping their wings and threatening to take flight. Bracing a hand on my abdomen, I faintly echo his words, "And may peace be with you."

With him so close, I realize he has to be nearly a foot taller than my five feet three inches. His light chestnut hair curls over his ears and at the nape of his neck.

Without taking his calloused hand from mine, he bends his neck so I don't have to look up as much and murmurs, "Tell me your name."

Only now, as I stare up into his captivating light green eyes, do I realize they're less sage and more like a dreamy sea glass—not simply green, nor blue, but a beautiful, calming combination of the two.

Before I get the chance to answer him, my father comes up to wish us peace, while quirking a stern brow at Jackson's hand still in mine. When he finally lets go, I quickly wipe my hand on the side of my sweater dress as if doing so will erase the feelings still twisting inside me.

We recite the Lord's Prayer before Holy Communion commences, and I retake my position at the piano, where I decide to remain for the rest of the service. But it doesn't seem to matter where I'm sitting, I can still feel his piercing gaze on me and it's causing a swirling in my stomach I'm not used to. I'm not quite sure I like it, but I don't necessarily dislike it either.

After the service, I make my way to the back of the church, where my father is shaking hands with the last of the members to leave. I tell him I'm going home to make some lunch before zipping up my jacket and starting the walk through the small flurries left over on the sidewalk.

It's pretty pathetic that at eighteen years old, I still don't have my license, but my father managed to guilt-trip me into waiting until the summer after high school to take my driver's test.

Once I get it, I'm gone.

I'm pulled from my thoughts when the smooth baritone voice from earlier says, "I think you forgot something, Miss Gray."

Staggering to a stop, I spin on my heels to find Jackson making his way toward me with his hands tucked into the pockets of his wool coat. With sunlight reflecting off his hair, it looks as if he has caramel highlights, and as he gets closer, I'm once again captivated by the puzzling shade of his eyes.

God, he's beautiful.

No. I shake my head and scold myself for thinking that way. I know boys as beautiful as him are no good for inexperienced wallflowers like me.

My thoughts are further solidified when he stands before me and smirks as if he's proud of himself for finding me again, because I swear, when he smiles, it's like I momentarily forget how to breathe.

"I don't believe I did," I tell him.

He rocks back on his heels, and his face seems to light up at the sound of my voice. But that can't be right.

"Oh, but you did. I didn't get your name," he clarifies.

Standing on my tiptoes, I try to look over his shoulder, but quickly realize he's too tall, so I look around him instead and find my father's watchful gaze on us.

"Look, Jackson," I start, and take a deep breath. "You seem like a nice enough guy, but I think it's best if we keep to ourselves when we're at church."

"So you can know my first name, but I can't know yours?" he questions.

Biting my lip, I fumble over my response. "It's—"

"Jackson! We're leaving. Now." Jackson's shoulders stiffen from the rough command.

He briefly closes his eyes, and when they open again, he softly says, "I'll be seeing you, Miss Gray."

As he retreats to join his family, I realize Jackson's intimidating presence isn't one I welcome at my church. I'm immediately ashamed and hit with guilt for feeling that way, but I can't help it. He threatens to disrupt the only place I've felt at peace since my mother passed away three years ago. It's within these walls that I still feel her here with me. Don't get me wrong, I know she's with me wherever I go, but it's in this church, a place we spent so much time together, that I feel her most.

There's this nagging feeling in the back of my mind, a strange pull toward him, urging me to get closer. I repress those thoughts and continue my walk home, cursing myself for almost getting ensnared by Jackson's tempting gaze. Nothing good could come from befriending a boy this close to me leaving this town, let alone one who looks like him.

2

Jackson

Although my family attends church every Sunday, I've never considered myself very religious. At eighteen and a senior in high school, I'm probably the furthest thing from a holy man there could be.

But I'm pretty sure the devil is tempting me right now, or maybe I've actually done something right in this life, and this is divine intervention, placing the girl from church in my path once again.

Not only is she in my path, but she's stepping out onto the ice at my playoff hockey game to sing the national anthem.

Taevin Gray.

That's what the announcer said her name was just before she stepped onto the ice.

My eyes don't leave her petite frame as she lifts the microphone and begins singing "The Star-Spangled Banner" a cappella. She looks adorable in her black, quilted parka that comes down to her knees and black leggings with crisp, white tennis shoes that match a white knit beanie with a fluffy ball on her head. My fingers itch to run through the silky strands of her long, raven hair curling past her waist. And I know if she were facing me right now, I'd get lost in her depthless chocolate eyes the way I have for the past month my family has attended her church.

I hone in on her, taking note of each detail and creating a mental snapshot of this pivotal moment—the first time I've seen her outside the

"

walls of our church. I've asked around about her at my school, questioning if perhaps she was younger than me. No one had heard of my nameless obsession, which made me wonder if she was homeschooled. Now, as she sings the national anthem at my hockey game against our rivals, the Christian private school in our town, I put the pieces together.

Visions of her in a royal blue jersey and hanging out with one of the guys on their team don't sit right with me. If she is wearing one of their jerseys, she's covering it up right now. She's always seemed so shy in church that I have a hard time picturing her dating an athlete, which doesn't bode well for my chances.

As if a player like me has a chance in hell with a good girl like her.

I'm pulled from my thoughts as she begins belting the bridge of the song, and the crowd erupts in cheers filled with hoots and hollers for her singing. I've only ever heard her sing at church accompanied by a piano and choir, but hearing her sing a cappella right now sends chills down my arms and spine. She's insanely gifted and vocally talented. Even the way she performs is mesmerizing, it's as if she were born to stand center stage and captivate an audience. I haven't looked at the flag once since she opened her mouth, and I doubt any of my teammates have either.

The crowd roars as she finishes the closing note, and I don't waste any time skating over to her before she can get off the ice.

"You're incredible," I tell her, stopping beside the door she's about to walk out of and leaning my hip against the boards.

I'm going for calm and collected when I'm feeling anything but. Seeing her this close again, breathing in her sweet, floral scent, has my heart beating in overdrive.

She looks shocked to see me. Her eyes widen as she looks side to side, like she's trying to find a way out of conversing with me.

Clearing the nerves from my throat, I continue, "I mean, I knew you could sing from church, but your voice is beautiful and your range is insane."

"Uh, thanks," she says shyly.

"Are you sticking around for the game?" I can't stop myself from asking her.

"I wasn't planning on it. I've never watched a hockey game before. I'm just here because my choir teacher asked me to sing the national anthem," she explains.

"Will you stay? Pretty please?" I bring my gloved hands together in pleading.

She tries to muffle her laughter behind her fluffy mittens, but I catch a glimpse of her small smile. The fact that I made her smile makes my chest swell with pride as if I'd just scored the game-winning goal.

"How about this? If you stay to watch your first hockey game, I'll score a goal for you," I suggest.

Lowering her mittens, she raises her eyebrows at me. "That's awfully pretentious of you. Are you always this cocky, Jackson?"

"Not cocky, confident, *Taevin*."

A slight gasp escapes as her name leaves my lips. It's the first time I've said it out loud, and I have to admit I love the way it rolls off my tongue.

"Why do I get the feeling that only someone who is cocky would make that correction?"

"Stick around and see if I can put my money where my mouth is, Tae." The nickname slips out, and she narrows her eyes slightly while fighting a grin, and it's probably one of the cutest things I've ever seen a girl do.

"Alright. I'll stay for the first half. But if you don't prove yourself, I'm leaving."

Standing to my full height, I inch closer to her. "There's no halves in hockey. Stick around for the first two periods, and if I score in one of those, you have to stay for the third and meet me after the game by the concessions."

She bites the inside of her cheek. "I don't know. That's a big ask."

"Wilson, let's go!" my coach barks out.

Sighing, I make one last attempt to get her to play along with my wager. "Come on. It's a big game for me. I could use some motivation."

Taevin gently shoves my shoulders back toward my bench. "Alright, alright. I'll stay, okay? Just go before you get me in trouble."

I smile widely, likely making me look like an idiot, but I can't find it in me to care. She's staying for the game, and I'm going to score her a goal.

My eyes trail her as she exits the ice, and instead of listening to my coach's final pregame pep talk, I watch her until she takes a seat in the opposing team's student section.

Well, hopefully, that won't get too awkward for her when she cheers for me.

Who am I kidding? I'll be lucky if she even stays.

I'm still riding the high from our victory as I walk out to the concession area with my hockey bag slung over my shoulder. I stop in my tracks when I notice a girl with long, jet-black hair waiting in line at the concessions.

Even as she turns and smiles up at me, I'm still convinced my mind is playing tricks on me.

Taevin's smile widens as she closes the distance between us and takes in my astonished expression. "Have you always been such an overachiever? Not one, but two goals, and a classmate of mine said you got an assist, which he told me is a good thing."

I'm slow to answer because I'm a bit surprised by her sudden willingness to talk to me. In each of our few—okay, two—interactions prior to tonight, she's been so shy and reserved. Clearing my throat, I nod. "He would be correct. And I've never been much of an overachiever, but I'm highly competitive, and knowing I needed to score in order for you to stick around gave me all the motivation I needed to play my ass off tonight. You must be my good luck charm."

I notice her cheeks redden, and I'm not sure if it's because I cursed or if it's because I called her my good luck charm. Either way, I make a mental note to refrain from swearing as much as possible, even though the sight of her blushing is cute as hell. *Heck*. Ah, shit. *Shoot!*

Nodding to the concessions that are closing, I ask her, "What were you planning on getting?"

She follows my gaze and sighs as they shut the rolling door of the concessions. "I was craving a sugary treat. But I guess it wasn't meant to be."

"Did you drive here?"

Turning back to face me, Tae shakes her head. "No, I don't have my license yet." Her cheeks heat further to an adorable shade of red.

"How about you let me drive you home, and on the way there, we can stop for ice cream? It's my guilty pleasure I only allow myself when we've won."

She looks hesitant, biting down on her bottom lip. "I'm not sure that's a good idea. I mean, no offense, but you're a complete stranger."

"Text one of your friends my name and picture or something, and tell them we're going to The Sprinkled Cone," I suggest.

Her eyes sparkle at that. "Oh, I haven't been there in years. My mom used to take me there every Sunday after church while my dad finished up his work."

I smile at her excitement. "See, now we've got to go. Go on, get your phone out," I tell her as I turn to the side and do my best Zoolander impression.

Her face scrunches up adorably like she's tasted something sour. "What are you doing? What's with that face you're making?"

"I'm posing for the photo you're about to send to your friend."

"That face you're making has you looking very suspicious. She'll probably think you've already abducted me and taken my phone."

"How about a FaceTime call then so she can see you're willingly going with me?"

"Am I though?" she questions.

"Are you not?" I toss back, loving this new back and forth.

"I'm pretty willing to get ice cream and have a warm ride home, but the jury's still out on the company I'll be keeping."

"Oh, Taevin," I say as I sling my arm around her shoulder. "I think you and I are going to get along great." As she taps on a contact and holds up her phone, I ask, "What's your friend's name?"

"Ryan."

My stomach sinks. Shit, did I read this all wrong? Does she have a boyfriend?

Before I can overthink this any further, her friend accepts the call, and on the screen appears a girl with short, blonde hair that's so light it almost looks white. Alright, so not her boyfriend. Her head is angled down, looking away from the screen, so I can't make out her facial features.

"Hey, Ryan!" Tae greets her overly enthusiastically.

Without looking up, the girl sighs. "Is it your dad? Do you need me to come do damage control again—oh, hello," Ryan says when she notices me now standing behind Taevin. "Who do we have here, bestie babe? And does he have a brother?"

Taevin's eyes widen to a comical size. "Oh my goodness, Ry! Stop it. This is Jackson Wilson. I just wanted you to see his face in case he turns out to be a serial killer instead of a high school hockey player taking me out for celebratory ice cream at The Sprinkled Cone."

I choke back a scoff. "If I were a serial killer, I wouldn't have suggested you call your friend or send a picture of me to her. And to answer your question, yes, I do have a brother."

"Semantics. You probably want to seem reasonable instead of the crazed psychopath you are," Taevin notes.

Her friend Ryan, whom I forgot was still on the phone, clears her throat. "You seem willing to go to your favorite ice cream place with him, but just in case your paranoia is correct, either call me or send me a proof of life picture later. Love ya!"

Shaking her head, Tae chuckles at her friend. "Alright, I will. Love ya too! Bye, Ry."

"Nice meeting you, Jackson Wilson, hockey player and hopefully not serial killer. Have Tae send me a picture of that brother of yours," she says before hanging up.

Tae slips her phone into her purse and turns to face me. "So, that wasn't weird at all."

"I agree, it wasn't. I liked meeting your friend. Hopefully, when you call her later for proof of life, the conversation is filled with how hard you're crushing on me." I toss her a wink before slinging my hockey bag back over my shoulder and making my way toward the rink exit.

"As if. I'm just in this for the free ice cream. What sane person would turn down free ice cream from a cute boy?" Her eyes widen and her blush spreads to her neck when she realizes what she's just said.

I can't stop myself from smiling like the Cheshire Cat. "And what sane person would turn down the opportunity to offer a cute girl he's shamelessly crushing on a ride home?"

Taevin bites her lip, hesitating for a moment, before she follows me out of the rink as we head toward my truck.

"Is this yours?" she asks.

"She is."

"She?"

"My sweet Frannie girl here is a 1975 Ford F-150 Supercab."

"You would have a red vehicle," she teases.

"What's that supposed to mean?" I ask, rounding the truck and opening the passenger door for her.

Instead of hopping in, she turns to face me, which puts us in closer proximity. There's something about this girl being in my orbit that twists me up inside, but in a good way. A way I'd like to get more accustomed to. Rolling her eyes, Taevin says, "It means I'm not surprised you'd have a flashy colored vehicle."

She's so fucking cute, I can't help but chuckle. "Ah, see, that's where you're wrong. My older brother Bennett and I have been working on restoring her for the past three years, and because of the sweat equity he put into her, I let him choose the paint color this past summer. He went with Candy Apple Red, of course."

"Of course," she echoes my sentiment. "So, does this thing even have seatbelts?" Tae questions as she hops into the cab of my truck.

"I wouldn't have allowed such precious cargo if it didn't," I tell her, leaning in and pulling said seatbelt across her lap before latching it and ensuring it's secured.

My cheesy as hell line has her rolling her eyes. "I'll bet you use that line on all the girls you give rides to."

I pinch my face in disgust. "That'd be weird considering the only other girl I've allowed inside Frannie has been my little sister, Walker."

I'm still standing between her and the open passenger door when her brown eyes shine up at me in disbelief. "You can't be serious?"

"About what?" I say somewhat defensively.

"You've never had another girl in the cab of your truck aside from your sister? Who, by the way, has one of the coolest names I've ever heard."

I smirk down at her. "You're the only girl I've ever even asked to get in my truck, Taevin Gray. Now, let's go get you that ice cream cone."

Shutting the passenger door, I quickly round my truck and slide in beside her to start it, making sure to crank up the heat when I do. Rubbing my hands together to warm them up, I bring them to my mouth and blow on them, before turning to Taevin and asking, "So, what's your favorite flavor of ice cream?"

Looking her over, I try to guess before she responds. My money is on her favorite flavor being vanilla with sprinkles on it, but she surprises me when she says, "Monster cookie in a waffle cone—there's just nothing better than the peanut butter flavor hitting my tongue followed by the crunch of the frozen M&Ms. What's yours?"

I'm left somewhat stupefied imagining said ice cream hitting her tongue, but I think she's completely clueless to her effect on me, so I try to pull my shit together. Clearing my throat, I reply, "Mint chocolate chip."

"Like your eyes," she murmurs under her breath, but with the way she's facing me, gazing into my eyes, I'm able to catch what she said.

"I've got mint eyes?" I ask, amused by how easily her cheeks heat.

Biting her bottom lip, she nods in response. "They're not quite blue, but they're not simply green either. They're almost like sea glass, don't you think?"

"I guess they kind of change in different lighting, so that'd be a good comparison."

"And the color is rare," she points out, and the breathlessness in her tone, combined with the way we're leaning toward one another, is leaving me heady.

I wonder what she'd do if I leaned in and kissed her right now. Would she turn away and get scared off? Would she tell me to get lost?

Before I can ponder that further, Taevin's phone lights up with an incoming call. She looks at the screen and says, "It's my dad, I'd better get this."

Swiping accept, she answers, "Hey, Dad. The game just ended, and I'm going to grab some ice cream on my way home."

I can't quite make out what is being said on the other end of the call, but when Tae lies about who she's getting ice cream with, I stiffen beside her.

Sure, her father is our pastor, but I didn't take Taevin as the lying teenager type. The thought that maybe she's only lying because she's with me, and perhaps I'm someone to lie about, is unsettling.

When she hangs up, she turns to me and it's as if she's read my mind when she says, "I'm sorry I lied about who I'm with to him. It's just that my dad is overbearing and extremely strict. If he knew I was with a boy right now, regardless of the fact that he's a member of our church, he'd come pick me up and drag me straight home. And then he'd likely ground me for the rest of senior year."

"So you're a senior?" I ask.

She shakes her and giggles at me. "Yes, I am. But is that all you got out of that?"

"No, I heard every word. Look, I get it. My dad is . . . strict too. I'm not upset you lied to your dad about me, just a little surprised by the action, is all."

She mock-gasps. "Oh, no. Don't tell me you've already put me in the perfect Taevin Gray, church choir girl box. How will I ever live up to your expectations now?"

I'm fucking obsessed with this little bit of personality I'm seeing from her. It's unexpected, yet refreshing at the same time.

Shifting into reverse, I rest my arm on the back of her seat and turn to pull out of the parking lot. "Come on, let's get you that waffle cone before I put you on a pedestal, Tae."

3

Taevin

Now

A steady beeping accompanies the pounding in my head and the heaviness of my eyelids as I struggle to open them.

It takes me a few moments to register that I'm in a hospital bed. And I'm clearly not alone because my right hand is warm and someone is holding onto it for dear life.

I slightly turn my neck and am surprised to find someone is hunched over with his head in his hand that isn't holding onto mine. And I'm even more shocked to realize that someone is not my manager, Kyle. No, this man before me has far too broad of shoulders to be Kyle.

"What happened?" I ask him, my voice hoarse.

He jerks his head up, and even though deep inside I'm not surprised, I'm still startled to see him next to me—holding my hand, no less—after all these years.

Jackson Wilson's mint green eyes lock on mine after almost a decade, and I'm stunned speechless by the desperation in them.

"Tae," he breathes my name as he takes my hand in both of his, bringing it to his lips, and then resting his forehead on our joined hands, before letting out what sounds like a sigh of relief. Placing one more chaste kiss on my hand, he meets my gaze again. "I was so worried. You were singing at my brother's wedding, and then you collapsed as you came off stage."

My brows furrow as the recollection sets in. What I'm still confused about is how I wound up performing the first dance song for his older brother's wedding in the first place.

"I thought the wedding was for a Mr. and Mrs. Carlisle?" I question.

"Yeah, Bennett decided to take his wife's last name," he clarifies, and I don't miss the slight twitch in his cheek as if he wants to smile. If he did, I know I'd get a glimpse of that gorgeous crescent dimple on his right cheek.

"That's sweet. I'm still not sure why I was asked to perform," I admit, albeit sheepishly. There's something about being in Jackson's proximity again that has me spinning.

"I'm honestly not sure why you were asked yet either. I didn't have any time to ask him before you collapsed."

"Yeah . . . about that—" I start but stop short when I realize *he* is the person beside me right now. "Where are Kyle and Braidy?"

"I'm going to guess that Braidy is your bodyguard who tried tackling me to the ground when he got to the hospital with your manager Kyle?" Jackson questions, brushing his hand down his jaw.

I take a moment to really take him in after all this time. His light brown hair is trimmed shorter on the sides now, but the top is still longer with tousled curls styled in a way I'm sure no one else could pull off. Instead of a clean-shaven face, he now sports neatly trimmed scruff that complements his features even more. His frame is broader, his muscles more pronounced after years of dedication to his sport. He looks sinfully handsome in a black tux with the bow tie undone, hanging around his neck. But those eyes, those piercing green-blue eyes, haven't changed. They're still framed by long, thick lashes most women would kill for. And they're still staring at me, pleading like they were when I ruined everything all those years ago.

"Braidy is still a bit green when it comes to the job—he's only been with me for about a week. I told Kyle a trip abroad probably wasn't the best orientation," I explain but bite my lip when I realize what I'm doing right now—making conversation with the one person I used to swear would never become a stranger, and yet, here we are.

A man in navy blue scrubs and a white jacket comes into my room and greets me, cutting off our reunion. "Hello, I am Dr. Dubois. How are you feeling, Taevin?" he asks with a French accent.

Swallowing past my dry throat, I tell him, "I won't lie, I've been better."

He nods and asks, "Do you know why you possibly fainted?"

I bite my lip and take a deep breath, trying to calm my nerves, though nothing seems to do that these days, or at least not since I received the news over a week ago.

"Yes, I know why." I pause, clearing my throat and trying my hardest not to sneak a glance at Jax as tears prick my eyes. "I was recently diagnosed with endometrial cancer, and I believe I may have fainted due to the pelvic pain I've been experiencing, along with possible side effects from a new medication my gynecologist started me on."

I don't miss the strangled gasp coming from where Jackson sits beside me.

The doctor nods pensively in acknowledgement. "I'm sorry to hear that. Do you have an oncologist you're seeing back home? I see you're from the United States. I've got a colleague who is a world-renowned gynecological oncologist."

"Thank you, but I'm scheduled with an oncologist in Nashville right when I get back," I inform him.

"Okay. Let me know if you'd like her information for a second opinion. She works out of Mayo Clinic in Minnesota," the doctor offers.

This all feels so clinical, almost making me feel detached from the reality at hand.

"We'll take her information, please," Jackson surprises me by joining the conversation, his voice gravelled with emotion. My head snaps to look at him, and I don't miss the way his shoulders have stiffened and there's a look on his face I haven't seen in years, though I can't quite place it at the moment.

The doctor gives Jackson her information and then asks if I have any further questions. When I tell him I don't, he excuses himself, and as soon as the door clicks shut, I turn on Jackson.

"We'll take her information? No, *we* will not. You heard the doctor, he said his colleague works in Minnesota." I huff in exasperation.

Jackson's penetrating gaze meets mine. "Yes, you're right, I heard him correctly. And isn't it a great thing that you have family who live in Minnesota?"

I scoff at his audacity. "I can't live with my dad to receive treatments. I have a plan back in Nashville, one that involves me living in my own home while I go through treatment and recover."

"I wasn't referring to your dad, Tae. I was referring to your husband. You can live with me—"

Now it's my turn for a shocked gasp to escape. "My *what*?" I shout, cutting him off.

"Husband," he repeats matter-of-factly.

My head spins, and I feel as if I'll be sick. "That's not possible. I signed the annulment paperwork nearly ten years ago," I whisper.

"Which would've been fine had I filed the paperwork. But considering our wedding was completely legal, without any mental incapacity or intoxication, we didn't qualify for an annulment in Minnesota," he explains in a monotonous tone.

"So what you're trying to tell me is that you and I are *still married*?"

"It would seem so, which means I'd like my wife to move in with me so she can receive the best care at our disposal." He flexes his hand as if he wants to reach for mine again.

I don't give him the chance as I toss mine in the air. "You expect me to just upend my life and move in with my estranged husband after not being together for the past decade?"

When he speaks again, his tone is softer. "How long have you known? Do you know what stage yet?"

Wringing my hands together nervously, I tell him, "I was diagnosed a little over a week ago. From the testing and biopsies they've done, they've diagnosed me with stage two endometrial cancer. They've confirmed it has spread to my cervix, but otherwise, it seems to have been contained. I'm scheduled to have surgery in two weeks, and then I'll begin chemotherapy after I freeze my eggs. It's going to be okay. *I'm* going to be okay. I've got a plan, and that treatment plan will be carried out in Nashville, not Minnesota."

He takes a moment to rake his fingers through his hair before he sighs and says, "I'm glad you have a plan, but respectfully, I think you should seek a second opinion. How about this, if you come back to Minnesota with me and you see this world-renowned oncologist, I'll give you the divorce no questions asked after you finish treatments."

Narrowing my eyes on him, I ask, "Why after I finish treatments?"

Jax sighs, closing his eyes as if he's trying to regain his composure. When he opens them, I feel his serious gaze burning into me like a brand—one I was once proud to bear. "Because I'll respect your wishes to their full extent while you're receiving treatment. As your husband, I'll be able to make decisions on your behalf if need be. And if we were to divorce *now*, those decisions would likely fall on someone else's shoulders."

"You'd respect all of my wishes, no matter if you agree with them or not?" I question, my tone riddled with disbelief.

"Aside from you seeking treatment alone in Nashville, yes, I will respect all of your wishes." He says the words so simply, though if he's anything like the guy he used to be, I know Jackson Wilson is the most stubborn man alive, and he will ask me to bend to his will.

"What if trying to see this new surgeon delays my treatment?"

"I think the fact that you're a famous country star and I'm a professional hockey player may help us pull some strings."

"Why are you so hellbent on me moving in with you? You understand I'm going to have a major surgery and will need to recover, right?"

"Meaning you'll need someone there to help you while you're recovering. That someone will be me."

I fold in on myself at the thought of needing someone else to care for me. It makes me feel weak and desperate—feelings I've recklessly run from over the past decade. "But it won't be. Don't you start your season soon?" I question, a little put out by his insistence.

He sighs heavily and pinches the bridge of his nose. "I'll have to report to preseason training camp in mid-September." He drops his hand and continues, "But I play professionally for Minnesota now, so I'll work out a schedule. If I need to take a leave of absence, I can do that too."

Jax tells me this as if I haven't followed his career since he left for Harvard.

"No. Jackson, no," I say firmly. "A leave of absence won't be necessary. If this world-renowned surgeon is still able to do my surgery the first week of August, I should be back on my feet like normal before your training camp."

He gives me a tight-lipped nod and focuses on his folded hands in his lap. "I'll go make some calls and see if I can't get an appointment scheduled for Monday morning."

"That's not going to work, J. The medical field doesn't bend to your whim."

"My father has a lot of influence in Rochester," he explains, and my stomach sinks and twists just thinking about the senator.

"No, please don't use his name. If you have to throw around ours, be my guest. Just not his," I plead.

He lifts his head and narrows his eyes at my pinched tone. I feel naked under his searching gaze until he finally nods curtly in acknowledgment before asking, "Can I get you anything?"

God, and there he is. The sweet, caring guy I fell head over heels in love with at eighteen. How, after all this time, is he affecting me in this way? My stomach somersaults at the thought of being in his proximity again. Of *living* with him.

But it's also the perfect reality check that I'm far from the innocent, put-together girl he loved back then. So as I shake my head, I remind myself: no matter how successful I've become, I'll always be an empty shell of the girl I once was. Too much has happened—keeps happening—for him to ever see me as he did at eighteen under the stars in the back of his pickup truck.

4

Jackson

Now

In the back of the ambulance on the way to the hospital, I remember thinking I'd never felt more helpless in my life.

But I was so fucking wrong.

Had I known what I was about to hear, I would've told myself to brace for earth-shattering news and the crushing fear now consuming my every thought.

Cancer.

One single word has forever changed my life—will forever change *her* life. The woman I've loved for over ten years has stage two endometrial cancer and there's not a damn thing I can do to make her better.

Well, that's hopefully not true. I refuse to remain helpless. I still can't believe I convinced Taevin to get a second opinion in Minnesota.

They kept her overnight for fluids and monitoring, and she was discharged a few hours ago.

I got my shit from my hotel suite and booked a private jet while she grabbed her things and tried to brush off Braidy's protections and evade Kyle's interrogation. I'm not sure what the deal is between her and Kyle; she said he's her manager, but he seemed more upset about the prospect of her going with me than that she wasn't going back to Nashville with him. He didn't even argue the fact that she said she didn't need Braidy to come and draw more attention to her when she had me to protect her, just seemed more upset that he too was being left behind.

Looking over at the plush seat beside me, I'm still shocked to see her just right there, sitting within reach and breathing the same air as me, after all this time.

Her raven hair is piled into a messy bun on top of her head, and some time over the past few hours the plane has been in the air, she got overheated and ditched my hoodie she'd borrowed. Now, as she uses said hoodie as a pillow, I take in her resting form. She looks so peaceful, and I hope for her sake she's able to sleep for the remainder of the flight.

Instead of taking a nap, my eyes trace the lines of her face, noting the differences of the woman sleeping before me from the girl I fell in love with a decade ago.

In place of her typically makeup-free skin I saw when we were together, Taevin has dark eyeliner framing her eyelashes and to top off the look is what has become her signature berry lipstick that has had my mouth watering since I watched her apply it on the way to the airport. It almost felt like she was applying her armor as she prepared for battle; though, I'm not sure if she was going to war with the paparazzi that waited for us at the private hanger, or if she's gearing up for her battle with cancer.

My stomach sinks further at the daunting prospect of her impending fight. Taevin shouldn't have to do this, especially not after watching her own mother wither away from cancer when Tae was only a teen.

And what the fuck was that back at the hanger? I knew Tae was famous, but I don't think I quite comprehended just how renowned she is globally. Both paparazzi and fans swarmed her at the private airport, and I had to step in front of her several times to shield her from the masses.

Blinking back to the present, I continue to take in the differences between eighteen-year-old Tae and the woman beside me. Possibly the most noticeable change from the church-going choir girl I knew back then is the half-sleeve of black ink covering the upper half of her left arm.

I'm no stranger to tattoos myself, and have them covering a lot of my body's landscape, but even knowing she had them doesn't prepare me for seeing them up close. Sure, everyone with eyes knows the famous Taevin Gray has these as well as several others covering her back, but as I take in their intricate detail, I'm mesmerized.

Her upper arm and over her shoulder is filled with black and white roses. I don't miss the way the stems weave together and are full of thorns. The sight throws me back in time to when I gave her that nickname.

"Your perfume drives me crazy," I tell her, inhaling deeply before placing open-mouth kisses on her collarbone. "Roses." Kiss. "Cinnamon." Kiss. "And hazelnut." Kiss.

I'm spurred on when she leans her head to allow me more access to her neck, and the adorable snort she lets slip has me chuckling against her skin before she informs me, "That's my hazelnut coffee creamer, not my perfume. And the roses are an homage to my mom; they were her favorite. Alright, back to the matter at hand, Superman. Less talking, more kissing."

I gently bite down on her collarbone at her use of that ridiculous nickname. "Why do you insist on calling me that all of a sudden? I don't have a hero complex."

That comment seems to spur another snort from her. "You totally do! You're always looking out for everyone but yourself. But that's not why I call you that—well, not the only reason."

Motioning for her to continue, I say, "Come on, spill. Why do you call me that?"

"Aside from the fact that you're so selfless, you're also like Clark Kent to me. Hockey player by day, musician by night. I can't believe you've been holding back the truth from me for so long."

"Does that make you my Lois Laine?"

"Nah. I'm more of the helpless heroine you have to save."

"And what am I saving you from, Thorn?"

"Thorn?" she questions instead of answering mine.

"Yeah, you're being a thorn in my side right now by delaying my reward for winning my game this afternoon. Also, I think I prefer when you call me Bear."

"Wow . . . How sweet of you. You're a real modern-day Romeo."

"Romeo and Juliet's love story ends in tragedy, Tae. There are no tragedies in the cards for us."

My stomach sours at how wrong I was to say that back then just as Taevin stirs beside me. She blinks her eyes slowly and stiffens slightly when she realizes where she is. Then she sits up and, to my disappointment, puts my sweatshirt back on, covering her skin I hadn't finished detailing to memory.

Once she settles, I shift in my seat to face her. "I've been thinking about something you said yesterday. You mentioned your surgery isn't scheduled for two weeks—was there a reason they needed to wait?"

She yawns before answering. "No, there's not a medical reason. I have a summer festival I'm headlining this weekend in Texas."

"The Summer Stampede Festival?"

"Yeah, how did you know?"

I shrug, feigning nonchalance. "You've performed there for the past six summers."

There's a slight frown on her face now, but she slowly nods her head. "I guess it has been that long. Wait, how'd you know that?"

I roll my lips together as I mull over whether or not I want to disclose my secret to her. "I was in Texas six years ago for Carson's wedding, and I may or may not have watched you open for Mason Corbin."

Her eyes widen in shock. "What? Jax, that was my first big show. It was when I sang—"

She starts and cuts herself off when she realizes what she was about to tell me, but she doesn't need to continue for me to know what she was going to say. That was the first time she sang her debut single "Martyred." I'm not sure she realized then that it would become a hit that shot her into stardom. Taevin had already signed a three-album deal with Tambourine Records, but that single was what started her on the path to becoming a household name.

"Back to my original question—why are you delaying surgery?"

"I can't just back out of my commitments, Jackson. My fans are counting on me to perform."

She sure didn't have a problem backing out of her commitment to our marriage the moment she thought she had a better opportunity. Instead of saying that, I swallow past the bitter taste of resentment threatening to surface. "I believe you once told me sometimes you have to put yourself first, or am I remembering that wrong? It's been so long since the night you left."

"Jax—"

"It's fine, Tae. I just think if there were ever a time to put yourself first, it'd be when you're about to endure the fight for your life."

"My gynecologist in Nashville assured me a week or two would be okay."

"But it's not just a week; it'll be almost three between when you were diagnosed and your surgery."

She places her hand on my forearm, and the moment her skin touches mine, goosebumps ripple up and down my arm. When she realizes what she's doing, she pulls away far too quickly for my liking.

Sighing, she says, "I've made my decision regarding the festival, J. You said you'd respect my choices in this."

Closing my eyes to hide my frustration, I reply, "Fine. You're right, it's ultimately up to you. But I'm coming with you. I don't like the thought of you performing a full set after what happened yesterday at Bennett's wedding."

I don't point out the fact that yesterday was only one song, not a full set list, because she knows as well as I do the difference the festival in the summer heat will be and the toll it will take on her body.

"If you insist," she replies, rolling her eyes.

"I do," I answer curtly, narrowing my eyes at her snark.

Now it's Tae's turn to shift in her seat to face me. "Perhaps I should put you to work if you're coming along. Wanna be my water boy? Hmm, no, maybe you should be my bodyguard since you've taken it upon yourself to dismiss Braidy while you're with me. Or, no! You can grab your Gibson when we're in Minnesota and you can bring it to Texas. When's the last time you played, J?"

Shaking my head, I don't answer her and look ahead at the seat in front of me instead.

"Come on, don't go quiet on me now. You got to ask your questions, don't I get to ask mine?" she pushes.

"It's been a while since I've played," I answer her without elaborating, which only further spurs her on.

"A few days? A week? Wait, why didn't you perform the first dance song at Bennett's wedding? Why did I?"

She huffs in annoyance when I don't respond.

Rolling my eyes at her insistence, I tell her, "He asked, and I turned him down. I haven't performed since around Griffin and McKenna's wedding."

"Oh my goodness, I didn't realize they got married. They were so cute together the summer they started dating," Tae gushes before asking, "When did they get married?"

Clearing my throat, I mutter, "Seven years ago."

Tae's eyes widen with shock, and it'd be comical if the truth weren't so pathetic. "I'm sorry, I think I misheard you. Seven months ago?"

I shake my head once. "Years."

She smacks my arm. "Jackson Charles Wilson! Why on earth haven't you performed in seven years?"

"Can we just drop it?"

"No! Tell me right this instant."

"Because of you!" I whisper-hiss.

She shrinks back. "Me?"

"Yes. Because every time I strum a chord, or sing a line, I think of you and everything I'll never have because you left and didn't choose me."

Tears well in her eyes, and I'm immediately filled with regret. Regret for losing my composure and regret for losing her all those years ago. I don't know how to be with her now. I don't know how to hide my resentment and frustration with her for leaving me behind for greener pastures. My life has been nothing but depressing, muted grays since she left it. There are few things that pull me from the abyss I've spiraled into over the past decade.

When we land and I take my phone off airplane mode, it begins buzzing incessantly with incoming texts.

I take a deep breath and open the thread with my sister first.

Walker:

> Is Tae okay, J?

Walker:

> I'm thinking of you both. Please let me know if you need anything!

Walker:

> Also, don't think just because you had to leave that you're going to get out of talking about this!

Rolling my eyes at her antics, I close out of her thread without replying and open the message from my mom.

Mama:

> I love you, sweetheart. Please let me know when you land safely. Take care of our girl! Xx

My mom's message makes me smile. She always did love Taevin like she was her own. I'm sure I'll have a lot of answering to do with her about how her baby boy was married for nearly a decade without her knowing. Mom is the only one I told everything to before I left Paris, with Tae's permission of course. I send her a quick reply that we landed before exiting my thread with her.

My stomach sinks when I see my father texted me.

Senator Satan:

> My office when you get back to Minnesota.

He's a delusional prick if he thinks I'm going anywhere near his home office. I've managed to keep out of there for the past seven years, and I intend to keep it that way. There's a fucking reason he wasn't allowed to come to my brother's wedding after all.

Just then, my phone buzzes with one final text from my brother.

Benny:

> You're fucking welcome. Don't let her go this time, J.

I grit my teeth at his assumption. I never let Taevin go—not ten years ago, and I'm sure as hell not about to now.

When I made the offer to give her a divorce after her treatment, I did so knowing there's not a chance in hell I'm going to let her go without a fight. While she's battling for her life, I'm going to do the same for our future together.

Tae will always be the love of my life, and I refuse to let her be the loss of it.

5

Taevin

"**P**inch me!" I tell Ryan later that evening over FaceTime after Jackson dropped me off.

"Would if I could, babydoll, but considering you're there and I'm here, I'll just ask instead. What happened that I need to pinch you?" she asks.

Propping my phone on my nightstand, I roll onto my stomach and hold my hand up and begin counting. "Well, for one, I'm thankfully alive."

She steeples her hands together and laughs. "Whew, thank the big man upstairs."

Rolling my eyes, I hold up a second finger. "For two, I had the greatest night of my life." Now I'm kicking my feet in the air and trying to muffle my squeals so my dad won't hear.

"Girl, are you on an ice cream high? You literally only called me an hour ago to tell me you were going. Drop the dramatics, it was the greatest *hour* of your life. Which, props to him for lasting that long."

I cover my face with my hands, my cheeks flaming red with embarrassment. "Ryan! Oh my goodness! No, that's not what I meant!"

"Not yet, maybe. So, did he kiss you goodnight? Make out with you a bit? Oh, what kinda car does he drive?"

"An old Ford truck from, like, the seventies or something."

"Does that mean it has a bench seat? Oh my god, did you sit in the middle? Did he lay you down on it? Did you get to second base?"

Shaking my head somewhat solemnly, I whisper, "We didn't even kiss."

"Wait? *What?* It was the single greatest hour of your life and he didn't even kiss you?"

I shake my head again.

"Did he try to?"

"No. He did kiss my hand, though." My tone is somewhat defensive.

"Wait, like, he grabbed your hand and kissed it like some prince kisses a girl's hand?" Ryan questions.

"No, like he held my hand as he walked me to the house next door because I told him if my dad caught him walking me to my door, it wouldn't be good. And then just before we got to my driveway, he pulled me into him with our joined hands and kissed the back of my hand."

Butterflies swarm to life as I remember the coy smile that curved his lips right before he pressed them to my hand. I've got nothing else to compare it to—because what should be shocking to no one, I've got zero experience with boys—but it gave me the same rush as singing in front of an arena full of people.

"Oh em gee! That's big for you, T!"

"I know. And if I'm being honest, I kind of wanted him to kiss me." I hide my face behind my hand, embarrassed I admitted that out loud.

"Kind of?"

Peeking through my fingers, I see Ryan motion her hand in a circle as if to say *come on, out with it.* "Okay, I really, really wanted him to kiss me. Maybe I had bad breath or something. He had mint chocolate chip, so I know his breath wasn't the reason."

"Maybe he didn't want to move too fast?"

I scoff in disbelief. "Have you seen him? Of course you did, what am I even talking about? You saw him on FaceTime, and that was him right after a hockey game."

Ryan nods her head in agreement. "I will say, he is, like, stupid hot."

See, Ryan knows. I can't even find it in me to be jealous over her comment because it's one hundred percent accurate. "Exactly! So I'm sure girls throw themselves at him all the time. It can't be because he didn't want to go too fast. He just probably doesn't like me like that."

"Wait, did he ask you to get ice cream, or did you ask him to go with you?"

"No, he did after he asked me to wait for him until after his game, but only if he scored."

"That's quite the gamble. Did the hockey boy say anything else?"

Twisting a strand of hair, I think about what Jax had shared tonight. "He mentioned I was the only girl who'd ever been in his truck aside from his sister."

Ryan sits up and slaps her bedding. "Babe, that's major! And maybe you'll be the first and last girl he fucks in it too." She waggles her eyebrows in an exaggerated way that has me rolling over with laughter.

"What the actual heck is going on with you?"

"I'm pent up and doubly so when I think of how lonely you are."

"I'm not lonely, Ry!"

"Be so for real right now. You've never even been kissed. As far as I know, tonight is the first time you've held hands with a boy."

"So? That doesn't mean I'm lonely. Besides, I've got you."

"You do. For life. But I'm your ride or die, not the one who's going to get your blood pumping and heart thundering in your chest before you're kissed for the first time."

"I still don't see how that makes me lonely."

"I've just felt it since your mom, Tae. She was practically your whole world, and then in such a short time, she was taken from you. I'm not saying your hockey boy will become your whole world or be the love of your life, but you genuinely looked like you wanted to say yes to going with him tonight. And I think that's a really freaking big deal."

Pursing my lips, I mull her rationale over in my mind before admitting, "It is. But as much as I think he's cute and wildly talented being able to balance on tiny blades, I don't think I'm wrong in saying I don't think he's into me that way."

"Don't take this the wrong way, but if he met you for the first time at church, and he knows you're the pastor's daughter, you're probably giving off virgin vibes. I think he's into you and he's just respecting you by going at your pace."

Shaking my head at her foolishness, I mumble, "Gosh, I don't even know why I care in the first place. It's not a good idea to get involved with someone so close to graduation. You and I have said it from the start: when September comes, we're leaving this town for good and never looking back."

Ryan knows better than anyone my need to escape from this town. Since my mom's death, my dad has become even more overbearing and strict. He tries to control my every waking hour, and I've grown tired of trying to maintain my perfect persona around him. I'm a teenage girl who should be trying new things, testing the boundaries, and making mistakes. It's not like I want to go out and try drugs, for goodness' sake. But it also wouldn't kill me to talk to a cute boy and get ice cream with him—tonight being the perfect example. Here I am, still alive and well in my room after doing just that with Jackson.

"So don't make it something bigger than it needs to be with him. Keep things casual, start slow, and see where things go," Ryan suggests.

"Casual?" I chuckle as I roll back onto my stomach. "You say that as if I have any experience interacting with boys whatsoever. How exactly am I supposed to keep things casual?"

"I don't know. Tell him you're looking for someone to help you check off your *Tae's things to do before college* list. There are so many things on there I can't possibly help you with."

My brows wrinkle in confusion. "The only one on there you actually couldn't help with was going on a ferris wheel ride, though I think it'd help you get over your fear of heights like I'm planning to do."

"Yeah, about that. So, if you look at your journal, I may have added a few things to the list on your behalf. I felt like it was my duty as your best friend to push you outside your comfort zone."

"Ryan . . ." I draw out her name as I hesitantly open my bedside drawer and lift the bottom to grab my journal from the hidden compartment I'm fairly certain my dad has no idea exists.

Shuffling through the pages, I find my list.

Tae's things to do before college:

    1. *Go on a ferris wheel ride*

    2. *Go to senior prom*

    3. *Get my driver's license*

    4. *Sing solo in front of a crowd*

    5. *Perform at a venue*

"See, I'm just fine, I already checked off number four on my own tonight. I sang the national anthem in front of a crowd."

"I feel like that only half counts. It should be one of your original songs. Make that an addendum for number five."

However, now as I scan the rest of the list, I notice it has in fact been added to with five new items written in my best friend's signature, all-caps handwriting.

TAE'S THINGS TO DO BEFORE COLLEGE (RY'S VERSION):

1. LEARN TO PLAY GUITAR

2. SNEAK OUT PAST CURFEW

3. GO ON A DATE

4. HAVE FIRST KISS

5. HAVE A BIG "O" (hopefully from someone else)

"Are you kidding?" I ask as I turn the journal around so Ryan can see it, as if she doesn't already know.

She shrugs as if it's not a major violation of my trust, though at this point, there really are no boundaries to our love for one another, so she already knows there's no chance I'll be upset with her over this.

"Consider it a fun little social experiment before we leave in the fall. Besides, you should thank me that I kept things mostly PG."

I raise my eyebrows at her. "Number ten is most certainly not PG."

"Thus, I said *mostly* PG. I bet your hockey boy could help you with a few of those things." Ryan waggles her brows suggestively, and I wish I could shove her through the phone.

"I'm sure he could, but it doesn't mean it's going to happen."

"Never say never, bestie," she singsongs before we tell each other good night and hang up.

Setting my phone down on my side table, I grab a pen out of my nightstand and update my list as I cross off number four from tonight's game. I also add in parentheses that number five needs to be an original song.

Knowing sleep is going to evade me, I shut my journal and place it back in its hiding spot. Once I've changed and gotten ready for bed, I'm just plugging my phone into the charger when there's a knock on my bedroom door.

Without opening it, my dad says, "Good night, Taev."

"Good night, Dad. Love you."

He doesn't say it back, which isn't an uncommon thing for him to do. My mom was the one to show her love through hugs and cuddles, but she was also the one to express her love verbally every chance she got. I suppose I continue to tell him I love him, even when he doesn't say it back, because I strive to be like my mother in every small way I can be. I'm not sure if that's harder on my dad at times, because she was the love of his life, but regardless, I'll continue to tell him just the same.

Sighing, I dive under the covers and adjust my pillow before remembering I need to set my alarm. Just as I've set it, my phone buzzes.

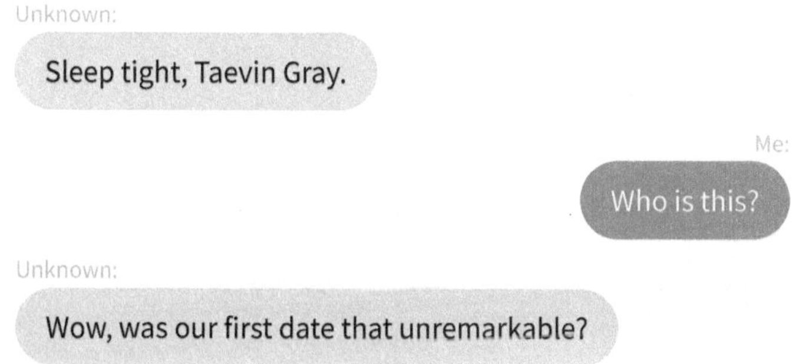

I smile like a fool and have to stop myself from squealing at the butterflies unleashing at the realization that Jackson somehow managed to get my phone number.

Me:

I learned another new hockey term tonight.

Jackson:

whew so you do know who this is.

Jackson:

What term is that?

Me:

Hat trick. And if you'd like to take me on my first date, I think you should have to score one first.

Jackson:

Did whoever taught you that term also inform you that hat tricks are really tough to get, especially during playoffs?

Chuckling to myself, I consider how to play this before typing my response.

Me:

Am I worth the hard work and effort?

Jackson:

Undoubtedly, yes. Consider it done. I've got a game Saturday afternoon. If my good luck charm is there, I'll score her a hat trick and take her out for our first *official* date after. What do you say?

Me:

I'll be sure to wear a hat I don't mind throwing onto the ice.

Jackson:

Atta girl! Sweet dreams.

I bring my phone to my chest and grin at my ceiling like an idiot. It's a long shot, but I think I may have my first official date this weekend. Look at me checking off one of Ryan's items like it's no big deal.

6

Jackson

I 'm still riding the high from our win and my hat trick when I walk into the lobby with my bag slung over my shoulder and holding a white knit hat in one hand and my hockey sticks in the other.

My face lights up when I catch sight of her dark hair as she stands with her back to me while talking to Ryan. I take her in for a moment, loving the way her puffy coat nearly swallows her whole, before making my way over to where the two of them are laughing together in the corner.

"You have the best laugh I've ever heard," is what surprisingly slips from my lips when I reach her instead of literally anything else.

Taevin startles, but when she realizes it's me who gave her the compliment, an enigmatic smile lights up her face.

"If it isn't Mr. Hat Trick himself," Ryan says in a teasing tone. "Maybe if you're funny on your date tonight with my girl, you'll earn more of her laughter."

I quirk a brow at Ryan. "Your girl?"

"Yep, Tae's my girl. And you're the lucky son of a gun who gets to take her on a date. I will say, though, you made that hat trick look easy."

Taevin nods in agreement. "You did. Almost too easy—makes me wish I would've challenged you a bit more."

"Not easy at all. I was just highly motivated," I admit, shifting my bag on my shoulder to compensate for the sheepishness threatening to take over. This feeling is not one I recognize, as I typically toe the fine line between confidence and cockiness.

Almost as if Taevin knows I need it, she pivots the conversation. "I overheard someone say there's scouts here."

It's my turn to nod once. "Yeah, from Harvard and Emery University."

"Aren't those both near Boston?" Ryan asks before aiming a knowing smile Taevin's way.

"They are. Well, Harvard is in Cambridge, but Emery is right in the heart of Boston."

"What a coincidence. Taevin happens to plan on attending—" Ryan is cut off when Taevin slaps a gloved hand over her friend's mouth.

Taking a mental note to ask her about that later, I shake my head at their ribbing. They remind me a hell of a lot of how my friend Carson and I act around each other.

Speaking of my best friend, he spots me from across the lobby and saddles up beside me.

"What the heck, J? You flew out of the locker room like a bat outta hell before we even got to celebrate. It's not everyday a guy scores three goals in one game—let alone a playoff game that earns us a ticket to state," he says, playfully shoulder checking me.

It's only then that he notices the two girls standing in front of us. "Well, hello ladies. I'm Carson, or Carsey as he likes to call me. And you are?" he asks them.

Tae holds out her gloved hand for him. "Taevin. And this is my best friend, Ryan. Pleasure to meet you, Carson."

"Pleasure's all mine. Wait, did you say your name is Taevin?"

"I did."

Carson's eyes widen to a comical size before he slowly turns to look at me. He's the least subtle person I've ever met, and it shows when he mouths, "Like *the* Taevin?"

I roll my eyes before nodding once.

"Oh, shit. You're the girl that has my Jaxy Bear completely smitten."

See? About as subtle as a gun.

Taevin's melodic laughter fills my ears again and I'm already obsessed with the sound. "Jaxy Bear? Oh, I think I like that. Might need to borrow that one," Taevin tells him.

Carson sends her a playful wink. "Stick with me, kid. I've got all the best gossip and embarrassing stories about our boy."

"Noted," she says, tapping on her temple. "But I wouldn't say he's *our* boy. We haven't even had our first date quite yet—it could go horribly."

"It won't," I state with more confidence than I feel. It's very possible that I blow it with her—she already has a way of knocking me off kilter. I'm just hoping I got a good enough feel for what she might like when we got ice cream the other night that she enjoys herself tonight.

Holding out her hat, I step toward her. "I believe this is yours. And speaking of our first date—we'd better get going."

She grabs her hat from me and a slight blush creeps up her cheeks. "Thanks." Turning to Ryan, Taevin asks, "I'll see you tomorrow morning at church, right?"

Ryan wraps her in a hug and murmurs something in Taevin's ear I can't quite make out, but I think she said something about checking things off. Again, I find myself wondering what that's all about.

Once they say their goodbyes, I place my hand on the small of her back to lead her out to my truck. And while there's a massively puffy coat between us, being this close to her is still a heady feeling.

Only after I've made sure she's buckled into my passenger seat and I've turned the key to start my truck does Taevin turn to me and ask,

"So, where are we going? You could've given a girl a head's up. All your text said when I asked what I should wear was something that made me feel comfortable, yet here you are in a suit."

"We have to wear suits for playoff games. I brought a change of clothes but then I left them in my truck so I figured I'd just change once we get there."

"And where is *there*?"

A sly grin spreads across my face. "You'll just have to wait and see."

I grab my phone to put some music on before pulling out of the parking lot as the playlist I selected quietly plays in the background. After Bennett and I got Frannie running like a dream, my next big investment was installing an updated sound system.

Taevin and I talk about school and what classes we're in, but as I take the exit for our first destination, "Just To See You Smile" by Tim McGraw comes on and I can't resist turning up the volume.

I'm drumming my thumb against my steering wheel as I sing along when suddenly Taevin turns off the music, leaving silence to linger between the two of us.

"Don't tell me you don't like country music," I say after a few moments have passed.

I chance a quick glance at her and find her shaking her head. "No, I do. It's actually my favorite genre."

I'm pleasantly surprised by that. "Even more so than Christian music?"

Her face turns down with a slight frown at my question. "I'm allowed to be more than a pastor's daughter."

My cheek twitches with a smirk. "I couldn't agree more."

The statement has barely left my lips when she lifts her gaze to connect with mine before I focus back on the road. "Really?"

"Yeah, Tae. I also get what it's like to be put into a box because of a parent's occupation."

"I suppose you're right. My dad told me yours is a senator. Is this his first term?"

I nod once. "He's up for reelection next year, so I've got to be on my best behavior."

"And have you?"

"Have I what?"

"Been on your best behavior?"

I chew on my bottom lip as I weigh my answer. Finally, I ask, "What's your definition of best behavior?"

"Have you done anything that could bring shame to your family?" she questions, though a giggle slips past her lips.

I bark out a laugh. This girl's going to keep me on my toes.

"I feel like I've heard something like that in *Mulan* before. My little sister made us watch every Disney movie a hundred times growing up. But to answer your question, no I don't think I've done anything to shame the family lately. I have been known to host a party or two when my parents are out of town, but the parties are pretty tame."

"Alright, I think I can work with that."

"You think?"

"To be determined, Bear."

"Bear?"

"Yeah, I think I liked Carson's nickname for you. Thought I'd test it out."

"You can call me whatever you'd like. So, if you love country music, then why did you turn it off? Not a fan of Tim McGraw?"

"Love him and his music"—she turns in her seat and faces me—"I just didn't think you'd have such a beautiful singing voice."

I'm not sure what to say to that, so I go for something playful. "You think I'm beautiful?"

"I said you have a beautiful voice. Don't get it twisted," she retorts, adding a roll of her eyes for good measure.

"Like listening to me talk, do you? We can turn our nightly texts into phone calls if you'd like to hear more of my voice." I send her a playful wink as we roll to a stop at a red light.

Taevin gives me a slight shove on my arm that does nothing. "I feel like you're deflecting right now. So tell me, are you in choir?" she asks.

"Me? No, I prefer not to sing in front of other people if I can help it," I admit.

"But you just sang in front of me," she points out.

"Guess that means I'm getting comfortable around you. But seriously, I don't know how you sang in front of a packed arena the other night. Which, you killed by the way."

"Thank you." I'm not sure if it's the red light or the compliment, but her cheeks take on a red hue. "It was actually a first for me, but I'm glad to have checked an item off the list," she murmurs so quietly I almost miss it.

"And what list is that?"

Her eyes widen before she says, "Oh, it's nothing really. Just a silly list Ryan and I put together for things to do before the fall."

The light changes and I focus back on the road. "Sounds fun. Can I ask what else is on there?"

"Mmm, I don't know, that kind of sounds like something that'd be classified until the second or third date at least."

"Here's to hoping I don't make a fool of myself tonight, then."

"I don't think it's you we have to worry about in this scenario. You're far more experienced than me—I'm the one who's never been on a date before, remember?"

Taking one hand off the wheel, I scratch the slight stubble on my cheek before admitting, "This is actually my first official date too."

Taevin chortles at that. "Good one."

"I'm being honest. I've hung out with girls in group settings that I'm guessing they classified as a date, but I've never done anything like this."

"And what's different about this?" she questions.

"Well, for starters, I've never picked a girl up and drove her to a date I planned out from start to finish. And I've never spent time alone with a girl like this trying to get to know her. Ultimately, you're the difference."

When I'm met with silence, I sneak a glance and see Taevin's eyebrows are raised skeptically. "I mean, I did my homework on you a little bit, Jackson. You've got quite the reputation as a ladies' man. It's actually why I made it what I thought was nearly impossible to take me out."

With my focus back on the road, I admit, "Look, I'm no saint. But I can say with complete honesty that a girl's never knocked me on my ass the way you have. I was captivated by you the moment I laid eyes on you in church. My reputation precedes me, but if you give me a chance, I can prove it wrong."

She doesn't respond, and instead smiles at the neon sign lighting up the building we've just pulled up to. I put my truck in park and look over at her. "If you tell me I don't have a chance in changing your opinion of me, I can take you home right now. But if you're up for a night of fun together, I think you'll get to know the real me."

I'm surprised when Taevin unbuckles and turns to face me. "I've got faith in you, and I agree, I think we can have some fun tonight." When she reaches for her door handle, I reach across and she halts her movements when I place my hand on hers.

"Let me start the date off right by opening your door."

"Okay. I'd like that very much," she says, tucking her hair behind her ear.

Keep me on my toes was right. For our first date, I brought Taevin to the arcade that's seen thousands of nickels between my siblings and me over the years.

We were both hungry when we got here, so we ordered a pizza and ate first. Then, for the first hour or so, we played arcade games and raced go-karts.

Now, though, I'm being bamboozled by Tae as she walks around the pool table to chalk the end of her cue stick again. She's beaten me twice in a row—about to be a third time—and all I can do is sit here completely dumbfounded. How is it that when we first walked up to the pool table, she grabbed the cue stick and acted like she didn't know what to do with it? She had me bent over, showing her how to line it up and where to place her hand to get the best shot, and yet she's an absolute pool shark.

And what's worse? She's calling her shots before making every last one of them. I'm not just getting beaten by the girl, I'm getting obliterated. So much so, that a small crowd has gathered around to watch her run the table.

"Thirteen ball in the far corner pocket," Tae calls before pulling back and making hard contact with the cue ball, sending her last striped ball into, you guessed it, the far corner pocket. It doesn't take much for her to sink the eight ball and then it's game over for the third time in a row.

"Damn. You really had me with the whole *I've never played before* act you had going. Where'd you learn to play like that?"

"We may or may not have a pool table in our basement. My parents used to play together a lot when I was growing up, and my mom was a bit of a pool shark when she and my dad met. Her father owned a bar, and I guess I picked it up from her."

"And the whole playing me for a fool?"

"My pathetic attempt at flirting?" she answers back in question.

I can't help grinning like an idiot. "I think you just wanted to have an excuse to check me out."

"Maybe . . . Could've gone better had I not kicked your butt."

"Touché. You've got me there."

Once we've racked up our sticks, I suggest we go next door where there's a candy store for dessert. Taevin chooses two white chocolate-covered Oreos, and I select half a pound of cookies and cream fudge. And because that won't quite induce a sufficient sugar coma, I convince her to try their ridiculously good old fashioned cream soda.

After I pay, we sit at one of the booths at the front of the store. Snow begins falling outside the window in thick, cottony flurries, and Taevin lets out a dreamy, contented sigh.

"What's got you sighing like that?" I ask her.

She focuses her gaze back on me and gives me a soft smile. "The snow. It was a good sigh. I love living here and getting to experience all of the seasons. Do you like winter?"

I take my time answering her question, too preoccupied taking her in. Her hair falls in waves from beneath her white knit hat that matches her sweater. I can't see them right now from where she's sitting across from me, but her dark jeans looked like they were painted on her while she was bent over the pool table earlier.

After openly checking her out, I remember she asked me a question and I clear my throat. "It's my favorite season, which is sometimes a scary thing to admit because to the wrong person, it probably makes me sound like a psychopath, but my favorite things happen in the winter."

"Oh, duh. That was probably a silly question considering you're a hockey player."

"Nah, I think it's a fair question. I could've said summer is my favorite because I love to golf or go wakeboarding."

"Do you like to do those things?"

I nod, and then she asks, "What other things do you like to do?"

"In the fall and spring I love to go hunting, and in the summer if I'm not golfing or wakeboarding, you'll probably find me fishing. Have you ever been?"

She shakes her head. "Nope, I've never been hunting or fishing before; my dad isn't much of an outdoorsman. The only golfing I've done is during gym class and I am not athletic enough to stand up on a wakeboard."

"I feel like that's a challenge I'd be willing to take on."

"What challenge is that?" she asks, quirking a brow.

"All the above. I think I could teach you to wakeboard. Golfing might take time. Hunting would require you to get a license, but you could tag along as my good luck charm. Fishing is pretty easy once you get the hang of it."

"You're pretty sure of yourself, aren't you, Jackson Wilson?"

"Not so sure of myself yet when it comes to you. But we'll get there."

"I have the utmost confidence," she assures me.

We sit there and talk for so long, I don't notice the time until the store is telling us they're getting ready to close for the evening. I help Taevin into her coat before taking a chance and grabbing her hand in mine. My heart launches into my throat when she turns to give me one of the most radiant smiles I've ever seen.

Just as I've opened the passenger door of my truck, I spin her toward me, and end up having to catch her around the waist when she slips on some of the freshly fallen snow. Holding her like this has thoughts I've never had suddenly filling my head. In the short span of time we've spent together, I've come to the conclusion that Taevin Gray isn't the type of girl you can easily let go of. Where do we go from here? What would it be like if she were mine? Am I boyfriend material? Am I capable of being more than just someone's fun night? Should I ask her to be my girlfriend?

Do it. Ask her.

"Listen, I don't really know how all of this works, so I'm going to just go with what feels right." I pause and grab her hands in mine, rubbing slow circles on the backs of hers. "Will you be my girlfriend, Taevin?"

Her eyes widen, and I hope the shock on her face isn't a bad kind of shock, like the kind where she's trying to figure out how to let me down easy. I feel a slight sense of relief when a slow smile tugs at the corners of her mouth.

She surprises the hell out of me when she points out, "You haven't even kissed me yet. How can you expect me to agree to be in a relationship with you when I don't know if you're a good kisser or not? For all I know, you could be terrible at it. I would hate to tie myself down to someone who uses too much tongue, or worse, none at all."

My eyebrows are to my forehead and I'm sure it's comical how wide my eyes are right now. It takes me a moment, but I manage to regain my composure.

"If you wanted me to kiss you, Tae, all you had to do was ask," I tell her as I drop her hands and take a step closer so I can wrap an arm around her waist, using my other hand to brush a stray piece of hair behind her ear before angling her face up to look at me.

She looks into my eyes for a moment before hers flutter shut at the same time as she lifts onto her toes, drawing her lips that much closer to mine. I hesitate for a moment, not only to make sure this is what she wants, but I also want to capture a mental snapshot of this moment in time. As thick, cottony flakes fall down around us, I'm captivated by the sight of Taevin's dark lashes coated with white snowflakes. Her black hair flowing out of her hat is the perfect contrast to the winter wonderland surrounding her, giving her an almost ethereal look.

When I lean down and finally press my lips to hers, I realize in an instant that my life has irrevocably changed. From this moment on, my life will be measured in moments that I'll designate as before Tae and after Tae.

A soft hum leaves her lips as I glide my tongue along them for entry. I let out a low groan of approval when she opens for me. Our kiss isn't frenzied, it isn't rushed. It's purposeful—an exploration that leaves me wanting to discover so much more. I wish I could freeze this moment in time—wish I could spend the rest of the evening doing this and only this.

She breaks the kiss when her phone alarm goes off, signaling that it's time to get her home before her curfew. I'm not sure where she told her dad she was going tonight, but I know it wasn't the truth. She said she needed to give him more time to come around to the prospect of her dating before she told him about me.

I lick my lips, savoring the way I can still taste her there. Tae tracks the move, causing her to bite down on her bottom lip with heavy-lidded eyes, and it takes everything in me not to pull her in for another kiss. Instead, I plant a soft kiss on her forehead and tell her, "I should get you home."

She wraps her arms around my waist and gazes up at me. "You should. But first things first, I've got to answer your question."

"And what question is that?" I ask as my mind tries to play catch up.

"Yes, I'll be your girlfriend." She gives me a quick peck before hopping into the passenger seat.

I stand there with my hand holding the door open, stunned—fucking stupified—at the fact that she said yes. When I asked, I honestly thought there was no chance in hell a girl like her would give a fuckup like me the privilege of calling her mine.

The beautiful sound of her laughter fills the crisp night air, snapping me out of my daze.

Taevin said yes. She's my girlfriend. I'm someone's boyfriend—no, not someone, *the* one.

Shutting the door, I round the back of my truck and pump my fist in the air. "Let's fucking go!" I shout into the void, to absolutely no one but myself.

I thought after I started my truck maybe I'd come down from cloud nine, but Taevin had other plans. The smile on my face only grows as she slides across the bench seat to tuck herself beneath the arm I had slung over the seat as I reversed out of the parking spot. Two contrasting things happen in that moment—my chest swells with pride at the same time my heart pinches in fear. I barely know this girl, and she's already turned my world upside down. If there's one thing I know for sure, it's that I'm going to do everything in my power to not fuck this up.

7

Jackson

Now

"So, where's home, J?" Taevin asks me as I grab her bags from where the flight attendant left them on the tarmac.

I hesitate, not knowing how exactly to answer that at first. For one, I haven't felt a sense of being home since she left me. And secondly, I'm not sure how to explain that I've got two places of residence—the condo I purchased from Bennett when he moved in with Scarlett last fall, and my house outside the city. I've been working on building the house for the past five years, and it's more than just a labor of love to me. I'm anxious for her to be in my space after having pictured her there hundreds of times over the years. I haven't stayed there since construction finished on it because it didn't feel right without her there.

Instead of elaborating, I just say, "We're going to make a quick pit stop at my condo in the city so I can grab a few things and then we'll stay at my house that's just outside the city."

"Oh, two places. Look at you making the big bucks," Tae teases, waggling her eyebrows so the ball cap she has on rises on her forehead.

I scoff at that. "Not at all. I think you have me mistaken for Bennett or Griff. I'm pretty replaceable, but Benny's the top defenseman and G has been a top goal scorer in the league for the past three seasons. I really thought this was our year to win it all."

Toeing the ground and refusing to make eye contact with me, Tae murmurs, "I may have noticed Minnesota made it pretty far in the playoffs this year."

Shaking my head, I playfully shoulder check her to get her attention. It works, and when her gaze locks on mine, I have to fight the urge to pull her into my chest the way I so naturally did once upon a time. Clearing the sudden nerves from my throat, I test out mirroring her teasing tone, "Been keeping tabs on me, Thorn?"

The nickname easily slips from my lips, because at one point calling her that and pulling her into my arms was second nature.

Tae's spine stiffens but I welcome the thought of her being as affected by me as I am by her. Going from having all of her to her becoming a ghost in my life has fucked with my head for years now, but nothing compares to having her so close physically again while remaining lightyears away emotionally. There's a void in my heart that will never be filled—years of my life wasted thinking about what could've been.

Loving her from a distance all this time was like trying to catch hold of a ghost—my heart felt as hollow as my hands did empty.

I know things are only going to get worse as she enters a space I've built from the ground up. Each room in my house was designed with her in mind. Every decision, down to the smallest of details, was made with thoughts of Taevin. I won't be able to talk my way out of it. As soon as we pull into the drive, she'll know this is the home she and I dreamed up when we were still practically kids.

I'm so in my own head, I hardly realize we've walked out of the airport and through the parking garage until I hear Taevin ask, "Is this . . .?"

I nod when I realize she's asking if this is my truck. "It is."

"You've still got Frannie girl? How is she still holding up after all this time?" she asks in disbelief.

"She got a bit of a facelift since you last saw her. I could never replace my sweet Frannie, she's been the best girl to me over the years. And she still has a lot of years left in her, don't you sweet girl?" I run my fingers across the newly painted tailgate.

"You painted her black?" It comes out more of a question than a remark.

I don't answer her because the truck color speaks for itself.

"Why?" she asks, though it's more of a whisper so I don't know if she actually wants an answer, but I decide to give her one anyways.

"Some things change, while others don't. Black became my favorite color a decade ago and it stuck."

She sucks in a shaky breath. "You said you didn't have a favorite color at the time so you adopted mine."

Yeah, that, and I became obsessed with the way her black hair looked laying across my chest. But I don't tell her that, instead I point out, "I said I'd adopt it, not borrow it."

Tae nods once before awkwardly shifting her weight like she's not sure what to do next. After tossing our bags in the bed of my truck, I open the passenger door for her. "Let's get you settled in. That was a long flight," I tell her as she slides into the passenger seat and I have to ball my hand into a fist to keep myself from buckling her in the way I used to.

After shutting the passenger door, I give myself a mini pep talk as I round the bed of my truck. I've got this. I can spend time with her in closed quarters while keeping my composure. I need to be her support right now, if I don't, I risk scaring her away, and I have no doubt Taevin would hightail it back to Nashville.

I hesitate a moment when I turn the key in the ignition, almost afraid that if I look over in my passenger seat I won't find her there. Scared that maybe this whole thing has been a figment of my imagination and the woman I've never for one second gotten over won't really be sitting beside me in the very spot she was in when we dreamed together as we drove down neighborhood streets under midnight stars.

Taevin

Jackson has been quiet, eerily so, since we left his condo and started driving out of the city toward his house. He mentioned it was just outside the Twin Cities, but we've been driving for over twenty minutes and the freeway has now turned into a back road that winds through fields of tall green grass and corn.

Apparently the condo was Bennett's until he moved in with Scarlett last year. As he walked me through it, he told me he bought it so the commute was shorter, and that was where he stayed for most of the season last year. I was shocked because it was fairly empty and cold, void of any pictures or signs that someone actually lived there, which is the opposite of what I'd pictured him in.

But aside from those few remarks back at his condo, he's been silent.

Shifting in my seat, I face him. "Are you getting hungry?"

He shrugs in reply, giving me nothing once again. His grip tightens on the steering wheel with one hand while his other runs through his hair for the dozenth time. He's clearly in his own head, and normally I'd respect someone's need for space, but I'm only in Minnesota right now because of him. So if I have to put myself through this discomfort, he needs to at least talk to me.

With a huff of annoyance I suggest, "We could order something for dinner. Wait, do they deliver food this far out of the city?"

"They do," he confirms, his curtness has me gritting my teeth until he flips his blinker and slows before taking a left-hand turn.

A cloud of dirt follows us up a gravel driveway as a massive dark house surrounded by evergreens comes into view, and my heart seizes in my chest as the memories come flashing back to me.

"If you could live in any color house what would you choose?" Jax asks me as he drives us through an older neighborhood near my house.

I don't hesitate with my answer. "Easy, a black house with a pitched roof and weathered oak wood and stone accents throughout."

"Wow, that was quick. How much have you thought about this?"

"As you know, black is my favorite color. And I've got at least a dozen Pinterest boards dedicated to my first apartment, first home, and ultimately my dream home. Oh, I almost forgot. Our dream home will be on a big plot of land where we can hunt and fish and sit out on the back porch to watch our kids play in the field behind our house."

"Is that all?" he drawls with a dopey grin on his face.

"No. I suppose not. I want it to feel cozy year round, but when it's Christmas time I want it to feel so magical, we never want to leave. A Christmas tree in every room and dozens to fill our front porch. Then when you come home from a long away trip, you'll feel our embrace from the moment you pull into the driveway."

"You're using the word 'ours' a lot to describe your dream house."

My eyes widen and my cheeks heat.

He shakes his head, grabbing my hand and bringing it to his lips. "Stop. Don't get embarrassed. I love this. Keep going. Tell me everything. How many bedrooms will there be?"

"Well, we're having at least three kids, so the house should probably have four bedrooms."

"Five."

"Five bedrooms? Seems excessive, but okay."

"No, five kids."

"Five?! Are you crazy?" I ask incredulously.

"What? Too many?"

"Yes! Most guys would look at me like I had two heads talking about three kids this day and age."

"Call me traditional then, baby. I want you barefoot and pregnant as much as possible."

"You just want to have your wicked way with me as much as possible."

"They say practice makes perfect," he croons, and I lightly smack his chest.

"You're crazy. So, tell me, what's on your wishlist, J?" I ask as we pull up to a stop sign, and he turns to face me.

"Aside from the five babies, not much. A hot tub tucked away from the main house where we can sneak off to go stargazing for a little alone time once the kids go to bed." He waggles his eyebrows, and I roll my eyes before he continues. "Oh, and a sauna too to help me recover my sore muscles after a game."

"That sounds glorious," I sigh in contentment, imagining someday our every wish and dream coming to fruition.

I'm dizzy as I snap back to the reality before me when he parks his truck in front of the large, black mansion with multiple roof pitches and stone and wood accents that looks like it was plucked straight from my dreams and placed on a huge plot of land.

How did he do this? *Why* did he do this? It's been so long . . . and yet every moment is still engraved in my mind like no time has passed at all. Has it been the same for him too, even after all this time?

When I turn to take Jax in, he's staring off into the distance, and I know the flashbacks of the many conversations about our future are playing out for him like a movie right now too.

Breaking the stifling silence, I ask, "What is this?"

After a deep breath he faces me, and when he does, his eyes rove over my face, studying every detail as if he's taking note of every difference. "My promise to you."

My breath hitches in a gasp. "I never expected you to keep it. I mean, we were eighteen-year-old kids with stars in our eyes thinking we were invincible, Jackson."

"Come on, Tae, not you too," he says, looking pained, as if what I just said struck him straight in the chest. "I'm so sick of everyone telling me I should've gotten over my high school sweetheart by now. They don't get it because they weren't there. But you were—you know how I felt about you—I'm surprised this is such a shock to you. Our future meant everything to me, and once upon a time, it did to you too."

"Yeah, well, maybe not everyone is meant to get a happy ever after," I hear myself whisper. Some of the most epic stories end in tragedy, but they're still worth telling because there's beauty in the breakdown.

And aren't I about to become a shining example of this? Spending the rest of my life living with the fact that I'll be incapable of living out the fairytale we once dreamt of. A fact that will become glaringly true for the both of us in a few weeks' time.

8

Taevin

Now

I'm just finishing hanging up the last of my clothing from my suitcase when my phone rings with an incoming FaceTime request. My shoulders slump and I let out a heavy sigh when I see Kyle's name light up my screen. Swiping, I accept his call.

"To what do I owe the pleasure, Kyle?" I ask him when he comes into view. He's wearing the pair of large, wire-rimmed, blue blockers I told him make him look like a creep, and I don't try to hide my exaggerated eye roll. "You're ruining your perfectly good face, you realize that, right? It's also extremely hard to take you seriously when you wear those things."

He takes them off and makes a show of feigning frustration with me. Though, maybe he really is frustrated considering the fact I just up and left Paris yesterday and flew to Minnesota with my estranged husband instead of flying back to my place in Nashville. Oh, and he's been texting me incessantly since I left about how furious he is with Jax for dismissing my security. I should probably feel guilty for the extra work he's complaining of, but I honestly can't find it in me to.

"Yeah well I don't have time to fret over whether or not my glasses are up to your fashion standards when I'm dealing with a PR crisis surrounding your sudden disappearance right before you're due to perform at the Summer Stampede."

With a huff of annoyance, I murmur, "Oh stop with the theatrics, Kyle. You can spin a story better than anyone I know. Besides, I told you why I'm here." The last part is a bit clipped because, lately, my patience is wearing thin with him.

Kyle's eyebrows shoot up his forehead; he's not used to me speaking my mind with him. But doing so feels right—freeing. "And I support your decision to seek a second opinion. What I don't understand is your reasoning behind staying with the man who crushed your heart without a moment's pause. You're a millionaire. If you can't find a short-term rental, buy a house, for god's sake. One with an extra bedroom for Braidy to stay in."

I can't mask my sassy reaction to his suggestion, which Kyle definitely takes notice of. "And who would help take care of me while I'm healing from surgery? It's not like I can ask that of Braidy, especially considering I hardly know the man."

"I'll look into an in-home nursing agency to give you round the clock care. Because I can assure you, Jackson is not the guy to rely on at a time like this. He will hurt you again, Taevin. Mark my words."

Something about Kyle's words and the way he said them doesn't sit right with me. I don't need his warnings; besides, they're completely unwarranted. "Hard to hurt me when I plan to keep him at a distance."

He breathes out a sigh of exasperation. "I sure hope you're right. Now, can you please tell me what the hell the plan is for the festival?"

An idea spins to life as I think back to what Jackson admitted to me on the plane. He hasn't played the guitar in seven years because of me. The person who taught me how to play my first chord hasn't played or sang because of *me*. If he insists on coming along, I'm going to make a few demands of my own.

Instead of sharing the plans swirling in my head, I ask Kyle, "How many rooms are there in the hotel suite I have booked for Summer Stampede?"

"Two, why?"

"Just wanted to make sure there was a separate room for Jackson to stay in."

Kyle's face turns down with a frown. "Why would he be coming?"

"My apparent husband wants to make sure I'm not overexerting myself. See, maybe you've judged him too quickly for the boy he was instead of the man he is now."

Kyle narrows his eyes. "Yes, about that. When were you planning on telling me you're married?"

It's my turn to sigh in exasperation because I knew this conversation was coming. If the dozens of texts awaiting me after I woke up in the hospital were any sort of indication. "Well considering I didn't know I was married, I'm not sure how I would have told you."

His brows wrinkle as he looks off to the side of his phone, likely typing away at an email on his computer. "What do you mean? Were you drunk when it happened?"

I roll my eyes at that because he knows damn well I wasn't much of a drinker prior to entering the spotlight. "No. I remember marrying him perfectly fine. I also remember signing annulment paperwork that was apparently never filed."

That seems to garner his attention because he snaps his focus back to me. "Do you need me to get legal up to speed?"

I shake my head. "No. I'm handling this on my own."

"Taevin—" Kyle starts, but I'm in no mood to be placated.

"I've got to go. Big appointment tomorrow morning. See ya."

Before he gets the chance, I end the call and toss my phone onto the giant guest king bed I can't wait to crawl into. I'm obsessed with this guest room, though, it's weird—one would actually think it feels more like the primary bedroom, what with the largest walk-in closet I've ever seen, the en suite bathroom, and it being on the main level.

Speaking of which, I walk into the en-suite and admire the oversized soaking tub I very distinctly remember telling Jackson I wanted in my dream home someday. And this one is beyond anything I could've dreamed up.

It's dark, yet cozy instead of cold. The walls are a slate gray marble tile from the floors to the vaulted ceiling with thick, dark wooden beams contrasting against the white paint. And a black stone tub sits in the middle of the room as the focal point in front of the most beautiful window that has to be at least ten feet. On either side of the bathroom are dual vanities, only further making me believe this was meant to be the primary bedroom.

I wonder why Jackson wouldn't sleep here—it's perfect down to the very smallest detail. Though I guess I haven't seen the rest of the house. There's a very real possibility his bedroom is even more serene.

When we pulled up to the house earlier and Jackson saw how overwhelmed I was, he bypassed the front door and instead led me to the back patio's entrance to the guest room, assuring me he'd give me a house tour after I got unpacked while he made us something to eat.

Unsure of how seeing the space he so clearly built with our dreams in mind will affect me, I walk to the beautiful tub and turn on the faucet before going in search of some bubbles or salts.

My breath hitches when I find rose petal bath bombs and rose scented bubble bath. When would he have had time to get these? Clearly he's had these for a while, considering we just landed in Minneapolis only hours ago. Or maybe he has an assistant that ran to the store for him while we were getting our bags and some of his things from his condo?

Instead of wasting any more time on the logistics of how or why he has these items, I grab them and soak in the bath until my feet are pruned and the alarm on my phone goes off reminding me to take my meds with dinner.

I'm exhausted and jetlagged, but this appointment tomorrow morning is the sole reason I'm in Minnesota right now. It's time to set aside my grievances with Jackson and focus on my health. Or, at least, that's what I try to tell myself as I towel off and get changed with anxiety's thick burden weighing heavy on my chest.

Dr. Stephanie Prescott is a petite woman with an overpowering presence. I'm not sure how she managed to pull it off, because I was dead set on not liking her just to spite Jackson, but when I met her, she immediately put me at ease. I quickly came to the conclusion I couldn't fight this battle without her on my team.

We're sitting in her office at Mayo Clinic in Rochester, Minnesota after I've gone through a number of tests and had imaging completed for her to review.

It's already been a long day with the drive here this morning, and a quick lunch break that left me feeling even more exhausted from the awkward tension between me and Jax. And the topic we're currently discussing is one I would rather steer clear of while my estranged *husband* is in the room.

"This is a lot to process at once, but I strongly urge you to reconsider delaying surgery. We could get you in as soon as tomorrow," Dr. Prescott informs me.

"I have a prior commitment, and my medical team in Nashville had said I could have my tumor resection once I got back from my performance. They didn't mention I'd need a full hysterectomy," I explain, completely numb from the news I've just received.

The tumor has grown. The cancer has likely spread beyond just my cervix. Hysterectomy is the best treatment option.

"Could you still wait to do the tumor resection until after my egg retrieval surgery?"

"The time for aggressive surgical intervention is now, Taevin. I apologize if your previous team was willing to delay surgery for a round of egg retrieval, but I strongly advise against it. Your images today show the larger tumor in your endometrium has grown since your last imaging. Based on the biopsy done at the Nashville facility, they determined your tumor is a grade two, meaning we can anticipate the cancer cells to spread at a moderate rate; therefore, I do not recommend delaying surgery any longer than we already have. When do you get back from your performance? We could schedule you the Monday after."

My throat swells and my stomach churns with bitter regret. I never should've waited. Now I may have missed my only shot at ever having children of my own.

As if she can sense where my thoughts have wandered, Dr. Prescott explains, "If we find the cancer has not spread to your ovaries, we'll keep them, and after you've recovered from your hysterectomy, you could attempt an egg retrieval to use for IVF with a surrogate if you choose."

"Do the eggs need to be fertilized with sperm upon retrieval?" I ask in a faraway voice I don't recognize as my own. I feel so detached. So cold. "If so, I'll need to find a sperm donor. Do you have resources you could provide me with?" There's a scoff from my side, though I don't pay it any attention.

I can see Dr. Prescott, but it mostly feels like I'm staring straight through her. She glances to my side before clearing her throat. "They do not. We can do egg freezing versus embryo freezing, though embryo freezing has a higher success rate for pregnancy than egg freezing."

Jackson grabs my hand in his, and for a moment I almost forgot he's here beside me. "Can we get more information on embryo freezing?"

My head snaps up to meet his gaze but I'm met with his profile instead as he continues to face the doctor.

"Jackson, I can't ask that of—" I start but he shakes his head and turns, giving me a look that says we can discuss this further later, which we most certainly will.

How could he possibly want to have children with me? My eggs are probably compromised by now anyway. And that's *if* they'll even be able to retrieve any. If I'm even able to keep my ovaries. I choke back a sob threatening to escape.

Not here. Not now. Keep it together.

I silently repeat the mantra to myself as Jackson continues to ask Dr. Prescott further questions about my surgery, my anticipated recovery timeline, when the egg retrieval process will begin, and when we'll know more about my treatment options post-op. His questions have clearly been researched, and he asks some of them after glancing at a note on his phone.

He took notes.

The scene before me is too overwhelming. Jackson, the first and only man I've ever loved, is sitting in an oncologist's office with me. He's asking questions on my behalf—questions I should've thought up on my own—and taking notes on his phone with my doctor's responses.

I block out his questions and her answers for the most part, but my back stiffens and my ears perk up when I hear him ask, "Can you walk me through more of what we can expect after the egg retrieval? How long will we have to wait to know how many eggs were successfully retrieved? When will we know the number of embryos? And at what point do they become blastocysts?"

We? Why is he asking all of these questions with the word "we" in them?

"Blastocysts?" I hear myself echo the word in question.

"Those are great questions, I'm glad you asked." Dr. Prescott focuses her attention on me as she continues. "Taevin, you will know how many eggs were retrieved upon waking up from anesthesia. We then will take the eggs and fertilize them if that is what you choose to do. It typically takes one to two days for a fertilized egg to become an embryo. You can anticipate knowing how many viable embryos become blastocysts five to six days after fertilization. Blastocysts are embryos which have reached a more advanced developmental stage, and have a higher chance of implanting successfully. We typically freeze at the blastocyst stage because they have a higher success rate with thawing and implantation."

I feel as though I'm frozen in time, watching my life happen as an outsider looking in. I'm filled with anguish as I sit here in an uncomfortable chair across from an oncologist, wishing so many things could've gone differently in the past decade that didn't leave me here on the verge of being infertile.

If there's one thing I've always hoped and prayed for in my future, it was to become a mother. And now, the ability to grow and carry my own child is being stripped from me. *Again.*

Breaking News

Country star Taevin Gray rumored to have checked into rehab
Where oh where is Taevin Gray?
By LARA BRADLEY

In the days following her onstage collapse, Taevin Gray hasn't been spotted in Nashville, or anywhere else for that matter. So where is she?

The country music star, 28, is rumored to have checked into an exclusive rehabilitation facility somewhere in the Dominican Republic for substance abuse.

Country Know Now has reached out to Gray's reps for comment, but have not yet heard back.

To stay up to date on all the latest country celebrity news, subscribe below.

9

Jackson

How is it that Taevin has been mine for eight weeks already? Time has flown by but nothing has ever felt so right. Every moment we spend getting to know each other, I swear is my favorite, only for the next day to roll around, taking over the top spot.

Right now being the perfect example. We're nestled together in the bed of my truck, parked in a random field off a country road as we celebrate our two month anniversary—yes, I'm well aware I'm a complete sucker for this girl and celebrating a monthiversary may be cheesy as fuck, but I'm too far gone for her to even care.

There's not a word in the English language strong enough to describe my fascination—my utter obsession—with Tae. We've been nearly inseparable since the night of our first date, sneaking away at every opportunity to spend time together. My friends are pissed I've ghosted them outside of school and hockey, and I know her father has to be suspicious of how much time Taevin is spending with "Ryan" lately.

In the matter of a couple months I've fallen fast and hard for the girl I've got wrapped in my arms. As I play with a strand of her long, inky waves, I say, "I feel crazy asking this, because I feel like it's something I should already know but I'm gonna ask anyway. Where are you planning to go to school in the fall?"

"I got nearly a full ride to Berklee—" she starts, but I cut her off.

"As in Berklee College of Music?"

"The one and only," she tells me as she turns onto her stomach and rests her chin on my chest.

Tucking my forearm behind my head as a pillow, I smile like a fool at her, and she quirks a brow in confusion at my expression. "Tae, that's amazing. Wait, why haven't you said anything? How am I only hearing about this now?"

"I'm still not sure if I'm going to go or not." Her confession is hushed, full of uncertainty.

My face falls slightly. "What has you questioning it?"

"It's not a full scholarship, and with out-of-state tuition and living expenses not covered, I'd graduate with a lot of debt I'm not sure is worth the risk when I'll most likely end up a struggling artist after graduation. My dad doesn't agree with me wanting to pursue a career in music."

How can't he see how incredibly talented she is? Even if he's only ever heard her sing at church—which I can't imagine is the case with how much joy she gets from singing—her dad should see how special she is.

"Some might call it fate that we could end up going to two separate colleges in the same city," I suggest, but my stomach sinks at the thought of that reality potentially scaring Taevin. I've come to the conclusion that now probably isn't the best time to bring up the fact that she could live with me off campus after our freshman year to save on living expenses. Hell, I'd ask her to move in with me freshman year if it weren't for us both being required to stay in the dorms our first year.

"What are you talking about?" she asks, and it's only now I realize I haven't told her yet.

"I'm going to sign my National Letter of Intent tomorrow afternoon. My school is putting an assembly together for me, Carson, and a few of my other classmates."

Her brows crease adorably in confusion. "Jax, you know me enough by now that I don't have a clue what you're saying. What is a National Letter of Intent?"

We haven't discussed what we're doing next year yet because our relationship is so new, and yet my chest squeezes in hopeful anticipation of what this could mean for us. My head is spinning with all of the plans I can envision us making together in Boston.

"Essentially, I'll be signing my commitment to play hockey for Harvard next year. Which means if you do go to Berklee, we'd be like a fifteen minute drive away from each other."

Taevin's eyes widen for a fraction of a second before she quickly sits up and stares out at the field surrounding us. I follow her, wrapping my arm around her bent knee. When I chance a look at her, her bottom lip is pulled between her teeth, seemingly lost in thought.

"Care to share what's going on in that gorgeous head of yours?"

She turns her gaze on me. "I'm not sure what to make of the thoughts that ran through my head just now."

My stomach sinks with dread, and it must be written all over my face because Taevin is quick to add, "No, not like you're thinking. They're not bad thoughts—well, depending on how you look at it, I guess they could be."

"T, you're killing me right now," I groan.

"I'm sorry, I'll try to explain, it's just, I'm not even sure how to process how I'm feeling at the moment," she clarifies.

"Did I scare you?" I ask, playing invisible chords on her shin to distract me from the nerves I'm riddled with.

"The opposite, actually," she admits sheepishly, and my head snaps in her direction so quickly, for a moment I think I've given myself whiplash.

"What does that mean, baby?"

Goosebumps erupt down her arms and shin at the term of endearment. She doesn't need to admit it because I know she *loves* it when I call her baby.

"Like I said, I'm not sure what to make of it, but the moment you said we could potentially be fifteen minutes away from each other, all of these images ran through my head." She hesitates a moment, so I give her leg a gentle squeeze of assurance.

"Like?"

"Like . . ." Tae sighs before continuing. "Like an image of me attending all of your home hockey games while I drown in a Harvard Hockey sweatshirt—"

I cut her off with a scoff. "Please, you'd definitely be wearing my jersey."

Tae gives me a shy smile as an adorable blush heats her cheeks. "And images of the two of us grabbing lunch between classes. Or holding hands as we walk around Harvard Square."

I nudge my shoulder into hers, nearly knocking her onto her side. "Keep 'em coming. Matter of fact, think bigger, Tae. Wanna know what I see?"

She nods in response. "Tell me."

Licking my lips, I gaze longingly into her eyes before I say, "I see the two of us experiencing our freshman orientations and then telling each other all about it over pizza afterward—we're going to go to as many pizza places around Boston as we can until we decide on our go-to by our sophomore year." Pausing, I debate whether or not to go there, ultimately deciding: fuck it. Taking a deep breath, I murmur, "Speaking of sophomore year, you'd graduate with a lot less debt if the two of us saved on rent and lived together."

A small gasp escapes Taevin as the words leave my mouth, but I don't have it in me to regret them. I know this is fast. I know I probably just put my foot in my mouth. But I can't find it in me to care. I want her to know how I feel about her. This thing between us isn't just a high school fling that'll fizzle out after the summer. We have a real shot at a future together. Taevin Gray is my end game, and it's about damn time she realizes it.

Taevin

Being in a relationship with Jackson is everything and more. But I think he may be certifiably insane—at least he's talking that way right now.

What does he mean I could save money if we rented a place together my sophomore year? I mean, don't get me wrong, I love the idea of the two of us going to college together in Boston and getting to see each other. But the way he just suggested it—with so much confidence we'll still be together a whole year from now—has me realizing I may be in a relationship with an actual crazy person.

Pretending as if he didn't just suggest the most deranged thing I've ever heard, I roll my eyes and nudge his shoulder. "Tell me more about these pizza tastings we'd be having if I choose Berklee."

Jax gives a small shake of his head. "It's alright if you're still a bit scared. We can circle back to discussing our living arrangements some time next year."

"Over pizza?" I question.

"Obviously. Is there any other way?"

"Yes, but none as superior as discussing my boyfriend's irrational thoughts over pizza."

Jax decides to let my teasing comment go, instead shifting the conversation. "I got you a little something."

With a quirk of my brow, I ask, "Did you?"

"I did," he says before reaching to his side and handing me two long-stemmed red roses. "For you, my sweet Thorn."

Inhaling them deeply, I sigh in contentment as the familiar scent floods my system. "Thank you, Bear. I love them."

"And is that all you love?" he questions with a playful lilt to his tone.

Leaning over, I give him a quick peck and watch with rapt fascination as he slowly licks his lips and lets out a low groan. "God, I love that you taste like cinnamon and hazelnut."

"And is that *all* you love?" I mock.

Before I can stop him, Jackson grabs one of the roses out of my hand and plucks a petal off. "She loves me." *Toss. Pluck.* "She loves me not." *Toss. Pluck.* "She loves me." *Toss. Pluck.* "She loves me not." *Toss. Pluck.* "She loves me." *Toss. Pluck.*

Before he can grab another petal, I snatch it back and then drop the roses onto the truck bed and tug on Jackson's coat to pull him on top of me. He wraps his hand around my head before laying me on my back. My breathing picks up speed as he hovers above me, perfectly content with staring into my eyes.

"I'm pretty sure I left off at 'she loves me.' Does that mean what I think it does?" he asks, a hopeful glint in his eyes.

"It does. I do. I'm not sure how you've managed to steal my heart in only a couple months' time, but you did."

"Say it," he demands.

"I love you, Jackson."

He hums in approval before brushing his nose against mine, but holds back on giving me the kiss I'm craving.

"Baby," he whispers against my lips. "You make me so damn happy. I love you so fucking much, Taevin. I've never said those words to anyone outside of my family, but I needed to tell you. Just like I need to kiss you right now."

"Then kiss me already. Please," I beg, barely able to get the words out before his lips crash against mine.

Our bodies become a panting, frenzied mess of tangled limbs and crashing lips. We get so lost in the kiss—I'm so intoxicated in the feel of his body moving against mine in a way I've only dreamed of experiencing—we don't hear the crunch of earth beneath tires as the police cruiser approaches. Or the sound of footsteps padding through the dried-out tall grasses, still dead from the long winter. No, we continue to make out hot and heavy until a throat clears at the end of Jackson's tailgate.

Breaking the kiss, Jax lazily pulls back and moves to a sitting position. I shoot up so quickly I narrowly avoid headbutting him.

"Good evening," the officer starts, tipping his baseball hat at the pair of us. "I'm sorry to interrupt, but are you aware you're trespassing on private property?"

"Good evening, Officer. My apologies, I thought this was public land according to my hunting app that shows public hunting land in the area."

"The public land was recently rezoned and this property now belongs to the Minnesota State Government. I'm going to have to ask for both of your licenses so I can issue the two of you a written warning."

"I don't have my license, but I do have a photo ID," I tell the officer as I scramble to reach for my backpack.

Jax places a hand on my arm and shakes his head. "There's no need."

Without saying another word, I watch as he hands the officer his license along with what looks like a business card, and within moments, understanding dawns on the officer's face.

"I'm sorry about this misunderstanding, Mr. Wilson."

"It's okay, Officer. I won't say anything if you don't."

"I won't. But would the two of you mind finding somewhere else to fool around so we can avoid any more unnecessary run-ins?"

"Say no more, sir. We're headed out now."

"Have a good evening, and stay safe," the officer says before walking back to his cruiser.

As Jackson's helping me out of the truck bed, I ask, "What the heck was that about?"

"My dad gives me this card that's essentially a 'get outta jail free' card to hand to an officer if I'm ever pulled over for speeding or something like that. I've never had to use it before, and I wasn't planning to, but I didn't want you to get into deep shit with your dad."

"J, you didn't have to—" I start, but he cuts me off.

"I know I didn't have to, Thorn. I was protecting you."

"You seem to have a way of doing that lately," I tell him. On the way back to my house, I can't help but feel guilty knowing he had to use that card. He hasn't talked too much about it since we've started dating, but from what I gather, Jackson's dad is a control freak—even more so than my dad. I hate the thought of him having used anything from that jerk.

Instead of stewing about it, I focus on settling my heart rate from having been caught in a compromising position. I bask in the memory of his hands on mine as we were sitting in the back of his truck, and I'm suddenly curious to know if I've missed something major about Jackson.

"Hey, before we got . . . caught up, I noticed you were strumming your fingers on my shin. What was that about?"

Clearing his throat, he taps his thumb on the steering wheel before stealing a glance over at me. "I may or may not play the guitar."

"Wait, what? For real?"

"Yeah, my mom was adamant we each learn an instrument growing up and when Bennett chose the guitar, I followed his lead."

Okay, but how did I not know this about him?

"Do you remember on our first date how you asked me about the list I made with Ryan for before I leave for college?"

"Yeah, you said I needed to make it to the second or third date at least before you'd disclose the items on said list; though I think we're beyond that by now. Fess up, T—what's on this list?"

Biting the inside of my cheek, I debate whether or not to tell him the full list, including the items Ryan added. Ultimately, I decide to step outside my comfort zone and tell him about the entire list.

"Some of the items are ones I added, like go on a ferris wheel to get over my fear of heights, get my driver's license—though that one is my goal before the end of the summer—perform an original song at a venue, and go to senior prom. And some are ones Ryan added on my behalf like go on a date, sneak out past curfew, kiss a boy—all of which you've helped me check off."

"Okay, is that the whole list?"

I fidget my fingers together in my lap. "No, there's two more items on the list Ryan added."

"And they are . . ." he drawls as a slow smile spreads on his face.

"Well, she's always known I've wanted to learn to play guitar. So I've been saving up for a few months now to try to buy my own and then teach myself or do tutorials or something."

"No need to do that, you've got me now," he assures me, bringing our joined hands to his lips and trailing soft kisses along each of my knuckles. "I'll teach you."

My stomach clenches at the way his voice turns to gravel.

"What's the last item?"

"Oh, um, I don't remember."

"Is that so? Then why are your cheeks so red, T? What is it? Come on, you can tell me," he goads.

Covering my face with my hands, I mutter, "Have an orgasm."

I peer between my fingers at him when I feel the truck slow to a halt. Jax puts the truck in park before turning to face me and slinging his right arm over the back of the bench seat. With his other hand, he unbuckles me and pulls me toward him.

"What does that mean?" he asks, his voice raspy and sexy as hell.

"It means I–I've never . . ." I start to stammer so I take a deep breath. "I've never had one before."

"Ever?" he questions, and I nod in response.

"Like even by yourself?"

Shaking my head, I whisper, "Never."

Jackson faces forward and drops his head back against the headrest. "Baby," he groans, dragging his hands down his face.

"I figured you knew I was a virgin . . ." I tell him, trailing off awkwardly because this conversation is so outside my comfort zone.

"I mean, yeah, I figured that." Turning to face me again, he takes my hands in his. "And regardless of your virginity, I never want you to feel like I'm pushing you for anything—you set the pace with everything, Tae. I mean that."

Biting my bottom lip, I feel my cheeks heat further. "I know that," I murmur, looking down at our hands.

Lifting my chin, he says, "I'm serious, T. You're in charge."

Chuckling, I shoot him a wink. "As if I didn't already know that."

"There's my girl." Jackson brings me in for a hug, but before he pulls away, he whispers, "Don't you worry about the last item on your checklist—I'm making it my life's mission to be the one to give you your first orgasm. When the time's right."

My stomach knots as heat pools in my core, and the only relief I find is rubbing my thighs together. But what hits me like a drug to my system is the love swirling in my heart for this boy.

10

Taevin

Now

*R*ushing up the steps to the front porch, I nearly fall as I slip on the snow-covered cement. But I just couldn't help myself, everything looks so beautiful. There's got to be nearly two dozen pine trees of all shapes and sizes, each lit up and standing in planters on the front porch.

Snow flurries whip around us, giving the feeling of being in a snowglobe. But I don't feel trapped here in this moment the way I imagine I would if I were truly stuck in a glass bubble. No, instead, I feel freer than I've ever been. Tossing my arms out wide, I spin in circles as I throw my head back in a fit of carefree laughter. This. This is what living is for. These moments of complete clarity with no one but my best friend by my side.

I tell myself to stop acting like a fool—to try to play things cool—but I can't help myself.

"Please be careful. I don't want you to get hurt," he pleads, his voice laced with worry. I stop dead in my tracks as the deep baritone caresses my eardrums.

He? Wait, why is my best friend a he? Where is Ryan?

"Are you alright, baby?"

Baby? Why is Ryan calling me baby?

"Fuck, what's happening? Should I call the doctor?"

No! No more doctors. I'm tired of fighting.

"Thorn! Baby, stay with me."

Thorn? Oh, fuck. Jackson. Jackson's my best friend. And I need to stay with him. He wants me to stay with him. But why is he so blurry? And why do I feel like I'm falling?

I'm always falling when it comes to this boy. But he's no longer a boy; he's a man now. A very handsome, beautifully broken man. It's only now, as I somehow lay in his arms and he brushes his warm, calloused hand against my bare scalp, that I realize I must've fallen and he's caught me.

Jackson's always catching me.

Shooting up in bed, I clutch at the covers on my bed to try to ground myself.

It was a dream. Only a dream.

My throat is dry and my hands won't stop trembling, so I shove off the covers and make my way down the hallway that leads from my bedroom to the kitchen.

Jackson's house is my dream home I envisioned at eighteen, only amplified and modernized to everything I didn't know I'd want and need in a home at twenty-eight. I cling to every detail all over again to bring my heart rate back down and distract me from my racing thoughts.

The beautiful engineered oak wood floors are throughout the house, the only exceptions being the four bedrooms upstairs and the basement. The walls are either painted black or the perfect off-white color. There are wooden and stone accents everywhere, my favorite of which being the antique beams on the vaulted ceilings in the main living spaces and my bedroom and bathroom.

When he was giving me the full house tour earlier this week, Jackson pointed out small details most people wouldn't appreciate knowing, but I was fascinated by each and every one of them.

Like when he pointed out how he worked with the builder to make sure to prioritize energy efficiency, and he suggested making the home a net-zero one, meaning it produces as much energy as it consumes. Or that he implemented as many smart home systems as he could, with advanced security measures, voice-activated controls for lighting, thermostat, and appliances, and the fact that he can manage almost everything in the home from an app on his phone. After showing me the app, he had me download it and added me as a secondary user on his account.

I still can't quite wrap my head around the fact that he built my dream home on my dream plot of land—large enough to raise farm animals as well as children like we often used to talk about.

My mood sours at the reminder that it doesn't matter if I'm staying in my literal dream home when it's going to be more like a prison of a reality I'll never have.

Letting out an exaggerated sigh when I take in the dimly-lit kitchen, I drag my fingers along the custom concrete countertop of the island. If Jax hadn't told me, I'd have guessed the island was made of wood with its dark wood tones and the live edge. The countertop is cool beneath my finger tips, causing goosebumps to peak across my flesh. This is my dream kitchen—almost as if he stole the ideas straight from my memories—with black cabinetry and a stone backsplash.

"T? You good? Do you need anything?"

I turn, unsurprised to find Jax standing at the base of the stairs. From what I can remember, he never could fall into a deep sleep; I guess some things never change. Yet again, maybe they do. As he moves closer, my eyes stay fixed on the ink displayed across his bare chest and continues down his left arm while the right arm remains ink-free. A transposition to what is happening inked on his right leg from his ankle up to where the ink swirls and disappears beneath his dark athletic shorts.

It's not only the ink that's changed—this man has grown into himself. Long gone is the somewhat lanky teenager, and in his place is a deliciously sculpted man. His chest is so much broader, his pecs more defined, and I'm not sure what possesses me to do so, but I have to fight the urge to take his light brown nipple into my mouth and suck on it.

I bet it still drives him wild.

Instead of berating myself for those salacious thoughts, I double the fuck down. My breath hitches as I take in the masculinity coming off of him in waves. God, I'm pretty sure he's gotten taller too. He's got to be over 6'3" now. I'm miniature-sized in comparison with my 5'3" frame.

I used to love the way he'd so easily pick me up, practically manhandling me every opportunity he got. And even now, I can't stop myself from wondering what he could do with those extra inches of height and pounds of muscle. Hell, I'm half convinced that maybe his new tattoos should be factored into the endless possibilities.

Only as he stands right before me do I get a better glimpse of them, though I can only make out the faintest of details in the dim lighting. Like the way the sleeve of his left arm has the most beautifully intricate roses shaded in black and white ink. There are thorns throughout that extend down onto his hand, wrapping around his left ring finger.

How had I not noticed that?

I'm so mesmerized by the artwork displayed on his hand, I almost miss the flock of ravens adorning his Adonis belt on his left side. A place I know all too well. A spot I used to lick a trail over that drove Jax crazy.

"Jax," I breathe, unable to come up with anything more intelligible than his name.

He's close now, so close I watch in utter fascination the way his throat works when he swallows and I damn near moan when his Adam's apple bobs. His jawline is shadowed by scruff after not shaving since sometime before his brother's wedding. My fingers ache to run over the stubble and grip into his curly locks. Instead, I reach behind me and grip the edge of the island to stop myself from doing something foolish like touch my estranged husband.

"Tae," he draws out the single syllable, his voice full of gravel. My nipples pebble beneath my sleep tank, and it takes everything in me not to reach for him. It's been so long since I've yearned for another's touch, so long since I've been held in someone's warm embrace.

Nearly every night since I was last in his arms, I've craved the feeling of being tangled up in bed with him. And it's no one's fault but my own that we're where we are today. I was the one who chose to leave and never look back. *At least, that's what he thinks—all he can ever know.*

The realization hits me like a bucket of ice water, and thank fuck for that. I was a hot second away from dropping to my knees to beg for forgiveness.

Oh, fuck. Abort, abort! Get out of here, T!

Knowing I need to get out of this room and put some much needed space between us, I let go of the island and open a cabinet I'm pretty sure he told me holds the glasses. Before I even realize I opened the wrong cabinet, Jax passes me with a glass in hand headed to the refrigerator.

"Water?" he asks.

Clearing my throat, I nod before realizing he has his back to me. "Yes, please," I say, my voice shaky from the mixture of lust and uncertainty.

When he turns to hand me the water, there's a cocky smirk etched across his face, the very smirk that headlines in my dreams each night and used to incinerate my panties. "Thirsty, T?" he questions, bemused and completely self-assured.

Reaching up, I push my palm to his forehead. "You're the cockiest little shit I've ever met. Some things never change."

"Thank god for that. I missed the way your tits lit up when they saw me." The fucker waggles his eyebrows at me.

"Jackson!" I guffaw, shocked he just went there.

Bending over in laughter, Jax sets the glass down on the counter before clapping his hands in amusement. "You should see your face right now." Standing to his full height, he tilts his head to the side and rolls his bottom lip between his teeth. "Damn. Are you mad at me? Come on, T. I thought I fucked the prude outta you when we were eighteen. You grew to love my raunchy humor. Some might go as far as saying you craved it."

I did. Probably still do. But fuck that, we're not going there right now. We can't.

"For the next few weeks while I'm staying here, consider me a born-again virgin," I grit out, narrowing my eyes at him.

"Aye, aye, captain," he says sarcastically as he salutes me.

Rolling my eyes in exasperation, I go to pick up the glass of water, but it's only as it's in my hand that I realize my mistake. My chest rubs against his bicep, my pebbled nipples growing impossibly hard from the accidental contact.

I can't be sure if I've imagined it, but I think a low groan escapes Jackson. A buzzing electricity thrums through my body as heat floods my belly.

Knowing I'm no longer worthy of hearing such noises, I tuck my tail between my legs and make my way to my bedroom.

Jax chuckles. "Night, Thorn."

"Night, Bear." The old nickname slips past my lips, and I should regret it immediately. Instead, I slip beneath the covers and trace my lips as if doing so will resurrect the memories of feeling his pressed against them.

After a restless night of little to no sleep, I'm surprised to hear Jackson's doorbell ring at the crack of dawn. Rolling over in bed, I check my phone and see it's not necessarily first thing in the morning. Shit, we need to leave for the airport in the next two hours to catch our jet to Texas for the Summer Stampede.

I decide to see who came over, my guess is Carson considering he and Jackson have always been so close, and he happens to now play on the Wolverines with Jax. Hesitating in the doorway of my bedroom for a moment, I peer down at my robe and decide the fluffy material covers everything and is far from immodest.

By the time I hear the feminine voice floating through the space, it's too late for me to backpedal out of the open living space. Shit, I've been spotted!

"Oh my gosh, you're Taevin Gray!" a drop-dead gorgeous woman with platinum blonde hair and the brightest smile I've ever seen says far too cheerily for this time of the morning.

"Tis I," I for some terrifying reason respond with. For fuck's sake, can the floor please open and swallow me whole? *Tis I?* Who the hell says something like that? How about, a quick 'yep, that's me,' or, I don't fucking know, 'I am and who are you?' Because as I take in this bombshell before me with tanned, toned legs that go on for days and perky breasts that have me wishing I could lay on them like a pillow, I suddenly realize I'm incredibly invested in finding out who she is and what she's doing at Jackson's house.

"Is it weird if I hug you? I'm a hugger and also the biggest fan of your music—well, and just you in general."

"Lex, breathe," Jackson chides while biting back the laughter shaking his shoulders.

Lex?

It's only then that I notice he's taken a spot on the sectional in the living room, looking far more relaxed than I feel in this moment. His tatted leg is sprawled on the L of the sectional with his opposite tatted arm resting against the back of the couch. How he can manage to be so blasé about who I presume is his girlfriend meeting his estranged wife who happens to be staying with him while she receives cancer treatment is beyond me.

Taking an exaggerated deep breath, Lex relaxes ever so slightly before offering her hand and introducing herself. "I'm Alexa Collins. I went to college and played volleyball with McKenna, that's actually how I was adopted into the group."

She gives me a handshake that is somehow firm yet gentle at the same time and I find myself perplexed by this woman. I can already tell she has a beaming personality I'll love, and even though it kills me to admit it, I think I could find myself becoming friends with the woman who is taking on the only role I've ever wanted.

Clearing my throat and giving myself a mental pep talk to not sound like a fool, I say, "Nice to meet you. I'm Taevin."

I squeeze my eyes shut, annoyed with myself for repeating my name when she clearly already knows who I am.

She lets out what I'm going to deem an adorable snort—damn her, and her adorable snorts are winning me over. "I think I'd have to be living under a rock for the past decade to not know who you are. I'm seriously, like, your biggest fan. When you performed the national anthem at Madison Square Garden for the NBA finals five years ago, I was there and nearly passed out on the sidelines."

I can't help but join in her laughter. "Which team were you there to watch? I don't remember Minnesota being one of the teams in the finals, but I'm pretty awful with sports."

Alexa's smile kicks up another notch, if that's even possible. "Oh, no, I wasn't there as a spectator. I was there as a sideline reporter. Between you and me, I really don't prefer to cover basketball, but we were down a few reporters at the time. I mostly do sideline coverage for football now. Every now and then I get to fill in for hockey, so that's always a treat to get to see Jax and the guys."

Recognition sets in. "Oh, yes, that's why you look so familiar. You covered the Thanksgiving football game this past year, right?"

"Yep! I'm still sour over not getting Brody Meyer to change his mind about a pre-game interview, but he's stuck in his ways regardless if I'm now besties with his little sister. The guy gives zero fucks about reporters, and it is what it is, I guess." Alexa shrugs as if she's unbothered, but her tone is laced with annoyance. "I also might look familiar from the Fourth of July lake trip we all took at McKenna's family cabin. I came up with our other teammate, Brooke."

"Oh my gosh, yes, you're right!"

"Anyway, enough about me," she says before turning to face Jax. "I came bearing bad news and wanted to offer it to you in person."

"And what news is that?" Just as the question leaves Jax's lips, his phone starts buzzing on the coffee table. When he moves to pick it up, Alexa rushes over to sit beside him and places her hand over his to stop him.

Irrational jealousy I know I have no right to feel fires through me, heating my skin and twisting my stomach in knots.

"Oh, come on. It can't be that bad. What's going on?" Jax slips his arm playfully over her shoulder and brings her into his chest almost as if he's putting her in a headlock or some type of wrestling move.

With her head trapped between his bicep and chest, I'm barely able to hear her murmur, "Calvetti signed a four-year contract with Minnesota."

Jackson lets go of Alexa's head as soon as the words leave her mouth. "You're joking, right? If this is a prank you and the guys are playing on me, this isn't funny."

Calvetti? God, why does that name sound so familiar?

Alexa sits up and after glancing at me out of the corner of her eye, she faces Jackson. "I'm unfortunately very serious. I caught wind of it about an hour ago and the station likely will be breaking the story on their eight o'clock broadcast that starts in a few minutes. I'm guessing that was Bennett calling to inform you of the deal."

"Wait, how would Bennett know?" I ask as I take a seat on the far edge of the sectional, attempting to give them their space but too curious not to ask. Jackson is far too worked up right now for this to not be a big deal.

With his head in his hands, he runs his fingers through his curly locks, gripping onto the strands and looking like he's about to pull it all out.

Alexa looks at Jackson as if she expects him to answer my question, but when he doesn't after a moment, she takes it upon herself. "As you know, Bennett just got married. You did an amazing job performing their first dance song, by the way."

"Thanks," I reply sheepishly, suddenly filled with guilt for Jax missing the rest of his brother's wedding reception on my behalf. Also, confused why Jax would rush to the hospital with me and then leave his girlfriend in a foreign country with his family.

"Anyway, Bennett married Scarlett Carlisle who recently became the owner of the Minnesota Wolverines. I believe she's been in talks with Calvetti for a couple weeks now. The one thing Minnesota is lacking currently is a solid goaltender who can play in high stakes games—" she pauses to nudge Jax's shoulder. "You and I both know that even though there's history with the two of you, signing Calvetti was the right thing to do. You guys may have made it farther in the playoffs than ever before this year, but one of the main reasons you lost is because you don't have a goaltender with playoff experience. Calvetti has won a cup with LA, and for most of his seasons playing with them they made a deep playoff run. Whether you like it or not, you're stuck with him for the foreseeable future."

Jackson's head shoots up. "Four fucking years? How could Bennett let her do this? It's bad enough he was my sister's celebrity dance partner this summer but there was nothing Walker could do about that. *This* was Bennett's choice to sign off on."

"Come on, Jax. That's not fair to either of them. Bennett doesn't get a say, and Scarlett has a business to run. Do me a favor? Before you talk to Bennett, try to set aside your beef with Calvetti and see it from Scar's perspective. Regardless of what you think, he's a top-five goaltender. You played with him at Harvard almost a decade ago, I'm sure the guy has done some growing up over the years just like you have. Or at least, I think you have." Jax grunts at her, and Alexa rolls her eyes in exasperation.

My world comes to a screeching halt as I finally realize why the goalie's name sounds so familiar. It was the goalie Jackson played with his freshman year at Harvard. He was also the teammate of his that was almost a little too happy to help me find him at one of the house parties in Boston.

Fuck, I don't think I can sit here and listen to Alexa console Jax any longer. Especially not before I've had any coffee in me. Excusing myself, I make a quick cup of coffee before escaping to my bedroom to finish packing.

Thoughts of the two of them sitting out there together have me spiraling as I toss my essentials for the trip into my luggage. Each rift of laughter I hear echo down the hall has me shoving things unnecessarily hard into my suitcase.

She's put together, professional, and everything I'm sure Jackson's family would want and expect out of their daughter-in-law while I'm sitting here throwing a jealous fit, about to become infertile, and attempting to fight cancer.

Yeah, I'm a real fucking catch. More like a disaster—the train wreck you can't look away from.

11

Taevin

"**W**hat do you miss the most about living in Minnesota?" Jackson asks me, and I pause warming up my vocal chords for my morning soundcheck.

I'm pretty religious about my vocal exercises and rest the day before and day of a performance to prevent strain or damage. But having Jackson accompany me to the Summer Stampede Festival has slightly thrown me off my routine. For one, I've been completely scatter-brained since spending our entire flight steering conversation away from anything and everything even remotely 'Lex' or goalie related. And now, instead of complete vocal rest for twenty-four hours leading up to my soundcheck, he has me answering silly little questions like this one to get to know me again. And against my better judgment, I've played along because I've felt sorry for him since Alexa broke the news to him of Calvetti signing with the Wolverines.

"Probably the food," I admit somewhat reserved as I scroll through my playlists to find the perfect song to cover. Typically during my soundchecks, I like to cover an old favorite of mine, or a current hit from the charts.

"What? How is that possible? I love when we've got a game in Nashville and I can get some hot chicken," Jackson tells me.

"I'm not much of a spice girl," I murmur, continuing to scroll on my phone. My slight irritation with him is highly irrational, I realize this—somewhere in the back of my mind, I'm trying to remind myself I have no right to be jealous of the fact he's moved on. Hell, I should've done so by now too. But it doesn't stop the green monster from rioting within me.

"Oh, I remember." He lets out a deep chuckle and I wonder if he's remembering the time we went to get his favorite curry for his nineteenth birthday only for me to be sick to my stomach the rest of the afternoon with him having to take care of me. Jackson's always taken care of me. And in only a few days' time, I'll have to depend on him more than I ever have in my life.

My only saving grace is that Ryan was able to get some time off work to stay with me at Jackson's house for a few days. I'm not sure what I'd do if I needed to depend on him to help me immediately post-op. Or my dad, who only just found out I have cancer before we left. I couldn't bring myself to tell him in person, so I left him a voicemail when I knew he'd be teaching confirmation classes.

I'm a coward, I know. But at the same time, we haven't spent much time together in the last several years. I pushed him away little by little when I ran to Nashville.

"What foods do you miss the most? Wait, let me guess . . . I know it's not your dad's pathetic attempt at a meatloaf. I'm not trying to be an ass, but that was the worst meal I've ever had."

My face wrinkles in disgust on instinct, giving Jax his answer. I do my best to push the memories of that awkward night to the back of my mind.

"Alright, alright. Oh, I know! You used to love it when my mom made tater tot hotdish." He claps his hands in celebration when he sees the dreamy look on my face at the thought of his mom's hotdish. He's not wrong, I'd love a hearty serving of that.

I wonder if Alexa has had his mom's hotdish. His mom adored me when we were together, but I haven't had the chance to talk to her since being back in Minnesota because she went straight from Paris to California to help Walker move her things back home—something that Jackson was not thrilled to learn.

Kyle interrupts my spiral, reminding me I've got to get my sound-check over with before the next performer gets here. Turning, I shout, "Okay boys, I've selected the cover we're going to play this morning."

Pressing send in the BandPlay app, each band member's phone pings a moment later. With a hand on the very lowest part of my back, Kyle leads me over to the piano, and once I'm seated on the bench, he comes up beside me to adjust my mic as if I'm not perfectly capable of doing so on my own.

"You're sure about the song choice?" Kyle questions me in a hushed voice.

"There are no fans here. It's what I'm feeling right now, Kyle." With a quick nod, he gives me a soft smile, one I haven't had aimed my way in far too long.

My stomach twists when he brushes a stray strand of hair behind my ear and leans in to whisper, "You're always right. I should know that by now."

Only after he's standing offstage do I take a deep breath and shake my hands out before giving my lead guitarist, Sterling, a nod.

My band begins to play a slightly alternative version of Britney Spears's "Everytime" as my fingers fly over the ivories.

Closing my eyes, I get lost in the song as the lyrics pour out of me. I'm unable to hold back the rush of feelings that swell to the surface. Overwhelming anxiety and fear consumes me as I think about my upcoming hysterectomy. There are so many unknowns that I won't know the answers to until after surgery, and then if I'm able to keep my ovaries, after the egg retrieval. What's worse is that's all before I start chemotherapy. And don't even get me started on my soapbox about how cruel it is that I'm to go through this all while living with my ex, who just so happens to not be my ex, and is indeed still very much so legally my husband. My husband, who is dating the most wonderful woman, and I can't even be mad about it because I'd date her too if I was into women.

Instead of stewing on that tidbit, I do the only thing that brings me relief and put my everything into singing this song. I shouldn't push my vocal chords, but I do. I shouldn't pound my fingers into the keys, but I do. I shouldn't break in front of him, but I do. Pouring all of my fear, doubt, and anxiety into the song, I break on stage.

My vocal chords pull tight from the emotions welling in my throat, especially when I open my glassy eyes and look offstage to find Jackson with his arms crossed, only breaking his stance when he drags his thumb beneath his eye as if to wipe a stray tear away.

The damn bursts open as tears stream down my cheeks. Straining, I manage to sing the last lines of the song through the thick emotion closing my throat. My choked sobs echo through the microphone, and within seconds Kyle rushes over to me from offstage and Ollie, my bass player, is beside me asking what's wrong.

Ollie, being the manchild he is, doesn't know what the hell to do when a woman cries in front of him. Kyle, on the other hand, doesn't hesitate to scoot onto the piano bench beside me, wrapping me in his arms. He rubs his hand up and down my back in a way that I'm sure he means to be soothing, but actually leaves my skin crawling. His touch feels all wrong—always has.

Aside from Ryan, there's only one other person who has ever been able to be my anchor in the storms that threaten to pull me under.

"I'm going to need you to get your hands off my wife. And unless you never want to be able to use them again, I suggest you keep them to yourself from here on out." Lifting my gaze from Jackson's fist clenching at his side, I revel in the way his jaw feathers in tempo with his fist. His murderous gaze is laser focused on Kyle's hand resting on my shoulder.

So much for a quiet divorce that'll be kept out of the media because no one knew about our marriage in the first place. I'm still not sure how Bennett and his bride were able to keep that tidbit under wraps after Jax declared I was his wife in front of their wedding guests, but so far there hasn't been a single story about it.

While I can trust my bandmates, I can't say the same for the festival staff assisting with soundchecks. My speculations are valid, I realize, when I see one of the stagehands hugging a clipboard to her chest with her jaw nearly touching the floor.

Kyle's body stiffens beside me and I turn in time to see his head shoot back as if he's been struck, eyes briefly widening before narrowing on Jackson. "Down boy. No need to mark your territory." He pauses, turning to look at me. "But it's the oddest thing, I don't see a ring on her finger."

My former—yet apparently current—bodyguard, Braidy, rushes to the stage to deescalate the situation, but I raise my hand to stop him and tell him, "Braidy, we're fine here. I'll deal with this. Thanks."

Letting out a deep sigh, I shrug Kyle's hand off my shoulder and take out my in-ear monitors as Kyle helps take off my wireless pack from where it's attached to the back of my top. Pushing to stand, I go toe-to-toe with my *husband*. I grab him by the wrist and he placates me, allowing me to drag him offstage and through the back lot where my tour bus is parked.

I drop his hand and round on him, shoving my palms against his muscular chest. He doesn't move an inch and that only seems to fuel my unbridled anger.

"Let's get a few things straight, *Jaxy Bear*. One, I'm not your wife in anything but name." Holding up my hand in his face, I lift a second finger. "Two, you've gone and pissed me right the fuck off with that caveman claiming bullshit you just pulled. What the fuck was that, J?!"

"What the fuck was that?" he repeats my question, his voice filled with condescension as he lets out a low chuckle. Throwing his hand up, gesturing toward the stage, Jax growls out, "*That* was me being nice. *That* was me showing restraint. *That* was me letting fucking *Kyle*—" He pauses to make a face of disgust as if saying his name alone might make him sick before continuing, "—off the hook far too easily after he dared to touch what's *mine*."

I scoff, hoping my own growing disgust is evident. "So that's what this is about? A pissing match so you can puff out your chest and lay claim to me? Well guess what? I haven't been *yours* in ten years, Jackson Wilson!" I'm screaming the words at this point. Even knowing we're likely causing a scene, I'm unable to let this go. "I'm not just another one of your one night stands you can use and discard, Jax. I'm in the spotlight twenty-four-seven. Do you even realize what you just did back there? You may as well have called the tabloids yourself to tell them we're married. God, how could you be so selfish?"

Narrowing his eyes, his chest heaves as he points his finger at his chest. "Me? Selfish? No, darling, if that's either of us, that's you. Or did you forget that you broke my goddamn heart to move onto bigger and better things when we were supposed to live out our dreams together?"

My heart cracks down the center, reopening old wounds almost as if they'd never healed at all.

"That was a low blow—" I start, but before I can say anything else in response to his outburst, he goes off again.

"Oh, come on! You stand there and try to use my *alleged* sex life against me but I can't bring up what you did to begin with? Where do you get off? You're the one who broke our marriage—broke me—and then left town and never looked back."

"I did! I fucking did come back," I splutter through the sobs wracking me. My stomach twists so violently at the flash of memories that night triggers for me that I fear I'll be sick. Bracing a hand over my lower stomach, I take a staggered step back.

His face pales to a sickly shade of white and his shoulders drop.

"You know I came to Boston, but it didn't matter then and it's beside the point to bring up now," I whisper, too drained to continue this conversation.

"Fuck! T–baby, I'm sorry," he says softly, but I turn my back on him and swing the door to my tour bus open, entering before securing it shut and locking it behind me.

Throwing myself face down onto my usual bed in the back, I debate whether or not I'll choose to sleep here tonight instead of the hotel suite I'm sharing with Jax.

My mind whirls as I try to figure out what the hell that was. What happened out there just now wasn't us—not the inseparable Taevin and Jackson I remember. The version of us I'd branded myself with and clung to the memory of like it was my lifeline.

It's only after my tears have dried and I'm drifting off to sleep that I realize I don't recognize that version of us because that was our first actual fight. Even when I broke us, we didn't try to cut each other like that.

12

Jackson

Now

F^{uck!} I'm not sure how things escalated so quickly earlier, but I know I took it too far.

It was like I couldn't stop myself from pouring out my feelings to her, even though I knew it wasn't the time or place to do it. She drives me wild—completely fucking mad. It's like I'm a hormonal teenager all over again. Tae went from bringing out my cheesy as fuck passion as a teenager to bringing out a new possessive side of me now. She went from making me want to girlfriend her up and spoil her to making me want to win her back and take care of her at all costs.

One minute she has me reminiscing about what it was like to hold her in my arms, wishing I could've done just that the other night in my kitchen. Then the next morning, she's giving me the cold shoulder. Actually, she's been practically ignoring me every second she can since I found out about Enzo fucking Calvetti. And then when I finally got her talking to me before her soundcheck, I had to go and fuck it all to hell.

I couldn't help it—I saw red when Kyle touched her. A foreign possessiveness I'm not sure I've ever felt fueled me to threaten her manager, and in hindsight, I know I was out of line.

"

Which led me to the position I'm in now, standing outside our shared hotel suite like a dog with its tail tucked between its legs, unsure if I should go inside or give her more space. Taevin texted me about two hours ago to let me know she had to come back to the hotel to get her hair and makeup done by her "glam squad," whatever the fuck that is.

Braidy gives me a nod as I stand there awkwardly and weigh my options. "Boss lady said you were free to go in. Guess that must mean she's forgiven you."

I shake my head. "Afraid I haven't done anything to earn her forgiveness yet." Holding up the tray in my hands, I add, "Hoping these will help me take a step in the right direction."

He chuckles. "I think you'll do just fine. She's been texting every ten minutes asking if I've seen you or if you've stopped by yet."

"That's not necessarily a good thing, Braidy."

Finally, I decide to man the fuck up and go inside the suite, and when I do, I question whether I walked into the wrong one. A rack with dozens of sequined and bejeweled outfits is set up right near the door, damn near blocking the entryway. The kitchenette countertop is covered with shoes and boots, cowgirl hats, and more jewelry than someone could probably wear in their lifetime. But none of that compares to the lit up vanity that wasn't there an hour ago when I left. Its countertop is filled with dozens upon dozens of makeup brushes and products. And sitting in front of that on a barstool is Taevin in an oversized, white hotel robe, hugging one knee to her chest while the other leg dangles over the edge of the stool tapping to the beat of the music playing in the background.

Dumbfounded, I stand there and take in the scene of her in hair rollers, bopping along and lip syncing while a woman looks like she's beating Tae's face with some orange thing. She has her eyes closed, so she hasn't noticed me standing there staring at her like a creep with a bag of lunch in one hand and a drink carrier in the other.

After her hospitalization in Paris, and hearing what her doctor in Minnesota had to say, I've been an anxious mess when it comes to Taevin's performance tonight. She mentioned on the flight here that she has had more inflammation than normal due to her tumor, and she was worried about it affecting her vocal chords.

A faint gasp leaves the woman's lips before she shrieks, "Oh holy shit! I was about to scream but then I realized who you were. You *are* Taevin's secret husband, right? Well, I guess it's not so secret anymore since the news broke about an hour ago."

My hackles rise. "What are you talking about?"

Taevin's eyes shoot open before she narrows them at me through the reflection in the mirror. "Oh, just what I told you would happen. You let the cat outta the bag, and now we'll have to suffer the public disgrace and scrutiny when you inevitably give me my divorce."

Eyeing the makeup artist suspiciously, I shuffle my feet from side to side, unsure if and how I should respond to that.

"You don't have to worry about Elsie, she's like a sister to me and has been with me for five years now. Even so, she's signed a big, fat NDA so she won't say shit. Right, Else?"

"Damn straight, beautiful," Elsie agrees as she looks me up and down. "So, Mr. Secret Hubby, are you going to continue to stand there like a weirdo with those mysterious drinks in your hands, or are you going to take a seat and join our conversation we were just having about you?"

"Else, what the fuck?" Taevin grumbles, lightly shoving her friend's shoulder.

"Oh, come on. Like he doesn't probably already know he made you cry yourself to sleep earlier? And if he doesn't, he needs to and does now. You're welcome."

"Elsie!" Taevin admonishes, now covering her face with her hands.

Steering the conversation just slightly, I hold up the bag and drink carrier in my hands. "I brought provisions. I wasn't completely sure what you liked to drink before a performance, but I got you a green tea and a berry smoothie—both listed as beverages that help reduce inflammation. I also brought you a leafy salad with tomatoes and walnuts to try to help. If I was completely off base, let me know and I can go get you whatever else you'd like."

Taevin's face crumbles into what looks like uncertainty. She's likely questioning my motives because my current actions don't match how I behaved earlier.

"Hey, Else, could you please give us a few minutes?" Taevin asks.

"Yeah, no problem. I can go downstairs for a coffee."

"I've got an iced one and a black one here if you want either of those," I tell her, holding up the drink carrier. "You don't need to leave. Taevin and I can just go talk in the other room," I suggest, nodding in the direction of Taevin's closed bedroom door.

Elsie looks to Taevin to gauge her response. Tae nods once at Elsie then rises from the barstool and marches toward her room, but not before making sure to shoulder me on her way past. I follow her into the room and shut the door behind me, standing there with my back against the wood as I work through what I want to say to her.

Taevin beats me to it when she asks, "Are you sure she'd be okay with you coming into my room like this right now?"

I blink, my brain trying to catch up. "Who are you talking about?"

"Alexa, your girlfriend." Taevin states it so detached, as if she's unaffected by the fact that she thinks I have a girlfriend.

"Alexa is not my girlfriend," I assure her.

Rolling her eyes, Taevin corrects herself, "Fine, your friend with benefits."

"Not that either. Last time she and I spoke, she said she had just started seeing someone." Pushing off the door, I eliminate the space between us until I'm standing toe-to-toe with her like we were earlier.

Taevin's face scrunches up. "But the two of you seemed comfortable together—you two were cuddling on your couch."

"I'd hardly consider giving her a noogie cuddling. Bit of a stretch, don't you think? But good to know I can't put my arm around a friend because she's a girl without that meaning we're either dating or fucking." I can feel myself getting worked up, so I take a deep breath.

She crosses her arms and quirks a brow. "Oh, that's rich coming from you, considering you threatened my manager only hours ago for doing just that."

Breathing out a sigh of defeat, I rub my hand down my jaw. "Shit. You're right. I'm sorry."

"And you know that's not what I meant. The two of you seemed *familiar* with each other." I don't miss what she's getting at, and if I'm not mistaken, I'd say there's a hint of jealousy in her tone.

Instead of calling her out on that, I try to put her mind at ease. "Alexa and I got closer this year because we were sick of being the only two single ones in the group. I did ask her out, and after one date we both agreed we're better off as friends. But then when the rest of the group assumed we were something more, we didn't correct them because it was easier to let them make their assumptions than explain that we'd become really good friends. We've gone to a few events together so her parents stay off her back about needing to settle down and I got my brother and friends off my back about needing to move on and forget about you."

Taevin is silent at my admission, her hands dropping to her sides.

"There's just one problem," I say as I take another step into her space, crowding her as my chest brushes up against hers.

"What's that?" she questions, now sounding a bit breathless.

"There's no moving on from you, Taevin. You made that impossible when you tattooed yourself on my soul."

"You can't possibly mean that, J. Especially not after the things you said earlier today—"

I cut her off. "About that. I'm so sorry for fighting with you. There's no excuse for my behavior. Was I jealous? Yes. But that doesn't justify the way I spoke to you earlier. I'm so fucking sorry, T."

She's silent for so long I worry she won't forgive me. Finally, she whispers, "Want to make it up to me?"

"I'd do anything to make it up to you," I tell her, because it's god's honest truth.

"Play with me."

"Wait, w-what?" I barely stammer the question out.

Her eyes widen when she realizes what she said. "I-I meant play *for* me. As in play your guitar for me—*with* me on stage. I'd like to sing a duet with you tonight."

"You want me to perform on stage with you tonight in front of thousands of people?"

"Yes," she states simply as if asking me to do so isn't one of the most bizarre ideas she's ever had.

"I already told you I haven't touched my guitar in years."

"You and I both know it's like riding a bike. And if you didn't intend on playing it, why did you bring your beat up guitar case? Is it empty?"

"No, it's not. But I only brought it because you threatened my life if I didn't bring it."

"Hmm, did I?" she asks, feigning innocence.

"You most certainly did. I believe you said something like, 'if you don't bring your guitar I'll kill you or put your balls in a meat grinder.'" Instinctually, a shiver runs down my spine at the memory. She had the craziest look in her eyes, but it was the only thing she had said to me for hours before we left, so I did as she asked.

"So what song should we sing?" she asks without me ever agreeing.

"What makes you think I'm getting on that stage?"

She shrugs her shoulders, and I don't miss the way that little movement has her robe falling open ever-so-slightly. "You said you'd do *anything*. This is my request."

"You know I don't like playing, let alone singing, in front of crowds. Could I maybe just play here with you after you're ready? Like when you're warming up your vocal chords? Besides, if the two of us perform together on stage, won't that only shove our marriage further into the spotlight?"

She pulls at her bottom lip while she thinks it over before saying, "Fine. I suppose that'll do."

Leaning down, I whisper in her ear, "Do I get to pick the song?"

"Sure," she whispers, breathless.

"Then I choose 'Landslide,'" I tell her without hesitation.

"The original version or the one by The Chicks?"

Looking into her eyes for as long as I can, I brush a stray strand of hair that's fallen out of her curlers behind her ear and say, "Whichever was the version you used to sing me to fall asleep over the phone or while you ran your nails over my scalp as we laid in bed."

Her breathing picks up, and it takes nearly all the restraint I have to resist looking down to watch her chest rise and fall. "That was so long ago I'm not even sure I remember, but I think it was sort of a mix of the two."

"It was ours, and that's the one I choose."

"Stripped down, just you and me?" she questions, and my stomach tightens involuntarily.

"That's the only way you'll ever get me to do it, T," I tell her, looking into her deep brown eyes while fighting the urge to kiss her.

"Okay, just the two of us. Now go take a steaming hot shower and warm up those vocal chords while I tune your guitar."

That little tidbit seems to break me from my spell. "Since when did you learn to tune a guitar?" I ask, a playful teasing in my tone.

"I might've picked up a few things in the last several years. You'll just have to stick around to find them all out." She shoots me a playful wink and I think maybe that means she's forgiven me, even though she shouldn't.

"Looking forward to it, Thorn." As if on instinct, she looks down at my left hand and stares at the tattoo wrapped around my left ring finger. I clear my throat to regain her attention. "Some day I'll tell you about them." When she just stares back at me in confusion, I clarify, "My tattoos. I've gotten too many to count by now, but I'll tell you the story behind them."

There's really not much to tell. They're an homage to her. Every last one of them has to do with the girl who stole my heart at eighteen.

Without another word I step back and make my way toward the door before hesitating with my hand on the handle.

"The third hanger in," I murmur softly over my shoulder.

Confusion knits her brows. "What?"

"The third hanger in—the black dress with black jewels covering the bodice. If I were choosing an outfit for you tonight, that's what I'd want to see you in."

"And what makes you think you get a say in my wardrobe?"

"I know I don't. It was a request. Do me a favor and grant me it?"

She scoffs. "Why would I do that?"

Lowering my gaze to the floor, I smile softly at my shuffling feet. "Because seeing you in a version of the dress you wore to my senior prom will have me feeling nostalgic, just like playing for you will now. It'll be a full circle kind of moment."

Chancing a glance, I look up at her. She tilts her head side to side before answering, "Yeah, I guess you're right. It will be a full circle moment considering the time you sprang a surprise performance on me while we were at the fair. Consider this a decade's worth of payback."

"Hey, look where it got us." I take a moment to let those words sink in, and while our future didn't work out for the two of us the way I'd planned, I could never regret that night and the success it led her to.

Taevin breaks our eye contact, gazing off to the side of the room and I take that as my cue to leave her alone.

As I suds up in the shower, I try to give myself a mental pep talk for our little private performance. Basically the only thing I can come up with is, *don't fuck this up.*

Taevin

Yeah . . . so I fucked up.

I messed up in the worst way.

After I tuned Jax's guitar, he came back into my room smelling so good it left me reeling—a mixture of his laundry detergent, his bodywash, and the cologne I got him as a wedding present. How is it that he still has it after all this time?

As he approaches the bed where I'm sitting with his guitar in my lap, I clear my throat and try my best to subtly breathe him in when he takes a seat beside me.

"You, uh, smell familiar."

Jax quirks a brow, bringing the fabric of his shirt to his nose and taking a whiff. "Familiar in a good or bad way?"

"The best way," I mutter under my breath but he definitely heard it if the cocky smirk he's wearing is anything to go off of.

Looking over at him, I can't help but ask, "How is it you smell exactly like the cologne I got you on our wedding day?"

"Because I still wear it. Well, lately only for special occasions so it doesn't run out. When I got my first signing bonus, I bought a ridiculous amount of bottles because I heard they were discontinuing it."

His cheeks heat in the most adorable way, so I question, "How many bottles is a ridiculous amount?"

"Twenty-five," he murmurs.

My eyes widen. "Jax! That cologne was like two hundred dollars. You spent five grand on cologne?"

He grabs the back of his neck, looking so bashful it takes everything in me not to throw myself into his arms right now. I've never been able to resist him when he gets like this—the way he looks right now is like an aphrodisiac personalized just for me. "Yeah, I know. When Bennett found out because we were living together at the time, he just about blew a gasket and gave me the biggest lecture on being smart with my money. It was another example of me doing something to keep the memory of us close that he just couldn't comprehend."

"How many bottles do you have left?" I ask, my voice hushed.

"I've got plenty—I think I've only gone through about six or seven. But I wanted to be able to wear it for the rest of our lives, so when I realized I was going through about a bottle a year when I wore it everyday, I started to cut back and only wear it on game days and special occasions."

"And right now is a special occasion?"

"It is," he assures, nodding his head.

It's only then I take in what he's wearing. A familiar camouflage baseball hat I got him when we were dating causes another wave of nostalgia to hit. To anyone else, the simple combination of a camo hat and a spritz of cologne wouldn't damn near shut them down and turn them on all at once. Well, if anyone saw Jax right now, they would definitely feel the same.

He's paired his backward hat with an olive green Carhartt shirt, fitted light-wash jeans, and a pair of chestnut, square toe Tecovas.

Essentially, he looks the exact way I'd imagined him in all of my fantasies over the past decade.

So, yeah, I'm completely fucked.

How am I supposed to resist him when I've already been hanging on by a thread?

Knowing I need some space, I shift his guitar beside me and stand. "I'm going to finish getting ready quickly," I tell him.

Nearly a half hour later, once Elsie put the finishing touches on my hair and makeup, I walk into my bedroom where Jackson was waiting for me. He's got his guitar perched on his thigh as if he's been playing, but I know he hasn't since I haven't heard anything from the other room.

He looks up, and when he takes in my chosen outfit, he shakes his head as a slow smile spreads across his face. "Should've known asking you to wear something for me would only make you do the opposite."

Slowly, I lower my gaze from his and try to take my outfit in from his eyes. I'm wearing a lightwashed denim corset, a short, black leather skort, a belt with an oversized turquoise buckle, and my favorite black and turquoise cowboy boots. My ears, neck, and arms are covered in turquoise and silver jewelry, and I'm still debating whether or not I'll wear my signature black cowgirl hat or not.

The dress Jax requested wasn't right for this festival, but I did tell my stylist I was taking that one home with me to save for another performance in the future.

"I tend to stray from being the people-pleasing girl I once was the farther I get from Minnesota," I inform him.

"Does that mean you'll want to please me when we get back home?" His question is meant to be teasing, but it causes my heart to stutter.

Home.

He said when *we* get back home.

And, god, what I wouldn't give to go back in time and make that a possibility.

But I can't.

All we have is here and now.

Giving my head a slight shake, I lick my lips and gesture to his guitar. "Shall we?"

Jax gives me a curt nod before looking down at his guitar—well, more like glaring at it.

"You know you can't just will it to play itself, you actually have to strum your fingers," I tease, and when he shuts his eyes, hanging his head, I almost feel bad. That is, until I see the shake of his shoulders from his muffled laughter.

He throws his head back so the beautiful sound echoes off the walls, and suddenly I wish I could freeze time. I'd give anything to stay here in this bubble with him like this—his smile the only thing I see and his laughter playing like a record on repeat.

When he finally composes himself, he gives me a slow perusal; the way he longingly takes me in feels like a physical caress. "God, I've missed you. So damn much," he rasps once his gaze finally meets mine.

My heart lurches in my chest at his admission. As if I have no control of my body, I'm suddenly across the room and sitting on the edge of the mattress next to him. Close enough to feel the heat radiating from his skin.

"Do you need me to sit behind you and show you where to place your fingers on the frets like you did for me my first time?" I ask. What was meant to sound sassy completely misses its mark, my sultry tone eliciting goosebumps on his arms.

Jax swallows roughly, and I watch the way his throat works with rapt attention. I used to love sucking, licking, and biting the skin there. As if he knows exactly where my mind has gone, he begins strumming the opening chords of the song. His playing isn't practiced like it once was, but it still works to throw me back in time just the same.

The moment he sings the opening line of the song, I'm suddenly no longer sitting on this bed in a hotel room in Texas with him. Instead, we're sitting in the bed of his pickup truck beneath a blanket of July stars twinkling against the midnight sky.

As if I can't help but do so, I join him, singing in perfect harmony. Our voices shouldn't blend together so beautifully after all this time, but they do. Almost like we've been performing together for years instead of the reality of our situation.

Even as I get lost in our song, I don't take my eyes off his. I'm branding this moment to memory, knowing with absolute certainty this will be what I think of to get me through the hardest of times about to come my way.

My body inches closer to his with each verse, and by the closing lines of the song, I'm nearly on his lap—my chest pressed against his upper arm and one of my crossed legs resting atop his thigh closest to me.

When the final chord hangs between us, our mouths are only a breath away. I can nearly taste his sweet, mintyness. And when he licks his lips with his eyes locked on my mouth, I decide to throw caution to the wind.

"Taevin! We need to go. Now," Kyle booms from the other side of the door. Squeezing my eyes shut, I curse under my breath. The interruption working like a bucket of cool water being dropped over the two of us.

I just about kissed my husband. My first and only love. Undoubtedly the one who got away. But it's only because of my decisions that we're in this situation. If I had chosen differently—picked him over anything else—there's no doubt in my mind we could've been *everything*.

But I didn't. So we aren't.

Breaking News

Country star Taevin Gray married to Jackson Wilson
Everything we know from the couple's secret marriage.
By LARA BRADLEY

There was quite a reveal during Taevin Gray's soundcheck ahead of her performance this evening at The Summer Stampede music festival.

The country music star, 28, has been secretly married to professional hockey player, Jackson Wilson, 29, for nearly a decade according to court documents obtained by *Country Know Now*.

Sources revealed the pair had a heated exchange onstage following her band's soundcheck, in which Wilson referred to Gray as his wife.

Country Know Now has reached out to reps for both Gray and Wilson, but have not yet heard back.

To stay up to date on all the latest country celebrity news, subscribe below.

13

Jackson

I'm late. I've never been late to pick up Taevin, and today of all days isn't the day to start.

Of course my father chose today to berate me about needing to prioritize hockey over, in his words, "some high school fling that will inevitably flop." Not sure why it took him nearly three months to realize I had a girlfriend, but it did. My mom was gushing about Taevin and prom being today, and it unfortunately set my old man off. Which meant I had to take a lengthy meeting in his home office where he proceeded to threaten to cut me off financially if I fucked up my scholarship with Harvard.

I try to put his threats behind me as I pull into Taevin's driveway. I've got enough to worry about as today's going to be one of the first times I'm sitting down with her father as Taevin's boyfriend. She told him about us last month. Some time after we'd declared our love for one another, she decided it was time to stop sneaking around and be truthful.

To say he wasn't pleased to learn his daughter is dating would be an understatement. And when he saw I'm the lucky bastard who gets the privilege of dating her, well, let's just say the guy proved that even pastors aren't immune to passing judgement.

As I approach the front steps of her mid-century house, I can't help but fidget with the bowtie threatening to strangle me. I knock on the front door and then tighten my fingers around the plastic box holding the corsage I got for Tae. The only thing she told me about her dress was that it's black—not shocking at all—so I got her a black corsage with a black bracelet and myself a matching boutonniere since I'm decked out in black from head to toe from my Ray-Ban sunglasses to my Tom Ford dress shoes.

The front door opens to reveal Pastor Gray and a scowl that I've come to learn is reserved just for me.

"Good afternoon, Pastor Gray," I say, aiming to start the conversation off as politely as possible.

"Make sure to have her home by ten o'clock sharp," he grumbles, not bothering to greet me.

Caught off guard, I try to reason with him. "Oh, um, I thought perhaps Taevin's curfew would be pushed back a bit considering it's senior prom, and I don't know if Taevin told you, but my school's dance doesn't get over until ten thirty."

"You're lucky I'm even allowing her to go. I thought for sure when her school refused to let you attend hers, that it'd mean I'd be able to avoid her going to a prom with you. But it seems like public schools will let anyone through their doors."

I don't say it out loud, but considering my high school's prom is in a local hotel's ballroom, yeah, I think we're a little more lenient than Taevin's private, Christian school. Instead I say, "I'm thankful we're able to experience this milestone together, though I would've gladly gone to her school's prom over my own so Tae could dance with her friends."

He grunts and I'm not sure if he's agreeing or just mocking me. "Well, it seems she's made friends with some of yours," he notes dryly.

"She has—my best friend Carson's twin sister, McKenna, and her best friend Katie have adopted her into their group. They'll both be with us tonight."

Pastor Gray simply grunts, again, in reply.

"So, um, may I come in?" I ask him, shuffling side to side on my feet. My collar feels like it pulls even tighter as he stares me down for what feels like a full minute before he steps back and waves me inside.

Walking into the entryway of their home, I take in the interior, having never been inside until just now. All of our dates thus far—at least since she told her father about us—have ended with me walking Taevin to her front door and telling her good night after thoroughly kissing her in my car seconds before.

The entryway consists of a den with glass-paned french doors to the right, and a staircase on the left side, and a hallway in between. All of the walls are filled with dozens of pictures of a young Taevin, making me wish we had more time for me to look at them all. Dark wood floors run the length of the hallway, but the den and the steps share the same dark burgundy carpet that reminds me of that in the *Home Alone* house.

What I'd give to have Taevin home alone with me for a few hours, let alone a few days.

I must have a dumb smile on my face because Pastor Gray turns to me, and almost as if he read my mind, grumbles, "Wipe that smile off your face. This is the first and last time you'll be invited into my home."

Noted. Though, I don't need to be invited in by him in order to visit Taevin. Sneaking in could be fun.

Before I can strategize how I'd manage to do that, the breath is stolen from my lungs when the most beautiful vision appears at the top of the stairs. Taevin looks drop-dead gorgeous in a black gown that is beaded and fitted on the top with a sparkly bottom that flows to the floor. As she walks down the steps to me, I don't miss the slit on the side of her dress that showcases a teasing amount of her thigh. The dress isn't overtly sexy, still having straps and a skirt that doesn't cling to her curves the way it certainly could, and yet I'm having the most impure fantasies about me inching the dress up and exploring what she's got on underneath.

When she reaches the last step, she giggles at me before placing her hand beneath my chin and closing my mouth. Wiping the side of my mouth and giving me a wink, she teases, "You had a little something there."

You bet your ass I did, I think to myself. I mean, how could I *not*?

This dress.

Taevin.

Fuck, I've never been so awestruck.

"T, you look stunning—you're quite literally dazzling in this dress," I tell her, holding her hand in mine as she takes the last step down the stairs. Lifting her arm, I twirl her around so I can see the back of her dress, loving the way it moves as she spins.

"You like?" she asks, lifting the bottom of her dress to show me her black Converse sneakers. Waggling her foot side to side, she says, "I had to go for comfort over fashion on the shoe choice, though."

"I love it. The dress. The shoes. All of it. Everything," I assure her, completely in awe.

"Oh, can I see the flowers? I promise I'll try not to poke you when I pin your boutonniere on," Taevin swears as she gestures to the plastic box I forgot I was even holding.

Clearing my throat, I open the lid. "Yeah, here you go. The florist said she stuck the pins right in the back of it."

She grabs the boutonniere and slips one of the pins out, placing it between her lips while she takes the other and lines it up on the lapel of my jacket. As she rearranges it to where she wants it, I gaze down at her and take in the details I missed when she was walking down the steps. Her raven hair is curled and pulled back into some sort of wispy bun. And instead of her typical makeup-free look, she told me she was going to get her makeup done this morning with Kenna and Katie. Whatever they did somehow makes her brown eyes even more enchanting.

I'm entranced as I take in her bold, burgundy lips that are still wrapped around the second pin. If we weren't standing right in front of her dad, I'd claim those lips without a care in the world about getting the dark lipstick all over me.

She smiles brightly when she successfully pins the boutonniere on without poking me. "Alright, my turn," she tells me as she holds out her right hand.

Bringing it up to my mouth, I place a chaste kiss on the back before grabbing the corsage out of the box and looking around for where to set it down.

Her dad reaches his hand out, signaling for me to hand it to him. "Thanks," I murmur and then slide the corsage onto her wrist.

"It turned out perfect, J. I love the black roses. Thank you so much." Turning to her dad, she holds out her wrist. "Look, Dad. Jackson got Mom's favorite flowers in my favorite color. Wasn't that sweet of him?"

"Yeah, Taev, it was. She'd probably be beside herself with tears seeing her baby girl all grown up and going to her senior prom." Her father is looking at her with a faraway look in his misty eyes, and it's one of the first times outside of church I've seen him look something other than stern, though I can't quite get a read on the fleeting emotion before his face neutralizes as he glances at me.

"That was, uh, kind of you to think of Taevin's mom." Offering his hand out to me, I shake it as he says, "Have her home no later than eleven o'clock. I'll be up waiting, you hear?"

"Yes, sir."

"Robert. You may call me Robert."

I'm shocked but hopeful to see a sliver of progress in getting him to like me.

"I'll have her home safe and sound by eleven, Robert. Thank you."

He turns to Taevin, and at first I think he's holding out his hand to shake hers as well, but he holds hers in his for a moment before pulling her in for a side hug. The gesture looks like it catches Tae off guard, and I'm not surprised considering what she's told me of how their relationship has been since her mom passed away.

"You look beautiful, Taev. Be safe tonight and have fun." Robert steps away and just as we step out the front door, he calls out, "Oh, before I forget. Could I get a picture of the two of you?"

Taevin looks to me and blushes when I nod and shoot her a quick wink.

Wrapping my arms around her waist from behind her, I position us in the typical prom pose and smile at her dad as he snaps a few photos of us on his phone before thanking us and seeing us off.

Once we're inside the cab of my truck, Taevin turns her wide eyed gaze to me. "Okay, that was weird, right? He hasn't gotten sentimental like that since my mom died—at least, not in front of me he hasn't."

Grabbing her hand in mind, I intertwine our fingers and press a kiss to the back of her hand. "It's progress. And did you hear him say I could call him Robert? I feel like I'm living in the twilight zone right now. Between him saying that, and the fact that I'm lucky enough to call a staggeringly beautiful woman like you mine, I'm feeling invincible."

That earns me a giggle and a little shoulder shove. "Oh, quit it. I was so surprised that a boy as handsome as you was taking me to his senior prom that I realize now I haven't even told you how hot you look."

"Wait, you think I'm hot?" I retort.

She rolls her eyes. "I can't even with you."

"Yeah, but you still love me, so what does that say about you?"

"You're right, I do love you. I think it says I'm a hopeless fool."

"Ditto, baby. Now, let's go dance the night away." Placing another quick peck on the back of her hand, I shoot her a quick wink before taking off.

"Dangerous Woman" by Ariana Grande is playing, and holy fuck, the way Taevin is moving her back against my front right now is headed toward a very dangerous situation.

We haven't gone *there* yet, and not for her lack of trying. "There" being literally anything farther than making out, dry humping, and a lot of heavy petting. I'm not even sure how I've managed to stay strong with holding out this long, but my willpower to resist her is slipping by the second. Especially with how fucking gorgeous she looks in this dress.

Think of bad things. Gross things. Literally anything but the way her ass is grinding so perfectly against your raging hard-on.

I back up ever-so slightly to adjust myself before gripping her around the waist. "Tae, you've got to stop grinding on me like that or I'm going to bust in my fucking pants."

She giggles and looks at me over her shoulder. "Is that even possible?"

"You're about thirty seconds away from finding out," I grit out, telling myself to stay strong.

Getting checked against the boards. Those sad pet infomercials. Falling off a horse. Getting kicked by a horse . . . in the dick!

Nothing is fucking working, I'm bricked up beyond belief.

She spins in my arms to face me, pulling on my neck to bring my ear to her lips. "What if I want you to come in your pants, J?"

I'm fucked. Jesus, I'm so fucked.

Being the little minx she is, she bites the shell of my ear and that along with her warm breath tickling my neck just below my ear, has me nearly coming undone right then and there.

"Baby," I half groan, half plead. "Have a little mercy on me."

With her arms wrapped around my neck, she pulls her head back to look into my eyes. "I'm ready."

"Taevin," I murmur, pressing my forehead against hers.

"I want you, J. I want you to be my first," she whispers softly and I feel my resolve slip farther.

She steps back when I don't immediately respond, and I snap out of the mind-fuck spiral I was going down.

Pulling her back into my chest, I place a kiss on her temple and whisper against her skin, "And I will be. Trust me, T, I want you more than anything. It's not a matter of me wanting you. I refuse to take your virginity on prom night—it needs to be special, not a teenage cliché."

She pouts. "But we're at a hotel, and we've still got a few hours before I need to be home. It's not a cliché if I want this. Besides, who knows when we'll get another opportunity to be alone like this again?"

"There's no rush, T."

And there's not. I'm not sure why I'm being so protective of her virginity, it's not like I'm a virgin myself; before Taevin, I was definitely known as a player. But with her, everything is different. I've wanted to take things slow—to take our time and get to know each other before we cross the lines physically.

"It's not rushing when we've been together for over three months and we love each other."

I agree with her, I think we're both ready to take the next step. Still doesn't change my mind. So I tell her, "Trust me, it's taking everything in me to wait right now, but I can't tonight."

"So let me get this straight, if it were tomorrow, you'd be okay taking my virginity, but because it's prom night, you won't?" She scoffs.

Tucking a stray piece of hair behind her ear, I hold her gaze. "Correct. Because when I make love to you for the first time, I want to take my time with you. I want the moment to be special, not rushed in a hotel room on prom night so I can get you home before your curfew. I want to be able to hold you in my arms after and take care of you," I explain to her, hoping like hell she understands where I'm coming from.

"Oh," is all she replies.

"Yeah, something like that," I mutter against her cheek before kissing it.

"What?" she questions.

With a deep chuckle, I clarify, "Something like, '*Oh, Jackson! Yes, Ja—*'"

I catch her hand midair—by now, I can anticipate the swat she was aiming at my chest—and bring it to my mouth where I place a whisper of a kiss on the inside of her wrist.

"I love you. Do you know that?"

A dreamy sigh leaves her lips as a soft smile appears. "I do know that. And I love you too."

Turning her around so her back is to my front again, she murmurs over her shoulder, "Now let's see if I can make you come in your pants so at least one of us has a happy ending tonight."

"Such a thorn in my side," I whisper against the shell of her ear, eliciting a shiver to run down her spine.

"You'd probably love it if I scratched you up a bit."

I throw my head back and groan as images flood my head of me hovering above Taevin while she claws at my back to keep herself anchored as I drive in and out of her.

My dick twitches in my pants just as Taevin does some twisting motion with her hips, driving me mad with desire.

Yep, I'm completely fucked.

14

Taevin

"What do you mean you've never flown a kite?" Jackson asks incredulously.

"I don't know, okay? I just realized it myself when you told that guy after your game to 'go fly a kite,' that I've never actually flown one."

With one hand on his steering wheel and the other on my thigh, he tells me, "Well, that's unacceptable. We're going to the store to buy one right now and then we're going to fly a kite, dammit. I know the perfect place."

"Like, today?"

"Yes. Right now."

Peering out his windshield, I point to the darkening sky. "It looks like it might rain."

"Nah, I think it's just supposed to be windy and cloudy. Which is perfect kite-flying weather."

I look down at my white sundress covered in yellow marigolds and shrug my shoulders. Well, if it rains maybe I'll see that restraint of his slip. Especially considering I couldn't wear a bra with the way the neckline plunges and the straps criss-cross in the back. Actually, now I'm praying for rain.

After a quick stop at the convenience store, we park his truck in the big prairie behind his house. Tall green grass stretches acres across the rolling hills that butt up to a line of trees in the distance. Patches of wild flowers are sprinkled throughout and I can't help but stand in awe of the beauty of it all once I hop out of the cab.

"Jackson," I gasp, taking it in.

Coming up behind me, he wraps his arms around my waist and rests his chin on my head. "I've been waiting for the wild flowers to bloom so I could bring you out here." After placing a kiss on my temple, he spins me around in his arms. "Let's fly this kite, baby."

Baby. He knows I'm putty in the palm of his hand when he calls me that. I don't know why, but the way he says it and the way he looks at me when he does, makes me feel like I'm just as much his everything as he is mine.

The past three months have been a whirlwind of extreme highs as we've fallen head first, inexplicably in love with each other. I realize that likely everyone feels this way when they're with their first love before it inevitably falls apart. But something about this feels so different from the young love my friends have experienced. It feels as if we've been tethered together and nothing and no one can tear us apart.

That's why I'm ready for us to take the next step—I want him to make love to me. No, I *need* him to. I'm dying for us to make that connection. It's all I've been able to think about since his prom last weekend.

I'm so lost in thought as I gaze into his sea glass eyes, I hardly hear the first roll of thunder. Blinking out of my haze, I ask, "Should we be out here if it's going to storm?"

"I'm not too worried about it." Jax shrugs. "Still sounds pretty far off in the distance to me. Besides, the wind is picking up just right to not only fly this kite, but for me to potentially catch a glimpse of what you're wearing under that little sundress—which is tempting the fuck out of me, by the way." He bites his bottom lip and scrunches his face as if he's in pain.

Rolling my eyes at his theatrics, I shove his shoulder before clapping my hands together. "Alright, let's do this if we're going to do it before we get soaked."

Jax waggles his brows suggestively. "Oh, I plan to get you soaked, alright."

"I'm going to kill you."

"Nah, you love me too much to hurt me."

"Is that so? Then why do you call me Thorn? Thought it was because I'm such a pain in your side."

He reaches into the back of his truck to grab the kite. Once he's unpackaged it, he avoids eye contact with me at first. But when his smoldering gaze locks with mine, I feel the warmth of it throughout my core. "I don't call you Thorn because you're a pain. I call you that because thorns symbolize so many different things, and you're nearly every one in my eyes: sin and redemption, pain and protection, hardship and resilience, strength and unique beauty. I figured you knew by now that you're my everything, Tae, but if not, I'll do my best to show you each day from here on out."

I'm breathless as his words sink in. Boneless as his love seeps through me. Hopeless when it comes to ever loving anything or anyone as much as I love him.

"Jax—" I start but he cuts me off when he drops the kite to the ground and lifts me up, my legs wrapping around his waist just before he presses my back into the cab of his truck. His lips are on me seconds later. This kiss is fiery desperation. Our bodies mold together in the most divine way. When his hips grind into me, I feel his belt buckle imprinting my bare thigh and I want nothing more than for him to brand me—to mark me as his permanently.

Thunder rolls again, this time not so far in the distance, just before the skies open up and heavy rain comes pouring down. But we don't stop kissing, nothing could distract me or make me hesitate.

I need him right now.

It's only as I think this that he breaks our kiss, and I whimper at the loss, causing him to let out a low chuckle.

Jax throws his head back, and as the rain soaks his face and hair, I'm mesmerized at the sight of his throat working as he continues to laugh. And when he lowers his chin, shaking his hair out of his eyes, so he can make eye contact with me again, I don't think I've ever seen something so captivating—so *tempting*.

Instead of begging him with my words to finally make me his, I show him what I want with my body as I dig my fingers into his shoulders and slowly grind my hips against his in circles. I watch with fascination as his eyes change from twinkling in playful delight to growing heavy with devious desire. Throwing my head back against his truck, I arch my back so my breasts rise and brush his chest. The damp material rubs against my hardened nipples, and I'm aching for him to touch me—*claim me*—where I want him to most.

"You might actually kill me if you keep doing what you're doing with your hips, baby," he gruffs out.

"In that case, maybe I do want to kill you," I retort, continuing to rock my hips against his.

"Fuck it. It's not like we're going to fly a kite in this weather anyways."

Unsure of what he means by that, my confusion quickly dissipates when Jax steps back, still holding me with my legs wrapped around his waist, and begins walking toward his house.

"Put me down, J. I'm too heavy and I can walk perfectly fine."

"Tae, be so for real right now. You're pint sized compared to me." Nodding across the lawn he says, "No one is home. My parents left this morning with Walker for one of her dance competitions in New York. I've got the place to myself for the entire weekend." A slow, seductive smirk spread across his face, leaving my chest heaving at the sight.

This is it. It's finally happening—that's why he said fuck it.

Before I can think any further, he says, "Now hold on tight. I'm not sure if you know this but you're super wet." He tries for all of two seconds to hold back his laughter.

"I hope you're laughing at how pathetic of a line that was. I'm honestly reconsidering letting you take me upstairs to have your wicked way with me," I deadpan.

He stops walking and stares at me intently. "Tell me what you want, Thorn. Remember, you're in control here. Always."

"I need you to stop wasting time talking and get me upstairs to your bedroom. I'm sure about this, Jackson. I'm ready—I've *been* ready and you know that. Are you sure this is what you want?" I question him, though I regret it when his eyes narrow on me.

"Am I sure that I want to be the guy privileged enough to have all of your firsts? Yeah, I've never been more sure of anything in my life."

With that, he begins moving again toward the house, this time with a quicker pace than before.

"Someone's in a hurry. Thought you were going to take your time with me," I taunt as he nearly slips trying to take the steps two at a time.

"Trust me, I plan to take my time with you." Digging his fingers into the undersides of my thighs, he carries me the rest of the way up to his bedroom, and with every step my breath becomes more shuttered. My heart is pounding so hard in my chest, I fear he'll hear it and think I'm having second thoughts.

He opens his bedroom door and swiftly kicks it shut before walking over to his king size bed covered in plush, navy bedding. To my surprise, Jax doesn't set me on the comforter like I thought he would; instead he sets me on my feet before him, taking a step back and staring at me.

"May I?" he asks. I lift my arms in invitation, hoping that's all the answer he needs.

He lifts the hem of my dress at an achingly slow pace, dragging his fingers across my skin as he does so. I melt at his touch, so much so that I'm honestly concerned my legs will give out on me. And when he bends down to trail open mouth kisses up my thighs, to my hip bones, and my stomach as he lifts my dress, I think I'll combust from the heat he's sparked inside of me.

We've messed around plenty, but always with our clothes on. This is the first time his hands and lips are on the expanse of my bare skin.

Impatient, I lift my sundress the rest of the way over my head. I'm left topless and I find him marveling at my chest. He kneads my breast in his hand, tweaking my nipple before moving to the other and giving it the same attention.

"You're so beautiful, Tae. I meant it when I said I'm going to take my time with you—I want to kiss every inch of your skin."

I always imagined I'd feel self conscious the first time I was completely naked in front of a guy, but with the way Jackson's looking at me right now, I feel more confident than I've ever felt.

Kneeling down before me, he grips my thighs and places one singular kiss over my satin-covered center. "Jax," I gasp at the foreign feeling, immediately wanting more of the sparks he's eliciting inside me. He pushes my panties aside and slowly drags a finger up my slit. Forget sparks—he's ignited a raging wildfire in my core that's spreading through my chest. And when he follows the same trail his finger just made with his tongue? My skin burns with need everywhere. I've truly never felt more alive.

Resting his forehead against my stomach, he groans as if he's in agony.

"Fuck!" he murmurs, squeezing his eyes shut before he presses his lips against my stomach.

"What's wrong?" I'm quick to question, praying I didn't do something wrong. Oh shit—do I taste bad? Oh my god!

"Nothing, aside from the fact that just the sight of you and the briefest taste of you just about had me coming in my goddamn pants."

"W-what?" I stammer, unsure I heard him correctly.

"Lay back on the bed, baby," he tells me, gently pushing me backward until the backs of my knees connect with the mattress.

Jackson kneels between my legs, stripping me from my underwear at a torturous rate. When I squirm, trying to ease some of the ache he's created, he spreads my legs apart and asks, "Is this okay?"

"Y-yes," I stammer, somewhat flustered.

"How do you want me, T? Tell me and I'll do whatever you want me to, baby."

Sitting up, I rest my weight on my elbows so I can take in the sight of him kneeling before me with his big hands gripping my thighs to hold them open. He has a cocksure smile that would normally irritate me, however, it only amplifies his sex appeal right now.

Biting my lip, I hesitate what I want him to do to me. What I need is *him*. But I know that answer won't suffice. I take a deep breath and tell him, "I want you to do what you were doing before." When all I get in response is a cocked brow, I huff out a breath of frustration. "W-when you kissed me and then licked me there."

"There?"

"*There*," I growl out in annoyance, gesturing to the place between my thighs that's splayed out before him.

"You mean here?" he asks before placing a whisper light kiss on my clit and blowing on it. My core clenches with need for him to do that again.

"Yes," I pant breathlessly and watch with rapt attention as he slowly drags a finger down my slit before circling my entrance, toying with me I'm sure because of my impatience.

He did say he'd take his time with me, but this is torture.

"I-I need more. Please," I plead with him to give me what I want.

"Is this what you want, Thorn?" he rasps the question as he slowly pushes a finger inside me.

The intrusion is foreign but welcome as he slides it out and then back in again. I've never fingered myself, all I've ever tried was playing with my clit, but that never brought me to orgasm.

This—Jackson touching me in this way—has me regretting never trying it. Though, now that I think about it, I'd rather he was the first.

As if his finger moving inside me wasn't enough to make me combust, Jax lowers his mouth back to my core all while keeping his eyes locked on mine, only breaking our stare when he closes his eyes and groans against my clit.

Gasping, I fist his bedding to anchor myself as I throw my head back in pleasure. Jackson flattens his tongue, lapping my slit before flicking my clit with the tip of his tongue.

When Jax adds a second finger and finds the most delicious rhythm with his tongue, I lace my fingers through his hair to hold him in place as I begin to rock my hips against him.

He breaks his pace and lifts his lips just enough to rasp, "That's it, T. You're doing so good for me, baby."

Picking up right where he left off, Jax sucks my clit into his mouth and that, in combination with his fingers, is all it takes to make me detonate.

My orgasm crashes into me like a tidal wave, cresting and threatening to pull me under. I'd gladly drown in Jackson's current if it meant I got to hold onto this feeling forever. With trembling legs, I'm boneless as Jax continues to pump his fingers in and out of me, prolonging my release.

"That was the hottest thing I've ever experienced," he murmurs against my thigh before pulling his fingers out of me. The sight is so debaucherous, yet I can't get enough.

If this is what it always feels like—like my heart will beat right out of my chest and my core will combust from the intensity of the climax—then sign me the heck up for a lifetime supply.

Part of me loves the forbidden aspect of what we're doing, but my god, I don't know how something that feels this euphoric could be deemed unholy.

All my life I've been raised to think sex only exists in the marriage bed, but there's nothing about this that feels wrong. Every part of me felt whole while I fell apart at the hands of Jackson.

He crawls up the bed and pulls me into his arms before delicately kissing along my temple. "How are you feeling?" he murmurs.

"Better than I've ever felt," I admit, nuzzling my head into the crook of his neck and placing whisper-light kisses against his jaw, neck, and collarbone.

We sit like that for a moment, wrapped up in each other's arms, legs intertwined when he whispers, "So I did okay? I've never—

My head shoots up. "Never what?"

He rolls his bottom lip between his teeth. "Never gone down on anyone before."

That simply cannot be true. Yet, I know I have no reason not to believe him. What would he have to gain from lying to me? "I'd have thought the fact that you gave me my very first orgasm would've been answer enough."

The cocksure smile I've come to love takes over his face, and I can't even berate myself for stroking his ego.

Suddenly, I realize I haven't returned the favor.

Pushing Jax onto his back, I throw my leg over his waist and straddle him. When my bare core rubs against his boxer-clad length, I let out a soft moan. "I believe it's your turn to feel good now."

"This isn't transactional—that's not how this works."

"Then tell me how this works. Because the way I see it, you gave me my first blissful orgasm and I'd like to show my appreciation by returning the favor."

"Trust me, watching you fall apart from my fingers and tongue was more than returning the favor."

I can't help the laugh that slips out, but really all I want is to continue this feeling, I rock my hips against him, and Jax grips my hips to halt me in place.

"Tae, we've got plenty of time. Or we could if you'd stay."

I chuckle softly at his suggestion.

"Can you ask your dad if you can sleep over at Ryan's tonight?" he asks.

Bending down, I place a quick kiss on his lips. "Yeah, so I'm pretty sure now that he found out we're dating that he'd never believe that lie."

"Then tell him the truth. Say you're staying here. Hell, say you're staying the entire weekend. We're eighteen, what's he gonna do?" he presses as if he doesn't know exactly what he'd do—ground me for life.

"We've got two weeks left of school, Jax. He's not just going to let me stay here all weekend with you."

"Fine, just tonight, then." He punctuates that suggestion by bucking his hips against mine.

Rolling my eyes, I ask, "Are you delusional? He'd never let that fly."

"Tell him you're helping me with a school project that I need to finish in order to graduate."

"You're one of your class's valedictorians."

"So? He doesn't need to know that."

"Your mom went on and on about it to him at church last Sunday."

"What if you text him where you are and then say we fell asleep watching a movie or studying together?" he suggests, continuing to rock into me.

"Mmm," I moan in appreciation. "You're *very* persuasive when you're doing that."

"Is that so? In that case," he says as he rolls me onto my back and drags his boxers down. When he runs his thick length through my drenched core, I whimper in response. "Just think, baby. If you stay here, you can get this any time you want. All hours of the night."

Part of me wants to scream yes, but there's a part of me that's holding back, and I'm not sure why. Yet I quickly realize part of the reason when I can't stop myself from asking, "Have you ever stayed the night with a girl?"

"No," he responds, and I must do a poor job of hiding my shock because he cracks a smile. "What? Is that surprising to you?"

"Well, yes. You said you've thrown parties here before, and I'd have assumed you brought girls up here and they stayed the night with you."

He shifts his weight, pitching himself up on his elbows so he can hold my gaze as he hovers above me—the sight is beyond intoxicating.

"Let's get one thing straight: I've never had a girl in this room. Ever. Not in this bed, not in my shower, not alone in the kitchen where I plan to feed you later. And I've never stayed the night with anyone at my house, or anywhere else for that matter. You'll be the first and only girl I want to do that with, T."

His sage eyes remain locked on mine, and I feel myself being pulled even farther into Jackson's current. And it's then I decide to jump head first without giving it another thought. "I'll stay tonight, but I'm not sure I'll be able to convince my dad to let me stay the entire weekend. Tonight will be reason enough to ground me for the rest of the summer, I'm sure."

"I'll break you outta jail." Chuckling, he places a quick kiss on my forehead, and another on each of my collarbones before hopping off the bed.

Sitting up, I watch as he tucks himself back into his boxers before I ask, "Where are you going?"

"Your stomach was growling, so I'm going to feed you some dinner."

When I quickly look down at his pitched boxers, he shakes his head. "Trust me, there's plenty of time for that, baby."

Tossing me his shirt, he sends me a sinful wink before heading out of his room. "Come on, Tae. I've been told I make a wicked-good grilled cheese," he calls from down the hall.

With a huff of annoyance at my stomach's greedy interruption, I pull his shirt over my head and breathe in his heady scent—a spicy, woodsy blend that's entirely *him*.

Forgoing my panties that lie on the floor, I decide right then and there that if I'm going to take the risk of breaking my father's rules by staying the night, I better make the most of it. I'm going to make it my mission to drive Jax wild.

Jackson

Shutting off my bathroom light, I freeze in my tracks as I take in the sight of my heartbreakingly beautiful girlfriend sitting on the edge of my bed with nothing but a thin sheet covering her body and my Gibson guitar laid across her lap.

Taevin frets a few chords, and my heart swells with pride with how quickly she's picked up on what I've taught her. She's been practicing every chance she gets, and I make a mental note to get her her very own guitar for her birthday. Or maybe like a four-month anniversary present? People do that, right?

I listen for a moment, loving how lost she is in the music, but I can't remain inconspicuous when she begins percussive slapping the guitar—something I hadn't taught her yet.

"And how, my little Thorn, did you learn to do that?" I question.

She startles for a moment before giving me a soft smile once she sees me. "I may or may not have been practicing with my choir teacher's guitar at school during my study hall."

"You're going to become an expert in no time."

"Sometimes the student becomes the teacher, but I don't think that'll be the case with us," she explains. Taking her hand off the neck of the guitar, she pats the space on the mattress beside her. "Come sit, I want to play you something I've been working on."

I move to her on instinct, marveling at the sight of her completely naked in my bed with a guitar in her hand. I've never seen a sexier scene in my life. Taevin's tousled hair falls to her waist, giving her a freshly fucked look, which causes my dick to thicken beneath my boxers.

"Show me what you got."

She shifts excitedly toward me, causing the sheet to fall to her waist, leaving her perky tits on display for me, and I have to literally bite my knuckle to hold back the groan that wants to slip from the sight. "Okay, so I've been playing around with these lyrics for a few weeks now, but the composition just kind of came to me when I was messing around in the choir room earlier this week. It's rough, and I think you could help make it so much better because you're an insanely talented guitar player, but anyways, it goes a little something like this," she explains as she begins strumming the opening chords of the piece she's been working on.

The melody is beautifully spellbinding. And the moment she opens her mouth to sing the opening lines of the song, I'm entranced. My girl has me completely bewitched within the first verse. Closing her eyes as she plays, Taevin gets lost in the lyrics. She sings about finding your first love and falling fast and hard, and I quickly realize she's written a song about the two of us.

Taevin's song ends with a beautiful guitar slide that she seems to have mastered in no time, and I'm stunned silent. When she finally opens her eyes, I stare into her big brown eyes that shimmer with nervous excitement, and I realize I literally can't speak. I don't have words for what she just did, and when she misinterprets my silence for indifference, I curse myself for being the reason the twinkle in her eyes diminishes even temporarily.

Just as she moves to set the guitar aside, I manage to find my voice. "Tae," is what I manage to strangle out, and I immediately feel like an asshat. As if merely saying her name would be a sufficient response to the woman I love pouring her heart into a song for me.

She moves to tug on the sheet pooled at her waist, and my brain finally snaps the fuck out of the haze she put me in. I take her hands in mine, closing the space between us as I rest my forehead against hers. There's an innate need to be as close as possible to her, and this just isn't cutting it.

"Come here, baby," I whisper against her lips, pulling at her waist. Tae climbs into my lap, and I brace her head in my hands as I kiss her forehead once, twice, and a third time before resting mine on hers once more as I search for a way to put what I'm feeling into words.

"How are you real?" is what I finally decide on.

Tae's cheek twitches like she's fighting back a smile, and that just won't do.

"I'm sorry, I'm just having a hard time coming up with words when I can hardly comprehend that you're real and you're so incredibly talented and you're *mine*." Pulling my head back so I can stare into her eyes, I cradle her face in my hands like she's the most delicate thing in the world. "What you just did was truly remarkable. I've never seen a more breathtaking sight in my life and I've never heard anything like it."

"Really? You're not just saying that?" she questions hesitantly.

"It was so raw and beautiful. You're right, the student has far surpassed the teacher at this point," I admit in awe.

The light in her eyes reappears with a vengeance, causing my heart to swell with pride.

Tae walks her fingers up my arm and over my collarbone with one hand until she wraps them both around my neck. "Well I had a really good teacher. He was very diligent in his teachings," she teases, throwing her head back in laughter.

"Laugh it up while you can, Thorn," I taunt, gripping her hips and tickling her as I stand up and spin us around. Her laughter turns into squeals as she begs for me to knock it off.

Laying her on her back, I settle between her thighs, and when her warm skin scorches my bare chest, our laughter dies, quickly transitioning into heavy breathing.

I hover above her, not wanting to hurt her beneath my body weight.

With a trembling hand, Tae reaches up and palms my cheek before dragging her finger tips over my stubble, then along the edge of my jaw, before raking them through my hair. "Kiss me already, would ya," she whispers, and how could I resist?

Our lips come together, meeting eagerly, yet nothing about this kiss is rushed. My chest tightens at the tenderness in which our mouths move together, the way she timidly opens for me before our tongues tangle.

If I had to choose between never playing another hockey game again and never getting to kiss Taevin Gray again, I'd happily say my goodbyes to the ice.

This girl has quickly become my whole world—consuming my every waking thought and fulfilling all of my wildest dreams.

I can't wait to graduate and start our lives together in Boston this fall. We're going to make this work, I know it.

Our kissing inevitably turns into more. Unable to resist her bare breasts sitting before me like they're on a silver platter, I knead one in my hand, tweaking her nipples in the way that had her moaning earlier. Taevin grinds her hips against mine, and I groan into her mouth at the feel of her warm heat against my hardening length.

Breaking our kiss, I bring one nipple into my mouth while continuing to tweak and knead the other.

"Oh my! Yes—" Taevin gasps when I gently bite her nipple. "Take these off," she murmurs, pushing the waist of my boxers down.

Deciding I need to give her more, I kiss a path down her stomach until I've got her legs spread over my shoulders and shed my boxers the rest of the way.

"Is this okay?" I ask, meeting her lust-filled gaze.

She nods eagerly before I swipe my tongue through her slit. God-damn, she's already soaked. Remembering what drove her wild earlier, I push a finger inside her, pumping it a few times before working a second in and hooking them upward. That seems to nearly throw Tae off the edge because she moans loudly in response.

God, that's fucking hot. The noises she's making, the way her body responds to my touch, it's all too much yet not nearly enough. I'm so turned on I find myself rutting into the mattress to find relief. Fuck, I think I could come just like this—she turns me on like never before.

When I suck her clit into my mouth while feverishly pumping my fingers in and out of her, Taevin comes apart on my fingers and tongue, pulsing and soaking them.

Only after she's ridden out the last ripples of her release do I kiss a path up to her lips once more, hovering above her as I do.

Pulling her lips from mine, she looks up at me with blown pupils and a hazy smile on her lips. "I fear you've turned me into an addict."

"Oh yeah?" I question, chuckling against her lips when she wraps her legs around my waist and urges me closer to her.

"Yeah. And I'm ready for my next hit," she tells me as she circles her hips so the slickness between her thighs coats my dick.

"Tae," I whisper in warning because if she continues to do that, I won't be able to resist.

As if she can read my mind, she pleads her case. "Stop resisting me. Please. I want you so badly. Don't you want me too?"

"Of course!" I assure her.

"Then why won't you show me how badly you want me? Maybe you don't want me as much—" she starts, but I cut her off with a hum of desperation in her ear when she moves her hips and I nearly slide inside her.

"Mmm, do you know how bad I want you?" I pant out the question, my desperation making me breathless. "So bad—I want you so *fucking* bad, baby," I whisper the last word into her ear as she moves her hand between us and glides the head of my cock through her drenched slit.

That feels so good. Fuck, too good. "Oh, shit! Tae, wait."

"What are we still waiting for Jackson?" she huffs out in exasperation.

"How about a condom for one?"

Her hips halt their movements as her hand freezes on my dick. "I-I didn't really realize. Sh-should you have already put one on? I don't know how to do any of this."

"Shh," I whisper soothingly against her lips as I tangle one of my hands through her hair as I cup her cheek. "No, it's okay. I haven't entered you or anything, but even though we both got tested and you started birth control, we should still use a condom to be safe."

She nods and presses her cheek into my touch. "Yeah, you're right. I'm sorry, I just got caught up in the moment."

"You don't need to apologize. It's my job to keep you safe and protect all of your dreams." Reaching over her, I open my bedside drawer and feel around until my fingers close around the foil wrapper I'm looking for.

Sitting back on my knees, I bring the foil to my mouth but hesitate. Looking down at her, I urge her to be honest with me. "Are you sure about this?"

"Yes, I'm sure. I want you, Jackson. Please," she begs her consent, and I don't have the willpower to resist her any longer.

I rip the wrapper open with my teeth and sheath myself before resuming my position of hovering above her. With shaky hands, I grip my length and give it a few pumps before guiding it to her entrance.

Taevin braces her hands on either side of my face and stares into my eyes as she gives me a nod of encouragement and assurance. It's only when she whispers "make me yours" against my lips that I finally nudge the head of my cock inside her.

Shuttered breaths escape me as I brace my arms beside her head and gently tangle my fingers through her hair. Without breaking her lust-filled stare, I inch inside of her, going slowly to try to ease her discomfort as much as possible. I've never been with a virgin before, but I know once I push past her barrier, it'll be painful at first for her.

She's so tight that it feels like I can't move further. "Take a deep breath for me, baby," I encourage her, and when she does so, I pull my hips back before slowly pushing my length back inside her, causing her to gasp when I push past her tight barrier.

I halt my movements to give her time to adjust, my entire body quivering against hers as I take in her pinched brows.

"Are you okay?" I manage to rasp out the question between my gritted teeth. I'm hanging on by a thread right now as I continue to tremble above her.

"Yeah, I'm good," she assures me.

"Does it hurt? Do you want me to stop?"

"Gosh, no. It was a pinch of pain, but I'm good now. Please don't stop." Raking her fingers through my hair, she grips my neck and brings my mouth to hers.

When I press my lips against hers, I push inside her further until I've nearly bottomed out. "You feel so perfect. It's like you were made for me," I groan in pleasure. "I love you."

"Mmm," she moans before nipping at my bottom lip. "I love you too. Now move, J."

And so I do.

I pull out so only my tip is still sheathed inside her warm heat before pistoning forward until my hips collide with hers, and when she pivots her hips so her clit brushes against my pelvis, she bites down on my shoulder to keep from screaming.

Shaking my head against hers, I demand, "Let me hear you, baby. We're the only two here. I want to hear every sound I pull from you."

She does as I request and it spurs me the fuck on. I have to remind myself to hold onto my restraint so I don't hurt her, but when she rakes her nails down my back and roughly squeezes my ass, my control slips and I drive into her faster. My frantic thrusts make her moan louder, and I fear I may come from the sounds she makes alone.

Not yet. Not fucking yet.

My silent commands are useless though because as I continue to piston my hips in and out of her, my balls pull taught with the telltale sign that I'm rearing toward release.

"Jax!" Taevin chants my name, and when I finally feel her pussy pulsing around me, squeezing me so tight it feels like I won't be able to pull out, I drive into her one last time and unravel with her.

My cock twitches as I spill into the condom, which only seems to further Taevin's release. Our breaths and moans sound harmonious as we ride out the waves of our orgasms.

I've never come simultaneously with someone before and I realize now I've just picked up the same addiction as Taevin.

Nothing has ever been better than this feeling—my body pressed against hers, our chests brushing as we fight to catch our breath.

It's euphoria in the purest form.

A vice I'll never willingly give up.

"You've ensnared me, Thorn," I whisper against her neck before placing a delicate kiss against her pulse point.

"Good, because I don't plan on letting you go," she murmurs as she rakes her fingers through the hair at my nape, keeping me in place.

"I'm yours for the taking," I admit as my heart beats wildly in my chest.

"Then I'll take forever."

"I think I'll hold you to that."

"You do that."

I will.

15

Jackson

Now

My legs bounce incessantly as I hold onto Tae's hand from my spot beside her bed in the post-op recovery room a nurse led me back to moments ago. This room is giving me deja vu to her hospital stay in Paris.

"Hey, sleepyhead. How are you feeling?" I ask as her eyes flutter open.

Tae's brows crinkle but when she manages to keep her eyes open long enough to focus on me, her face transforms with a radiant smile eclipsing the fog from anesthesia.

"Well, *hello* handsome," she rasps, her voice hoarse.

"Hello to you too, gorgeous," I reply, failing to bite back a chuckle.

"You think *I'm* gorgeous?!" she squeals like a schoolgirl and it's honestly one of the most adorable things I've ever heard.

"Of course. From the moment I first laid eyes on you to our wedding day to now. You're the most mesmerizing woman I've ever seen."

"Shut. Up. I'm married to you?!"

Alarm bells go off in my head, I shoot a look at the nurse but she's too busy laughing at Tae's animated expressions.

"Don't worry," the nurse assures me when she senses my anxiety. "This is totally normal when people are waking from anesthesia. Sometimes patients are groggy and sometimes they practice a little comedy routine for us."

"Who are you?" Taevin asks the nurse.

"I'm your nurse. My name is Whitney."

"Whitney. My girl! Do you *see* him? This sexy man just said he's my husband. No wonder my stomach hurts so bad. He's probably packing a weapon down there."

"Taevin, oh my god." I don't manage to bite back my chuckle, instead my cheeks heat and I fall into a fit of laughter.

That is, until I realize she said her stomach hurts. My face falls and I rush to grab her hand. "Are you hurting, baby?"

She hums a sigh of content. "Have I ever told you how sexy it is when you call me that?" she asks, completely ignoring my question. "Makes me putty in your hands."

"I'm going to go grab her something for the pain. Be right back," the nurse says, leaving us alone.

I focus back on Tae, giving her a small smile. "You may have mentioned it a few times while we were dating."

"And then we got married." She sighs with a smile.

My lip twitches at the corner. "We did."

"And you told me all about the babies you were gonna give me."

An ache explodes in my chest. Before I can answer, she continues, "And now, I'm guessing I'll never be able to do that. Bummer because I would've died to have your babies. They woulda been so cute. Your curly hair, my dark eyes. Could you imagine?"

I can. I really can.

"There's still a chance, baby."

Now it's her turn to be interrupted because before she can speak, the surgeon comes in.

"Good morning, Taevin. Jackson, nice to see you," Dr. Prescott greets us.

"Good morning, Dr. Prescott," I greet her while Taevin's eyes close and her head bobs as if she might fall back asleep before her eyes shoot back open and she blinks a few times.

Dr. Prescott stands next to the bed. "Taevin, I realize things may still be a bit foggy for you from the anesthesia, but I wanted to stop in to give you an update on how things went before I head back into the OR for my next surgery."

"Thank you," Tae rasps, her eyes fluttering open and closed as she struggles to stay awake.

"As you know, prior to surgery we discussed the plan for a partial hysterectomy, meaning we would leave only your ovaries and we'd remove your uterus, fallopian tubes, and cervix. Your ovaries were viable and there was no evidence of disease on them. We did, however, have to remove several lymph nodes near your cervix. If you choose to do a round of egg retrieval, you can begin the process after your two-week post-op check-up. Once the egg retrieval surgery is complete, you would then begin chemotherapy treatments."

"Well that's just—" Taevin starts but cuts herself off to puff out a breath before her lip begins to quiver. "Thank you." Her voice breaks and it's as if the news has snapped her out of her fogginess.

"If you think of any questions or you have any complications, please be sure to reach out to the care line that will be listed on your discharge paperwork," Dr. Prescott informs her.

Taevin still looks overcome so I reply for her, "We will. Thank you, Dr. Prescott."

"You're welcome. Rest up, and I will see you in two weeks for your next appointment."

Once Dr. Prescott is out of the room, Taevin's walls come crumbling down, and for the first time I'm seeing the devastation and fear consume her.

"Baby," is all I manage to whisper, standing up so I can lean over her and kiss her forehead.

"I-I still h-have a ch-chance. I-I c-can st-ill be a m-mom," she stammers through the sobs.

My heart fissures down the center for her, and I make a silent vow to do everything in my power to help her egg retrieval be a success.

The next day, I take off at a sprint toward the front door, opening it and placing my pointer finger in front of my mouth in a hushing motion. If I didn't know she was coming to stay here, I wouldn't recognize the woman with the bright pink pixie cut standing in front of me as Taevin's best friend, Ryan.

Though recognition would soon set in because when she sees it's me who answers the door, she says, "Oh, hello, hockey boy. Did you miss me?"

Shaking my head, I gesture for her to come inside while I grab her suitcases. Yes, suitcases being plural, as in she packed three large ones. "Ryan, good to see you. Thanks for coming."

"Thanks for letting me stay here a few days while Taevin's getting up and going."

Shutting the door, I scratch the side of my face before gesturing to her luggage. "Of course. But are you sure you're only staying for a few days? Seems like you've got enough baggage to stay indefinitely."

"Pretty sure you're the one with all the baggage." She waves me off over her shoulder. "If you just show me around quickly and let me know which room is Taevin's, you can get back to whatever team training or puck bunnies are waiting for you. I've got my girl."

Yeah, that's not going to fly. Like, at all. Knowing I need to set her straight, I inform her, "I don't have any plans or training, and I've never hooked up with a puck bunny. And like I said, thanks for coming to help take care of *our* girl."

That's right. She's not just Ryan's girl; she's mine too.

Ryan scoffs and rolls her eyes. What's with these women and rolling their goddamn eyes? "Never say never, Jackson. I may have seen you in a compromising position one night in Boston when *my* girl was coming to get you."

All color drains from my face when I realize the night she's talking about. "You were there with her?" I ask and when she simply nods in reply, I can't stop myself from wishing I could punch Enzo Calvetti in the face right now. "So then tell me you stuck around long enough to realize I was drunk out of my mind, and even in my inebriated state, I practically tossed her off of me."

A slight frown appears on Ryan's face. "Unfortunately, no. I left the party with Taevin, and then everything went to hell after that."

"What do you mean?" I question.

Now her frown turns to, I don't know, panic maybe? It's been so long since I've seen her, I can't get a good read on the emotions playing across her face. "Nothing. She was just brokenhearted and in a city she thought she'd be living out this epic love story with you, and instead her heart shattered on the pavement."

"I'm so fucking confused right now. Taevin's the one who changed all of our plans to take her record deal. And instead of letting me come with her or attempt a long distance relationship, she's the one who broke my heart."

"Is that how you remember it? It was so long ago, by now it's all so fuzzy, I guess." Ryan hums before shrugging as if me having my heart broken by Tae was no big deal. And I don't know why I let it get to me, but the condescending little hum she did sends me damn near over the edge.

"Not long enough ago for you to still send me bags of dicks monthly," I mutter under my breath, but she must hear me because she breaks out into a shrill fit of laughter.

"Oh, fuck. I almost forgot about that. I've had it on subscription since you purchased this house."

"One, how the hell did you know I purchased this house?"

"Property records, duh. You should've put it under an LLC or something if you didn't want people to find your home address."

"Noted. I'll look into changing that immediately," I growl out.

"You should, otherwise the paps will be out here sniffing around after they saw the two of you together at Summer Stampede. I'm surprised they haven't already found you."

I sigh in frustration just thinking about those vultures closing in on us. I can't let that happen. Maybe I should look into upping my security systems too. Fuck, maybe Taevin should look into Braidy staying here while I'm on the road for away games. I kind of hate the fact that Kyle hired him though. Maybe I can convince Taevin to let me hire someone else to be her bodyguard while she's in Minnesota.

"I'll get right on it," I say gruffly, mentally adding things to my to-do list.

Ryan huffs out a breath. "You do that. But could you show me where I'll be staying and bring my bags with you while you're at it?"

"Did Boston take all the manners outta you?"

"No, I just lose them from time to time when I'm dealing with my best friend's estranged husband."

"Nothing estranged about me—I'm right here, aren't I?" I ask, holding my arms out wide.

She shrugs. "For now. Jury's still out as to whether or not you manage to win her back. My money's on you making a complete fool of yourself a time or two before that happens."

"You know, I almost forgot what a joy you are to be around," I deadpan.

"I've been told I'm a real fucking ray of sunshine," she retorts.

"What a stretch that is," I murmur as I grab two of her suitcases and march up the stairs to show her to her room.

"Knock, knock," I call out, standing in the open doorway of Taevin's room.

Taevin's lying on the bed, propped up by half a dozen pillows, as Ryan runs a brush through her damp hair. At the end of the day, the one thing I can admit when it comes to Ryan is she's a hell of a friend to Tae. She's been so on top of everything when it comes to helping Taevin these past few days.

"To what do we owe the pleasure, hockey boy?"

"I was wondering if the two of you would like to have dinner in here, or if you'd like to join me and my mom in the dining room?"

Taevin's eyes shoot up to meet mine. "Wait, your mom's here?"

"She is. You said you missed her tater tot hotdish, and she's been chomping at the bit for a chance to see you again, so I figured two birds, one stone. If you're not feeling up to company and eating in the dining room, I totally get it, just thought I'd offer."

A soft smile spreads across her lips. "I've missed your mom, and I was just telling Ryan I need to get up and move around a bit. Give me, like, five minutes and we'll be right out."

Knocking twice on the wooden doorframe, I nod and say, "Sounds good. She'll be excited to catch up. But if she's being too much, use a code word or something so I know if I need to kick her out."

"And what code word would that be?" Ryan asks on Tae's behalf.

"I don't know, like, crown, or something like that."

"What if the word crown naturally comes up in conversation? You'd just throw out your mother?" Ryan questions.

"I'd rather kick out my mom by accident—politely, of course—than have Taevin uncomfortable or overwhelmed." Turning to fix my gaze on Taevin, I say, "I'll see you in a bit."

Walking back down the hallway, I turn into the kitchen and find my mom setting the table.

"Here, let me help," I tell her, grabbing the utensils from where she set them out on the kitchen island.

"Thank you, sweetheart. What'd she say?" my mom asks eagerly.

"Tae said she and Ryan would be out in a few minutes."

"Oh! I'm so happy!" my mom squeals and I can't help but smile at her excitement. She loved Taevin like she was her own while we were dating. Not that she'd ever admit it, but I know she was devastated when we broke up and Taevin moved to Nashville.

Just as we've finished setting the table, Taevin comes slowly shuffling out of her bedroom with Ryan following closely behind her to join me and my mom at the dining table.

Before I can say a word, my mom hightails it toward Tae.

"Ma—" I start just as she freezes in front of Taevin.

"Taevin, oh my gosh! Honey, I've missed you! Can I hug you? I don't want to hurt you."

"Kathy, it's so great to see you; I've missed you too. You can hug me, but maybe a side hug would be best for now?"

"Of course, sweet girl!"

I watch in awe as my mom hugs Taevin and Tae's eyes well, full of emotion when my mom starts rubbing her hand up and down her back. Once my mom has hugged her to her heart's content, she takes a step back and says, "A little birdie told me you've been craving my tater tot hotdish. Well, honey, all you had to do was ask and you shall receive."

Turning to face the table, my mom gestures at the steaming pan of Taevin's favorite meal.

"It smells amazing. The second Ryan opened my bedroom door, my mouth started watering. Thank you so much."

My mom waves off her thanks. "Anytime, sweetie. I mean it; it's my pleasure."

I pull out a chair for Taevin that's next to mine and Ryan helps her ease into her seat.

"Is this okay? Do you need anything from your room to help you be more comfortable? Maybe that front pillow thing you ordered?" I suggest, noticing the slight pinch to her brows as if she's in pain.

"Yeah, that'd actually be great. I'm not sure why, but I've been sneezing today and holding the pillow against my stomach to brace myself has helped ease a bit of the pain," Tae explains.

She doesn't need to say another word. I'm up and on my way to her room in an instant, damn near running to grab said pillow.

Taevin has been in so much pain since her surgery, and I'm terrified she'll have a post-op complication if we're not careful. I don't want anything to set her back from the egg retrieval process she hopes to begin soon. The timing needs to be perfect so she can begin chemotherapy as soon as possible.

When I'm in her room grabbing the pillow, I notice a worn leather-bound journal laying open on her nightstand. She has a mechanical pencil sitting beside it, and it's only then I notice the lyrics scrawled across the pages in lead.

I'm so goddamn tempted to see what she has written about, but I know it'd be a major violation of her privacy.

Sighing in frustration, I'm about to turn to walk out the door when I make out the title written across the top of the page. "Revival" is written in a slightly darker handwriting than the rest of the page.

Is my Thorn writing about me?

Is it possible that I could still be her muse after all we've gone through? I'm not sure, but I'm anxious as hell to find out. I walk out of the room with a dopey smile on my face, because not only am I hopeful that Tae's writing about me, but I can also hear the tail end of the conversation between my mom and the woman I've never stopped loving—and I hope I never will.

"Have you seen your dad more since you've been back?" my mom asks, and I'm eager to hear Tae's reply because so far she hasn't seen him. I haven't wanted to push her to talk about it, but she did tell me she told him about her diagnosis before we left for Texas.

"No, he and I have had a strained relationship for years now. If I'm being honest, he hasn't been the same since my mom died. I was so scared to tell him I have cancer like my mother did, that I told him over a voicemail."

"Oh, honey. I'm sorry to hear that. If it is something you want, maybe your time spent back home will help bring the two of you closer again."

"Yeah, maybe," Tae agrees.

Remaining hidden in the shadows of the hallway, I run my hand through my hair. Tae doesn't know this, but her dad texted me the day of her surgery. I'd honestly kind of forgot he did with so many other friends and family texting to check in on Taevin that day. I need to tell her about it.

"Okay, enough of the heaviness. How's my boy been treating you?"

"He's been so good to me, Kathy. Ryan had never had the cheesy potatoes y'all used to make for family get-togethers, and just the thought of them had my mouth watering and finally gave me the urge to eat something in days. Until then, they practically had to force-feed me. But his cheesy potatoes seemed to do the trick. Then he made chili and that was to die for."

"If I were a betting woman, I'd say he's trying to win back your heart through your stomach."

"Hard to win back something he's had all along," Taevin murmurs in a hushed tone, no doubt hoping I won't overhear.

Too late.

My heart pounds in my chest.

Up until now, I was playing it safe when it came to easing Taevin back into my life, thinking that would be the least likely way to scare her. But after hearing that, I'm done holding back my feelings.

I'm going to do everything in my power to show Taevin how badly I want her to stay.

Not just through the remainder of her treatments—forever.

16

Jackson

Now

Tae's feeling the best she's felt since her surgery a little over a week ago so we're going to a coffee shop down the road from my house before heading to Target to get some things she's running low on. Ryan stayed for the first week following surgery to help her with pretty much everything from washing her hair to sitting in bed and holding her while she cried.

I've been trying to research as much as I can about the ways to help her recover and what to expect when caring for someone who had a hysterectomy, but I'm pretty sure from what I've picked up on that Tae's crying has more to do with the fact that she's unable to carry her own children and the uncertainty for how her egg retrieval will go. The meds they prescribed her can only help with her physical pain, but they can't heal the emotional heartbreak she's experiencing.

When she told me she was feeling better this morning, I couldn't help but smile and feel hopeful that today would be a good day for her. I'm also not sure if she's put two and two together on what today's significance is.

"Are you sure about this? I don't want you to push yourself too hard before you've healed," I say to her, opening the door to my truck and helping her step up into it.

"I'm sure. Stop being such a worry wart. If I start to feel like I'm overdoing it, you can always carry me with your big, beefy muscles."

"Hey, I am not 'beefy.' I'm fairly lean as far as muscle tone goes, especially in comparison to Bennett."

"Yeah, but he's a giant. You're still bigger than both Griffin and Carson," she points out and then rolls her eyes when I reach across her to buckle her seatbelt.

Before she can give me shit for that, I quirk a brow and ask, "And how would you know I'm bigger than both Griff and Carson? I certainly wasn't bigger than Griffin last time you saw him."

I wait a moment for her to answer, and when she signals as if she's zipping her lips, I shut her door and get in the driver's side. Starting my truck, I turn to her. "Have you kept tabs on me all these years?"

"Define keeping tabs . . ." Taevin trails off.

"Have you watched me play on TV or something since I've been in the league?"

She bites the inside of her cheek, debating whether she wants to disclose that information or not. "I may or may not have caught a game or two over the years."

"Caught as in you *came* to a game or two?" I question, eyes wide at the thought that she could've actually been in one of the crowds I'd continually searched without really thinking I'd find her.

"A few times when you played in Nashville, and then if my tour schedule happened to align with your away game schedule, I'd make an appearance."

"A few means more than one or two. How many are we talking exactly?"

Tae shrugs as if this is no big deal. "I don't know, maybe a dozen."

"There's no way. I've searched the crowds for you over the years and if you'd been to a dozen games, there's no way I wouldn't have seen you—no way that you wouldn't have been on the jumbotrons or had a news story leak that you were there."

"Yeah, about that . . . I always purchased nosebleed tickets and made my former body guard, Josh, dress normal and wear a jersey. And then there's the disguise I have with a blonde wig and jersey to hide my tattoos."

"Whose jersey do you wear?"

"What?" she questions, stammering over the word.

"Which team?"

"The Wolverines," Tae murmurs reluctantly.

"And whose name is on the back of your jersey?"

Folding her arms over her chest, she sighs. "Wilson."

Yeah, I don't even try to hide my smile. "What I wouldn't give to see that."

I don't even know how many times I've imagined her wearing my Wolverines jersey with my name splayed across her shoulders. So everyone in the arena would know Taevin Gray is mine.

"How come you didn't ask me which number was on my jersey?" she asks, folding her arms across her chest.

"Because I know my own number," I state blankly.

"That's great, but the number on the back of my jersey is seven."

Did she just say *seven*? As in my big brother's number? Nah, she's fucking with me.

"Sorry, I think I misheard you—you said *twelve*, right?"

"No, I never did care much for double digit numbers."

"Lies. Your birthday is on the twelfth."

"Doesn't mean I have to prefer the number. By the way, what a weird coincidence that your hockey number is my birthday. I could've sworn you were always seventy-seven."

"That was taken when I got signed by the Wolverines, so I went with my favorite number instead."

"Since when did twelve become your favorite number?" she questions with a teasing lilt to her tone. That is, until she must realize the answer to her own question.

Instead of waiting for her to say the conclusion I'm sure she's come to, I let one of my secrets spill. "Since the day I found out your birthday is on the twelfth, and then we went ahead and got married on the twelfth of August. It appears I've been pining for you all these years, Thorn."

Leaving her to process that little tidbit, I press the playlist on my phone and turn up the volume as "Dreams" by Fleetwood Mac plays through the speakers. I drum my fingers on the steering wheel to the bass as I contemplate how I want things to play out today.

Since I brought her home from her surgery, I haven't tried to hide behind my feelings for her; I've decided to go for it. Besides, it's not like she can hurt me more than she already has. And if all I get is this one shot while she's forced to be in my orbit again, I'm taking it.

I just wonder if she's also remembering today is technically our tenth wedding anniversary.

"T, you just had major surgery and this is the first day you've been feeling okay, I feel like this is too much too soon," I tell her as we pull into the Target parking lot. "Besides, do you really think your baseball hat and sweatsuit are going to disguise you from your borderline-psychotic fans? I swear with the way the teenage girls at the coffee shop were gawking at you, they had to have taken pics and shared them all over the internet already." I've been trying to plead with her the entire drive from the coffee shop to Target, but she's a stubborn little thing.

Tae pats me on the arm. "Ah, that's cute that you think those girls were looking at me. They were most definitely drooling over you. You're Jackson freaking Wilson, after all." She leans her head against the headrest and turns to face me with a dopey look on her face. "Makes me feel nostalgic thinking back to all the times girls would try to throw themselves at you while we were together."

I quirk my brow at her. "And how did that turn out for them?"

She smirks before trying to hide her reaction by biting the inside of her cheek. "Hey, I never told you to damn near stiff arm them." Shaking her head, she throws it back and braces her hands against her lower stomach. "Oh my god, do you remember that time you yelped and nearly fell off your deck when Rosie Phillips tried to hug you at your beginning of summer party?"

I guffaw at that. "I did *not* yelp."

"Oh, you yelped, Bear. But let's drop it and go inside before I rip a stitch from laughing."

"I'll take the small wins where I can get them." I smile at her and then get out and quickly round the truck so I can help her down.

I've got to give it to her, Tae does a pretty good job of keeping a low profile for the most part while we go through the first few grocery aisles.

"Do you think they have your latest album on vinyl here?" I ask her, tossing a package of Double Stuf Oreos into the cart. Then, thinking better of it, I grab three more packages and toss them in too.

Looking up, I see Taevin shake her head at me. "I see you haven't gotten over your addiction."

"Why give up a good thing? Oreos have always been there for me."

"You're something else, you know that?" she mutters as she slowly turns the corner.

"Hey, you never answered my question. Do you think they have it here?"

Instead of answering me, she walks toward an end cap a few aisles down that's filled with the exact thing I'm looking for. Grabbing one of the special edition vinyls in my hand, I turn it over and marvel at the black and white portrait of her. She's got her head turned slightly to the side with a black cowgirl hat lowered over her eyes and her long, raven hair is windblown across her face. I swallow past the emotion clogging my throat and breathe, "Tae, this is so fucking cool. Seeing you like this—knowing you got to live out your wildest dreams—it's surreal."

Biting my quivering lip, I try to compose myself so no one sees me losing it in the middle of Target. Turning to her, I pull her in my arms and kiss the top of the ball cap she's wearing. "I know you've probably heard this a million times from everyone around you, but I'm so fucking proud of you. God, you really did it. Everything we talked about all those years ago."

In spite of everything she put me through so she could get where she is today, I like to think I'm still one of her biggest cheerleaders. She admitted she came to several of my games over the years, and someday I'll tell her how I went to as many of her concerts and performances as I could, hoping like hell she'd somehow see me in the crowds that grew unbelievable in size each time I'd go to see her.

Watching her live out her dreams while I was going through the motions—paralyzed by the loss of her—was bittersweet in the worst way. I mean, yeah, I worked hard to become a professional hockey player, but if I'm honest, I've been a shell of the man I was when I was hers.

With Tae's arms wrapped around my waist, I feel anchored in a way I haven't been in years. She was my stabilizing force back then and now it's my turn to step up and be hers.

Patting my chest, she pulls away and starts walking toward the registers. I place her record in the cart and follow after her, nearly running into her when I don't realize she's stopped short.

"T?" I question, looking around to make sure no one's recognized her. When I don't find a reason for her abrupt stop, I realize we're in front of the baby section just before I watch Tae's shoulders shudder. She brings her hand to her mouth to muffle the sob that escapes while tears stream down her cheeks.

Fuck. I need to get her out of here.

Leaving the cart right where it is, I put my arm around her shoulder and hold her against my chest as I guide her out of the store.

Once I've got her securely in my truck and I've started it, I run back into the store to grab our cart and check out. Rushing to get back to her, I nearly run straight into Alexa in the parking lot.

"Woah, sorry!" she apologizes before looking up and realizing it's me. "Hey, stranger. How's it going?"

Some of the panic that was squeezing my chest subsides from seeing one of my friends. And that's exactly what Alexa is to me. In fact, over the past year, she's become one of my closest friends that isn't one of my teammates.

"Hey, Lex. It's going." I nod over to where my truck is parked, and say, "Sorry I nearly ran you over. I was just hurrying to get back to Tae."

"Ah, I see. How is she?"

"She's had a long morning already so she's waiting in the truck for me. I think she may have overdone it a bit."

Sympathy floods her face, and Lex reaches out to give me a reassuring squeeze on my arm. "That's too bad. Well, I won't keep you. Get your girl home so she can rest up."

Warmth fills my chest and I can't help but smile from her words. My girl. Home.

I give Alexa a quick hug and as she steps away, she does what she does best, she shows how big her heart is. "Please let me know if there's anything you or Tae need. Anything at all, any time of day or night—I mean it. You've got a village, Jackson, and now that Taevin's back where she belongs, we're her village too."

Pulling her in for another hug, I take a deep breath to fight back the fear that threatens to take over whenever I think about everything Tae has already gone through. And this is only the beginning.

"Thank you, Lex. You don't know how much that means to me."

She turns to walk away, but not before reminding me, yet again, to call her if I need anything.

I load the groceries into the back of my truck and get into the driver's seat, apprehensive of what state I'll see Taevin in. To my surprise, Tae isn't crying anymore, which I think is a good thing.

That is, until she avoids meeting my eyes the entire ride home and doesn't say more than a handful of words to me. If there's anything I know about women, it's that one-word responses are never, ever a good sign. It's not long before I realize I probably just need to give her space and think of something to cheer her up in the meantime.

"Remember when we used to pull pranks on my brother and sister?" I ask Tae as we sit in the living room and eat goulash together. When she said she was craving it, I was more than happy to make it for her seeing as it's my favorite meal of all time. Add in my nana's homemade sauce my mom brought over last week, and it's the best damn thing to ever exist.

Chuckling, she scoops a big spoonful of noodles into her mouth and chews it up before responding. "I used to love doing that. And then Walker loved it so much she wanted to start doing more prank calls so she'd have us use funny voices to call the numbers on the back of the cereal boxes or random companies in town to enter formal complaints for the dumbest shit." A soft smile spreads across her face. "Those were some of my favorite things to do."

"Want to try to prank call some of the guys now? I saw this video earlier that had me laughing pretty hard. Essentially, a group of girls were calling their exes, and when they'd pick up they'd just tell them they were calling to say goodnight."

"That'd actually be hilarious. Would the guys just be like what the fuck are you doing?"

"A few of them might catch on since I've become the team prankster."

Pulling my phone out of my pocket, I scroll through my contacts and tell her, "Alright, I'll try Bennett first."

"No, you shouldn't. Aren't they on their honeymoon right now?" Tae questions.

"They are, but I'm still pissed at them for signing Calvetti, so this is a little appetizer of what's to come for him." I'm sure the smirk taking over my face looks as devious as I feel.

The phone rings and I put it on speaker so Taevin can hear.

"This better be a fucking emergency," Bennett grits.

"We've talked about this—that's no way to greet your favorite brother."

"I swear to god, J, if you don't start talking, I'm hanging up and not talking to you for a year."

"Well that's just not true. Preseason starts next month, you'll have to talk to me then at least."

"Five . . . four . . . three . . ."

"Alright, alright. I just wanted to call to tell you goodnight."

A click sounds on the other end of the line before the call disconnects.

"He's such a grumpy asshole sometimes," I tell Taevin, shaking my head at my phone.

She giggles and then her face crumples in pain.

"What's the matter?" I'm at her side in a second.

Tae shakes her head. "I'm fine, promise. I guess laughing still doesn't feel the greatest."

Throwing myself down beside her, I rest my head against the back of the couch and breathe a sigh of relief. "Should I stop? I don't want you to be in pain or pop a stitch."

"No, I'll be fine. I'll give you a signal if it's too much." I turn my head just as Tae grabs one of the throw pillows and hugs it to her chest, bringing her legs up to better support her core.

Quirking a brow, I ask, "And what signal would that be?" When she flips me her middle finger, I narrow my eyes and shake my head at her. "I should've known."

I scroll down my contacts and dial Griff next.

"Hey, J. What's up? You good?" he answers the phone.

I press mute and whisper-hiss to Taevin, "See, that's how my brother should've answered the phone."

Unmuting my phone, I say, "Hey, G. Yeah, I'm good. Not much, just getting ready for bed. You?"

"Ah, man, I feel like it's early for you. Are you sick or something?"

I smile at how much of a *dad* he's become to the group. "Nah, just been tired is all."

"Right, that makes sense. How's Taevin doing after surgery? Have you guys tried the chicken pot pies yet?"

"We ate them last night for dinner and they were bomb—perfect amount of flaky crust on top while not being dried out in the center. Not sure how you did it, man." I pause, eyeing Taevin as she shifts to get comfortable. "Tae's doing good, resting up and healing."

"Nice! I'm glad they turned out. And that's good to hear about Tae. We've been thinking of you guys."

Tears of gratitude well in the corners of my eyes when I think of how great of friends I've got. Clearing my throat, I say, "Thanks, G. How's staying at the cabin and working at Camp Katie? Sorry I couldn't make it up this year."

"It's going really good. We've got a few new counselors and we just kicked off the figure skating camp. It's filled up to capacity already in year one, so that's great news."

"That's awesome!"

"Yeah, it's pretty awesome to see what Kenna and Carson have come up with to honor Katie. Anyway, I think I got us off topic. Why'd you call again?"

My attention is momentarily pulled back to Tae when she gasps. Clearing my throat, I answer, "I was really just calling to say goodnight, man. And that I miss you."

Griff sniffs on the other end of the phone. "Fuck, buddy, I think you might make me emotional."

"Don't go crying over me calling you," I tell him, chuckling because he's not giving me shit right now, he's being completely serious.

"I won't, but I miss you too. Say hi to Taevin for us. We'll be back in the city in time for training camp and Bennett's cookout in a few weeks."

"Sounds good, bud. I'll let you get back to the fam."

"Thanks, J. Love you."

"Love you too, G. Night."

"Sleep tight, fucker," he says, and I chuckle as I hang up the phone, stopping short when I see Taevin has tears streaming down her cheeks.

Panic flares in my chest at the sight of her in pain. "T, what's wrong? Fuck, I said I shoudn't have called him."

"No, it's not that."

"Then what is it?" I press.

"It's just, I didn't realize the camp you were missing for me to be here was a camp dedicated to Katie's memory. When did they start that?"

My heart sinks thinking about Katie's accident and her funeral. Both of which happened only days after I left for my freshman year of college. Swallowing past the emotion swelling in my throat, I run my fingers through my hair. "Carson and Kenna, uh, they started a summer sports camp in honor of Katie. It's up north on the lake where we spent the Fourth of July with them. They bought a former resort that had closed down and fixed it up so the cabins could house the campers and counselors."

I take a deep breath to combat the weight of grief pressing down on my chest before continuing, "I believe this is the sixth summer. They originally started by offering only hockey, golf, and volleyball camps. I'm pretty sure Katie played a hand in the fact that there just so happened to be an older hockey rink down the road from the campsite. McKenna made it a priority to have both beach and court volleyball offered the second summer. From there, it's grown year after year. It sort of went viral and got all sorts of attention last summer when Nathan Connelly filmed part of his *Hockey Visionary* documentary there after he was drafted."

Tae's breath hitches. "Wow. That's a beautiful tribute to Katie—to continue her legacy in a way that benefits young athletes."

"Yeah, I agree. And they've made it their mission to make the camp accessible to kids from all walks of life. There's a scholarship program where a professional athlete can sponsor kids, or even entire teams, to cover their fees and travel expenses."

She catches me off guard when she asks, "What's been your favorite part of working the camp?"

I scratch the scruff covering my jaw as I think about my answer. If I were being honest, I'd tell her that working with the kids is undoubtedly my favorite part, but I don't know if that would upset her. So instead I respond with my second favorite part. "I love being back at their family lake house. That's where I spend most of the offseason. It brings back good memories."

Taevin inches closer to me, giving me a dreamy smile, and the sight has me feeling like I'll never be more victorious than when I've earned one of her smiles.

"We did make some pretty amazing memories that week, didn't we?"

Nodding in agreement, I'm at a loss for words. July nights by the fire, visions of Taevin in the sun and covered in sand, and watching in awe as she came to life in the glow of the festival lights all come rushing back.

I think she's just as lost as me because as her face inches closer to mine, her eyes flutter shut only momentarily before her breath hitches in a nearly silent gasp.

She shifts on the couch, moving slowly to a stand. "It's been a long day, I think I'm going to head to bed."

Wanting to make sure she makes it there safely, I stand and place my hand on the small of her back, but with the way her sleep tank has shifted, my palm is met with her bare skin. I feel her tiny goosebumps rise beneath my hand, and from only the slightest touch, it feels like lightning has struck my heart, sending chills of my own straight down my spine.

God, I've missed her. When it comes to Tae, my body's in tune with hers as if no time has passed at all. But time has passed. Too much of it, in fact. So much that it has me dying to feel her lips pressed against mine. *Would she taste the same?*

Thankfully, Tae moves toward her bedroom before I do something stupid like press her against the wall and find all sorts of answers to all sorts of questions I've got.

"You don't have to walk me to my door, you know," Tae tells me.

"Oh, I know. I don't plan to just walk you to your door. I'm going to tuck you in too."

She scoffs at that. "No you're not."

"I most certainly am. Just like old times." I give her a wink. When she sticks her tongue out at me in response, I throw my head back in laughter. "Always the thorn in my side."

Spinning to face me once she gets to her door, she pushes playfully at my chest. "Hey, you were the masochist who kept coming back for more," she teases before her smile falls and her eyes drop to her hand lingering over my heart.

She moves to pull it away but I catch it and bring it back to my chest, needing to hold on to the feel of her touching me for just a moment longer. Lifting her chin, I gaze into her eyes. "I think you're mistaken," I tell her.

She swallows. "Is that so?"

"Yeah. You see, you used the past tense when you said that. But the thing is, I'll never stop coming back for more when it comes to you. You've ensnared me for life, Thorn."

Lifting onto her toes, our faces inch impossibly closer. When she licks her lips, my stomach clenches in anticipation.

"Sounds painful," she murmurs, and I feel her warm breath against my lips like a caress.

It's taking all the restraint I have left to hold back in this moment, but I need her to be the one to take this step.

"Good night, Bear," Tae whispers against my lips as she presses the lightest kiss against the corner of my mouth.

When she pulls back just enough to take in my reaction, I lace my fingers through her hair and bring her mouth back to mine. Our lips don't crash together in a passionate frenzy, no this is a long time coming—ten years, in fact—and I plan to take my time reacquainting myself with her lips. Gliding my tongue along the seam, she opens for me. Tae's body sinks against my chest as we moan in harmony at our first taste of each other in nearly a decade. I savor every moment, slowly rolling my tongue against hers.

Nothing has ever felt as right as *this*. This is where I belong—who I belong with.

Tae reluctantly breaks our kiss, grabbing hold of my forearms to regain her balance as she sways on her feet. Fear instantly replaces my lust, and I grab her around the waist to anchor her to me. "Are you okay?"

She buries her head in my chest and I think she's crying when her shoulders begin to shake, until I hear her soft laughter. "I'm alright. Turns out your kisses still make me weak in the knees."

I breathe a sigh of relief, placing a kiss on the top of her head. "You scared me, baby."

Lifting up onto her tiptoes, she wraps her hands around my neck and pulls me down for a brief kiss. "I'm sorry for scaring you."

"Is that all you're sorry for?" I ask, immediately regretting opening my dumb mouth but needing to know her answer.

With her fingers threaded through my hair, she pulls back and looks me in my eyes. "If you're asking if I'll regret kissing you in the morning, the answer is absolutely not. In fact, I think knowing I might get another tomorrow will be the only thing that helps me sleep peacefully tonight."

I rub my hands up and down her rib cage. "I'll kiss you whenever you want—every hour of every day if you'd like."

She flutters her long lashes. "I'm not sure if only once an hour will satisfy my needs."

"I don't remember you being so gluttonous."

"Ten years without you will drive a woman mad with greed."

"We can't have that," I hum in response, tucking a stray hair behind her ear.

"No, I suppose we can't," Tae says, bringing me in for another quick kiss. She steps out of my hold and opens her bedroom door, turning to peek at me through the opening. "It's probably best if I tuck myself in tonight."

"You sure?"

"I am," she assures me. "Good night."

"Night, Tae. Sweet dreams."

I turn and start down the hallway when she says, "You too. Try to get some sleep."

"I will."

"Oh, and Jax?"

Halting, I look over my shoulder at her. "Yeah?"

"Thank you for the kiss goodnight."

I smirk at her. "You don't have to thank me."

She bites her bottom lip and leans against the doorframe. "It was the best way to wrap up our tenth anniversary."

My shoulders sag in relief when her words register. "You remembered."

"Always," she murmurs, giving me a shy smile before closing the door.

As I walk up the stairs to the guest room I've been sleeping in since Tae came to stay, I can't seem to wipe the dopey smile from my lips. Even after I've gotten ready for bed, I lie there and smile up at the ceiling.

My phone buzzes on the nightstand, and I'm quick to check to see if it's Tae saying she needs anything. It isn't her; instead I find a text from Griff in our group chat.

Pucking Legends:

G-Baby:

> It was good talking to you tonight, J. But now that I think about it, was that one of those clock app trends?

Me:

> You bet your sweet ass it was. But it turned out to be more than I could've ever hoped for. Thanks for being a good sport . . . unlike Bennett!

Me:

> I was trying to get Tae to smile. Turns out laughing one week post-abdominal surgery still hurts.

G-Baby:

> Glad I could help, man. Love you and thinking of you guys. Let us know if you need anything.

Benny:

> Please apologize on my behalf to Taevin for my grumpiness. It wasn't directed at her.

Me:

> Wow, you're able to be nice to someone just so long as it's not me?

Benny:

A thousand percent.

Me:

You grumpy motherfucker!

Benny:

I'm a happily married man trying to enjoy my honeymoon. I think it's perfectly acceptable to be grumpy that I'm getting prank called by my brother on my fucking honeymoon.

Carsey:

Um, what the fuck? What prank call trend is this? And where was my call?

Me:

After I realized how much it hurt her stomach to do the calls, I stopped.

Carsey:

And I was third on your list?! Jaxy, buddy, come on. It's you and me against the world!

Instead of replying, I click call on his contact. The phone rings once before he answers. "I've been awaiting your call, Jaxy Bear."

I shake my head. "Sorry I made you wait all of five seconds."

"The wait was unbearable."

"You're such a dick."

"Am not. That title is reserved for Bennett."

That earns him a chuckle from me. "You're right."

"How is she?" he asks, likely knowing exactly why I called. Carson has this weird ability of being in tune with what I'm thinking or what I need, often times before I do.

"She's, uh, she's doing okay," my voice breaks on the last word and it doesn't get past him.

"What's the hardest part right now? Break it down for me."

"Her physical pain seems to be manageable at this point. But I think she's struggling most with her infertility as a result of her surgery."

"Shit. I get that. The invisible scars are the hardest to help someone overcome, but I know you can help her through this, Jax."

Pinching the bridge of my nose, I breathe a sigh of frustration. "It's killing me, Carse. She breaks down crying every time we see a baby. Whether there's a video on social media, or like today, when she saw the baby aisle in the store, she sobs. It breaks my fucking heart. And I feel like it's only going to get worse when we begin the egg retrieval process."

"You just said we . . ."

"Yeah. I'll be helping her through the process, and, uh, you know, giving her my . . . sperm."

He clears his throat on the other end of the line. "Are you—have you two talked about kids? I mean, having kids together?"

"Of course. Well, I mean, we used to talk about it all the time when we were dating. We both wanted to buy a big plot of land somewhere where we could have a bunch of kids and animals and let them roam around. She wanted three and I wanted five, which she said made me crazy."

"I'm sure I don't need to tell you this, but there's no way you could only be her sperm donor with all of your history. Have you talked about what that means for y'all?"

I blow out an apprehensive breath. "No. I guess I don't want her to second guess having me be the one to help her. And in light of everything else she's dealing with right now, it seems futile to ask her about something we don't even know will have success right now."

"Shit, Jax. I'm sorry man. Have you talked to her about it since she had her surgery?"

"No, not really. Each time I tried before she had her surgery, she shut me down. But she has her first post-op visit in a few days, and her doctor's going to give us a better idea of when she'll begin the injections and the timeline for her egg retrieval. They want to try to get it done as soon as possible so she can start chemotherapy."

Carson blows out a breath on the other end of the phone. "I may not know much about the medical side of things, but here's what I do know: there is no better teammate than you. When the guys are feeling down, you lift their spirits with your humor and lighthearted personality. I know it's probably hard as hell to be uplifting when you feel like you're drowning in the unknowns, but there's no one better than you to be by Taevin's side through all of this."

"I still love her, Carse," I admit, surprising myself when the words leave me.

"You and I both know you've never stopped loving that girl from the moment you laid eyes on her."

"I'm terrified I'm going to lose her again," I choke out.

"She's prepared to fight, Jax. You just have to make sure she knows she's not going to war alone."

He's right.

This battle may be hers, but I'll be damned if she fights it alone.

17

Jackson

Now

There's a faint sound of music drifting down the hallway coming from Taevin's room that I can hear even over the crackling of bacon.

My phone buzzes on the counter and when I look down, I see Tae's dad texted asking for an update on how she's doing. He's been doing that a lot lately, though I suppose it's because he said Taevin hasn't been responding to him.

I quickly type out my daily update on how she's feeling then set my phone back on the counter.

I stop in my tracks when I hear Taevin singing, causing a smug smile to tug at my lips. Turning off the stove, I move the bacon off the burner and toss the dish towel slung over my shoulder onto the counter. Tae hasn't sang since her surgery because she said it had hurt her stomach and chest too much. I'm dying to hear her better.

My feet move of their own volition until I'm suddenly standing just outside her bathroom right as her beautiful mezzo-soprano voice begins to sing the chorus of the song.

I can't stop myself from inching closer and spying through the crack in the doorway as she continues to belt the lyrics to Céline Dion's absolute banger, "It's All Coming Back to Me Now."

It's likely due to my foolish heart, but I assure myself that she's singing this song right now because she's thinking of our kiss last night. The kiss that had me up most of the night replaying it in my mind over and over again.

So it's all coming back to her, is it? I love this far too much, and the cocksure grin that spreads across my face can't be stopped as she continues to sing the bridge of the ballad.

Oh, I've come back, Thorn. And I'm here to stay.

Taevin

You know what no one told me about getting a hysterectomy? The fact that my boobs still hurt like hell around *that* time of the month and I'll still go up nearly a full cup size. Like now, as the shower water sprays down and pelts my nipples, I feel like I could cry from how sensitive they are. I should ask my doctor about this at my appointment this afternoon, because surely this can't be normal.

And I *need* chocolate. Would Jackson just make himself useful and get me some goddamn chocolate? Oh, and some salty as fuck chips with guac, like, right this minute.

My mouth waters as I towel off from the shower, but when I look up, I shriek at the sight of Jackson standing in the doorway of my bathroom looking far too casual with his hands in his grey sweatpants, legs crossed at the ankles while he leans against the doorframe like this isn't a major invasion of privacy.

"What in the hell do you think you're doing?" I squeal as I do my best to cover myself up and hide my hideous surgical scars behind my towel.

Jackson doesn't move a muscle of his beautiful, unblemished body, instead he bites his bottom lip and quirks a quizzical brow. "Céline Dion? What has you feeling so nostalgic, Tae?"

It's nearly impossible to be upset with him when he has that dopey smile on his face and his curly hair is disheveled from sleep.

I do my best to muster up a growly tone when I tell him, "You seriously need to get out. I don't want you to see me like this."

With his hands up in surrender, he backs out of the bathroom, but he doesn't leave my bedroom. Through the crack in the door, I watch him move across the room to the armoire where he pulls out some sheets.

Humming the tune to himself that I was just embarrassingly belting, he strips the bed before remaking it with fresh sheets. Knowing there's crisp, clean sheets on my bed makes me want to crawl right back in.

And can I take a moment to praise this man's taste in sheets? They're luxurious beyond compare.

Walking into the closet, I shut the door behind me and pick out an outfit that won't press too snug against my healing incisions. As I throw on a pair of pants, I feel my resolve to be upset with Jackson slipping further away until I'm huffing in annoyance with myself while pulling on my shirt.

"Seems I'm not the only one feeling wistful," I interrupt his humming once I've finished getting dressed and step out of the closet.

He stands beside the bed and shrugs before continuing to change the pillow cases. Something as simple as changing my bedding—because he knows it's still difficult for me to do much of anything at this point—shouldn't have tears welling in my eyes, but it does. "The last time we sang that was on the way to McKenna and Carson's cabin, which was also the last time I heard that song. Makes me feel hella nostalgic."

"You did not just say 'hella,' did you?" I ask incredulously, quickly wiping away a stray tear before he can see.

"Isn't that what the kids say these days?" he tosses back over his shoulder with a cocky little smirk on his face.

Tipping my head side to side, I act as if I'm pondering that. "I'm pretty certain it's not."

"What if I told you it's what I say these days?"

"Then I'd say you should probably quit if you want to have any chance at kissing me again," I taunt.

At the mention of our kiss, his face lights up as songbirds simultaneously take flight in my stomach. Our kiss last night was a decade overdue.

Jax stands up straight and saunters over to where I stand across the room from him. The amount of swagger this man possesses at this time in the morning is unfair. With his shirt off, I'm able to greedily take in the ink covering his left arm that bleeds onto his left pec, right over his heart. His chiseled body is so far from the lankier, eighteen-year-old version I once memorized. I mean, sure, he used to have a six-pack, but the man closing in on me now has *abs* full of definition that ripple to the waistband of his sweatpants.

He was once upon a time a cocky little shit, but now he oozes confidence that he's rightfully earned by working his ass off both on and off the ice. And, yeah, I've still seen glimpses of that cockiness in him, but it errs more on the side of sexy conviction now.

Jackson steps into my space, closing any remaining distance between us, and his presence is all-consuming, intoxicating. He cups my face in his hands and for a moment he just stands there gazing into my eyes.

"I'm going to kiss you again, Tae. Are you okay with that?"

"Thanks for the play-by-play," I sass back. "Yes, I'm okay with that." To prove my point, I wrap my arms around his waist, pulling him impossibly closer and loving the feel of his warm chest and stomach heating my skin even through my shirt.

"Come here, baby," he whispers against my lips, and when his lips press against mine once more, all is right in the world.

Somehow the sterility of the exam room is welcoming instead of stifling. I guess that's at least one positive, considering I'll be spending so much of my time in and out of exam rooms over the next several months.

I adjust how I'm sitting on the exam table and the paper that was stuck to the back of my legs and ass crinkles as I do, drawing all attention to me.

"Do you need anything?" Jax asks for about the dozenth time. He's so helpful and caring and normally I would be so appreciative of that, but right now my emotions are all over the place. The discussion of my future fertility is one that sends me spiraling to the point of no return.

Knowing he's not to blame for the hand I've been dealt and all he's trying to do is be thoughtful, I take a deep breath before responding. "No, I'm okay. Thank you, though."

Then, focusing my attention back on my doctor, I ask, "I'm sorry, what were you saying? I think, if I remember right, you were talking about timing out the start of my next cycle."

"Yes, I was saying that because you aren't going to get a period anymore, we're relying on your labs and imaging. Based on today's bloodwork and ultrasound, I can confirm you're at the stage in your cycle where you'd begin menstruation within the next day or two.

Before you leave, we'll send the scripts to your pharmacy for you to pick up your prescriptions for your injections. You'll want to make sure you get them in your refrigerator, and then you'll begin injections three days from now."

With a growing pit in my stomach, I take a deep breath and say, "As your nurse can attest, I'm not a huge fan of needles or the sight of my own blood." I wince thinking about nearly passing out earlier when they took my blood. "Is there a way I could come here to get the injections instead of having to self-administer them at home?"

"Or can you teach me?" Jackson cuts in. When I look at him sideways, he shrugs. "What? If the injections can be self-administered, it's not like I couldn't be the one to give them to you."

"You're right, Jackson. Typically if someone isn't comfortable with needles, we recommend a support person help administer them," Dr. Prescott tells us. "We also recommend doing the shots between six and nine o'clock at night, and to try as best as you can to administer them at the same time consistently each night leading up to the egg retrieval surgery. The daily injections will last ten to fourteen days, depending on what your lab work tells us. Then we will schedule the trigger shot to be done exactly thirty-six hours before the retrieval."

Wringing my hands in my lap, I look over to where Jackson sits beside me and worry my lip. "I don't want to mess with your schedule too much, you're already doing so much for me throughout this process. I couldn't ask that of—"

Placing his hand on mine, he cuts me off. "Let me stop you right there. You're not messing with my schedule. All of my training is in the morning and early afternoons. I'll be able to give them to you. And you're not asking anything of me, remember? I want to do this with you, T."

It's nearly impossible to fight the tears welling in my eyes as I take in what he's just said. He wants to do this with me. What does he mean by that? He wants to be beside me as I fight this damned cancer? Or does he want to support me during the egg retrieval process that could possibly result in *our* future children? Or maybe, just maybe, he wants to be there for me through it all.

But I'm not sure Jackson is ready to stand by my side when there's still so much I'm keeping from him—so many ugly truths he's yet to discover. If he learns them, would he still feel the same as he does now? Or will he turn his back on me when the harsh realities come to surface?

18

Taevin

Somehow our high school graduations weren't on the same day, so yesterday Jax attended mine and today was my turn to watch him walk across the stage in his cap and gown.

His high school colors are green and yellow, and I've come to realize I much prefer my school's royal blue and white. But even with a bright green cap and gown, Jax looks handsome as ever with his grown out curls spilling out the sides and the back of his cap.

The ceremony just closed, and with his little sister Walker's hand in mine, we walk down the gymnasium bleachers and out onto the gym floor where some of the graduates are still collecting their caps after tossing them in celebration. When Jax spots us, he nods at the friends surrounding him before taking off in a run toward us.

"Come here, baby," he yells as he closes the distance, and without giving it a second thought, I unclasp my hand from Walker's and kick off my sandals to run to him. Once he's close enough, I leap into his arms, crashing against his chest and wrapping my legs around his waist even though the dress I'm wearing could possibly make doing so indecent. But I couldn't care less right now. All I want in this moment—well, every moment really—is to be in his arms.

Jackson kisses me silly in front of a gymnasium full of his peers and their families, and I know him well enough by now to know that this is an intentional display of affection, an act of staking his claim. I'm not sure what it says about me, but I love when he does things like this—essentially telling everyone that I'm his and he is mine.

Only when a throat clears behind me does Jax break our kiss. He lowers me to the ground and throws a protective arm around me, likely preparing to go toe-to-toe with his father.

"PDA is beneath Wilson men, son. Don't let me see anything like that again. Am I understood?"

"Yes, sir," Jackson bites out, doing a poor job of hiding his disdain for his father.

My interactions with the senator have been few and far between since Jax typically only brings me to his house when his father is out of town or he's certain he won't be around. I'm not sure how his mother Kathy has managed to stay with such a cruel-hearted man. Especially considering how considerate and loving she is. The way her husband treats Jackson and Bennett is abhorrent. From what Jax has told me, his dad is fairly decent to Walker, thank god. The poor girl is only eleven after all.

Even with my limited interactions with Senator Wilson, I get a clear sense that he doesn't approve of Jax being in a relationship with me. I'm honestly not sure he'd be okay with Jax being in a relationship period, regardless of who it was with. But he seems especially upset that I'm the one his son has chosen to fall for.

Jackson has already told me his father tried to forbid him from dating me, stating a relationship would distract him from his goals, which doesn't make any sense considering he has a full ride to Harvard. What really surprised me was that when he told Jackson he had to break up with me, Jax told his father that if he tried to tell him what to do again or threatened our relationship in any way whatsoever, he'd quit hockey and sabotage not only his scholarship, but any shot he has at going pro.

Without giving his dad another opportunity to lecture him, Jax turns to hug his mom, sister and older brother, Bennett, who I only met for the first time in person today. He's called and FaceTimed Jax a few times when we've been together, and from what I've gathered, he's a pretty great big brother to his siblings, even with the stress of being a professional hockey player at such a young age weighing on his shoulders.

Jax has talked a lot about the upcoming NHL draft that he's eligible to enter. He told me Bennett was drafted at eighteen, and instead of going on to play college hockey for a few years, he was signed by the Minnesota Wolverines right away. From what I've been told, that's rare, especially for a defenseman. Jackson decided to enter the draft this year, but being a forward that might not go in the first or second round, he knows he'll likely play a few years of college hockey before he signs with whatever team drafts him or possibly play for the AHL.

I'm excited for him and beyond proud, but I'd be lying if I said the unknown of where he'll end up and when doesn't scare the heck out of me. It's probably naive of me to believe we'll be together forever at such a young age and only having dated for a handful of months, but I can't stop myself from believing with every fiber of my being that Jackson Wilson is my end game.

"Turner, what's up man?" Jax hollers from his parents' kitchen island when he spots a tall guy with brown hair, tanned skin, and brown eyes approaching us. He's walking over with Carson, but I don't think I've met him before.

The guy shakes Jax's hand and brings him in for a one-arm hug. "Not much, Jax. Just putting Carson through the grind, trying to bring him up to speed," he taunts, looking over his shoulder at Carson, where Carson flips him the bird. Turning back to Jax, he asks, "What about you? Something has to be keeping you busy if we haven't seen you at the rink or gym yet."

"Yeah, yeah. I hear ya. Not something, someone," Jackson says, wrapping his arms around my waist and kissing the top of my head. I melt into the embrace, slightly buzzed from the seltzer I've been sipping on, but more intoxicated from the way being in his arms makes me feel.

"This is Tae. Tae this is Griffin Turner, and of course you've met Carson."

"Nice to see you again," Carson says as he grabs a cup and fills it up with a rum and soda mix.

"Baby, Turner used to play on our high school team with us. Now he's big time at Emery before he heads to Colorado," Jax explains as he nuzzles into my neck.

I'm so lost in the feel of his lips against my neck, I forget we're in a room full of people. "You better watch yourself, Bear, or I'll have to take the host away from his own party and lock you away upstairs," I murmur to him over my shoulder.

"You wanna have your wicked way with me, T? All you had to do was ask. Let's go," he says as he takes my hand and leads me through the crowd of people standing in front of the steps that lead to the stairs.

Before we can make our escape, his friends McKenna and Katie stop us. Realization dawns on me as I take in Katie that Griffin must be her older brother, also known as the guy McKenna couldn't stop gushing about finally being home for the summer again when we spoke at their graduation. That makes a lot more sense now, I can see why she'd be hung up on him. Not only is he gorgeous, but the forbidden aspect of him being the boy next door and her best friend's brother has me itching to write a song about them.

"We're going to stop you right there, Jaxy. We need to steal our girl, Tae, for a bit of fun," McKenna tells him.

The girls pull me from his hold and into a group of their friends. Katie and McKenna have been so kind and have adopted me as one of their own since they met me this spring. I had the best time dancing with them at Jax's prom, and we've hung out as a group a few times.

"Tae! I've been meaning to ask if you have any plans over the Fourth of July? We have a cabin on a lake up north we typically go to every year with our families, but this year our parents have a charity gala, so it'll be our first trip there with just us four. They said we could invite a few friends along and we'd love to have you and Jax join us!" McKenna explains as Katie nods excitedly in agreement.

"You have to come! Pretty please," Katie begs with her hands clasped together.

"I'll see what I can do. I'm not sure if my dad will go for a full weekend without parental supervision," I tell them, knowing the only reason he let me stay at Jackson's house a few weeks ago was because I lied and told him his parents were there and that we would be sleeping in separate rooms. Maybe I could stretch the truth in this case, or maybe I'll get lucky and he won't ask for clarification and just assume there'll be parents there instead.

Yeah, keep dreaming . . .

"Well you can tell him that Bennett will be there, and he's an adult who definitely acts like our parental figure keeping us in line," McKenna explains.

"Yeah, Benny acts like a daddy to the group." Katie winks before waggling her brows suggestively.

"Gross, Katie!"

"Ugh, sorry. I know that's weird to say about Bennett. I just *need* to find a guy who knows what to do with his hands and doesn't suck my face like an amateur," Katie says, looking around the room as if she's searching for someone that might meet that criteria. "And the guys we went to school with aren't cutting it."

I laugh at the way she sighs in defeat. "I think you and my friend Ryan would get along."

"Really? Is he hot? Who am I kidding? With a name like that, of course he's hot. Please bring him!" Katie begs.

"*She* goes to her grandmother's house for their annual Fourth of July family gathering, or I definitely would," I assure them.

Katie waggles her brows. "Is *she* hot?"

I chuckle. "The hottest."

Katie shimmies in excitement. "Hell yeah! Let's go get another drink so we can cheers to all of Tae's hot friends."

Another seltzer and a couple awful songs later, Katie and McKenna pull me and Jax into a game of Never Have I Ever around the outdoor firepit with a group that includes Carson and Griffin.

After the game wraps up, I go to grab a bottle of water and get pulled into watching Katie and Carson play a game of beer pong. They're hilarious together, one minute fighting like cats and dogs, the next gazing at each other curiously making me wonder if they've ever crossed the line I know McKenna wants to cross with Griffin.

Speaking of said line, when the three of us walk out onto the back porch a bit later, we find them talking together by the fire.

"Aw, look at the two of them, lost in their own little world," Katie points out.

My confused expression must be written all over my face because Katie laughs when she sees my pinched brows. "Oh, we're well aware of their not-so-secret feelings for each other; however, the two of them remain clueless to the fact that their feelings are mutual."

I look to Carson for confirmation, and am surprised to see him nodding in agreement. "And you're okay with that? With one of your best friends wanting your sister?"

Carson's nose wrinkles in response. "Easy . . . I don't need to be thinking about the likes of anything nefarious happening between them. But as far as guys my twin sister could date go, Mack couldn't find a better guy than Griff."

"That's so far from the reaction I thought you'd have. But what would I know, I don't have any siblings. It's just that typically when I read a book with a brother's best friend trope, the couple usually sneaks around in secret."

"Shut the fuck up! Are you a romance reader?" Katie squeals.

"I am," I admit somewhat bashfully.

"That's it. You need to text me all of your fave recs so I can stock up on what to read at the cabin. Kenna and I love to read too. She likes more of the dark romance books and I'm a slut for a good age gap. What's your favorite?"

"Um, I like to be emotionally traumatized by whatever I'm reading," I tell her and she throws her arms around me, squeezing me in a tight embrace.

"We've just become besties, bitch."

Carson chuckles at the two of us and shakes his head. "What the fuck is happening right now?"

"We obviously just discovered we're about to become the best of friends, duh." Katie rolls her eyes at Carson before fixing her attention on something going on behind Carson.

Katie gasps. "Be so for real, are you going to let Rosie freaking Phillips be all up on your man like that?"

"Katie . . ." Carson admonishes.

"What?" Katie questions in a haughty tone.

"Looks like I don't have much to worry about," I tell them, gesturing toward where Jax is standing on the other side of the deck. They both turn, and together we all watch Rosie try to move in for a hug just as Jax yelps like he's on fire and backs away from her in such an exaggerated way, he damn near falls over the railing of the back porch.

"Aw, look at our little Jaxy growing up and falling in love," Katie coos.

"I could've told you both he's smitten as hell over you, Taevin. My guy has been a goner for months now," Carson assures me.

"Thank you for the vote of confidence, but he gives me all the reassurance I need," I say as a blush heats my cheeks.

"What do we have here?" Katie asks, pointing to where McKenna is straddling Griffin on one of the Adirondack chairs by the firepit.

Carson turns to Katie. "Should we mess with them a bit, Kitty?"

"I'd love nothing more, Carsey-baby. Let's go!" Katie and Carson take off down the steps just as strong arms wrap around my waist from behind. I love when Jax holds me against him like this.

"There you are. Are my friends done stealing my gorgeous girlfriend away from me?" Jax murmurs the question against my neck before sucking the sensitive skin into his mouth, likely leaving a light mark.

Spinning around in his embrace, I answer, "They sure are. They've moved on to messing with their siblings instead."

He looks over my shoulder to where Carson and Katie must be and he lets out a snort. "That's epic. It's about time G and Mack Attack get together."

"Am I a distraction for you? When it comes to hockey, I mean?" I ask the question that's been on my mind since Griffin brought up that they hadn't seen him at training lately.

Jax rears his head back, looking completely taken off guard. "What? No, of course not. Why would you ask that?"

"In the kitchen earlier Griffin had mentioned he and Carson had been training on and off the ice and they hadn't seen you around. And we've been hanging out so much lately, I can't help but assume it's because of me."

"T, it's the first week of summer. So what if I took a few days off for the first time in years? I already made plans with Carse and Griff to train with them next week." Stepping impossibly closer to me, he grasps my head in his hands and bends so he's at my eye level. "Listen to me when I say this: you're not a distraction, baby. If anything, you make me want to work harder than ever to make all of our dreams come true. The draft is in a few weeks, but after that you best believe I'll be prioritizing spending as much of my summer with you as possible. Make yourself a list of things you want to do together this summer, and I'll do my best to check them all off."

"Are you sure?" I ask him, worrying my lip between my teeth.

He releases my bottom lip and pulls it down with his thumb. "Am I sure that I can't wait to get lost in a summer haze with you for the next few months? Yeah, I've never been more sure of anything."

Swatting his chest halfheartedly, I tell him, "Be serious, J. Promise me I won't become a distraction for you. I'll be damned if your father is right about anything when it comes to us."

"I promise, baby."

I let out a squeal when he lifts me into his arms bridal style. He chuckles, telling me, "Okay, now that we've established you're my motivation, not a distraction, it's time for me to take my girl inside so she can have her way with me like she promised earlier."

As he carries me up the steps leading to his bedroom, I can't wipe the splitting smile from my face at yet another one of his loud displays of affection.

"Easy, caveman. I'm pretty sure everyone here already knows I'm yours. If anyone needs to mark their territory, I think it's me," I tease him.

"I'm just making sure everyone knows we're both taken. I think they all know now that I've got my claws sunk into you, baby."

Rolling my eyes, I hold onto him tighter and whisper in his ear, "If anyone's going to claw the other in this relationship, it'll be me Jackson Charles."

"Fuck, I love when you're demanding. It turns me on so much."

Before I can respond, he tosses me onto his bed before locking his door, and next thing I know his lips are blissfully on mine, right where they belong.

19

Jackson

I'm not sure how she managed to do it, but Taevin convinced her dad to let her come to the Wilder family cabin with us for the Fourth of July. We're headed up a few hours later than Carson, McKenna, Katie, and Griffin because I just got in late last night from Dallas, where I spent the past three days for the NHL draft.

We're riding with Bennett, but I'm picking her up from her house by myself first so I can get a few minutes alone with her. Especially because I just got the call from Wolverines management that the prospects development camp will take place on Monday after the Fourth, so we've only got a few days together before I'll be busy and staying away for another three.

When I pull up to her house, I kill the engine and round my truck, holding my arms wide open just as Taevin jumps into them.

"Minnesota. Can you believe it, baby?" I ask, picking her up and spinning her in my arms.

She squeals with joy and I stop spinning to rock her back and forth in my arms. "I saw! I'm so proud of you, J. So beyond proud of you." Taevin grabs my face in her hands and peppers a few kisses on my lips and cheeks.

"We'll be able to come back home after college once I sign with the Wolverines. The two of us can live out all of our dreams right here just like we've talked about." I don't think I'm imagining the look of apprehension on her face when I set her down, but she quickly schools her expression before I can get a good read on it.

"I'm so excited for you!"

"For us, right?"

"Yeah, it's almost too good to be true." She pauses to worry her lip before she says, "I thought you had said that Nashville was really interested in you and New York had put out feelers. Even Boston, but I don't remember you mentioning Minnesota," she says and alarms start going off in my head.

"Those teams were all interested, but I didn't want to tell you that Minnesota was showing interest because I didn't want to get your hopes up if they didn't end up drafting me."

"Is this where you hoped you'd get drafted?" she asks, looking down at her hands.

"I mean, yeah. It's a dream come true. Not only do I get to potentially play for my home state, but I also have the chance to play professionally alongside my brother. Do you know how rare it is for two brothers to be in the NHL, let alone on the same team?"

"I do. I guess that's why I hadn't even considered Minnesota as an option."

I won't lie. I can't get a read on how she's feeling and it's scaring the hell out of me.

Taking her hand in mine, I walk her up the steps and sit on the front porch swing, patting the cushion next to me for her to take a seat. Once she does, I ask, "What is it about the draft results that worries you?"

She pulls my hands into her lap, turns them over, and begins drawing lines on my palms. "There are still so many factors up in the air, and I'm worried about what that means for our future."

"The only questionable things are where we'll end up and when. As far as I'm concerned, there's no question in my mind when it comes to you and me that you're my future. At least, that's how it is for me. Do you feel differently?" I ask, panic evident in my voice at this point.

"What? No. No, of course not!" she assures me, squeezing my hands in hers.

"Then why are you worried?" I ask, mindlessly running my thumbs over the backs of her hands.

"I'm terrified that we'll wind up another high school sweetheart cliché," she admits, avoiding eye contact with me.

"What?" I question, ducking to meet her eyes.

She still won't look at me, and I'm beyond terrified at how this has taken a turn. "That we'll go away to college, try to make things work, and it'll probably work until you get signed or something else happens that could pull us apart. I mean, in your scenario, things have to work out perfectly as far as timing goes. What happens if you sign mid-way through your collegiate career and I'm still in school?"

I freeze my hands in place. "Then we'll make it work long distance, Taevin. Do you not want this to work?"

"Of course I do, Jackson. How could you even ask that?"

"Then don't give up on us before we've even got any hurdles to overcome."

"I'm not! I think I'm justified in being worried about what our future has in store for us. Not to mention, look at all the attention you get from girls now—won't that only amplify when you're at the collegiate level?"

I scoff because, no, that one doesn't feel justifiable at all. I've never given her any reason to doubt my faithfulness. "I don't know, but that is a non-issue for me. You know you're all I see. I'm crazy about you, baby. This isn't some high school fling for me. You are my entire future. I'd quit hockey tomorrow if it was what stood in the way of our future."

Tae shakes her head vehemently. "No. You promised you wouldn't let me become a distraction."

"Then tell me what I can do to make you feel secure in our relationship. You're scaring the hell out of me, Tae."

"I need to know that our entire future won't only be about your goals and aspirations, but that I have a say in our future too. What happens if I can't pursue a career in music while living in Minnesota?"

"Then I'll request a trade to wherever you want to go as soon as my rookie contract is up."

"It's not that simple—you and I both know that."

"Then I'd quit," I say simply and without hesitation.

"I can't ask you to do that. I won't *let* you do that."

Shifting, I turn so I'm fully facing her. "Then we'll make it work long distance for as long as we need to in order for us both to live out our dreams, T. I'm committed to making this work."

She silently stares into my eyes for so long I fear she doesn't believe me. She has to know how serious I am.

Finally, she breaks the silence. "We'll make this work. I'm committed wholeheartedly to not only making it work between us, but also putting our dreams and our futures first. I promise I'll never make you feel like you have to choose between me and hockey ever again—that wasn't my intention, by the way. I've just never imagined I'd stay here after high school."

My brows furrow in confusion. What does she mean by that? "Like living with your dad?"

"No, in Minnesota. Every time I imagined what my future would look like, it always played out with me living in a big city like New York City, LA, or Nashville. Before I met you, I swore I'd leave home and never look back. I mean, sure, I'd still come back to visit my dad; but I didn't see myself living in Minnesota beyond high school. It'll just take time for me to wrap my head around that possibility," she explains, gripping my hand in hers like she's scared to let go.

"Tae—" I start, but pause to consider what I want to say. Truth is, I'm at a loss for words. What does that mean for us? I don't want to make her feel like she has to live somewhere she was deadset on leaving just to make me happy and support my dreams. But I'd also rather not live long distance from her for longer than I have to. Depending on if and when I sign with Minnesota, I could spend one to three seasons playing for them. Selfishly, I'd love to stay at Harvard for as many seasons as I can just so I can stay closer to Tae; which is the exact opposite of how any other eighteen-year-old in my shoes would feel.

Before I can voice my jumbled thoughts, Taevin cups my face in her hands, rubbing her thumbs up and down my cheeks in a soothing motion. "We don't have to figure everything out right now. I'm so sorry I even mentioned this, I just got in my head. Let's get to the cabin so we can properly celebrate the fact that you were just drafted! I'm so proud of you, J." Tae's eyes shine with adoration, and without a moment's pause, I pull her into my arms and silently vow to do whatever it takes to help the woman I love achieve her wildest dreams.

With my arm slung over her shoulders, I turn and nuzzle my face against hers, placing a quick kiss on her cheek before leaning in and murmuring, "I can't wait to get you alone, Thorn. My plans for the evening consist of kissing every inch of your skin."

I pull back just in time to see Taevin's eyes widen right before she elbows me in the ribs. Her gaze remains fixed on the front of the truck where Bennett sits in the driver's seat.

Turning back to her, I tell her in a hushed tone, "Don't worry, Benny didn't hear."

She turns and cups my ear before quietly saying, "If he does hear you, plan on rooming with him instead of me this weekend."

I play along and cup her ear back. "Better make sure you moan into the pillow then, baby."

Her breathing turns rapid at that, and fuck if it doesn't turn me on. Turning her chin so she's facing me, I gaze into her deep brown eyes before bringing her in for a kiss that's far from indecent, but when I pull back and turn forward, I connect eyes with Bennett in the rearview mirror and he just shakes his head.

"Why the fuck did I agree to let you ride up with me again?" Bennett grumbles after he aggressively presses the mute button on his radio.

I smile, welcoming his grumpiness at this point. "No clue. I just assumed you wanted to spend more quality time with your little bro."

"Yeah, that's definitely the reasoning," he deadpans.

"You wanted me to have more time to spend holding hands with Tae?" I guess, waggling my brows at my brother in the rearview mirror.

He guffaws at my remark. "You're such an annoying little shit sometimes."

I shrug off his dig. "Yeah, but you've missed me while you were out on the road playing all season. Just admit it," I taunt, batting my eyelashes exaggeratedly just to piss him off.

"I'm not admitting to shit that ain't true, J." Instead of giving me the opportunity to rebuttal, he turns up the music loud enough to cut off any conversation. Fine by me, we've only got another twenty minutes until we're at the cabin anyways, and I intend to spend every second thoroughly riling Taevin up until she's begging me to stay in our room instead of hanging out with the group.

By the time we pull up to the cabin, Taevin is flushed and her breathing has picked up; essentially, I got her right where I want her.

"Wait, I thought you said we were staying at their cabin. Is this a resort?" Taevin asks, gawking at the mansion before us.

Cutting the engine, Bennett shifts in his seat and chuckles. "Not a resort. This used to be their grandparents' estate. Carson and McKenna's parents inherited it a while back, but they completely remodeled the place about four years ago. They call it their family cabin, but it's like over eight thousand square feet. I'm not sure anyone would consider that a cabin."

"Definitely not what I'd consider a cabin," she mutters before getting out of the car. She leans against the side of Bennett's SUV, taking it all in. The exterior of the place has a lodge aesthetic and is expansive from the front, with large stone and cedar beams that score to the second story. I've been here a few times over the years I've known Carson and McKenna, and I think Tae's mind is going to be blown when she sees the inside. While this house looks fairly stately from the outside, the exterior is somewhat deceiving for how big the interior really is.

Tossing my arm over her shoulder, I lean in and brush my lips against the shell of her ear. "Did I mention there's seven bedrooms? Meaning we're not sharing with anyone. And Carson being the best friend that he is, gave us the biggest bedroom in the basement with its own ensuite and french doors that open right to where the hot tub is."

"I'm afraid you didn't. Jokes on you, though, because if I would've known we weren't going to be sleeping on an air mattress all weekend like I thought we might be, I would've packed skimpier sleepwear."

I nip at her ear lobe before letting out a menacing chuckle. "It's cute that you think you're wearing anything to bed while we're here, baby."

With that, I swat her butt and grab our bags before following Bennett and Tae inside.

Instead of getting her all to myself, we're immediately swarmed by the rest of the group. McKenna and Katie introduce us to the only two people who are staying here that we haven't met, their two new teammates they'll be playing with at Abbott University, Alexa and Brooke. They seem cool and like they'll fit right in with our group.

But I can't stop myself from bending down and greeting my favorite guest of the weekend. McKenna's Golden Retriever, Ranger, is the dog I always begged my parents for but my dad always forbade us from getting.

Ranger rolls onto his back the way he always does when he sees me, knowing I'll give him the biggest tummy rub. "Hey, buddy. Who's a good boy? Yeah, you are, aren't you, good boy?"

"Um, this is the cutest dog I've ever seen," Tae says as she kneels beside me and joins in giving Ranger his favorite pastime.

"Do you want pets one day?" I ask her.

"As many as we can fit in our house. I was never able to have any growing up, and I've always been so jealous of Ryan because she has two dogs and her nana's house has a stable with horses she got to ride pretty much whenever she wanted growing up."

"Then it's settled, I'll get you however many pets you want," I tell her. "Consider that one of my future vows."

My eyes widen at what I've just let slip.

Taevin either doesn't register what I said, or she takes it in stride. Shit, now I hope she did realize what I meant by that.

She looks over at me with a radiant smile. "Then we better live on a big plot of land so I can fill it up with all the chickens, cats, dogs, and goats my heart desires."

"Goats?"

"Yeah, I feel like they'd be fun for our kids to chase around some day," she says wistfully.

I know I've got the dopiest smile on my face right now as warmth spreads throughout my chest. "I'm going to take our bags down to our room quickly. Do you want to check it out or stay up here with the group?" I ask, hoping like hell she'll agree to get away with me before I have my way with her right here and now.

Standing, I offer my hand out to help her up. "I'd love it if you gave me a tour."

"One grand tour coming right up."

Our grand tour is unfortunately postponed when the guys pull me into a conversation just as the girls whisk Taevin into the kitchen to do a welcome shot.

The draft is all Carson, Griff, and Bennett want to talk to me about, and after a while I can see it's making Taevin anxious when she catches snippets of our conversation, even though she won't admit it. I wish I had known she was hesitant about living in Minnesota after college.

I meant what I said when I told her I'd do everything in my power to sign somewhere else after my rookie contract. Hell, I was serious when I said I'd quit if it was in her best interest for her to pursue her dreams. I'm pretty sure that scared her more than anything, so I dropped it for the time being.

When it comes to how I feel about her, I want Taevin to have no reservations or confusion. I want her to be sure of what we have and secure in my love for her. I intend to do that, no matter what it takes.

20

Jackson

T wo days full of wakeboarding, boating, beach volleyball, paddle boarding, singing by the bonfire, and fireworks with our friends means I haven't had nearly enough alone time with Taevin as I'd like.

Thankfully that's about to change. I pull my T-shirt on just as Tae walks out of the bathroom in a pair of cutoff jean shorts, a white tank top, and black vans. The simplest of outfits does it for me every time, and she knows it. Especially when she catches me checking her out with a heated stare I'm sure could sear her skin.

"Change of plans. We're actually not leaving this room," I tell her, wrapping my arms around her waist.

She giggles as I pepper kisses across her face. "Jax! You promised we could ride the ferris wheel here so I could check it off my list."

"Did I? I mean, we don't have to leave for you to ride something . . ."

Before she can even attempt to swat at me, I slide my hands under her butt and lift her up. She wraps her legs around me, and I take a moment to run my hands over the smooth skin of her thighs.

"I believe I already rode what you're referring to this morning. Now it's time for you to take me to this fair I've heard so much about."

Throwing my head back, I let out a defeated groan. "Fine."

She's right, I can't go back on my promise. Especially considering the surprise I have up my sleeve for her.

Last night was the Fourth of July, and before the fireworks, Taevin and I played around the bonfire for our friends. I ate up every rightfully-deserved awestruck stare aimed my girl's way. After Kenna and Katie told Taevin about the nearby fair, I smiled at the plan I'd been formulating to help check off a few items off Tae's list of things to do before college officially was set in motion.

Ever since she told me her dad agreed to let her come up here, I'd been working on a covert mission behind the scenes. Thanks to Kenna and Katie's help, I'm pretty sure Taevin has no clue what I'm up to. I convinced her we had to go under the guise of checking off her riding the ferris wheel, but that won't be the only thing she checks off her list . . . or at least I hope not.

It takes us about a half hour to drive to the fair and find parking for Bennett's truck I borrowed. Part of the reason it took us longer was because I packed the truck bed full of pillows and blankets in case the stars are out tonight.

Hopefully she doesn't think it's all too much—I just want this to be special since it's our last night here together before we get up early tomorrow to head home for my developmental camp.

The sun makes its descent into the horizon as we walk into the fairgrounds, and the colorful lights on the rides surrounding us have me feeling nostalgic to when my mom used to bring me and my siblings to this same fair growing up.

Tae's hand shakes in mine standing in line for the ferris wheel after purchasing tickets. "You getting cold feet?" I ask, looking down and appreciating the way her eyes twinkle in the glow of the kaleidoscope of colors in front of us from the ride.

She worries her lip for a few moments before determination sets in and she replies, "No, I'm ready to check this one off. I might be a few more weeks out from getting my license, but this is the last one you can do with me."

Holding her hand in mine, I bring it to my lips and place a quick kiss on the back of it. "I won't let go of your hand the whole time. You've got this. If it makes it easier for you to get through the ride, I can always distract you."

Arousal heats my veins, and I use all of my willpower not to let images of Tae falling apart on my fingers cloud my vision.

She nudges me with her elbow. "You wouldn't."

"Oh, I definitely would and will if you let me."

Tae rolls her eyes, ignoring my proposition. "Just promise not to let go of my hand."

"I won't take my hands off you the entire time." She huffs so I add a wink for good measure.

As we get situated inside the gondola of the ferris wheel, Taevin squeezes my hand so hard I'm actually impressed by her strength and somewhat fearful she's going to break something.

Pulling my hand from hers, I wrap my arm around her shoulder and pull her against my chest. "Come here, Thorn."

She takes a shaky breath and looks out the open side of the gondola just as the ride jolts us into motion before promptly stopping so the next group of riders can get on.

"Shit, shit, shit!"

I can't help the chuckle that slips when she squeezes her eyes shut, shaking her head like she wants nothing more than to get the hell off this ride.

She just needs a little distraction.

Dropping my arm from her shoulders to her waist, I spread my legs and pull her into my lap. With one arm wrapped firmly around her torso, I drag my other hand up her thigh at a torturous rate.

"Relax, baby," I whisper against the shell of her ear, eliciting a full-body shiver that has her writhing in my lap.

Her eyes are hooded as she looks over her shoulder to see if anyone can see us, but I already know they can't. The gondola doesn't have windows, but the walls are high enough to cut off the view from any possible spectators.

"No one can see us."

She worries her lip between her teeth, likely contemplating whether or not the risk is worth the reward. I want to assure her it will be, but I'll also never push her if this isn't something she wants.

"I'll have to be quiet," she finally murmurs against my lips before leaning in for a kiss that gets my blood pumping and has me feeling like my heart will beat right out of my chest.

I take that as my permission to continue my trail up her thigh until my fingers brush just beneath the frayed hem of her denim shorts. When I drag my finger through her arousal, I'm not sure if it's her moan or mine that escapes. But I make a shushing sound to remind us both to stay quiet.

"You're so fucking wet," I rasp against her neck.

"Please," she pleads as I circle her clit, and the sound of her begging me to continue has me clenching my teeth to keep from getting too worked up.

"Tell me what you want, baby."

Before she answers, she nudges my fingers away and then swivels her hips, grinding against me. The friction. The soft moan that leaves her lips. The smell of her arousal mixed with her perfume. The combination of it all is enough to drive me mad.

"Make me come, Jax. Please."

I grab her hips, and she takes that as my cue for her stop; however, when I tighten my grip and move her hips forward, urging her to continue, she leans in and bites down on my bottom lip as she grinds up and down my length.

Holy hell.

"Is this okay?" she asks, and I can't fight back the low chuckle that slips.

"Okay? Baby, I'm trying my very best not to bust in my shorts right now. Keep going. I wanna make you feel good—watch you fall apart."

She grinds against me some more and her muscles tense as I lift my hips up and thrust up.

"Oh—" she gasps, throwing her head back. "That feels so good, J. Don't stop."

"I won't." And I don't. I continue my ministrations until Taevin's body convulses over me and I watch with rapt attention as she falls apart above me.

Pulling her down until her lips crash against mine, I swallow her moans.

I've never wanted to come so badly, but I refuse to ruin the surprise I have up my sleeve by coming in my shorts right now. After she's finished riding out her release, I halt her hips but continue to kiss the everloving shit out of her.

This girl—fuck, how is she even mine?

I need more than just this moment.

More than just this summer or next year.

I need forever with her.

Every first and every last, I want to experience all the big milestones and mundane moments in between with her by my side.

The ride slows before coming to a stop when we're at the very top, and it's only then with her straddling me and her arms around my neck that we both turn our heads to the side and look out at the view.

From here, we have a view of the entire fair, including a stage on the far end of the fairgrounds where a small crowd is forming as a band begins performing.

It must be nine o'clock.

Perfect timing.

A smile lifts my lips when Tae points to the stage. "Oh, look. There's a concert tonight. Did you know about that?"

I shrug, feigning nonchalance. "Yeah, there's live music every year."

"I wonder who's performing."

Pressing her closer against my chest, I hug her tight and murmur, "We can go check it out after we get off the ride if you want."

Her cheeks brush against mine and I can feel the smile that takes over her face. "Yeah, I'd love that!"

I knew she would.

And it doesn't hurt that this band is an up-and-coming one she recently discovered a few months into us dating. They quickly became one of her favorites, and when I saw they were performing at the fair this weekend, I couldn't help but ensure that we'd be here.

As soon as our ride ends, we make our way over to the edge of the crowd and she squeals when she realizes who is performing.

I grab her hand in mine, dragging her toward the stage. "Come on, let's get you closer to the front."

"I'm fine right here," she insists, but standing on the outskirts of the crowd doesn't bode well for what I've got up my sleeve.

I turn and murmur in her ear. "The band has to see one of their biggest fans up close."

Her cheeks flush as her eyes widen and she shakes her head.

Instead of listening, I tug her behind me as I weave a path through the crowd toward the front. Once we're a few rows back, just off the front edge of the stage, I pull Tae in front of me and press my chest flush against her back before wrapping my arms around her waist and lacing my fingers in hers.

The familiar song has to be the third or fourth song of their set, and I wrack my brain to try to remember if it was during this one or the next that my surprise would take place.

As if on cue, when the song comes to an end, the lead singer of the band announces there's a special performance in store for us this evening. "Ladies and gentlemen, please join us in welcoming a fellow Minnesotan to the stage. Taevin Gray! She's going to be performing an original song for you all tonight."

Taevin's entire body stiffens in my arms. Bending down, I whisper in her ear, "I figured since there's only two items left on your list now, you should check off performing in front of a crowd."

"I did when I sang the national anthem at your playoff game, remember?" she hisses through clenched teeth.

"That wasn't an original song, baby. Remember the addendum you made?"

"Semantics. I can't believe you did this, Jackson Charles Wilson."

Oh shit, she just full-named me.

Yeah, I probably fucked up, but there's no time to waste on that right now.

Guiding her through the rest of the crowd up toward the stage, I lead her to where the bass player is standing off to the side of the stage holding an acoustic guitar.

The new guitar I purchased for her a week ago and have been dying to give her.

It has a matte black body with a glittery black strap that Taevin reluctantly slings over her shoulders after she walks woodenly up the steps to the stage.

She's shellshocked and I pray to god she doesn't get stage fright.

Pride expands in my chest as Tae approaches the mic stand. I mirror the deep, calming breath she takes before she searches the crowd until her eyes lock on mine.

"Thank you for having me tonight." A few whistles give her pause before an enigmatic smile transforms her face. "I'm not gonna lie, I had no idea I'd be performing for you all tonight. But earlier this year, I made a list of things I wanted to do before I go to college this fall. One of the last things on the list was to perform an original song in front of a crowd. So if it's alright with y'all, I'm going to check this one off the list and play you a song I just finished. It's called 'Ensnared Hearts.'"

The crowd cheers when she strums the opening chords of the song, it makes her smile. Their encouragement heightens when she closes her eyes and sings the first lines.

The lyrics are familiar, taking me back to the night she sang them to me just before we made love the first time.

Taevin captivates the audience with her infectious energy just like I knew she would. She's a natural up there; it's as if she were born to be on stage.

When she gets to the chorus she first played for me months ago, my chest swells with pride. "It's a sin and you're redemption. Strength and beauty tangled tight. Hold me now, pain and protection. Lose myself in sea glass eyes. My heart won't be contained, I'm yours in every way. Ensnared hearts, you and me. Pull me free, but baby keep your hold on me."

Stagelights illuminate her petite figure, yet she doesn't look small right now; in fact, she looks larger than life with the way she commands the stage. It's amazing, actually—the way she's managed to ensnare the crowd with only her voice and a guitar.

Taevin Gray was born to dazzle the masses, and I'd give up everything if it meant I got to watch her shine like this for the rest of my life.

Taevin

I'm still shaking even an hour after performing.

In front of a crowd.

While playing guitar—a guitar that happens to be *mine*. Like, whose life is this? And who am I going to have to fight when they try to take it back?

I may have been riddled with nerves and on the verge of throwing up when they first announced my name. But then I got up on stage and looked out at the crowd. And my eyes landed on him.

Jackson was the focal point that kept me grounded during the entire performance. Then when I finished and the band asked if I wanted to perform my favorite song of theirs with them, I glanced over at Jax and his entire aura exuded pride.

I suddenly realized I'd do anything to keep him looking at me like that for the rest of my life.

And now here we are, snuggled in the bed of his brother's truck with a pile of blankets under a sky full of mesmerizing July stars.

The heat of his chest beneath my cheek, and the feel of his strong arms wrapped around me feels like home.

Jackson is my home.

He rolls me over onto my back and brushes his thumb against my cheek, staring down at me with eyes full of love and longing.

"I love you so much," I whisper, needing him to know that but unable to put into words just how much he means to me.

Jax peppers delicate kisses on my cheeks, my forehead, and over the bridge of my nose. "I love you too, baby. So fucking much. And I don't think I've ever been so proud of someone in my entire life as I am of you for what you did tonight."

Staring down at me, he licks his lips before shaking his head in disbelief. A huge smile takes over his face. "You were amazing up there, Tae. Truly. And I wasn't the only one who noticed. You managed to captivate the whole fairground with your performance."

I try to shy away from his praise but he tilts my chin back up to look at him. "I love what you did with the song. And if the way the crowd went wild for you was anything to go off of, I'm sure they loved it too."

"Only because you pushed me out of my comfort zone," I admit. And it's the truth. As much as I'd like to think I was going to check everything off my list, performing an original song in front of a small room of people—let alone a crowd of hundreds—wasn't something I really thought I'd accomplish before the fall. I'm not sure I would've ever had the nerve to do that without Jax's planning. The hope I saw in his eyes made me more determined than ever to overcome my fears and self-doubt.

He makes me want to be brave—to go after everything I've ever dreamed of.

When I look up at him again, he looks unsure and I'm not sure what I said to put that look on his face.

"I'm sorry if I pushed you too far too soon, that wasn't my intention, T."

"You didn't. I swear," I'm quick to reassure him. "If anything, I should get down on my knees and thank you for giving me one of the most memorable nights of my life. It was—" I take a deep breath before biting back a smile. "It was unbelievable. Being up there. The stage. The lights. The *crowd*. The adrenaline. Oh my gosh, J, I felt like I was high. And when they cheered for me, I was soaring. It was such a rush!"

"I wish I could relive this moment over and over again—you look so happy."

"I am."

"I know, it's written all over your face. Your joy is contagious. I'm so damn proud of you." He leans down and places a tender kiss on my lips that has us both smiling as he pulls away.

Looping my arms around his neck, I rake my fingers through his hair as he rests his forehead against mine. "J?"

"Yeah, baby."

"I'm not sure I've ever been this happy in my entire life. And I know that might sound crazy or dramatic considering I'm only eighteen and you'll be nineteen this month, but I don't care. It's the truth, and it's all thanks to you. I'm not sure what our future has in store for us but I know whatever comes our way, I want to experience it by your side. The good, the bad, the ugly, the joyful milestones, a house, pets, marriage, kids—I only envision you beside me."

Jackson is speechless as he stares into my eyes.

Just when I think I've gone too far and stunned him beyond belief, he sits up and rocks back onto his heels, reaching out his arm for me. "Come here."

He hops off the truck, and I scooch until my legs are dangling off the side of the tailgate.

It's dark now, but I can still make out his silhouette as he bends down to grab something out of the tall grasses that surround us. After a minute, he comes back and stands between my legs, placing his hands on either side of my waist.

I'm hesitant to wrap my arms around his neck after being so vulnerable. Ultimately, I do, and Jax hums in contentment.

"I don't think that sounds crazy or dramatic at all."

My brows pinch in confusion until realization sinks in. "You don't?"

He slides his hands beneath the hem of my tank top and then rubs his thumbs up and down my bare skin. The movement is soothing, though I'm not sure if it's more so for me or him, because when I take him in, he looks like he's contemplating something.

"Not at all—" Jax clears his throat and then takes a deep breath. "In fact, I only see you too. When I think of my future—I envision the two of us. Only ever us. What would you say if I asked you to make that dream a reality?"

Jax grips my waist and lifts me off the tailgate so I'm standing in front of him. Taking my hands in his, he shocks the hell out of me by dropping down on one knee.

"What are you doing?" I squeal because what the hell is happening right now? "Have you lost your mind? Stand up, Jackson. This isn't something to joke about." I try to pull him up but he doesn't budge.

"I've never been more serious in my life," he admits, running his thumbs over my fingers. Taking a deep breath, he continues. "Your future is so damn bright. Your hopes and dreams matter to me a hell of a lot more than my own do. But regardless if we wind up on different ends of the country while we're pursuing those dreams or we're together in the same home, I'm going to do whatever it takes to make this relationship work. Let me prove that to you by vowing to be by your side for the rest of my life."

"My dad would never let me get married so young—" I start, but he cuts me off.

"Then we'll elope. We're eighteen, Tae. We don't need anyone's permission."

I stare into his eyes, searching for any hesitation and find none. "You're serious about this?"

"I am. And regardless of your answer, I know we will make this work."

Biting my bottom lip, I shake my head once. "You're trying to tell me you want to go into your freshman year of college married?"

"You're damn right I do. I'd love nothing more than to introduce you to everyone as my wife."

"Your wife?" I repeat in disbelief.

"Yes."

"Well are you gonna ask me something then?"

Jax lets out a low chuckle while grabbing something out of the chest pocket of his T-shirt. When he opens his hand, a small bunch of grass is wound into a small circle. And the moment his beautiful, sea glass eyes meet mine, I know my answer before he even asks.

"Like you said, we're young. And to anyone else, we may look like fools. If there's one thing I know for sure, it's that I love you with my whole heart and I want to start a life with you. So, Taevin Gray, will you make me the happiest man in the world and marry me?"

Those beautiful songbirds only he can awaken take flight in my stomach again.

"Yes," I whisper, blinking away the happy tears threatening to spill down my cheeks.

"Yes?" he questions in disbelief.

"Yes!" I reply a little louder this time.

He lifts me into his arms and spins me around. "You'll marry me?" he questions again, and I can't help but giggle.

"You're crazy for asking, but I'm crazy enough to agree. Yes, I'll marry you, Jackson!"

Pulling me in for a kiss, my lips quiver against his. When I break the kiss, I rest my forehead against his and rub my thumb up and down his cheek. He grabs hold of my hand and slips the makeshift ring onto my finger. I press my lips to his and I can't stop the smile that lights up my face even as I kiss him with everything I have.

Holy hell! This can't be real life.

Jax finally breaks our kiss, and sets me back on the tailgate, spreading my legs so he can stand between them. With his head nuzzled against my neck, he breathes me in and asks, "So, when are we making this official, wifey?"

I can't help but chuckle. "Well, I suppose it depends if we're really eloping or telling our parents. I'm not going to lie . . . I'd prefer we elope and tell them at, like, Christmas break when we come home or something."

"I agree."

I quirk a brow. "Really? It's that easy?"

"I mean, I don't have the best example of a healthy marriage. But from what I've heard, there's this saying, 'happy wife, happy life,' and I plan to live by that."

I push his shoulders back. "In that case, I think we should celebrate."

Jax gives me the sexiest smirk. "Oh yeah?"

"Yep."

Wrapping his arms around my waist, he tugs at my hips so I'm barely resting on the edge of the tailgate. "And how do you wanna do that?"

A shy smile eclipses my face before I bite my bottom lip. "Make love to me under the stars?"

"Couldn't think of a better way to celebrate. Sit back," he tells me, nodding to the pile of pillows we were snuggling in earlier.

Once we're both in the bed of the truck, Jax kneels beside me as he helps me pull my tank top over my head before slowly inching off my shorts. The way he's looking at me and touching me—with gentleness and reverence—liquifies my stomach. And when his lips connect with mine, his tongue swiping inside for a taste, I become desperate to feel his skin on mine.

Trailing my fingers beneath the hem of his shirt, I lift it up his torso, only breaking the kiss so he can pull it over his head. While he does, I don't waste a moment as I unbuckle his belt and push his shorts and boxers off his hips.

"Need you," I whisper, wrapping one arm around his neck and the other around his waist so I can pull him on top of me.

"You have me. Always." Jax carefully lowers himself on top of me, my flesh burning where his touches mine. Goosebumps erupt across my skin, and my nipples pebble.

I kiss him again, though this one is brief, ending with my tugging his lower lip between my teeth. "I need you inside of me, Jax. Now." I punctuate my demand by gliding up and down his length.

When his tip slides inside of me momentarily, we both still. The silence is broken when Jax lets out a groan of frustration, hanging his head until his forehead rests against my chest.

"Shit! I don't have a condom. I left them at the cabin."

My mind whirls as I try to come up with a solution that gets me what I ultimately want. Which is him inside of me as soon as possible. "The glove compartment?" I question.

"It's not my truck."

I worry my lip between my teeth and shrug as if I'm not about to ask something cringy. "Think your brother would have any?"

He shakes his head. "Bennett just got this, and he's not exactly the kind of guy who hooks up in his truck."

"Okay, well I'm on the pill so we could go without . . ." My eyes widen at the same time as my lips fold shut so I won't blurt any other ridiculous suggestions.

His head drops again and he lets out a low groan that makes my stomach flip. "Baby, don't play with me right now."

My cheeks heat with embarrassment as I silently curse myself for suggesting the ludicrous idea in the first place. "I'm not, but I understand if you don't want to take the risk of going without."

"Taevin . . ." he groans my name like it's a prayer and he's begging for mercy. He lifts his head and our gazes lock. "It's not a matter of want. Of course, I *want* to. I just—" Jax pauses, licking his lips before a pained look eclipses his face. "I've never gone without one before. I just want to keep you safe, baby."

"We've both been tested and I've been on the pill for months now. If it makes you feel better, you could pull out."

Jax looks me over, scrutinizing whether or not I'm sure about this. "Would you be okay if I didn't pull out?"

God, that might be the sexiest thing he's ever asked me.

I lick my lips, desperate to end this conversation and have him do just that. "I'd be more than okay with that—in fact, I think it's the only way we should celebrate our engagement."

A deep moan vibrates from his throat as he pushes further inside me. "Fuck, Tae. Fuck! This feels too good."

Once he's fully seated, his dick twitches inside me, and without the barrier between us I feel everything. I'm so worked up I nearly come just from him entering me and that small movement.

He stills inside of me, breathing deeply as we tremble against one another.

"Please, Jax," I gasp without even really knowing what I'm pleading him to do.

"Want me to move?" he asks just as he pulls nearly all the way out and then slowly slides back in.

"Yes," I moan, raking my nails down his back as I lock my legs around his hips.

My eyes roll to the back of my head when he pistons deeper and then rolls his hips against my clit in the most glorious way.

"Baby, I've never—it's never been—ah, you're so wet. So tight." His gibberish confessions match my nonsensical thoughts.

"Don't stop. Please!" I'm fully aware I'm begging him at this point, but I'm on the very brink of my orgasm and if he breaks this rhythm I think I'll die of disappointment.

"Never," he rasps into the crook of my neck, and then I'm coming.

My orgasm pulls me under into a sea of ecstasy that is only made infinitely better when Jackson drives deeper and groans, his cock pulsing as he releases inside me.

I rake my fingers through his hair as he presses soft kisses down my neck and across each collarbone. When I open my eyes, I smile up at the sky full of stars and sigh in contentment as Jax rolls us over and pulls me into his arms.

"I love you, Taevin. No matter what our future holds, I promise you I'll never stop."

21

Taevin

Now

I'm not sure why I'm so nervous right now. It's not like it's the first time I'm meeting Jax's family. But it is the first time anyone aside from his mom has met me as his wife . . . his *estranged wife*, who didn't even know we were still married.

And we're not the only ones going to Jackson's brother's house—the entire team will also be there for their captain's annual preseason cookout.

Ugh. No wonder I'm so worked up.

God, I could use a drink right now but I'm not supposed to drink while preparing for my egg retrieval. These damned injections hurt like a bitch. I'm on day eleven of two shots per day to try to stimulate my ovaries to produce as many eggs as possible for my retrieval that's scheduled in only a few days.

With shaking hands, I finish applying a second coat of mascara to my eyelashes before putting the tube away in the vanity drawer. When I close it, I hold onto the edge of the counter for a moment and consider all the details Jax thought of when he was building this home. It's weird that for a guest bathroom he'd have such an extravagant set up with a custom vanity and the dreamiest soaking tub that could comfortably fit two people.

Grabbing my phone and my crossbody bag off the bench at the foot of the bed, I take a deep breath and walk out of the room, shutting the lights off as I go.

I walk into the kitchen and Jax startles me by saying, "T, relax. You look like you're about to throw up, and we both know that won't feel good with your healing stomach incisions." He looks so good standing there in the corner with a glass of water in his thick hands, legs crossed casually as the afternoon sun highlights him through the windows above the kitchen sink.

Jeesh, I really do have a shit poker face.

"I'm good," I lie, unconvincingly I guess, because Jax guffaw's at me.

"You look tense. Come here, baby." Jackson sets down his glass and gestures for me to come into his arms. Setting my things on the kitchen island, I move to him and melt into his embrace as he pulls me into chest and rocks me lovingly back and forth.

Jax rubs his hands up and down my back, and the simple act wouldn't be soothing if it were anyone else. But when it's his hands on me, my body comes to life responding in ways it hasn't in far too long. Placing a kiss on my temple, he murmurs, "What's got you feeling anxious?"

I bury my head into his chest and mumble, "Oh, I don't know. Only the fact that I'll be meeting your entire team at the same time as I'm reacquainted with your brother, sister, and best friends."

"Ah, that? That's nothing. I thought you were anxious about the fact that I'm going to have to participate in the annual Labor Day food eating competition."

I shoot my head up to look at him. "The what?"

"It's so stupid but a few years ago, the guys started this ridiculous competition where we eat foods that aren't overtly sexual in nature until we eat them. It's gotten out of hand at this point."

"Must've for you to say that. So, what are you eating this year?"

"Papayas."

I let out an unattractive snort as I laugh at the image playing in my mind of a group of grown men eating papayas.

"Ha ha, laugh it up," Jax says, feigning annoyance.

Once I've somewhat composed myself, I ask, "I'm sorry did you say papayas?"

"I did. And we've even got to eat them with our hands behind our backs."

"Oh my god, this is going to be so good."

"It should be, so long as you pay close attention." Jax waggles his brows and I just roll my eyes.

"There she is. It pains me to admit this, but I much prefer your sassy eye rolls to the anxious look you were wearing when you came in here."

I playfully swat at his chest and move to grab my things when he pulls me back in and wraps an arm around my waist, placing the other along my jaw. "Where you going?" he questions.

"Nowhere," I reply breathlessly.

"Good, because I'm feeling needy for your lips."

"Is that so?"

"Mhmm," he murmurs, brushing his lips against mine in a whisper of a kiss. I wrap my arms around his neck and pull him down for a kiss we can both get lost in. Our lips collide in a clash of burning need that can only be satiated by one another.

Ever since we kissed again for the first time nearly two weeks ago, things have certainly shifted between us. It's almost like no time has passed and we're picking back up right where we left off. Though, I can't entirely say that's true for me. For Jackson, sure, but that's only because he doesn't know what he doesn't know.

Each time he kisses me, and with each passing day where he looks at me with stars in his eyes, I fall into a deeper pit of debilitating guilt.

I'm snapped from my downward spiral when Jackson spins me, backing me up until I'm pressed against the corner of the kitchen cabinets, and without missing a beat, he carefully lifts me and places me on the countertop that chills my heated skin.

His hands grip my hips and I love the way his fingers dip beneath the hem of my shirt, testing me—tantalizing me—in the most delicious way. I wish for his fingers to drift higher moments before he grants my silent plea.

"Jax!" I gasp when he brushes his fingers over my nipple. The slight touch is taunting, making me want to turn this game of teasing right back on him.

"I see these are still as sensitive as they've always been," he rasps against my neck as he tweaks my nipple with his fingers, driving me wild with need. "Tell me, Thorn, do you think I can make you come just from nipple play?" Jax asks, and with how sensitive they've been due to the medication, I have complete faith that he could get me there.

Arching my back, I give him better access to do just that with my nipples, and in doing so, my hips inch forward until I find myself grinding against him.

"T," he groans as he thrusts his hips into me, gripping my hip tighter with his one hand while the other masterfully plays with my nipples, rolling, tweaking, and kneading them. When his mouth latches on to the spot of sensitive skin just beneath my jaw, I moan into his ear and quicken the pace of our hips. The combination of it all has me so on edge, so worked up, I feel as tight as a guitar string, my stomach pulls taught with desire. Longing. Aching. Need like I've never known courses through me and threatens to pull me under.

Lifting my shirt and bra up, he brings his mouth to my nipple, sucking it with a quick pop before blowing on it and doing the same to the other. When Jax latches onto one and then slides his hand off my hip and instead uses his thumb to rub rough circles over my clit, so I can feel it through the thin fabric of my skirt, white hot pleasure blinds my vision and I go *off*, coming harder than I have in years.

I breathlessly ride out my orgasm, desperately grasping onto the euphoria for as long as I can.

Once I'm thoroughly satiated, Jax lets go of my nipple with a pop and gives me a mischievous smirk. "I love the needy little whimpers you make just before you come."

I slowly push his shirt over his head. Not wanting to receive without giving him the same pleasure in return, I make quick work of unbuckling his belt and unbuttoning his shorts. Thank god he doesn't try to stop me when I push down his boxers and shorts enough so I can firmly grip his hard length in my hand. "If I recall, I'm not the only one who whimpers while I'm on the brink," I tell him.

He chuckles roughly, his chest rumbling against mine until it cuts off abruptly when I roll my thumb over the head of his cock, using the precum he's leaking as lubricant. Knowing it won't be enough, I spit onto the palm of my hand and resume pumping his length.

"Fuck, baby." He drops his head against my shoulder as he ruts into my hand, turning me on so badly with his loss of control. "Having you touch me again feels so perfect—so fucking *right*."

"I can't wait to have you fuck me again, J," I whisper into his ear. Continuing to pump him, I ask, "Whose cock is this?"

"Yours," he answers without hesitation. "Fuuuucck, always yours," he groans as I work his head and brush my thumb lightly over the thick vein on the underside of his cock—the one I used to love running my tongue over again and again until he lost all control.

"Good answer. And who's making you feel so good?"

"You," he whimpers, quickening his pace. "My beautiful wife is making me feel so fucking good. Too good. Taevin, baby, I'm gonna come," he warns moments before my hand and upper thigh are covered with his release.

Dragging my finger over my thigh, I take great pleasure in watching his eyes darken as I bring his release to my lips and suck my finger clean.

"Mmm, I almost forgot how good you taste," I hum before pulling him in for a kiss.

"When can I taste you again?" he asks against my lips.

Pulling my head back, I keep my arms wrapped around his neck, raking my fingers through the hair on the nape of his neck. "I'm not supposed to for six weeks."

"That's just penetration though, right? You just had an orgasm and it didn't hurt, did it?" he questions with an edge of apprehension.

"I did, and it didn't," I confirm at the same time as my pussy clenches in anticipation for the possibilities that are to come. Bringing him in for another kiss, I drag my finger tips over the scruff on his jaw. Pulling back, I tell him, "You never could grow facial hair when we were together."

He lifts his brows suggestively. "There's a lot that's different about me now, baby."

"I can see that," I retort, trailing my fingers down the column of his throat, across his chest and over his tattoos on his shoulder before moving them farther down to trace the flock of ravens just above his hip bone.

"As much as I'd love to explore all of those changes, we should probably get going to your brother's house. That is, unless you'd like to stay here instead?" I ask, hopeful to get out of the event entirely. "You said your parents won't be there, right?"

His brow creases momentarily. "I think my mom might come, but she said my dad is out of town." The tension that was growing in my shoulders eases slightly. Jax peppers kisses across my cheeks and the bridge of my nose before promising, "We just need to make an appearance for a couple hours. Honestly, we can only stay for like three hours max so we can get you home in time to do your shots."

The reminder of my shots doesn't produce the same unease it typically does because he just said he needed to get me *home*—as in this beautiful house he built with only me in mind.

The words flood my system and sink into my bones, causing a new melody to spring to life in my head. Knowing I need to get it on paper as quickly as possible, I push Jax back just enough to scoot off the counter.

"I'm going to get cleaned up and I'll be right back out," I shout over my shoulder as I rush to my room. As I run the water over a washcloth in my bathroom, I hum out the melody as lyrics begin to come to me.

You're my revival,
My place of survival,
Your arms are the home I never lost.
I might be fragile,
But you make me whole again,
Make me sing again, my muse.

I type the lyrics in my notes app, promising myself I'll put them to paper later when we get home. After adding a reminder to have Kyle ship my favorite songwriting guitar to Jackson's house, I walk out of my bedroom feeling lighter than I have in weeks.

My melodies are coming back to me, and instead of the heartbreak and grief they've been riddled with for so many years, I'm finally able to write about something lighthearted—like falling again for the boy who was once my whole world.

In all honesty, Jackson Wilson has always been my muse.

I'd say my heart's revival album is long overdue.

We make our rounds as Jax introduces me to his teammates and their significant others if they have one. So far, I haven't recognized any of them and I'm anxious for Carson and McKenna to arrive so I can see some familiar faces.

Just then, Bennett joins us on the back patio with a young boy on his shoulders and his new bride, who I recognize as Scarlett Carlisle, the newest and youngest owner of the Minnesota Wolverines, beside him.

Jax wraps his arm around my waist and pulls me in as they approach us with big smiles on their faces.

"Taevin, hey! I'm so glad you could join us today. How are you feeling?" Scarlett asks, surprising me when she brings me in for a hug.

Somewhat stunned, I pat her back awkwardly when Bennett tells her, "Little Red, not everyone is a hugger like you."

"Oh my goodness, I'm so sorry. It's just with all I've heard about you lately, I feel like we're old friends," she explains.

I side eye Jackson and the little shit winks back at me.

"It's alright, I don't mind the hug. I mean, I would've hugged you on your wedding day had I not made such a dramatic exit."

"How are you feeling now?" Scarlett asks me.

"My incisions are nearly healed, it's the exhaustion at this point. Add in the hormone injections Jax is poking me with each night and I am just a hormonal, tired mess at this point."

"What are the injections for? And why in the hel—heck are you trusting J to give them to you?" Bennett asks, and I'm somewhat surprised he doesn't already know considering how close he and Jax are.

"I'm getting injections to prep for my upcoming egg retrieval this week," I explain.

Bennett's eyebrows shoot up, and as he opens his mouth to respond, Scarlett cuts in. "Oh, I didn't know that! My stepmom did IVF to have Gemma, of course that was sixteen years ago and I was pretty young, but I remember the injections being tough on her. When is your procedure?"

"Thursday," I reply.

"Well now that we're back from our honeymoon, let us know if there's anything we can help with. I'd love to make you dinner sometime this week if that's okay with you."

"Really? That'd be amazing," I tell her, then turning to look up at Jax. "Do you think maybe we could have them over for dinner?"

Jax squeezes my hip, and the small gesture warms my chest. "Of course, baby."

I feel like I need to pinch myself right now. As if standing here with Jax, meeting all of his teammates and being introduced to his new family members, wasn't already making me feel overwhelmingly grateful, now he's claiming me in front of everyone once more with his arms around me and calling me "baby." I can't begin to explain how amazing that feels after convincing myself for years that I'd never get to experience any of this with him.

"Shut up! Is that my favorite secret sister-in-law talking to my other favorite sister-in-law?" a shrill voice asks just before her bouncing blonde curls come into view.

"Walker!" I squeal just as Jackson intercepts his sister moments before she was about to crash into my open arms for a hug.

"Dubs, be careful!" Jackson scolds her. "Taevin just had surgery a few weeks ago, and she's not even cleared to lift more than fifteen pounds."

Walker's eyes widen, and she brings her hand to her mouth to cover her gasp. "Oh my gosh, I'm so sorry, Tae! I didn't even think of that."

I can't stop the lighthearted laugh that escapes. "It's honestly okay, Walker. No harm done. I missed you so much!" Pushing Jax to the side, I bring Walker in for as tight of a hug as I can muster.

"It's been so long. Too long! And how in the hell didn't I know that my brother was married to my favorite freaking artist?" Walker questions, pulling back to take me in as she shakes her head at me and then Jackson.

"Well considering I didn't even know we were still married, you'll have to take that one up with your big brother."

"Wait, Uncle Jaxy is married to Taevy Gray?" the little boy on Bennett's shoulders asks, and I'm obsessed with the way he just said my name. Is it possible to change my name to Taevy now?

"Her name is Taevin Gray, Bug," Scarlett corrects the boy.

"And what's your name, handsome?" I ask him.

"Gunner!" he tells me.

Jackson points to a teenage girl who joins us, standing beside Scarlett. "Tae, this is my niece Gemma—she's like, your biggest fan—and that little man is my nephew, Gunner."

"Pleasure to meet you—" I start but bite my lip to hold back a laugh because Gemma is looking at me wide-eyed like she might faint at any moment.

Gemma turns in slow motion to her sister. "Scar! Why didn't you tell me my literal hero would be at our house?"

Scarlett and Bennett both chuckle and shake their heads at Gemma.

"Wait, you look so familiar. Did you by chance have backstage passes to see me this spring when I performed in Minnesota?" I ask her.

"I did! *Ohmygodsheremembersme!*" Gemma squeals, turning to Walker and hugging her around her waist. "Did you hear that? Taevin freaking Gray remembers me."

Walker rolls her eyes as she pats Gemma's head. "Sure did! You're pretty freaking memorable, Gems. Who could forget a personality like you?"

Jackson nuzzles his head into the crook of my neck, and I giggle when his scruff tickles my sensitive skin. "I'd say you worried for nothing. Not sure *the* Taevin Gray could mess up meeting my family and friends. Everyone here has stars in their eyes for my girl, and rightfully so."

Butterflies take flight in my stomach hearing the possessive way he calls me his girl.

Unable to resist teasing him, I taunt, "So your plan is to just skip right over the hard conversations and go straight to claiming me in front of everyone you know?"

I immediately regret my word choice when he stiffens behind me.

His deep inhale brushes against my back before he leans in and whispers against the shell of my ear, "We can have all the hard conversations whenever you want, Tae. Regardless, I'm not going anywhere."

I let his words sink in and ease any remaining anxiety I had about being here today. Knowing we can have the hard conversations later, I squeeze his hands that are wrapped around my waist. "I'm holding you to that, Bear."

"You do that, baby," Jax murmurs against my skin before kissing my temple.

Just then I spot McKenna and Griffin walking toward us with a little boy on Griff's hip. A smile lifts my lips as I take in how happy they look. When they get closer, a girl I vaguely recognize comes running up and holds McKenna's hand.

"Tae, I know you remember Griff and Kenna, but this is their daughter Cadence." He points to the beautiful blonde girl who looks much older than nine due to her height. "And this chubby little man is their son Rowen." I watch with a sinking heart as Jackson grabs Rowen from Griff's arms and lifts him in the air above his head before settling him on his hip as if he's done the move hundreds of times. "Cades is nine now and Rowen just turned one, didn't you buddy?" Jax tickles the little boy's chunky belly, and it's all so adorable but mostly overwhelming because how is Cadence already nine?

Nine years old. She's so tall, her smile is so bright, and from how she's greeting and interacting with both the adults and kids right now, I'd say she's probably a great kid.

Nine years.

How has it already been nine years?

God, I don't think I can do this right now.

God? What has he done for you in all these years except steal everything good and pure?

"It's so nice to see you both again, and it's a pleasure to meet you Rowen and Caden-ce—" my voice cracks as I say the girl's name. Bringing my hand to cover my mouth, I choke back a sob that threatens to escape. "Excuse me, I'm not feeling well," I say before taking off toward the house.

I make it to the entryway inside the house just as Jax calls out, "Baby, wait up."

Freezing in place, I brace my lower stomach, willing this uneasiness I'm feeling to subside.

Jax's arm comes around my shoulders when he reaches me. "Hey, what's wrong?"

Avoiding eye contact, I keep my gaze fixed on the floor. "You know what? I'm so sorry, it turns out I'm not feeling well enough to do the big party after all. I think I should probably go. You stay, though. I'll order a car to bring me to your house."

"You're not having a random stranger drive you home." Gently, Jax tilts my chin up, and when my watery eyes connect with his, a look of hurt flashes across his face. "Talk to me, T. What happened just now?"

"N-nothing," I stutter, looking over his shoulder to make sure no one is eavesdropping on us. Satisfied when I don't see anyone, I fix my gaze back on his.

"Please don't lie to me, baby. Was it my brother? Did he say something?"

Reaching out, I grasp his forearm and assure him, "No, it's not Bennett. I promise."

"Did someone make you feel uncomfortable?" he questions.

Dropping his arm, I grasp my stomach again with both hands this time, attempting to steady myself, but it's no use. I feel like the walls are closing in on me.

Stumbling backward, I bump into the entryway table behind me. "I'm so sorry, I'm just feeling a bit unsteady right now."

Jax is quick to reach out and stabilize me. With his arm around my waist, he gestures to their front door. "Here, let me walk you out to my truck and then I'll text Bennett that we had to go."

"No, Jackson. You haven't even been here an hour yet. Besides, that papaya-eating competition hasn't happened yet," I point out, trying my best to convince him to stay and let me get a ride.

"I don't care about anything going on or anyone here besides you, T. Now let me take you home."

I don't put up any more of a fight as he places his hand on the small of my back and guides me out to his truck.

There's a foreboding feeling sitting deep in my gut that everything is about to change once again.

"Here, let me," Jax insists, taking the ice cube from my hand and holding it against my stomach. "Do you want to pinch the area like last night or have me do it?" he asks in a gentle tone, causing tears to well in my eyes.

I hesitate, because how in the hell is this man being so good to me right now when I don't deserve it? I don't deserve his kindness or his selflessness.

"I can pinch it. Thanks," I murmur as I gather the skin between my fingers and squeeze right before he draws the needle to it.

"Close your eyes, T," Jax tells me just before he gives me the first injection. Drawing up the second round, he asks, "Are you doing okay?"

"Fine, thanks," I say, breathing deeply and keeping my eyes shut.

"This will all be worth it one day, baby," he whispers. I freeze, my whole body stiffening as his words register. This is the first time he's even hinted at the fact that if this is successful it will result in our future children. I mean, he didn't say that exactly, but that's definitely what he's insinuating.

I let out a low chuckle that evolves into something bordering on hysterical.

Jackson draws back the needle he was about to poke me with. Glancing up at me, he asks, "What's happening right now?"

A child or children I'll never get to grow in my own body.

My stupid, useless fucking body that has failed me in the worst way already.

Of course my hormonal rollercoaster of emotions chooses this moment to send me freefalling from laughter into choked sobs. Jax shoots up, setting the injection on the bathroom counter before wrapping his arms around me. He just stands there and patiently holds me as my worst memories come crashing back to the forefront of my mind.

Blood. There's so much blood. It's soaked through my pants. I fall to the ground and drop my head into my hands as sobs wrack my body with an unyielding force as the likely reality of my situation hits me.

"Oh my gosh! Tae, we need to go to the hospital. That's a lot of blood."

"I can't, Ry. Not yet. He doesn't know. Jackson doesn't even know."

My knees give out on me and I collapse, the only thing preventing me from falling is Jackson's strong arms wrapped around me.

"I'm so sorry!" I wail into his chest through the sobs that wrack my body.

"Shh," he hushes against my temple, bringing one of his hands up to wipe the tears steadily streaming down my face.

"It's all my fault," I admit, ashamed by my body's continued failure.

Pulling my head off his chest, he holds my face in his hands, his eyes flicking back and forth between mine. "What are you talking about, baby? You have nothing to be sorry for."

"I do!" I choke out, knowing I look as hysterical as I feel. "You wouldn't be looking at me the way you are right now if you kn-knew the t-truth."

He flinches at my words, just slightly, but calmly asks, "What truth?"

"I shouldn't have gone to Boston that weekend to find you. If I hadn't traveled, things could've been different. Maybe he would still be here with us."

As my words register, Jackson's eyes widen and he freezes in place, staring down at me with a look full of equal parts confusion and terror. "Who would be here with us?"

"Our baby," I whisper, fixing my gaze on the shower beside us, too ashamed to meet his gaze. My stomach sinks to the floor and my heart shatters all over again when I hear Jax's whimpered cry.

"No," he rasps, completely heartbroken, sounding every bit as pained as I imagined he would all those years ago.

It's one single word, but that's all it takes to break me forever.

"No," Jackson begs, dropping to his knees before me. When he rests his forehead against my lower stomach, I can't hold back the agonizing shriek of sadness that escapes.

I tell myself I've had nearly ten years to grieve—that I've got to be strong for him. It's my time to be his rock, but I can't. I'm breaking right alongside him. Only my mind is trapped back in that Boston hospital room again, hearing the news that my incompetent cervix is the cause of my sweet little one's early arrival to heaven.

Taking a deep breath, I try to muster up the courage to speak. "When I saw Cadence today, I already knew who she was. I knew McKenna had her during her freshman year of college." I pause, remembering when I heard she had a baby, I spiraled on the road, using alcohol as my only escape. Her baby lived and mine died because my body was too weak to keep him alive. Hiccupping back a sob, I continue. "Seeing her today—knowing our baby would've been the same age as her—it brought me right back to the worst day of my life."

The moment my fingers lace through Jackson's hair to anchor myself, it's as if he's momentarily thrust from his despair. Almost robotically, he grabs an ice cube from the cup on the counter and places it against my stomach. When he pinches the skin with silent tears streaming down his face, I turn away with a mirrored look of anguish as he administers my second shot.

I can't do this right now—not here, in the house he built for us, while the love of my life finds out about our shared tragedy for the first time. Almost as if he's heard my thoughts, Jax stands abruptly, apologizing before he excuses himself.

"Jax!" I call after him.

My feet move after him before I've even realized what I'm doing as I mindlessly follow him down the hall to the front door that he promptly slams behind him.

I halt in the hallway and take in the silence of the house that suddenly feels too large with rooms my body will never allow me to fill—not then and not now.

He said he wasn't going anywhere earlier, but I should've known better.

Why would anyone want to stay with me?

I'm a failure down to the very marrow of my being.

And now that Jackson knows that ugly truth, he could never truly love me again.

22

Jackson

Now

Miscarriage.

The word has continued to ring in my ears since I got the hell out of my house, leaving Taevin alone like an inconsiderate, selfish prick to go to the nearest bar.

And even now, after too many whiskeys to count, that one word has me spiraling.

Fuck!

Taevin miscarried a baby—*our* baby—and I wasn't there for her. Why didn't she tell me? How the fuck can we get a real second chance when the odds have been stacked so incredibly against us all along? Not only does she have cancer, is grieving the loss of her ability to carry her own children, and all along she was holding this secret loss of ours hostage.

Yet, here I am sitting at a bar drowning my sorrows while she sits alone at my house.

I'm such a fuckup. Even knowing that, it doesn't stop me from ordering another whiskey.

My drink is set in front of me on top of a coaster before the bartender turns to the customer that just sat down beside me.

I'm bleary eyed at this point, but as I turn my head, I take in the figure and squint. Huh, that's weird because the woman looks a hell of a lot like my best friend's wife.

"Hi, can I get a club soda, please and thank you?" When the bartender nods, I don't miss the way his eyes make a slow perusal down her chest.

Eyes up, motherfucker, I think to myself.

"Kenna? Is that you?" I question, squeezing my eyes shut, not entirely sure I'm seeing things correctly right now. Because there's no way my best friend's wife is sitting at a bar in a dress that looks like she's trying to get picked up, and very obviously *not* wearing her wedding ring on her left hand.

Yeah, that's right. I'm not too inebriated to miss out on that glaringly obvious detail.

"Jackson. Oh, hey," she says, apprehensive as she looks over her shoulder like she's trying to see if others have caught her out on the prowl like I just have.

What the fuck is going on right now?

Instead of asking her that, I try a more composed version. "What are you doing here?"

"Just, uh . . . you know, grabbing a drink."

"With who?"

"M-myself," she stammers, and even in my drunken state I can tell something is up.

"M&M, you're going to have to answer slowly so I can understand because I'm fucking turned up at this point, but, respectfully, what the fuck are you doing here by yourself without your wedding ring on?"

McKenna's eyes widen before she glances down at her left ring finger, almost as if she's just now noticing her ring is missing. Good, I hope all she did was lose it.

She runs her fingers over her left hand almost as if she needs to feel it to believe it's not there. "Oh, I must've left it in my jewelry box at home."

"Uh huh, and I'm just sitting here having celebratory drinks by myself for shits and giggles," I deadpan, narrowing my eyes.

When she just stares at me, I ask, "Shouldn't you be at home with your husband and kids?"

The words have barely left my mouth before a strong hand comes down on my shoulder and grips it a little too firmly for my liking. "I'm going to need you to apologize to my wife, Jax. Best friend or not, you shouldn't talk to her that way. If she wants to have a night away from me and the kids, she has every right to do so. In fact, I encourage it."

I turn sluggishly in my barstool until I'm facing Griffin. "G? Oh, hey man, I didn't realize you were here. I thought I was being a good friend by confronting your wife before she went home with another guy."

Griff pinches the bridge of his nose and shakes his head. "Liquid courage really makes you say stupid shit, J."

Realizing I haven't apologized to Kenna yet, I swivel back to face her. Too quickly, apparently, because I have to grip onto the bar to steady myself. "Sorry, Kenna. I know you'd never cheat on our guy. I mean, just fucking look at him. He's like the ultimate DILF and you're like—"

"Don't finish that sentence," Griff growls, cutting me off.

Throwing my hands up in surrender, I ping pong my eyes back and forth between them. "I won't. Anyways, I'll let you two love birds get back to your date night. I'm sure you don't want a sorry motherfucker like me to bring down the vibe."

"What's wrong, Jax?"

"What isn't?" I'm quick to retort.

Griff smacks my arm. "Do you need a ride home?"

"I'm not really sure I want to go home right now."

"You wanna sleep it off at our place and I can swing you back home later?" Griff asks.

"Yeah, that might not be a bad idea. But wait, I don't want to ruin your date night. Kenna was just ordering a drink."

"I'm not really feeling the best anyways." Kenna shoulders her purse just as Griff shrugs out of his jacket, draping it over his wife's shoulders. That's when I notice Griffin isn't wearing his wedding ring either.

Only after we're all securely in the confines of Griffin's Jeep do I insert myself in their business. "Why were you two acting so weird at the bar? And why are you both not wearing your wedding rings? You guys aren't like, having marriage troubles or anything are you?"

"You really don't have a filter when you drink, do you?" McKenna mumbles under her breath as an obvious blush heats her cheeks.

"Nope," I say, popping the "p" just for the hell of it.

"Well, if you must know, we were doing a little marriage experiment," she says, as if *that* clarifies anything.

"The fuck? Are you guys like swingers or some shit?"

"What? Jesus, Jax. No! I don't share my wife."

"And I most definitely do *not* share my husband," Kenna adds for good measure.

"Okay, okay, I just had to make sure you two weren't in some kinky sex club or something."

"So what if we were?" Kenna questions, her tone haughty.

God, I'm such an ass.

"Sorry, I'm not shaming anyone. I just figured you two weren't the sharing type."

"And you'd be right," they say in unison.

Freaky.

"Anyway, we read this article that says you should always date your spouse. And while we're pretty religious about date nights, we wanted to uh—" He pauses to clear his throat. "We wanted to try something new."

McKenna turns in her seat to face me. "We were there to pick each other up. That's why we both weren't wearing our rings and that's why I told you I was there by myself. The plan was to go to a random bar and hit on each other like we were strangers."

"Yeah, you know, to see if I can still woo my wife." Griff waggles his eyebrows at me in the rearview mirror.

"And does he still got it?" I ask McKenna.

"Jury's still out. He didn't quite get the chance to use his pick up lines on me."

I wince, scrunching my face up. "Ah, shit. Is that because of me? It's because of me, isn't it? Sorry for being such a cock block, Griff. I'll make it up to you, buddy."

"And how are you gonna do that?"

"I'll be the most upstanding house guest you've ever had. I'll go right to my room in the basement and I'll be so silent, it'll be like I'm not even there."

"For fuck's sake," he mutters, shaking his head.

I chuckle. "My point exactly."

After McKenna gets me settled in their guest room with a big glass of water, I thank her before throwing myself onto the bed. It's comfortable and I nearly pass out as soon as my head hits the pillow. Only as I'm drifting off to sleep do I curse myself for not checking in on Taevin.

The next morning my head feels like I've driven it through a brick wall. Repeatedly. The pounding only intensifies as I make my way up the basement steps to find music blaring from McKenna and Griffin's kitchen.

I watch in utter bewilderment as Griff stands next to their stove, shirtless, with a red, white and blue apron tied around his waist that says MY WIFE IS AN OLYMPIC GOLD MEDALIST, WHAT'S YOUR SUPER POWER? as he scream-sings into the end of his spatula along to Phil Vassar's "Just Another Day In Paradise."

Griff turns, flipping a pancake high in the air as Kenna drapes an arm around his shoulder, laughing at his antics.

It's as I sit there, a spectator to their happiness, that I realize whole-heartedly I want this with Taevin. If there were ever a couple to look up to when times are rough, it's them. Griffin and McKenna have been through hell and back with their heartache and loss, but when they found their way back to each other, they continued to grow and grieve together after working on themselves apart.

When Griff faces Kenna again, he places his palm on her lower stomach and brings her in for a kiss. My heart sinks in my chest momentarily, the ache only intensifying when I hear Griff, even over the music, assure Kenna when he says, "I'm so happy, Sunshine. We're going to be outnumbered, no more man-to-man coverage for the Turner household."

Kenna looks at him with stars in her eyes, so overjoyed in their moment together. I feel like an interloper to their moment of shared excitement. I try to make myself scarce, but as I quietly start down the steps to the basement, Griff calls out, "Morning, J. How'd you sleep?"

Not wanting to be rude, and also wanting to claim a stack of Griff's homemade pancakes all for myself, I greet them both. "Morning, G. Morning, Kenna. I slept great, thanks for letting me crash here."

"No problem, man. Anytime," Griff assures me.

"Coffee?" Kenna asks. Bless this woman's heart, she's one of my favorites. And I'm not just saying that because she's pouring me a cup of my tried-and-true hangover cure at the same time her husband sets a massive stack of pancakes in front of me all without me having to ask.

"You guys are the best, you know that?" I tell them.

"Oh, we know," Griff muses just as Kenna swats at his chest.

"Don't make his head any bigger than it already is this morning, Jaxy," Kenna jests.

"What's got your ego inflated?" I ask as if I don't already know the answer, not wanting them to know I accidentally saw their exchange earlier.

"You'll hear all in good time, buddy," Griff answers, shooting a wink at Kenna.

Subtly is not his strong suit either it appears. I wonder if becoming Carson's brother-in-law did that to him, or if he's always been that way and I hadn't noticed until now.

"Real smooth," Kenna murmurs to him, rolling her eyes for good measure.

"Anyways," Kenna starts, sidling up on the stool next to where I'm sitting at the kitchen island. "How's Taevin feeling after yesterday? I guess I wasn't surprised to hear she wasn't feeling well and wanted to go home. She is only a few weeks post-op, after all."

"She's feeling okay. Well, I hope she is," I answer.

"Wait. Why were you at the bar last night? You've hardly left her side since Bennett's wedding," Griff points out.

Thanks, wiseass.

"We, uh, got into a bit of an arg—" I pause, looking into my mug as I consider my words. "Actually, you know what? It doesn't matter. I shouldn't have been at that bar last night. I should've been home with my wife instead of running away from my problems." Lifting my head to meet Griff's gaze, I ask, "G, can you bring me home, please?"

"Yeah, man. Of course."

"How bad did you leave things? Is it a *bring spontaneous flowers home* kind of situation?" Kenna questions.

"I'm pretty sure she'd throw the roses back at me, thorns and all, praying I get cut," I admit.

"If she's a chocolate lover, you won't go wrong there. Just don't come home empty-handed after walking out," Griff suggests.

"Smart man," Kenna tells him just as the front door opens and Cadence comes running in with Kenna's parents behind her, her mom holding Rowen while her dad gets tugged in by the leash on their new Golden Retriever puppy, Minnie. I miss the hell out of Ranger, he was the greatest dog growing up. But I'm happy they decided to get a puppy for Cadence and Rowen's sake.

Seeing Cadence again after hearing how Taevin felt about meeting her for the first time yesterday has my heart cracking clear down the center. Tae kept calling our baby *him*. I'm not even sure how far along she was when she miscarried.

Because I'm an ass and didn't stick around long enough to ask.

Tae said he would've been the same age as Cadence. Nine. He or she would've been nine.

Would our baby have been tall like me or take on their mama's shorter stature?

Pain akin to a thousand papercuts slices through me as I think of all the questions that will remain unanswered.

And then I ask myself what the fuck I'm still doing here right now. I need to get home to her.

Almost as if reading my thoughts, Griff says, "Let me grab a shirt and my keys then I'll take you to your truck." He heads up the steps to their room without another question.

I make my way across the kitchen and wrap Kenna in a hug. "Thanks for taking care of me last night, M&M. Sorry I interrupted your big date night, and I'm even more sorry for ever doubting your faithfulness to Griff."

"I'm oddly okay with it—I know you were just looking out for him," she replies, a sleepy happiness present in her voice.

"Yeah, but you were my friend first."

"You're dang right. Try not to forget that next time you think I'm up to no good."

"Will do," I say, pausing just as I'm about to turn toward the front door. "Oh, and Kenna?"

"Yeah?"

"Congratulations," I tell her without elaborating as to what I'm congratulating her on.

Her face softens as a shy smile eclipses her face. "Thanks, J."

"And thank you for inviting Taevin to be a part of your book club yesterday. She told me you text her on our way home from the cookout. I'm sorry we had to leave early."

"Absolutely! I hope she'll take us up on it. It's nothing official, more so just an excuse for us ladies to get together."

"I'm sure she'll join if she's able," I assure her.

"Give her a hug from me when you get home, okay? She looked like she could use one yesterday just before she left."

Guilt weighs heavy in my gut as the repercussions of my actions sink in.

She looked like she needed a hug when she left the cookout yesterday, and that was before she shared one of the hardest things that's ever happened to her with me.

And then I left.

I was a fucking coward and I left the only woman I've ever loved to grieve and process on her own. She said seeing Cadence yesterday triggered her, just like it did for me just now.

I need to get home to her.

In Griff's Jeep, I do my best to avoid looking at him when I ask, "Can I ask you something kind of personal?"

"I mean you can ask, but I'm not sure I'll answer."

"Fair enough. Uh, I remember when you and Kenna were trying to get pregnant with Rowen that you opened up to me about it being more of a struggle."

"I did," he confirms.

Clearing my throat, I will myself to just go for it and ask him. "If you don't mind me asking, how did you manage to put aside your own fears and concerns to be there for her?"

When the vehicle rolls to a stop next to my truck in the bar's parking lot, Griff puts it in park before looking over at me. "Where's this coming from?" he asks.

"Uh, well," I start and my voice cracks. "Last night Taevin told me she miscarried our baby my freshman year. She said he would've been Cadence's age."

"Shit, J. I'm so sorry."

I manage to take a deep breath, keeping my tears at bay. "Yeah, last night, uh, was the first time I heard about any of it. And I just . . . walked out on her," I confess on a choked sob.

Griff grasps my shoulder firmly in his hand. "J, look at me."

With reluctance, I fix my blurry gaze on him, concern etched across his features. "It's never too late to fix things with the one you love. After Katie died, I walked out on the love of my life and missed two years of my daughter's life because of the chokehold grief held on me. Yes, you left last night. But I don't think Taevin will fault you for needing time to process the news of her miscarriage. You just found out you lost a baby ten years ago who you had no idea existed until last night. Go home to her. Apologize. Promise you'll show up and be there for her just like you have been, and then be a man of your word. You're one of the best people in mine and my family's lives, Jackson."

I swipe my knuckle beneath my eyes, catching tears before they fall.

"Let me ask you this. Does hearing the news you were told last night change the way you feel about her?" he asks.

I whip my head to look at him. "No. Never."

"Good. Then go home and tell your wife you still love her and you're never letting her go."

"How—" I start to ask but he cuts me off with a deep rumble of laughter.

"You're an open book, J. You always have been. The moment I saw you with her in your kitchen at your graduation party ten years ago, I knew you loved her and she had changed you forever. And, if how inseparable the two of you were that summer wasn't enough, the way you clung to her last night was a dead giveaway. You love her, man."

"I do," I admit.

"And have you told her that since she came back into your life?"

"No," I tell him, hanging my head.

"If you can sit here and admit to me you're still in love with her, then get home and do the same to her."

I bring Griff in for a hug. "Thank you, G. It means a lot."

"You don't need to thank me, J. You've been an unwavering support for me and my family for years. Showing up for you in any way I can is the least I can do. Love you, man."

"Love you too, buddy," I tell him as I get out of his Jeep and into my truck to haul ass back to my wife.

23

Jackson

Now

When I get back to the house, I don't immediately seek Taevin out. Instead, I head straight to the basement to unload the bags in my hands.

After another half an hour, I finally make my way upstairs to find her.

"Tae," I call out when I don't see her in the main living area. My anxiety spikes when I check her bedroom and bathroom and realize she's not in there either.

"Tae, baby, where are you?" I shout, taking the steps that lead upstairs two at a time.

My heart sinks when I find her curled up in a ball on one of the guest beds. As I get closer, I realize she's asleep. Her cheeks have dried tear streak marks down them and her eyelashes still look wet as if she cried herself to sleep.

Goddammit.

I swipe her cheek with my thumb and curse myself for doing so when she wakes up.

"Jax," she rasps in what sounds a lot like relief.

Unable to compose myself, my voice shakes as my apology comes spilling out. "I'm so, so sorry for walking out on you last night, Taevin. There's no excuse for me just up and leaving."

She grasps on to my forearm and tugs me closer. "I'm the one who should be apologizing. I kept that from you for so long."

"T, no." I shake my head. "No, baby. You have nothing to apologize for. I'm just so fucking sorry I wasn't there for you when it happened, and even more sorry that I wasn't there for you again last night."

"Where did you go?" she asks in a somber tone.

Staring down at her, I take a deep breath. "First to a bar. And then when Griffin and McKenna found me there, they took me back to their place to sleep it off," I explain, a mixture of regret and shame churning in my gut.

Taevin props herself up on one elbow and looks around the room, her eyes filling with tears as she does. "When you didn't come back last night, I came upstairs to grab one of your shirts to sleep in like I used to when we dated."

Looking down, it's only now that I realize she's wearing one of my faded Harvard T-shirts.

Tae's lip quivers as she continues, "After I left your room, I came down the hall to this one. I don't even know why, it just felt like something was pulling me here. This room is so beautiful, so full of light now that the sun is up. I love the window seats—" Her voice breaks, and I think I know why. Exhaling on a shuttered breath, she whimpers, "It's just like I always imagined it'd be. All that's missing is the furniture, but you had them build it just the way I said, didn't you?"

Tears stream down the tip of my nose and make dark spots where they fall on the bedding. "Yeah, baby, I did," I croak.

I remember the exact day years ago when she told me she wanted all the kids' rooms to be upstairs so they could take their pillows and blankets between rooms to sleep together when they were scared or wanted to make forts. She requested a dormer window in each bedroom so they could have a place to get lost in a good book, but two specifically for the nursery to let in all the natural light possible.

But there's no question what really tipped her off to the meaning of this particular space. I follow her gaze to the last detail of her dreams for the room of late-night feeds and endless snuggles. In the corner, catching all the natural light from the two deepest, largest dormer windows a man could draw up, is an antique rocking chair. Nothing fancy, and certainly nothing comfortable, but something she never skipped when describing the perfect, cozy nursery for our babies. I was a naive, hopeless romantic clinging to the possibility of a second chance with her the day I brought that home.

"Come lie down with me, Bear," she whispers, patting the comforter.

I lie on the bed beside her and pull her against my chest as we take in the room.

"It's even better than I could've imagined," she murmurs, her voice full of pain.

There's a reason I didn't show her this bedroom when I gave her a tour of the house. I knew it would cause her heartache, I just didn't realize then that seeing it together after learning she miscarried would break both our hearts.

"You said last night that our baby was a he?" I say, hoping like hell she's still willing to talk to me about everything.

She sniffs. "I wasn't far enough along to find out, but when I allowed myself to envision what could've been had I not miscarried, I always saw a baby boy. With your curly hair and my brown eyes."

I have to fight back the tears that threaten to escape. "When—"

Before I can finish the question, she answers, "Remember when I told you I came to Boston? That's when. I'd been planning to visit Ryan once she got settled at school. She's actually the one who made me take a test and came with me to confirm my pregnancy. I got to see him, hear his heartbeat for the first time only hours before it stopped. I was actually at the party that night to tell you about the pregnancy. That's when—"

A choked sob escapes her and my heart shatters into a million pieces.

I pull her further into my arms and we just sit there and cry together. I'm not sure how much time passes, but eventually Tae wipes beneath her eyes and then does the same to mine before nuzzling her head back in place.

"I have to have my trigger shot tonight at eight o'clock," she murmurs against my chest, which tightens in anticipation of her egg retrieval procedure tomorrow morning.

"I've already got an alarm set on my phone so we don't forget. One for eight o'clock and one for an hour before in case we weren't home."

"If it's alright with you, I think I'd prefer to just stay in today and have a lazy day," Tae says softly, almost sleepily.

Rubbing my hand up and down her spine, I kiss the top of her head. "I can't think of anything I'd rather do. But I do have a surprise in the basement for you if you're up for it. If not, we can do it on a different day."

Tae shifts so she can look up at me. "What kind of surprise?"

Bringing my arm beneath my head, I nearly get lost in her coffee-colored eyes. "A surprise I'm shocked I haven't given away yet."

That earns me a giggle, and the sound of her laughter heals me in ways I didn't realize was possible. "You always were terrible at holding in a secret, which meant you were shit at surprises or not immediately giving me a gift. Like when you gave me my birthday present three months early because you said you didn't know where you'd hide it in your dorm."

I join in her laughter thinking about my panic at hiding that guitar. "In all honesty, I don't think it would've been a birthday gift. I was too excited to give it to you and watch you play," I admit.

She squeezes me around my waist as she lays her head back on my chest. "So, what's this surprise? I'm intrigued," she says as she dances her fingers across my stomach, causing me to flex. Flattening her palm against my stomach, she inches her hand lower and murmurs, "These are certainly more defined now than I remember."

"If you keep feeling me up, we're not going to get to your surprise, baby," I rasp, grabbing her hand to stop it from trailing any farther.

Tae pouts and it's one of the most adorable things ever. "Don't give me that look." When she doesn't let up, I sit up and pull her off the bed with me. "Come on, you know I'm a sucker for that look."

"I do, that's why I'm not letting up until I get my way."

Using my hand as a blinder, I shrug in her general direction. "Then I guess I'm not looking at you until after I show you your surprise." Without looking back, I walk out of the room and down the steps to the basement. I smile when I hear her sigh and then follow after me.

The basement has been a work-in-progress. I've finished it in phases, prioritizing certain rooms over others. One of them being this surprise.

I lead her down the hall to where my home gym is. The glass wall of black-paned doors leading into the gym is one of my favorite features in the house.

"Where are you taking me?" she questions as I lead her through the gym doors. "I'm still on restrictions," Tae points out and I chuckle at that, because does she really think my surprise is bringing her to the basement to work out together?

"It's just through here," I explain, grabbing her hand in mine as I lead her to the far wall of the gym. When I gave her a tour of the house before her hysterectomy, I told her this door was for a changing room off the gym because I didn't have the surprise finished at the time. But over the course of her healing these past few weeks, the last of the materials arrived and it's finally ready for the big reveal.

Just as I'm about to open the door, she tugs on my hand to stop me. "Seriously, J. Where are you taking me? Oh, do you have some sort of kink about christening every room in the house? Because if so, I can think of about a dozen other rooms I'd rather do that in than the gym changing room. No offense."

"None taken. And I'll store that idea away for later, but that's not what this is about. I may have told a little white lie when I said this was a changing room." Reaching behind me, I turn the handle and watch her face register what I mean when the door opens to the dimly lit room.

She covers her mouth and gasps. "Jax, what is this?"

"I'm sure you're used to more state-of-the-art equipment, but I got the best of what was available to me in hopes you could record music here when the mood strikes," I explain, guiding her into the home studio I had originally built into the home but left empty. Standing behind her, I wrap one arm around her waist while using the other to point to different things in the room.

In place of the small changing room she was expecting is a room that spans nearly seven hundred square feet. I walk Taevin through the first part of the room where the production equipment is set up against a half-glass wall that leads into an enclosed studio that takes up nearly two-thirds of the space.

"When they were finishing the basement, they had to move the baby grand piano in here before they even put up the walls. They literally built the room around it, so I made it the focal point," I explain as we walk into the studio area. The entire back wall is filled with various guitars hung on the wooden acoustic paneling. "Over here is where you can record vocals, and the music producer I hired to help me with logistics and equipment assured me the room was big enough for your full band to be in here if you ever wanted to fly them out to record something."

Turning her around, I point back through the glass to the wall by the entrance. "And then I purchased and had as many pictures of you performing over the years as I could hung up on the back wall there. I figured the one on the side here would be a good spot for any of your albums and awards if you ever wanted to bring them here. If you ever, uh, you know, decided to stay," I end on a whisper, instantly regretting pushing her too far when I'm met with nothing but silence.

Instead of saying anything, Taevin leads me back into the control room. I'm about to apologize for overstepping when she pushes me down onto the couch against the far wall. "What—" I start, but am cut off when she straddles my lap.

"Sometimes words aren't enough to express appreciation—" Taevin starts as she slides my shirt up and over my head. "Sometimes expressing gratitude through action is the only way to show someone how truly appreciative you are of their grand gesture." My breaths come out strangled when Taevin places a kiss on my jaw and licks a trail down my neck before sitting up and wrapping her arms around my neck. Resting her forehead against mine, she shakes her head almost as if in disbelief, and the feeling is mutual, because what is happening right now?

With her lips brushing against mine, she murmurs, "And Jackson, I'm so fucking thankful for not only this beautiful room, but this entire house that I very much so plan to make our home. Because, if it's alright with you, I'd like to live with you here. Not just while I'm receiving treatment, but for the rest of our whole damn lives."

Reaching up, I grasp her face in my hands and lean back so I can look into her eyes while I make my confession. "Baby, nothing would be more right." My gaze flickers to her lips and back. "I love you, Tae.

I still love you. I've never stopped, not for a damn minute over the past ten years."

A strangled gasp leaves her as she wraps her arms around me, rocking us back and forth as she clings to me. Without breaking our embrace, she whispers against my neck, "I've never stopped loving you, Jackson, and I never will. I am yours until I take my very last breath, and even beyond that—my love for you is eternal."

Instead of giving either of us a chance to react to her declaration, her lips crash against mine in a kiss that expresses not only our love, but our forgiveness and promise to move forward in our second act together.

Our bodies move in sync as if no time has passed since we were last like this. Fisting the fabric of my T-shirt she's wearing, I slowly inch my fists up, only breaking our kiss so I can lift it off over her head.

"Tae, baby," I breathe, completely mesmerized by the feel of her silky skin beneath my palms once again. She's not wearing a bra, and the sight of her bare breasts in front of me is too tempting to resist. "You're so fucking perfect, T."

I'm prepared for the apprehensive look crossing her face and not surprised when she murmurs "No, I'm not."

"You are. You're perfect beyond belief. I've been obsessed with you since we were eighteen and my fascination has only grown with time. Come here," I tell her, pulling her closer so I can place open-mouth kisses across her chest, kissing up her neck until I come across her rose tattoo behind her ear. Drifting my lips over the delicate ink, I tweak her nipples between my fingers at the same time, earning me a sweet moan that sends blood rushing to my dick.

Taevin grips onto my shoulders, nails digging deliciously into my flesh as she begins rocking her hips over mine. I resent every ounce of clothing separating my skin from meeting hers.

As if she can read my mind, Tae lifts off of me before undoing the button on my shorts and pulling them and my boxer briefs down at the same time.

Taevin stands before me in nothing but a white, cotton thong, and the sight flips a switch inside my brain. I go feral, moving into action as if on instinct. One moment I'm sitting on the couch, the next I'm kneeling before her with my arms wrapped around the backs of her legs.

Staring up at her, she cups my cheek, and then drags her thumb across my jaw until she thumbs my bottom lip, pulling it from between my teeth. "I've nearly forgotten all of the sinister things my husband's mouth can do. Think you can remind me?"

I fucking whimper in desperation for her to let me do just that. I'd love nothing more than to taste her again. Eating her pussy was my favorite pastime.

I lick a trail up her thigh until I meet her thong-covered pussy. Hooking my fingers beneath the waistband, I slowly drag them down inch by inch, placing delicate kisses in their wake until she steps out of them.

Licking my lips, I prepare to devour her just as she presses her palm against my forehead.

"Lie down on the couch, J."

"What?" I ask incredulously as I look up at her.

"Be a good boy for me and lie on your back so I can sit on your face."

It's actually pathetic how fast I scramble to the couch, but I give zero fucks in this moment because my wife is going to sit on my face. I'm not sure where this newfound confidence of hers has come from, and I'm certainly not going to think on it too hard right now, but I'm a fucking fan of my wife telling me what to do. I'm not above begging and pleading with her to let me taste her at this point.

As soon as I'm lying on my back, Taevin straddles my chest, facing away from me. My mouth waters in anticipation but before she scoots back, Taevin bends over and places a soft kiss on the head of my cock, making it jerk in response.

I see fucking stars, and when her lips wrap around my length, my hips buck off the couch in response.

Holyfuckingshit. It's been far too long since I've been given a blow job and her lips feel like heaven. There's no way I'm going to last.

Knowing I need to do something to distract myself from the pleasure overload her mouth is providing, I grip Tae's hips and hover her above my face.

"Sit down and ride my fucking face, Tae," I command before placing her exactly where I've been dying to have her.

Within seconds of her pussy gracing my lips, she gets back to work, her head bobbing up and down my length, and it becomes a battle of who can make the other come first. I've got to remind myself not to finger her while I'm eating her out the way I know she loves because she hasn't been cleared for any penetration yet. But that doesn't mean I can't drive her crazy in other ways.

My hands wrap around her thighs, spreading them wider to gain better access. Just as I'm finding a rhythm she loves—if her moans vibrating against my cock tell me anything—Tae brings me to the back of her throat and the feel of her gagging around my length is enough to make me come right then and there.

I lift her hips slightly and warn, "Fuck, T. I'm going to come, baby."

That only further spurs her on, and her lips suction my cock just perfectly, sending me spiraling into an orgasm that almost turns into an out-of-body experience.

When I'm able to actually feel my limbs again, I slide out from where Taevin is kneeling above me and quickly lay her on her back.

I shoulder my way between her thighs and turn into a man obsessed, my sole focus on giving my wife the pleasure she deserves. There's a cadence that drives Tae wild, and when I find it, it's not long before she's coming undone beneath me. The taste of her release on my tongue is like an addict getting his first hit after being sober for years.

"Fuck. I've missed the taste of your sweet pussy," I tell her as I kiss a path up her stomach and over her breasts.

Lacing her fingers into the hair at the back of my head, Taevin pulls me to her mouth for a slow, sensual kiss that has my hips rocking involuntarily against hers, making my cock harden again.

"You always had a way with words that made me feel like I was an exception or something," Tae whispers against my lips.

She tries to pull me back in for another kiss but I stop her by pulling back so I can stare into her eyes. "You are my exception, Tae. You have been from the moment I laid eyes on you sitting alone on that pew at the very front of the church. I know love at first sight is something people think is made up, but I can promise you that you were my exception from the very first time I saw you. I haven't been with another woman since that day because there has never been another that's nearly as exceptional as you are."

Tae's brows draw together in confusion. "What do you mean not since that day? That doesn't even make sense. There were dozens and dozens of pictures of you kissing women over the years posted on social media. Those very photos of you would send me spiraling."

Nuzzling my face into her neck, I rake my teeth along her sensitive flesh and murmur, "It makes perfect sense. I kissed those women to get your attention, though it never seemed to work the way I intended. After a while, I realized that and from there on out I didn't even try. But it was never more than kissing, and only if I knew it would be blasted on social media in hopes that it would reach you."

Tae scoffs. "So, let me get this straight . . . you thought making it look like you'd moved on with dozens of women would send me running back to you?"

Propping myself up on my elbow, I hover above her and get lost in her chocolate eyes.

"Back then I was so mad at you for leaving me, I had hoped that me kissing someone else would tear you up so much that you'd come back to me—even if it were just to yell at me—I was desperate for anything you'd give me. Then when you didn't, the only way to satiate my need for you was to go to as many of your performances as I could over the years," I admit, hoping like hell she hears the sincerity in my tone.

Tae cups my cheek and rubs her thumb up and down my cheek in a loving way, but when our eyes connect, hers are filled with pain I wasn't anticipating to see. She worries her lips together before letting out a shuttered sigh. "I wish I could say I did the same, but that's unfortunately not the case. Your actions and seeing them all over social media sent me spiraling further than I already was after the miscarriage. I drank heavily for nearly two years in an attempt to drown out the grief. And when I drank, the loneliness would take over and I'd make poor decisions like allowing other men into my bed." Her voice cracks and tears slide down her cheeks.

Even though it pains me to know she'd moved on temporarily, I can't for one minute blame her. Everyone in my life thought I was insane holding onto the ghost of her for all those years. I can't even begin to put myself in her shoes at that time.

"Jackson, you have to know that if I knew we were still married, even though we were separated, I never would've done that. God, what you must think of me—" she starts before I swiftly cut her off.

"Baby, no. Please don't do that. It's not like you cheated, we weren't together. There were no vows you had to uphold when you thought we were no longer married. If anyone is sorry, it's me. I should've refused to let you walk out on me. I should've been there for you."

Taevin presses two finger tips to my lips and hushes me. "Shh. I don't want to do this again. We need to agree to leave the past in the past and move forward together. Yes, we both made mistakes that cost us years together, which is exactly why I don't want to waste another minute I have on this earth without you. Will you promise me?"

I stare down at her, taking in every little feature and detail of her face that has changed over our time apart so I can commit this moment to memory. "I promise, baby," I rasp out.

"Me too," she whispers and then tugs on my neck so we can seal our promises with a kiss that feels as though it separates time into then and now. A kiss in which I can feel Taevin clinging as desperately to me as I do her, the way I hope we always will from here on out.

For I will love this woman until my dying breath and in every eternity beyond this life.

24

Taevin

"**Y**our hands are shaking, baby. Are you sure about this?" Jax asks, holding my hands in his as we wait outside the courtroom for our names to be called.

Turning to look at him, I give him a reassuring smile. "I've never been more sure of anything. But I'd be lying if I said I wasn't nervous. I had a nightmare last night that our dads came rushing through the doors of the courthouse to stop us."

"Well considering we chose this day because it fell on a day my father would be out of town, I highly doubt it'll be the two of them stopping us together. But didn't you say your dad was doing a baptism this morning?"

I nod. "He is."

"Then I don't think your nightmare is coming true. Anything else I can put your mind at ease about?" He chuckles before placing a delicate kiss on my cheek.

"Well this is all feeling very Nathan and Haley-like, so does that mean we're going to move into a little apartment together after our wedding?"

His brows screw together. "I'm so confused right now."

"About what? Moving in?"

Jax shakes his head. "No. I mean, I have no clue who you're talking about, so I'm not sure whether or not we'll be like them."

"Wait. Are you telling me you've never watched *One Tree Hill* before?"

"No," he says hesitantly, likely knowing where this is going.

"You just signed yourself up for an OTH marathon on our honeymoon, Bear."

"Sounds like a dream come true. Can't wait," he deadpans.

I clap my hands like the overly excited fool that I am. "Oh, just you wait. I'm going to love this way too much."

Leaning in, Jax whispers, "If you think we're spending our nonexistent honeymoon binge watching a show, you've got another thing coming."

"Me. Hopefully I'm the thing coming." I hold my hand up to cover my laughter. "Oh my goodness, that was terrible, wasn't it?"

"It was, but I still love you." He laughs and rolls his eyes at my antics. "Don't worry, I'll have you coming plenty, baby. And to answer your question from earlier, we probably won't get an apartment until sophomore year. But if you want to live together before then, I could look into our options. I think most freshmen are supposed to stay in student housing, but maybe because we'll be married I could get an exception."

"I'm fine either way. Just knowing we'll be in the same city is enough for me."

"Married. We'll be married and in the same city."

Just then the courtroom doors open and our names are called.

Jax stands and buttons his suit jacket before holding his arm out for me. Holy smokes, he's beyond attractive in his tailored blue suit. He's attempted to tame his unruly hair in the most delicious way—somehow still tousled like he's run his fingers through it. I love the way his crisp, white dress shirt contrasts against his tanned complexion—that, in combination with the color of his blue suit, only makes his eyes more striking than they already are.

"Here's your last chance to run," he offers just as I stand and slip my arm through his.

"I'd never," I promise.

"Whirlwind days deserve to be celebrated with ice cream," I declare, holding up my waffle cone for Jax to cheers against.

His brows scrunch at first, but he smiles as he taps his cone against mine. "I feel bad that all I'm able to get you to celebrate is ice cream. On our two-year anniversary, I'm buying you an expensive bottle of champagne to celebrate," Jax promises, scooting closer to me on the bench we're sitting on at the park across the street from The Sprinkled Cone.

I pout at that. "I still won't be twenty-one on our two-year anniversary."

"Exactly why I'll be the one buying it," he says, adding a wink for good measure.

Taking a giant lick of my ice cream, I look up to find Jax watching me with hooded eyes. "You're a little temptress in that gorgeous white dress eating your monster cookie ice cream." I look down at my cotton, mid-length white dress with a square neckline that to me looked pretty plain when I picked it out, but with the way he's looked at me since he picked me up, I can't bite back the sultry smile that takes over my face.

Leaning into me, he places a kiss on my cheek before asking in a hushed tone, "Have I told you how stunning you look, baby? You took my breath away several times today—when I saw you walk out of your house earlier, when we recited our vows, and then when we walked back down the courthouse steps hand in hand, your hair was blowing in the wind and you looked so happy I knew right then and there I'm the luckiest man alive because I get to be yours for the rest of our lives."

Tears flood my vision as I absorb his words, wishing I could tattoo them on my soul.

I move closer, sitting on his lap to erase any remaining distance between us. Wrapping my arm around his neck, I lick my lips and gaze into his sea glass eyes glistening with adoration.

"Want to know what I was just thinking?" I ask him.

"Always," he's quick to reply as he takes one of the last bites of his ice cream cone.

Taking a bite of my own cone, I try to buy myself some time as I second guess whether or not I want to share my crazy idea out loud. "What if after celebrating with ice cream we did something a little wild?"

That catches his attention. "And what do you have in mind?"

Taking a deep breath, I decide to just blurt it out. "Let's get tattoos to memorialize this moment."

His chin shoots back in surprise and his eyes search mine for truth. "You're serious?"

"Yes. I've been dying to get one but I was hesitant about what I'd want to mark myself permanently with. I've always thought of getting a rose tattoo to memorialize my mom, but now it feels like that would be a good symbolism of our relationship too."

"Would we get matching ones?" he asks, taking the last bite of his cone before licking a bit of ice cream from his fingers.

A shiver runs down my spine at the sight. "We could. Or you could get something different. Up to you," I tell him, twisting my fingers through his hair.

A dazed smile turns his mouth up. "I'd like to get a rose to symbolize my *wife*."

My cheeks heat as those pesky songbirds flock in my stomach from the way he calls me his wife—so possessive, so proud, so damn solidified in his decision.

"Maybe I'll get your name tattooed on my forehead too so everyone knows who I belong to." I scrunch up my nose at his teasing and he throws his head back in laughter.

"You're something else," I tell him, shaking my head at his antics.

"Where are you going to get your tattoo, my little Thorn?" he asks, tugging at my waist to pull me in tighter to his chest.

Pulling my hand from his hair, I pull my own hair back to show him where I'm thinking. "I was thinking right here behind my ear."

"Won't your dad see that?"

"I'll just keep my hair down for the next month." I shrug. "Besides, I've gotten pretty good at covering the hickeys you're always leaving on me. And I'm already sad I have to forego wearing my beautiful wedding ring for the next month, so what's one more thing to hide?" Looking down at my left hand, I sigh in content as I stare at the black hexagon center stone with a halo of black diamonds set on a gold band. "It's so brilliant. You couldn't have picked a more perfect ring for me, J."

I glance down where his left hand rests on my thigh and smile. "Yours is perfect too. I love the black tungsten with the gold inlay."

"Thanks, I think I did a pretty good job aside from getting your ring size wrong. Who has fingers this small?" he asks, holding up my hand. "I told the lady at the ring store that you had really small fingers so she thought a size five would be best, but it's practically falling off."

"It is not," I correct him. "She was close, I think I'm like a size four, maybe four and a quarter for my left ring finger."

"Well, at least I have some time to get it resized over the next month while we're keeping our marriage under wraps," he points out.

"That's a good way to look at it. I can't wait for when I get to wear my ring everyday. Once I get it back, I'm never taking it off."

"God, I love you," he murmurs, bringing my hand to his lips and placing a kiss over my ring.

"I love you too."

"So, were you serious about the tattoo thing? Because if you were, I think I might be able to ask my cousin if he can squeeze us in today."

"Wait, you have a cousin who is a tattoo artist?"

"I do. He's saving up to open his own parlor. For now, he's a traveling tattoo artist. I mean, he's licensed and everything, he just doesn't have a storefront yet."

"I was serious. If he could do it, would you want to?" I ask him.

"I'll text him now," Jax tells me, grabbing his phone out of my purse because he said his suit pants were a bit too tailored after his recent growth spurt to hold his phone in his pocket. I'm honestly shocked he hasn't busted them open yet.

With a dazzling smirk on his face, Jax looks up from his phone. "Let's go get marked, baby."

"Anything you want to tell me, Taev?" my dad asks me later that evening as he comes into the kitchen where I've got my back to him as I finish fixing dinner. My stomach sinks to the floor with unease and I squeeze my eyes shut, cursing my foolish heart.

Shoot. Why did I think he wouldn't find out?

Trying to play it cool, I set the wooden spoon in my hand down. Turning to face him, I aim for denial. "No, should I?"

"I don't know. You tell me." His blank face in combination with his cool tone doesn't give anything away. I'm not sure what to make of it. If he knew I ran off, got hitched, and got a tattoo after, I think he'd be far more upset with me.

When I don't respond with anything he sighs and finally says, "There wasn't any parental supervision at the Fourth of July cabin, was there?"

Oh, thank the Lord. That was a close one.

Doing my best to muster up that I'd been caught doing the very worst thing I've ever done, I stammer out an apology. "No, there wasn't. I'm so sorry I didn't tell you, Dad."

"Did you know before asking me to go that there wouldn't be parents there?" he presses.

I pause to consider my options here. On the one hand, if I tell him the truth, I'll likely be grounded for the rest of summer. On the other hand, if I lie and he catches me in a second lie, I'll likely be grounded for the rest of my life.

I decide to go with, "I didn't. But Jackson's older brother, who is already in the NHL and very responsible, was there the whole weekend."

My father narrows his gaze on me, the way he does when he's trying to detect a lie. I must be getting better at selling a convincing white lie because he nods his head once and takes his hands off his hips. Guilt nags at my conscience, but before I can reflect on it, the doorbell rings.

"Are we expecting anyone?" my dad asks.

I shake my head at him. "Yes, Dad. You're the one who invited Jackson to dinner."

He clears his throat. "Oh, yes. That's right."

Cleaning off my hands on a dishtowel, I tell him, "I'll get the door. But, Dad, please be nice."

That earns me a gruff response. "I'm nice enough."

I wait until my back is turned before I roll my eyes. When I open the door, I'm barely able to see Jax behind the enormous bouquet he's holding in his hands. I gasp as I take in the beautiful floral arrangement filled with red roses, pink peonies and white hydrangeas.

"Jax! They're so beautiful!" I squeal, taking them from his hands, and as I do my fingers brush against his and my eyes widen in panic. Peeking at him from behind the arrangement, I whisper-hiss, "You're still wearing your ring."

Jax winces in realization. "Sorry, baby. I'll go put it in my truck so I don't lose it."

"Okay, I'll go set these down," I tell him. As I'm about to turn, he leans in and presses a chaste kiss on my lips.

"You look beautiful," he whispers before jogging to his truck.

I may have picked my sundress with him in mind. Okay, who am I kidding? I pick almost everything I wear these days with him in mind.

Just as I place the flowers in a vase, my phone rings. It's not a number I have saved in my phone, and typically I wouldn't answer it, but I question whether it could be my new roommate I was assigned from Berklee.

Swiping, I do my best for a cheerful greeting. "Hello!"

"Good evening, am I speaking with Taevin Gray?" a man on the other end of the line asks.

I hesitate a moment before answering. "Yes, this is she."

"Oh, good. I wasn't sure if I had the correct number. My name is Kyle Blackwood, I'm a talent manager out of Nashville." My heart rate picks up as he continues. "I happened to stumble across a video of you performing at a county fair last month. I've been looking to add another artist to my roster for a few months now, and I've got to be honest with you, no one has impressed me the way you did from that two-minute clip. I'd love to hear more of your work if you have an EP."

It takes me a few moments to snap out of the shock and answer him. "I-I don't have anything recorded. That was only like my second time performing in front of an audience." I snap my mouth closed, frustrated with myself for admitting that. I'm guessing talent managers aren't looking for someone as green to the music industry as I am. This sort of phone call wasn't supposed to come until after I'd had a degree from Berklee under my belt, if ever.

"Well that's alright. I've worked with a breadth of artists that range from having years of experience to diamonds in the rough looking for their big break. Is that you, Taevin? Are you the diamond in the rough I've been searching for? Because I think you just might be." Without giving me a chance to answer, he adds, "Of course, after seeing that initial video of you, I did some digging. I found a video of you performing the national anthem at a hockey game where you easily captivated the crowd. That was something else, truly spectacular."

I'm at a loss for words. I need someone to pinch me because what is real life right now?

"Th-thank you," I manage to stammer out.

"I'll tell you what, I'm going to be in Minnesota for a concert for another artist I work with next week. Do you think you'd have time to meet with me?"

My brows furrow in confusion. "I'm sorry, how did you know I was from Minnesota?"

"The internet unfortunately and fortunately in my case knows all, Miss Gray. Anyways, I'd love to meet you and go over some ideas I have to really shoot you into stardom. What do you say?"

I worry my bottom lip between my teeth. Closing my eyes, I take a deep breath before opening them and answering Kyle. "I say send me the time and place."

"Fantastic! Is it okay if I just text you the details once I get them ironed out?" he asks.

"Yes, that works just fine."

"Looking forward to meeting you, Taevin. Have a good evening."

"Thank you, you as well," I tell him before the line disconnects.

"What was that about?" Jackson asks, startling me from where he stands beneath the entryway to the kitchen.

I grasp my chest and take a deep breath. "Oh my goodness, you scared me." I pause, debating how much I want to tell him because I don't want to get his hopes up, or worse, give him any potential reason to worry. Today is our wedding day after all. I look past him to where I know my dad is likely sitting in the dining room. "Can I tell you later?" I whisper, hoping I can play it off like I don't want my dad to overhear.

Jax looks unsure but nods once. "Yeah, no problem. Can I help you with anything?"

"Yes, please. Would you mind grabbing the buns out of the oven for me? The oven mitts are in the second drawer to the right of the oven."

"Sure thing," he says. "It smells amazing in here by the way. Thanks for cooking, baby." Jax places a quick kiss on my forehead before heading to the oven.

We work our way around the kitchen as we finish preparing dinner. I attempted to make one of his favorites tonight. I even asked his mom for her goulash recipe so I could get it just right. She dropped off three jars of his nana's homemade sauce, so I don't think I could've managed to mess it up too badly.

And with the way Jax ends up eating thirds tonight, I'd say I did just fine. Though the entire time we're sitting for dinner, I have a niggling sense in the back of my mind that something big is about to happen. Even hours later as I stare up at my ceiling, I feel something akin to dread instead of the overwhelming joy I should feel on my wedding night.

25

Taevin

Now

I'm in and out of it as I wake up from the anesthesia, and at one point instead of Jackson being beside me, my mind plays tricks on me and I'm almost certain I see my father praying over me.

That's nice . . . I could use the extra prayers today considering it's my one shot at having children of my own. No pressure or anything.

Unsure of how much time has passed, I struggle through the haze to open my eyes. I've always had a harder time waking up from anesthesia, even general anesthesia like they used on me today.

When I finally come to, I realize Dr. Prescott is at the end of my bed holding a tablet in her hand while talking to Jackson.

"We were able to successfully retrieve fourteen eggs, which is on the higher end of average," she tells him.

"That's great, right?" Jackson asks, sounding hopeful.

Dr. Prescott nods her head. "It's a very positive result for the first phase of the egg retrieval. Now we will fertilize the eggs with your sperm. Tomorrow, the embryologist will check on the status of the fertilized eggs and by day three you will know how many embryos there are developing. We also typically recommend doing genetic testing at that point. Then on either day five or six, you'll get a call with an updated number of embryos that have reached the blastocyst stage, which will be the number of embryos they will freeze. If you choose to do genetic testing, the results won't come in for one to two weeks, so the freezing stage will happen prior to getting those results. Do you have any questions?"

"I do," I croak, swallowing past my dry throat.

Dr. Prescott and Jax both turn to look at me. "Hey, there she is," Jax says with a relieved smile.

"Hello, Taevin. I was just telling Jackson that we were able to successfully retrieve fourteen eggs," Dr. Prescott repeats for me.

"I heard that. That is great news. On average, how many eggs will reach the blastocyst stage?" I ask her.

"Typically between thirty to fifty percent," she answers.

My heart sinks. Because I don't like those odds.

Dr. Prescott must read my mind because she tries to reassure me. "This is why it is such great news that we were able to retrieve fourteen eggs today."

Jax pulls his chair up next to the side of my bed and takes my hand in his, bringing it to his lips and placing kisses along each of my knuckles. "I've got faith in our little ones, baby. They've got this."

It is quite possibly the exact wrong thing to say to me right now because my faith has been dwindling day after day since my diagnosis. It's actually pretty astonishing that I had any left after the depression I fell into after my miscarriage.

"If you two don't have any further questions for me, I'll let you get some more rest and the nurse will be in shortly to go over discharge instructions."

"Thank you, Dr. Prescott," we both say in unison.

"You're welcome. Have a great rest of your day," she tells us before walking out of the room they gave me. Typically they have patients in a curtained off area, but due to my safety and confidentiality, Jax requested I get a room instead.

Once we're alone, Jax rests his forehead on our joined hands. "Fourteen," he whispers. Looking up, his eyes find mine. "You're amazing, T. You've done such a great job."

Even with his optimism, I can't help the sense of dread that washes over me. This was my only shot at having children of my own. I've already been told that the chemotherapy I'll be starting within the next week or two will likely lead to infertility. And I know there's always adoption, and I'd honestly love nothing more than to adopt a child or several children someday, but it's the fact that so much of my autonomy has been stolen from me already.

This just needs to work out—it *has* to.

"It sounds like we'll hear of our future family's fate just as I'm about to start my first round of chemo. The timing is impeccable . . ." I say, my words dripping with so much sarcasm it's a wonder there isn't a puddle on the floor.

Jackson's eyes search mine. "Taevin, *you* are my family. *You* are my future. If we're able to have children of our own someday through surrogacy, that will be amazing. If we're unable to have children of our own and we adopt, that will be amazing too. If we decide we don't want any children at all, I would still be the luckiest and happiest man so long as I have *you* beside me."

Turning away, I try to hide the tears threatening to fall as my lip quivers. Taking a deep, steadying breath, I face Jax once again. "I could never ask that of you, Jackson. You were meant to be a father. And I need you to promise me something."

"Anything," he replies without hesitation.

"If we have any viable embryos, and for some reason I don't make it—if I don't win this fight—I need you to promise me you'll still go through with surrogacy."

He shakes his head. "Apparently I won't promise you anything because I won't promise you that."

"Jax—" I start but he just shakes his head, cutting me off.

"Listen to me, Taevin. While you're busy fighting for your life, I'm going to fight for us—for what our life could be, for everything it *will* be. Trust me when I say I'll never give up on our dreams. But there is no future for me without you in it. Now that we've found our way back to each other, I'm not letting you go. So together we're going to fight like hell, baby. We have to—" He doesn't finish the sentence, equal parts heartbroken and determined, but he doesn't have to.

Tears well in my eyes as his words sink in, and all I can do is nod in response. Clearing my throat, I croak out a weak "okay."

Jax sits up from his chair and brushes my hair out of my face before placing a delicate kiss on my lips. Cupping my cheek, he looks into my eyes and says, "I love you. You've got this, I know you do."

His voice is sure, filled with unwavering conviction that I wish I could offer him right back.

I'm not even sure how I got here. One minute I was sitting in Jackson's living room, and then when he left for his preseason camp this morning, I grabbed the keys to his SUV. It's like I blinked and here I am at the church where all these years later my father is still a pastor, standing at the altar with tears streaming steadily down my cheeks.

Before I left, just after Jackson had gone, I got a call from my doctor's office with an update on how many of our embryos made it to the blastocyst stage.

Never in my life have I wanted to curse God as badly as I do right now. Not even when He stole my mother from me far too soon. Not even when He so unforgivably took my baby.

If there's one thing I've always hoped and prayed for in my future, it was to become a mother. And now, the ability to grow and carry my own child was stripped from me. *Again.*

After my miscarriage, I remember thinking to myself maybe that was God's punishment for having sex before marriage—for not abstaining until we said our vows. Or maybe because we didn't get married in a church and instead had a courthouse wedding. Or because of how terrified I was when I first found out I was pregnant. Or worst of all, maybe I just wasn't meant to be a mother.

In hindsight, I could see that those weren't rational thoughts. But when I was six feet deep in grief, unable to climb my way out, all sorts of irrational thoughts consumed me.

And here I am again, thinking illogically after asking the impossible of Jackson. I can't believe I voiced my intrusive thoughts out loud. What I asked him to do if I didn't make it . . . it's unfathomable. Yet each night since my egg retrieval procedure, he's slept beside me and held me against his chest as if I hadn't asked the question of him at all.

"Why?" I hurl the question at the altar, falling to my knees. "Why me, huh? What could I have possibly done in this lifetime to deserve all you've cursed me with?"

Holding my head in my hands, I let the angry sobs wrack my body. I shake with fury as I mourn my body being ridden of my very female essence. I curse my body for failing me in more ways than one. Searing pain and invisible suffering accompanies my deepest sorrows for a life I envisioned but might never have.

I feel empty. Complete and utter emptiness entraps me, holding me to this altar as my heart begs to be set free from grief's torturous shackles.

I don't know how much time has passed, but I cry until my tears run dry and my fists feel bruised from slamming them on the altar. In a crouched position with my cheek pressed against the altar's floor, I open my eyes to find my dad standing off to the side.

Blinking rapidly to clear the resurfacing tears, I sit up when I realize I'm not hallucinating.

"Dad," I whisper, crying even harder when he comes closer and kneels beside me.

"Hi, Taev," he greets, his voice cracking when he says my name.

"I thought I saw you the other day," I tell him as tears stream down my cheeks.

He reaches a hesitant hand out and wipes away my tears before admitting, "I was there."

My brows pinch in confusion. "How did you know?"

"Jackson has been, uh, keeping me up to date."

I rear back slightly in surprise. Jax hadn't told me he'd been in contact with my dad. When I moved to Nashville after my miscarriage, I left everyone and everything from Minnesota in my rearview. Up until Jackson brought me back from Paris with him, I'd only come back here for concerts.

"So you know the two of us are still married," I say warily.

"I do. And I can't say I'm surprised that Jackson didn't file the paperwork for the annulment."

"I guess in hindsight, I shouldn't have been surprised either," I admit sheepishly. While Jackson's family may have all been shocked to find out we were married, my dad has known since just before I left. It was foolish of me not to follow up, but I probably would've had to ask for my dad's help again or go through Kyle, and whenever it came to Jackson, Kyle would turn cagey.

"Why are you here, Taev? What led you here this morning?" my dad asks.

Shaking my head, I look down at my hands in my lap. "I'm so lost, Dad."

I pause, worrying my bottom lip between my teeth. It's fitting, really—being here with my dad who also happens to be the man I grew up listening to each week as he gave his sermon. The man who helped raise me and guide me in my faith that I have since let go of.

God, I can't even remember the last time I was inside this church. It's been years.

Taking a deep breath, I decide to lay myself bare. "I'm broken, my heart is shattered and it hurts. I've never felt pain this visceral that wasn't physical. I'm wounded, but it's all invisible, and it makes me feel like I'm going crazy. Wave after unbelievable wave of grief and heartache crashes over me, and before I can rise to the surface to catch my breath, another one pulls me under. I'm drowning in agony all while the love of my life tries to pull me from the water. But I can't see past this storm of sorrows that keeps circulating. Help me understand, Dad. Why is God punishing me?" Gasping for breath, tears stream down my cheeks as I search my dad's eyes for the answers I'm seeking.

He reaches out to wipe more of my tears before taking my hands in his. "I'm not sure why you've been dealt these cards, Taev. I'd usually encourage those grieving to find solace in God's presence, but I'm not sure that's what you're willing to hear right now. What I will tell you is that when your mother died, I wavered in my faith. Tell me what brought you here, specifically."

"There are only two. There were fourteen but now there are only two. And that doesn't even mean either of those two embryos will become a baby I get to hold in my arms. For nearly ten years I've questioned why my baby was taken from me. My body keeps failing me, and I'm so damn *angry*. I only got one chance at an egg retrieval and now I may never have a child of my own. And I can't stop the intrusive thoughts from reminding me that Jackson would be better off without me. Not only am I holding him back with my cancer diagnosis, but now I'm burdening him with my infertility."

My dad doesn't hesitate as he throws his arms around me and holds me right there on the steps of the altar in a church that worships a God I'm not entirely sure I believe in anymore.

But maybe that's not true.

Something or *someone* placed Jackson back in my life after all these years apart. It wasn't just happenstance that I performed at Bennett and Scarlett's wedding after having just been diagnosed with cancer.

Maybe God didn't want me to go through this battle alone.

And maybe, just maybe, it isn't God that has stolen more from me, but the cancer.

Pulling my head from his chest, I look up at my dad. "I think I've been blinded by my opponent, Dad. I can't fight God, but I *can* fight cancer. Mom lost her battle but I refuse to follow in her footsteps in that aspect."

"You won't," is all he responds, and we sit in silence as I stare up at the light shining through the stained glass windows surrounding us.

We sit there for what feels like hours until I'm pretty sure my knees will never heal from the soreness. Finally, my dad breaks the silence. "I've got to get going now, Taev. But just know this: you are stronger than you could ever imagine. From the moment you came into this world prematurely yet still crying with piercing screams, you've been a fighter. Take strength in knowing you *can* overcome this. You *will* overcome this, I know it with every fiber of my being. And when it seems impossible, try to have faith that your two embryos will be fighters too."

"I love you, Dad," I tell him for the first time in far too long.

Instead of being met with silence like I had been for years, my dad wraps me in his arms one last time and whispers, "I love you too, Taev."

He helps me to my feet, and I walk down the aisle toward the back of the church, only turning to look over my shoulder once I've reached the doors. I watch as my dad, the last person I would have expected to pull me from this spiral, stands with his hands in his pockets staring up at the cross above the altar.

Maybe this will be a fresh start for us. Maybe I'll be able to beat this cancer. Maybe my two little reasons to fight like hell will be fighters just like me. But one thing is for certain: I *am* going to fight.

26

Taevin

"T, what are you doing? That is definitely not how to bait a hook," Jax admonishes as I nearly cut my finger trying to bait this stupid worm.

"Well, then help me," I tell him, completely exasperated by this whole experience. Jackson woke me up at nearly the crack of dawn to "go on an adventure" as he put it. I was surprised when he drove us to a lake about twenty miles out of town where his family keeps their three boats docked. And when I asked him why they'd possibly need three boats, he looked at me as if I were being unreasonable considering they apparently need different boats for fishing, wakeboarding, and then his parents have a pontoon. When I pointed out that the only other time I'd ever fished was while I was on a pontoon, he just rolled his eyes.

"Give it here," he says, gesturing for me to hand him the pole. He looks at it skeptically, and shakes his head before bringing the line in his mouth and biting the clear material in half. The move is not sexual, and I absolutely shouldn't find it hot, but for whatever reason I can't seem to get enough of my husband. I'm caught up in the newlywed haze, where I find every little thing Jackson does hot. Like the way his deft fingers work to thread and tie on the new bobber and hook he took out of his tackle box. Or the way he again brings the line to his mouth to pull it tight with his teeth.

Something is seriously wrong with me if I'm acting this depraved when he's already given me an orgasm this morning in his truck when I started whining over going fishing at the ungodly hour.

Without even looking at me, Jax shakes his head and mutters, "If you keep looking at me like that, woman, we're never going to catch our lunch."

"I'm not even hungry," I inform him.

"Yeah, I know. You're just thirsty as hell if the way you're ogling me from over there is anything to go off of."

"Ha ha," I mock, crossing my arms and rolling my eyes for good measure. "How long will it take us to get back to my house? I have an appointment this afternoon at two, remember?" I ask, remembering how long it took us to find his secret fishing spot that he swore up and down we'd catch a ton of fish at, but I haven't caught anything. Though clearly the fish are biting because they keep managing to eat the worms off my hook.

"There you go. All fixed up," Jax says, handing me back the pole now all ready to go. I take it from him and he says, "To answer your question, it'll probably take us an hour and a half, maybe closer to two if there are a lot of boats trying to dock at the same time as us."

I look down at my watch and bite the inside of my cheek as I try to calculate when we need to head out. "We should probably only fish for another half hour or so then," I tell him.

"Sounds good, baby," he says as he swivels on his chair to grab his pole and then stands to cast his line. Again, something that is not overtly sexy whatsoever shouldn't have me clenching my thighs together, but here I am trying to find relief anyway possible.

I stand up, giving it my best attempt at casting my line out. When I finally feel a strong tug on my line a few minutes later, I squeal in delight, "Bear! I think I've got one!"

Jax sets his pole down and makes his way over to me, standing at my back and wrapping his arms around me. "You've gotta set the hook like this," he explains as he helps me sharply yank back the pole before helping me reel it in.

"This has quite a bit of drag on the line," he says like I'd know whatever that means. "You're doing so good, baby. Keep going, just like that," Jax praises, and I stop momentarily as a chill works its way down my spine because the way he said that just turned me all the way on.

Clearing my throat, I resume reeling and I do a happy dance when I see there's still a fish on the line. "J, look! I'm actually going to catch one!" I squeak as I lift the line out of the water.

"Holy shit, you got a smallmouth."

"I didn't hear you complaining last night," I mutter.

"Bass. A smallmouth bass," he emphasizes.

"Right. I obviously knew that," I attempt to lie, though my laughter is a dead giveaway.

Jax makes quick work of unhooking the fish and holding it up to me with his thumb in the fish's mouth. "Here, hold it up and let me get a picture of you with it," he tells me as he sets the slimy fish in my hands and I nearly throw it out of the boat before he can grab his phone to take the picture.

Once he's satisfied with the number of pictures he takes, he takes the fish from me and places it back in the water.

"Hey, I thought you said that was going to be our lunch."

"I didn't think you'd catch a bass. But now that you've caught one, I'll just drive us back now and that way we'll have enough time for me to take you out to lunch before your appointment," he says.

I help him put our poles away and watch as he takes off his baseball hat to run his fingers through his hair. When he puts it back on but turns it backward, I'm officially feral for him. That, in combination with the way he manspreads in the captain's seat with one hand on the wheel and pats his thigh with the other, gesturing for me to take a seat, has me wanting to drop to my knees right here in the middle of the lake.

Biting my bottom lip to hold in the moan that threatens to escape from how freaking sexy he is, I take a seat on his thigh but he adjusts me, placing me right in his lap where I can feel how turned on he is as well. Jax's thick hands grasp my waist, raking me up and down his hard length, turning me on so badly and causing my nipples to pebble beneath my tank top.

"Take the wheel, T. But first, take off your shorts. You've got a swimsuit underneath, right?" he rasps the question, and the gravel in his voice causes full body goosebumps.

I nod and slip out of my shorts before taking my seat in his lap again, and when I do, he's quick to slide his fingers just beneath the waistband of my bikini bottoms.

Jax starts the boat with one hand and we take off just as he traces my clit with his fingers before going lower and sliding one inside my pussy and then adding a second shortly thereafter.

I can't concentrate on driving, though thankfully we're practically trolling with how slow we're going and it's just a matter of steering us in the direction we need to go to get to the dock.

From this angle, with the way he's sitting behind me, his palm rubs deliciously over my clit, and when he hears my moans of approval, he applies more pressure.

"I'm so close!" I pant breathlessly.

"You're doing so good for me, baby," he praises, and that causes me to clench tightly around his fingers as they work in and out of me.

"Fuck," Jax rasps before biting the back of my shoulder, and I can't hold in the gasp that slips out as he begins working his hand in and out of me faster, increasing the friction against my clit and causing the pressure within me to pull tighter.

"Yes, right there, just like that. Oh, god, don't stop," I plead desperately.

"I want you to beg me to let you come," he says gruffly.

I'm not sure what's gotten into him but I'm clearly here for it because I'm so wet I can hear it each time he pulls his fingers out of me just to thrust them back in deeper and deeper.

"Please, J. I'm so close. Please make me come," I beg, and he rewards me by snaking his other hand beneath my tank top and rolling my nipple firmly between his fingers.

The combination of what his hands are doing and the fact that anybody could catch us right now has me coming harder than I ever have. My pussy convulses around his fingers, causing his palm to rub rougher against my clit and it feels like my orgasm will never end.

"That's it, baby. Ride it out. You're so fucking beautiful when you come undone for me," Jax continues his praises before placing delicate kisses across the exposed skin on my back.

When he finally pulls his fingers out of me, I practically collapse onto the steering wheel as I fight to catch my breath.

His rough chuckle causes his chest to rumble against my back when he pulls me against him, wrapping his arm snuggly around my waist to keep me upright.

"Fuck, Tae. That was so hot," he murmurs against my shoulder.

"If this is what it'll be like every time you bring me fishing, consider me hooked," I say, and it's so cheesy but I'm in a post-orgasmic state of mind so I can't be held accountable for anything I say or do at this time.

I wiggle in his lap to get comfortable, and Jax holds firm on my hips to keep me in place. "Easy, T. I'm so fucking hard it hurts."

"Allow me to take care of that then," I taunt as I slide my hand up his thigh.

Jax is quick to catch my hand in his. "How about we wait until we're back in my truck. I want your mouth," he murmurs against the shell of my ear before biting down on it.

I look back at him over my shoulder and wink. "Oh, a little road head on the way to lunch?"

"You're nothing but trouble, you know that?" he asks, shaking his head.

"I wouldn't be doing my part as your wife if I wasn't a temptation, now would I?"

"You've been tempting me everyday since I first laid eyes on you, baby," he rasps.

"Ditto," I tell him as I shift onto his one thigh and wrap an arm around his neck so he can steer us back to the dock.

I love how easy our love is.

A little voice in the back of my head warns me that my appointment this afternoon could threaten that very ease between us, but I shove it to the far recesses of my mind as I run my fingers through Jax's hair and bask in this moment.

I shouldn't have lied to Jackson about where I was going. It's a terrible habit I've developed since the man sitting before me first called last week.

Kyle Blackwood looks nothing like I thought he would. I guess I had figured he'd likely be in his mid-thirties at the very least, but he can't be more than twenty-five tops.

He's dressed in a navy tailored suit and his hair is slicked back so not a hair is out of place. Kyle is polished from head to toe and I'm not sure what to make of him or the feeling deep in my gut that I shouldn't be here right now.

Pushing past that niggling feeling, I take a sip of my iced coffee and look up to find him staring back at me expectantly. Shoot, did I miss him asking a question?

"I'm sorry, could you repeat that?" I ask him.

"I was just asking if you'd ever consider relocating to Nashville since that's where the label I've been in contact with is located."

I glance down at my coffee cup and consider my answer. I mean, would I consider relocating? A few months ago I would've jumped at the opportunity to live in Nashville and sign a record deal Kyle said is practically a sure thing. Now, though? Now I'm a married eighteen-year-old about to move to Boston to attend college alongside my husband so he can live out his dreams of playing college hockey.

"Uh, I don't think I would at this time. Would that be a requirement from the label? Ideally, I'd like to still attend college at Berklee this fall. I got nearly a full scholarship," I inform him.

Kyle's eyebrows raise, and I think it's because he's impressed, that is until he responds. "Taevin, you do understand that an opportunity to sign a recording deal for multiple albums as a debut artist is extremely rare, right? So rare that I've never even heard of a deal like this."

I don't point out the fact that it's likely because he hasn't been in the industry that long, and instead murmur, "Perhaps it's too good to be true, then."

Kyle's eyes narrow slightly. "No, I don't think so. I think there's something else making you hesitate." Without breaking eye contact, he takes a slow drink of his tea. Clearing his throat, he admonishes, "Don't tell me you've got some high school sweetheart you're so hung up on you're about to miss out on a once-in-a-lifetime shot that's been placed in your lap."

Gathering my hands in my lap, I look down to avoid his skeptical gaze. "I do have a boyfriend who will also be attending college in Boston this fall," I admit the halftruth, though not calling Jackson my husband makes my stomach churn with guilt.

Why did I just lie again?

Kyle waves his hand dismissively. "Boyfriends come and go, trust me. The last thing you want to do is pass up this opportunity for college. Besides, what would a music degree get you that this record deal wouldn't immediately surpass as far as income and experience?"

He has a point; getting a record deal would mean I don't bury myself in student loan debt. But it could also turn out that I'm not ready to make this leap and my inexperience will lead to my career in the music industry tanking before it's even begun.

"Look, if you want to work together, I can get this deal signed by the end of the week, but I need to know you're all in," Kyle presses.

I worry my lip between my teeth and fist my hands together in my lap. Looking up at Kyle, I ask, "Can I have a day or two to think over my options and get back to you?"

Kyle sighs as if he's disappointed with my answer, but ultimately nods his head in response. "I suppose that'd be alright. But I need an answer in two days or I'm out. I'm a busy man, Taevin. I don't have time to sit around waiting on an indecisive, lovesick teenager."

Well that was uncalled for. I mean, sure, to outsiders I'm guessing Jackson and I look like lovesick fools, but what we have is unshakeable. We've made vows to be together for the rest of our lives.

I just need to talk to him about the record deal. He said so himself that we could make long distance work if we needed to, though I'm pretty sure he thought we'd have a few years before that was even a possibility.

Kyle hands me his business card, and after exchanging a firm handshake, I make my way out of the coffeeshop.

I'm just pulling my phone from my purse when I collide with a hard chest.

"Oh my goodness, I'm so sorry. I wasn't looking where I was going—" I start, but am startled to find I've run right into Jackson's father. "Senator Wilson, hello."

Taking a step back, he narrows his eyes at me. "It's Taevin, right?" he asks with a sharp edge to the question.

"Yes. I'm Jackson's girlfriend," I tell him, and there I go lying again. But Jax's father cannot find out about our marriage or things would spiral out of control for the last week before we leave for Boston.

"Is that so?" Senator Wilson questions. "Not for long, if I have anything to say about that."

I shouldn't be surprised by his condescending tone, yet here I am taken aback by what he's just insinuated. I'm furious, so much so that I let my anger get the best of me when I can't stop myself from pushing back. "Yeah? And what are you going to do about it? If I recall, your son already told you that if you interfere with our relationship, he'll throw his future plans at Harvard out the window. Is that what you want, Senator?"

He puts his hands in the pockets of his suit pants and rocks back on his heels. "I think I may have misjudged the seriousness of my son's fascination with you, and perhaps I've underestimated you, Miss Gray. But the thing is, if you want what's best for his future as well as your own, you should listen very closely to what I have to say."

Without warning, Jax's dad grabs me by the arm and drags me around the corner of the coffeeshop into the alleyway. Fear prickles at my spine as I run through my escape options. What is he planning to do to me?

Letting go of my arm rather roughly, he reaches into the inner pocket of his suit jacket and for a second I fear he'll pull out a weapon, but I'm relieved to find it's only his cellphone. My relief is fleeting when he turns the screen for me to see.

"Care to tell me what I'm looking at here, Miss Gray?" he questions as he swipes through a series of photos of Jackson and I in very compromising positions.

My heart sinks and my stomach churns as I take in the damning photos of the two of us in the woods when he took me turkey hunting with him in June. What's bad about that, right? Well, considering I have my back pressed up against a tree while Jackson's pants are around his ankles, I'm guessing it wouldn't be hard for someone to put two and two together.

And when his father continues to swipe through the photos that are getting increasingly worse, I gasp and push his phone away.

Oh, god, I'm going to be sick.

"How did you get those?" I ask once I manage to swallow past the bile in my throat.

"Well, you see, I've got these things called trail cameras all along my property. The boys use them for hunting; I, however, use them to ensure there are no trespassers on my property. *You*, Miss Gray, are a trespasser in the plans I have laid out for my son."

I brace my hands on my stomach to keep myself from throwing up, though it'd serve him right if I ruined his expensive dress shoes.

"So, here's what's going to happen. If you don't want these photos to be leaked, along with the video footage from this little afternoon delight, then I suggest you break up with my son. The sooner the better."

He clearly doesn't remember the fact that I'll be attending Berklee and therefore will be in Boston with Jackson anyways. And then there's the fact he's not been made privy to yet that I'm married to his son.

Finally able to find my voice, I muster up the courage to ask, "Why are you doing this? He's your son. Don't you want him to be happy?"

"Love and happiness are fleeting emotions reserved for weak individuals to cling onto in hopes that their pathetic little lives will have meaning. You've not only distracted my son, but you've made him believe in this fallacy that what you two have is something bigger than his future. And that's where you messed up. You've proven to be a roadblock, and I just can't have that."

I look up at him and whisper, "You're a monster, do you know that?"

"Ah, yes. I see we're finally coming to an understanding. I am, in fact, a beast not to be reckoned with. So, you're going to break up with my son. It will be a clean break. You will not speak to him after doing so, and you most certainly will not be moving to Boston with him. There are plenty of universities around the world, and because I know money is tight for your family, I'm even willing to pay for your education so long as it isn't anywhere near Harvard."

He's a crazy, narcissistic asshole.

"And if I don't do as you ask?"

"Then I'll have no choice but to leak these photos and both of your futures will go up in smoke."

"Why would you threaten Jackson's future? That doesn't make any sense for your plans."

He jams his pointer finger against his chest. "Because I know what's best for him. And if you aren't willing to let him go so he can have the future I've worked my ass off for him to get, then I'll sabotage any chance you have of a happy and successful future together."

"I've never met someone so vile," I tell him weakly.

A slow, sinister smile spreads across his face. "Do remember that whenever you consider contacting my son after you part ways. I'm sure it wouldn't be hard for me to conduct a thorough investigation into your father's church. You never know what might turn up—fraud or abuse? Could be quite the scandal. It wouldn't be a hard sell considering I'm a trusted member of the church and I'd only be doing my civic duty if I felt there was reason to investigate."

I try to run through my options, coming up with any alternative to avoid this. Maybe I could go to Jackson's mother and expose her husband's monstrous ways of interfering in his children's lives.

I'm not sure what she would do, though, Jackson said she's always turned a blind eye to his affairs and over-the-top punishments and treatment of Jackson and Bennett over the years.

The senator's eyes narrow on me. "Whatever scenarios you're going through in your head right now, let me just stop you. There is no escaping this fate, Taevin. I am the nightmare you can't outrun. I am a man who makes things happen, and I never bluff. End it with my son or these photos and videos go to every news outlet, gossip rag, and porn site out there."

He begins to step away from me and shoots me a menacing smile. "I'll tell you what, I'm feeling generous today."

Hope blooms in my chest.

"I'll give you until the night before Jackson leaves for Harvard. If you haven't ended things by the time we take off for Boston, I'll leak everything and launch an investigation into your father's church. See, isn't that kind of me to bestow that extra time?"

I turn to step out of the alleyway and look over my shoulder at him. "I'd normally never say something like this to anyone, but I hope you rot in hell one day, Senator Wilson. You're a disgrace of a man. You may think you can keep us apart, but mark my words, one day Jackson and I will find our way back to each other."

And with that, I hurry down the street and wait until I'm around the block to schedule a rideshare home. I'm in no position to call Jackson for the ride he offered me earlier. Besides, I need time alone to try to process and find a solution to this mess that doesn't involve breaking both mine and Jackson's hearts.

27

Jackson

Now

Taevin and I are just leaving her six-week post-op appointment where Dr. Prescott went over Tae's treatment plans for getting her port placed tomorrow and then her first round of chemotherapy will be administered right after they ensure the port's placement looks good.

Dr. Prescott told us Taevin will be doing a chemotherapy regimen administered at the cancer center every three weeks for the next four months.

After opening the clinic door for her, I take her hand in mine and bring our joined hands to my lips. "You're amazing, you know that?" I ask her as we make our way out to my truck.

Taevin smiles sadly at me, and I know it has everything to do with the news she received yesterday when I was unfortunately at practice instead of being beside her like I should've been.

Two embryos.

We have two little fighters.

And she was told the news about the future of our family alone.

I should've been there.

Which is exactly why as soon as she cried herself to sleep on my chest last night, I crawled out of bed and called Scarlett to inform her I'd be taking a leave of absence for each of Taevin's chemotherapy treatments. She told me to take all the time I need and to call her after

Tae's appointment today to let her know the frequency and duration of Tae's chemo sessions.

"What do you say to getting some ice cream?" I suggest, not even having to ask her where she'd like to go, but saying it anyway.

"The Sprinkled Cone?" we question in unison, causing us to both fall into each other in a fit of laughter.

"Is that even a question?" she finally asks moments later.

"It is, but not a very good one," I point out as I open the passenger door of my truck for her.

"I can't believe the place hasn't changed a bit since we were here last," Tae says in awe minutes later while we wait by the pickup counter for our cones.

When her gaze lands on me, I shoot her a playful wink. "You and I were both sporting new rings on our fingers the last time we were both here."

Taevin lifts her hand and frowns down at her bare left ring finger.

Clasping our hands together, I bring her left hand to my mouth and place delicate kisses on the back of it. "Don't be sad, baby. That was one of the best days of my life."

"I'm pouting because not only do I miss that version of us—so young, carefree, and in love—but I also miss the heck outta that ring. Whatever happened to it?"

I wrap my arm around her shoulders and pull her against my chest. "We're still in love and fairly young, just a lot less carefree than we were back then. As for the rings, I've still got them in my safe back at the house."

She looks up at me with her brows raised in surprise. "Really?"

"Oh, please. Don't look so shocked. You already know I never moved on and that I'm sentimental as hell when it comes to you. Of course I held onto our wedding rings. Hell, if our marriage wasn't a secret from everyone in my life, I would've worn the ring on my finger all these years."

"Yeah, instead you just secretly stayed married to me and then got thorns tattooed on your ring finger. When did you get your sleeve?"

I rub my free hand through my scruff, hesitating for a moment as I struggle to compose my thoughts. "Well when college me learned the hard way that kissing a bunch of girls wouldn't numb the pain after you left, I needed some other way to fill the void in my heart. And the one tattoo I had on my body was a reminder of the best day of my life, so I figured I could pass the time without you by inking your memory all over my skin. I started with my left arm sleeve, which took nearly two years to complete because I didn't have the time. Then I got my chest piece and my side tattoo. My right leg has taken the longest—almost four years in total, I think. My plan was just to tattoo every surface available until you came back to me."

"Glad I got to you before they touched your pretty face," she taunts as she bops me on the nose.

Our orders are called and I grab them before following Taevin outside to a bench I've always considered ours even through all these years apart.

Tae takes the first big lick of her monster cookie ice cream and sighs in content. "I've missed late September days in Minnesota."

"They're hard to beat," I agree.

"I love the brisk mornings where we need sweatshirts but then we get afternoons like this where we can be in T-shirts and eating ice cream. And nothing beats the maple trees we have here. The bright oranges, yellows, and reds of their leaves are like the perfect kaleidoscope of color." She looks so beautifully peaceful and at ease in this moment.

Taking her free hand in mine, I tell her, "I planted five maples about three years ago toward the back edge of the property. They're not very mature yet, but their leaves should start changing in the next week or two. I was thinking of building a hot tub and sauna out there so it was tucked away from the house."

"Will you take me out there when we get home?" she questions.

I smile at the way she so easily refers to it as our home now. "Of course."

"Oh! And can we maybe stop at an apple orchard on the way home? I was thinking of baking my apple muffins before my appointment tomorrow so you can have them for your game day just like old times."

How could I say no to that? My mouth waters just at the mention of her apple cinnamon muffins. What she doesn't realize yet is I have no intention of playing in my game tomorrow, but I'm not bringing that up right now.

Swallowing down a bite of my cone, I clear my throat and tell her, "Yeah, there's actually one a few miles down the road from our house. Could this be considered our second first date?"

I shoot her a playful wink when her cheeks heat an adorable shade of pink.

"We may have gone about things in a round about way considering we're already married."

"Griffin was just telling me he and Kenna read an article that said it's important to always date your spouse," I tell her, thinking back to what Griff and Kenna were talking about when we were on the way home from the bar the other week. The details are a bit fuzzy, but I think I got the gist of it.

Taevin's small smile at the mention of my best friends warms my chest. "I'll be sure to ask Kenna for all the marital advice she can give us. They seem like relationship goals from what I've seen."

"Yeah, I mean in their second act for sure. But they've had to work for it. After Katie died, Griff went a bit off the rails. He cut everyone out of his life, even Kenna. G didn't even know about Cadence until she was eighteen months old."

"Wait, really? I didn't realize that," she admits.

"Yeah, he actually found out he had a daughter after his game against Carson in Minnesota when Kenna happened to be there with Cadence."

Taevin shifts, tucking a stray piece of hair behind her ear. "Grief changes people and affects everyone differently."

I nod in agreement. "It does. And Griffin lost himself for a bit there after he lost Katie. But together Cadence and Kenna brought him back and breathed life into him again. Now the life they've built together is beautiful, but it didn't come without sacrifice and hard work to get where they are now."

"Then they one hundred percent are relationship goals. Life is messy, overly complicated, and often catches us off guard. Being able to find your person to share in the good times and hold onto throughout the chaos is the ultimate goal."

"Couldn't have put it better myself. I'm holding on and I'm not letting go, Tae."

"I'm going to hold you to that," she whispers, fidgeting with her cone and worrying her lip before looking up at me with teary eyes. "I thought about coming back home for the funeral, but I wasn't sure you'd want me there."

Pain slices through my chest at her admission. I rest my hand on her thigh and give it a gentle squeeze. "I would've wanted you there. In fact, I kept looking around the gymnasium where they held the memorial service for you."

"If I could go back in time and change how I went about things, I would in a heartbeat."

Licking my lips, I hesitate before saying, "What I still can't wrap my head around is why you left the way you did. I mean, I get that you were presented with a once-in-a-lifetime opportunity at eighteen, but we were so solid leading up to that."

She bites the inside of her cheek. "Do you remember when you brought me turkey hunting with you in the spring right before graduation?"

I give her a small smirk, remembering exactly what we did in the woods. "Yeah. How could I forget?"

Tae doesn't smile back. In fact, she winces. "Well there were, um, pictures of what we did. In a compromising position."

Confusion must be written all over my face because without waiting for me to respond, she continues. "There were trail cameras."

My stomach sinks and nausea takes over. "But those cameras were on our land," I stammer.

She nods once.

"What does that have to do with you leaving, T?"

Wiping a stray tear, her eyes search mine, bouncing back and forth like she's begging me to find the answer hidden in her gaze so she doesn't have to say it out loud. Finally she murmurs, "Your father approached me the day I met with Kyle for the first time. I was leaving the meeting thinking I'd turn Kyle down, or at the very least, that I'd consider the record deal only if I got to continue with my plans to attend school in Boston." She pauses, licking her lips and it gives me a moment to put the pieces together.

"Taevin, did my father blackmail you with pictures of us?"

Her lip quivers as she nods her head.

Holy shit. I didn't see that coming. At all.

"He said if I didn't break up with you, he'd release the pictures to the media and both of our futures would be ruined. Apparently he even had footage of us from the cameras. It was the hardest thing I've ever done, Jax. I was sick about it for weeks. You have to know, I never wanted to break us, but I didn't see any other way. I signed with Kyle and took the record deal because I didn't see any other way. But then when I found out I was pregnant, I knew I couldn't keep it from you. Even if it meant your father ruined our futures. So I sought you out when I was in Boston. I had planned to tell you about the baby and, well, you know the rest." She buries her head into my chest, and I rub my hand up and down her back in an attempt to soothe her while my world feels like it's crumbling around me.

How could he do this to his own son?

I've come to realize over the years just how controlling and manipulative my father is, but even knowing that, I never thought he'd do something this vile.

Blackmailing his own son with revenge porn? I feel like I'm going to be sick. Especially when I grasp that all the time I lost with Taevin was because my father stole it from us.

I'll never forgive him.

The urge to call my mother and tell her about what he's done subsides slightly when I feel Taevin's shoulders tremble against my chest.

As much as I wish she would've come to me about this then, there's nothing we can do to change the past. She must've been so scared. And felt so alone.

Taevin lifts her head and looks at me with tear-filled eyes. "I'm so sorry, Jackson."

Shaking my head, I take her hands in mine. "Don't be. You have nothing to apologize for."

She closes in on herself and looks down, avoiding my gaze. "I should've come to you. We could've tried to come up with a solution together."

Lifting her chin, I stare into her eyes so she can see how sincere I am. "We can't do the whole could've should've would've thing. We decided we're moving forward together, and I meant that. This changes nothing aside from the fact that my father is cut out of our lives for good."

I pull her into my arms and she lets out a heavy sigh against my chest. We stay like that—silently soaking in the afternoon sun—for I don't even know how long until I finally suggest, "We should get going to the apple orchard before it closes."

Taking her hand in mine, we make our way to my truck. Even though what she just admitted was hard to talk through, it's like a heavy weight has been lifted off her shoulders.

The apple orchard lifts both our spirits, and each time a soft smile lights up her face, I can't stop myself from kissing her cheek or tugging her under my arm.

I love this woman with everything I am, and I refuse to let skeletons from our past cast shadows on what we have. Letting go of what lies behind allows for brighter days ahead.

28

Taevin

Now

My hands shake slightly as I slide the lace garters into place on my thighs.

After a moment of hesitation, I lift my eyes to meet my reflection in the mirror. Blowing out a deep breath, I nod once.

I can seduce my husband.

Just open the door.

I've got this.

Jax loves me.

And he's going to love this.

My stomach twists with nerves as I open the bathroom door, but the nerves quickly turn to ribbons of lust when I take in the sight before me. I'm graced with the sight of Jackson sitting up in bed against the headboard with nothing but a sheet slung around his waist. He looks fine as hell sitting there with only a composition notebook in his hand, a pencil braced between his lips, and his guitar slung across his lap.

"Aren't you a sight for sore eyes," I murmur as I dig deep to find the confident, badass version of myself.

Jax looks up from his notebook and when his gaze rakes down my body, I have to stifle a laugh when the pencil plops out of his mouth as his jaw hangs open.

"You like?" I question, doing a slow spin so he can take in the black, lacy bodysuit I put on after my bath.

He swallows—actually no, it's more like a gulp because it's loud enough for me to hear from across the room.

"Baby, what are you trying to do to me?" Jax asks as he tosses the notebook and pencil on the bedside table next to him and sets his guitar on the ground. Flinging the covers off, he strides over to me at a pace that would be impressive if I were to focus on that. I can't though, because my focus is wholly on the man before me and the way his black boxer briefs hug his hockey thighs.

Jax closes the distance between us but instead of embracing me the way I thought he might, he stands before me and slowly rakes his gaze over me again, undressing me with his eyes.

He swallows and then rasps, "You look so fucking exquisite."

With one hand, he reaches behind me and palms my ass before giving it a squeeze while using his other to tip my chin up so he can steal a kiss. His kiss is hungry, frenzied, bordering on desperate, and I love that I can still get this reaction out of him.

Our lips move together and as his tongue delves into my mouth, I reach my hand down to rest against the waistband of his boxer briefs.

I trace the outline of his length above the fabric encasing him, reveling at how hard he already is. "God, I've always loved how hard you get for me before I've even touched you," I admit, breaking our kiss as I sneak my fingers into the waistband of his boxers before lowering them off, falling to my knees as I do.

Jax steps out of them and stands before me in all his tatted, naked glory. Running my hand up his inked thigh, I hum in approval as I take in the beautiful treble and bass clefs and lines of sheet music that travel up his quad. "Mmm, I love how intricate these are. You'll have to tell me more about them later."

"Later?" he questions, but it comes out as more of a taunt.

Looking up at him through my lashes, I wrap my hand around his length and give him a firm stroke. "Yeah, later. I've got other plans for you right now if you're alright with that."

"I'm more than alright with that," Jax rasps before cupping his hand under my chin so he can hold my stare. "But you better tell me now if you want me to come down your throat or somewhere else."

His gravelly tone sends a shiver down my spine and my nipples pebble impossibly harder.

"I want you to come inside me," I tell him somewhat shyly.

Jax's eyebrows lift in surprise. "Are you sure you're ready for that?"

"You heard Dr. Prescott today, I've been cleared for all sexual activities. And I'd like my husband to fuck me for the first time in ten years."

Pulling me to my feet, he walks us a few steps until my back is pressed against the wall and then he grips my hip. "Yeah, here's the thing. I'm not going to do that. Not right now, at least."

I pout but he just shakes his head at me.

"You see, the first time I take you again won't be a hard and fast fuck." He emphasizes his words by dragging a hand slowly up my inner thigh while keeping his other firmly gripping my hip.

"It won't?" I question on a gasp as shivers race down my spine.

"No," he answers, but it comes out as more of a growl. "Because the first time I take you again will be me making slow, sensual love to you. I plan to take my time and worship every inch of your beautiful body."

"I'm not so sure it's worthy of such worship right now," I admit shyly.

"See, that's where you're wrong, T. Your body is an alluring offering and I want to worship at your altar every day for the rest of our lives."

"How very holy of you," I say teasingly.

"There's nothing holy about the things I plan to do to you while I show you my devotion."

"Is that so? I think you better get to showing me then," I encourage him through bated breaths.

Jackson lifts me under my thighs and when I wrap my legs around his waist, my suddenly drenched core is lined up perfectly with his hard length and I can't help the moan I let out at the feel of him brushing against my lace-covered clit.

He walks me back to his bed and carefully lays me down before standing to his full height at the edge of the bed.

"We don't have to rush into this just because you were cleared by your doctor. If you want to take things slow while we get to know each other again, I'm good with whatever pace you want to move forward at," he tells me and the reminder of the way he's always put my needs and wants above all else has tears welling in my eyes.

"I love you so much, Jackson. No amount of time or distance has changed that and honestly, it never will. But I think I might die if I have to wait another minute to feel you inside me. So please, do me a favor and show me how much you love me."

Jax crawls onto the bed and works his way between my thighs until his body weight presses me deliciously into the mattress. He kisses me tenderly and just as I'm getting lost in the feel of his lips against mine, he begins mapping open-mouth kisses across my entire body starting at my neck down to my wrists and ankles, though he passes the place I'd love his mouth most. Well, really I want to feel his cock inside me more than I need to take my next breath.

"J, please," I implore, tangling my hands through his hair to halt him in place where he was kissing my hip bone.

"Please what?"

"I need to feel you inside me. Please."

He licks his lips and then smirks at my desperation. Instead of immediately giving me what I want, he licks a languid stroke over my lace-covered slit, causing me to whimper in response.

"There are snaps down there. Could you undo them?" I ask him.

With his deft fingers, he undoes the snaps before circling my entrance and easing one finger inside me. "Mmm, you're already so wet for me," he hums in approval. "Does this feel okay?" he asks as he pumps it slowly in and out of me.

"Yes," I drag out my whispered response.

"Do you think you can take another?"

Instead of answering with words, I nod eagerly. And when he adds a second finger, my eyes nearly roll to the back of my head with how full I feel. But it's still not enough. I need more. I need him. All of him.

"I'm ready," I assure him.

"Not yet," he counters, and I let out a growl of frustration. Jax has the nerve to chuckle. "Let me have a taste, baby. Please?"

"Well, when you ask like that—" I'm cut off when he places a single, gentle kiss on my clit.

He trails a path from my clit to my pussy with his tongue, and then he *devours* me.

Gripping the sheets, I throw my head back and moan while he fucks me with his tongue.

"Jackson, fuck, I-I *need* you inside of me. Now!"

That's all it takes, and then he's moving up my body, bringing his lips to mine once more and kissing me with a passion I haven't felt with anyone besides him.

He lines himself up at my entrance but hesitates as he takes a deep, shuttered breath. "You'll tell me if it hurts?"

"Yes," I promise him.

Jax nods once before nudging the head of his cock past my entrance. "*Fuck*, baby. I missed you," he groans as he slides inside me for the first time in over a decade.

He moves his arms beneath me, one hand tangling in my hair while the other grips my ass cheek with a claiming dominance. With our bodies wrapped around each other, he moves his hips at a languid pace as I trace my fingers over the lines of his back, noting how much more defined the contours of every muscle he has are.

"Are you okay?" he asks, locking his gaze on mine.

"I've never been better. I swear," I breathe the promise.

That seems to reassure him enough to continue. Jax drops his mouth to mine and sweeps his tongue along the seam of my lips until I open for him. We savor the kiss as he moves slowly in and out of me, grinding his pelvis against my clit with each thrust until my pussy flutters around his throbbing cock.

He groans in appreciation. "You're doing so good for me, baby."

The friction against my clit is devine, and I can tell I'm on the brink. "Yes, right there, just like that. Oh, god, don't stop."

Thankfully, he doesn't.

And when my body reaches the precipice, I tumble off the edge and freefall into the euphoria only my husband can invoke. Our bodies tremble in synchrony as we come together.

"You're my favorite addiction, Taevin Gray. I've missed you so fucking much." Jackson's soft admission warms my heart as he rolls us over and wraps me into his arms.

We sit like that for a few minutes until he carries me into the bathroom and starts a shower for us. As he washes me and holds me in his arms, it feels surreal to be like this with him again.

For the first time in far too long, I feel at peace.

When I'm in Jax's arms, I'm home.

29

Jackson

The sweet smell of cinnamon and sugar fills the air and it's like a beacon leading me to the kitchen where the sight of Taevin bent over in just my T-shirt and oven mitts as she pulls out a tray of muffins has me stopping dead in my tracks. My dick twitches in my gym shorts I threw on before I came out here as I take her in.

"Baby," I groan. "You look so fucking good in my shirt, and you know I can't resist you when you're baking. Let alone the sight of you baking in *our* home."

I close the distance between us, and once she closes the oven door and sets the tray of muffins on the stove to cool, I pounce on her, wrapping my arms around her from behind.

"It's about time you woke up, sleepy head. I was worried I wouldn't have enough time to seduce you before you had to head to the rink for morning skate."

"Seduce me, eh?"

"Yep," she says, popping the "p" and nodding her head once.

"What did you have in mind?"

"Wearing nothing but your shirt, for starters."

"I mean, I knew you weren't wearing a bra, but no panties?" I question, drawing the hem of the shirt up so I can see for myself. And,

Jesus, would you look at that—she was telling the truth and her pretty pussy looks like it's begging for another round.

"Are you sore after last night?" I ask her.

Tae shakes her head, but I quirk a brow in question. "I mean, I'm not sore but I do feel gloriously stretched."

"We can do other things. I seem to remember you loving my tongue and my fingers."

"I do, and you've already proven to me that I still love them. But I would like the one thing I haven't been able to have in far too long."

"You'll have to be a little more specific," I goad her.

"I want your cock. Inside me. Preferably right now. Is that specific enough for you?" She quirks one sassy brow at me, and my dick jerks in response.

Even though I want her, I can't help but question if this is the right move. "It certainly is. But I don't want to hurt you."

"I'm telling you, I'm not sore and last night didn't hurt me. Besides, I don't know how the chemo will make me feel." Tae wrings her hands together, and I rest my palms over them.

"We've got the rest of our lives, there's no rush," I remind her, rocking us side to side in our embrace.

"I know." She arches her back, causing her ass to rub against my erection, taunting me like she does best. "What if I told you that I'm just *really* fucking horny right now?"

I let out a low chuckle, leaning down to rasp in her ear. "Then I'd tell you that I'd hate to leave my wife feeling needy and unsatisfied."

She spins in my arms, wrapping her arms around my neck. "Good. Then do me a favor and give me your mouth, fingers, and cock."

"You don't have to tell me twice," I murmur as I lift her up and carry her over to the dining room. I lay her back on the table before pulling up a chair. "Spread your legs for me, T."

She does as I say, and I can't help but feel like the luckiest man alive to get to see her this way—in a way no one else ever will again. For some deep-seated reason, I have the profound urge to mark her. Scooting her hips toward me, I pepper light kisses along her right thigh before doing the same to her left. But when I reach the apex of her left thigh, I bite down on the soft, creamy flesh enough to leave a mark before soothing the skin with my tongue and lips.

"Did you just bite me and then leave a hickey?"

"I did."

"Jax!"

I shrug. "What? You're making me a feral beast."

Before I can continue to act on that, Tae looks at the clock on the oven and curses. "Shit! You need to go, you're going to be late for your morning skate. I'm so sorry we got carried away."

I chuckle and pull her closer to me, wrapping my arms around her waist in the way I've come to love so I can keep her close to me. "I'm not going to morning skate."

"What? Why not? Did it get canceled?"

"No."

"Then why in the world would you miss morning skate? If you miss, you'll be benched for tonight's game, won't you?"

"Yeah if I were planning on playing tonight. But I'm not."

Her eyes widen, and I find it cute that she's so shocked, but she really shouldn't be. "What do you mean you're not playing tonight?"

An adorable crease appears between Tae's brows and I brush my finger over it before placing a kiss on her forehead. "I'm taking you to your appointment this afternoon and then I'm taking care of you afterward."

She scoffs in disbelief. "You could still take me to my appointment this afternoon and not have to miss morning skate or your game."

I shrug off her comment. "I could. But I'm using my leave of absence time to take care of you."

"Jax, you can't miss your first home game to stay here with me. I'll be fine."

"You're having your port placed and receiving your first round of chemo this afternoon, there's no chance in hell I'm going to my game. Especially considering it's preseason. What if something happened to you while I was playing? You'll likely feel sick. I'm not going, T. I told Scarlett, Coach, and management that I'm not going to be there today or at practice tomorrow after I researched and found out the first two days after chemo are the worst."

Tears well in her eyes as she soaks in my words and my determined expression. There's no talking me out of this, and I think she realizes that. "I-I don't know what to say to that."

"You don't have to say anything, T. I'm right here." Pulling her in for a hug, I keep my arms wrapped snuggly around her as I inhale deeply. "Now, I don't know about you, but I'm about to eat at least half a dozen cinnamon apple muffins. Fuck, maybe even eight considering I don't have a game tonight."

Tae squeezes me tight around my waist and tips her chin, resting it against my chest so she can look up at me. "It's nice to see some things haven't changed."

"Baby, if you bake it, I'm gonna eat it. That will always remain true." I waggle my brows like an idiot and we both break out into a fit of laughter.

She shakes her head. "God, you're weird."

"Yeah, but you love me."

"You're right. I really do."

The nurse just left the curtained area we're sitting in as Taevin awaits her first chemo treatment. Her port was placed beneath her collarbone through an outpatient procedure, and after an X-ray ensured it was properly installed, Tae was wheeled to the cancer center wing. She's still a bit loopy I think from the light sedation though, because she keeps staring at me with the most smitten look and saying the most off the cuff things. Like telling the nurse to "look into my sea glass eyes because they're the most mesmerizing thing she'll ever lay eyes on." I managed to bite back my chuckle, but she had me full on chortling when she said "and not only does he look like *that* but he fucks like a god too. Some men have all the beauty but nothing to show for it. But not my husband—he's got the looks *and* the goods to back it up."

So it's only now as we're alone again and she's staring at me with hearts in her eyes that I lean in for a chaste kiss.

Tae tries to pull me back in to deepen the kiss but I turn my head and place delicate pecks along the inside of her wrist.

"I'm the luckiest woman in the world to have you."

Lacing my fingers through hers, I bring the back of her hand to my lips for a kiss. I'm so grateful to have her now, but I wish there wasn't so much of each other's lives that we'd missed out on.

But before I can say anything Tae asks, "Hey, Bear?"

I smirk at her use of my nickname. Playing along, I ask, "Yeah, Thorn?"

"I'm not sure I can do this alone." It comes out as a whispered confession, so quiet I almost miss what she's said.

My heart sinks at the fear in her voice, and an ache I've never experienced spreads throughout my chest. "And you'll never have to, baby. I'm right here," I assure her, rubbing slow circles on her hands before kissing her forehead, hoping like hell I can pour every ounce of my love for her into this kiss. I wish more than anything in this moment for the ability to ease her fears and assure her everything is going to be okay; but the thing is, I can't guarantee that. I don't know what this fight looks like for her, but the one thing I do know is that I'm going to be by her side. And beyond anything, Taevin will not only know but *feel* that she's not alone.

My phone buzzes incessantly on the bedside table, and I muffle a growl of frustration when I finally reach over and see Senator Satan on my caller ID. Standing from the bed, I leave Taevin resting in our room before making my way down the hall.

Swiping to accept the call, I sigh in annoyance at his interruption as I flop down on the oversized sectional sofa that takes up a good portion of the living room.

"Yeah?" I answer, not bothering with niceties since I know exactly why he's calling.

"What's this I hear about my son missing his game tonight? Tell me it's not true."

"Who's your source?"

He lets out a displeased scoff. "Does it matter?"

"I guess not, but considering your other son isn't on speaking terms with you, I figure it wasn't him."

"It doesn't matter who told me. What matters is that I had to have been misinformed because there's no way in hell you're missing your game tonight for some school yard crush you never managed to get over."

I see red. "See, that's where you're wrong, because I am missing the game tonight. And it's to be by my wife's side to take care of her. I know being faithful to your vows isn't something you take seriously or place importance in, but I meant every word; especially in sickness and in health," I seethe at him.

My sperm donor apparently can't comprehend my tone over the phone because he chuckles at that—fucking cackles like we're shooting the shit. "For fuck's sake. You were a teenager. No one expects you to uphold those vows."

I'm not sure I've ever hated someone more than I do at this moment. I clench my jaw three times before I finally grind out, "I do. It doesn't matter how old I was or wasn't, what matters is I am a man of my word and my mother raised me better than to turn my back on my family."

"Enough!" he shouts. "You will get your ass to the hockey rink and you will beg your coach not to bench you after missing your morning skate. And while you're at it, it would be a wise decision to evict all distractions from your home before your hockey career goes to shit."

A menacing chuckle escapes but honestly I could give a fuck less. "Get fucked, old man."

I hang up and smile, feeling proud of myself for finally standing up to the man who considers himself my father when he's been anything but practically my entire life.

"Jax?" Taevin calls out in question from the bedroom. I leap to my feet the moment I hear the weakness in her voice.

"I'm here, T. What's up?" I ask, pausing in the doorway when I realize she's no longer in our bed. That's when I hear her heaving echo off the walls in the bathroom.

Rushing to her side, I pull her long black locks back with one hand while rubbing her back with the other. Helplessness fills my chest mixing with confusion at the relief I feel that I'm able to be by her side right now.

This woman is the most important person in my life. There is no place I'd rather be tonight than right here caring for the girl who stole my heart at eighteen and so graciously never gave it back.

30

Jackson

Something is wrong.

I don't know what's going on with Taevin, but something has definitely been off the past several days since her appointment.

And whenever I ask her about said appointment, she gets cagey and changes the topic. It's driving me mad watching her distance herself from me for reasons I'm not clued in on.

"Jaxy, what's good, man? Thanks for hosting again," Carson greets me, slapping my hand and bringing me in for a quick hug.

"Carse, what's up? Yeah, of course," I tell him, looking behind him and only seeing Katie with him.

"Hey, Katie, thanks for coming," I greet her and bring her in for a side hug. "Are Kenna and Griff coming later?"

"Nah, I think Mack needed some rest after the first week of volleyball and Griff was going to hang out at her dorm with her since they don't have much time together before he heads to Emery," Carson explains.

"Right, that makes sense. I'm actually headed to Boston tomorrow afternoon to move into my dorm," I tell them.

"That's awesome! Is Taevin leaving tomorrow too?" Katie asks.

I shake my head. "No, her move-in day isn't for another week so she'll meet me there next week. I've got captain's practices for hockey starting early next week so they let the freshman athletes move in a week earlier than the rest of the students living on campus," I answer, looking around the main floor of my parents' house to see if I can spot Tae.

Katie joins me in looking around. "Where is she? I was hoping to hang out with her tonight."

"She should be here soon. She passed her driver's test today so she said she was going to drive herself here."

"That's awesome!" Katie squeals in excitement.

"Are you excited for hockey to start?" Carson asks me, and I should probably lie and tell him I'm stoked, but I don't have it in me.

"I mean, it'll be weird playing with a full team of guys I don't know. But I suppose it'll be nice having Taevin and Griffin in the same city as me."

Carson shakes his head. "It's wild how it worked out with the two of you both winding up in Boston. Is Tae excited for Berklee?"

I nod, even though I'm not entirely sure she's excited considering any time the topic of school or moving to Boston has come up in the past several days, she's quickly changed the subject or thrown herself at me. I'm not complaining about the latter, but I also don't love that she's avoiding the topic.

"Oh, there she is!" Katie points out, waving her arm in the air at Taevin to get her attention.

She looks sad. I can't quite put my finger on it, and she obviously won't tell me what's really going on, but she looks almost devastated to be here right now.

"What's up with our girl?" Katie turns to ask me.

"I'm not sure, she's been acting strange since an appointment she had earlier this week," I murmur as Tae approaches us.

"Well, what was the appointment about?" she asks.

"No clue," I whisper-hiss before rushing to close the distance between me and Taevin.

When I finally wrap my arms around her and lift her in the air, all is right in the world. "Congratulations on passing your driver's test, baby!"

"Thanks," she murmurs against my neck in a subdued tone.

Setting her down, I hold onto her shoulders and bend so I can look right into her eyes. "What's the matter? You looked sad when you came in and now you sound it too, but you should be ecstatic."

She tucks a stray strand of hair behind her ear and avoids my skeptical gaze, keeping hers focused on the stairwell. "Do you think we could go upstairs to talk?"

My stomach sinks as my brain processes what she's just asked. This may be my first relationship, but I've watched enough movies and shows to know when a girl says she wants "to talk" that no good comes from that.

"Yeah of course," I tell her, taking her hand in mind and leading her up to my room.

Once I shut the door behind us, Tae pulls her hand from mine and cracks her knuckles before shaking them out almost as if she's talking herself into having this conversation.

I take a seat on the edge of my bed and pat the mattress beside me but she just shakes her head and remains standing.

Wrinkling my brows, I ask, "What's the matter? You didn't answer me downstairs—" Pausing to consider, my eyes widen. "Wait, did you not pass your driver's test?"

She shakes her head. "No, I passed. That's not it."

"Then what's going on? I've gotta be honest, you're scaring me a bit, baby."

When Tae's watery eyes lift and connect with mine, I realize that my fears are valid.

"I've just been thinking a lot about my future."

"Okay . . ." I trail off because that's not what I was anticipating she'd say, though I'm not exactly sure what to expect right now with how hot and cold she's been all week.

"And there's something I didn't tell you. I—uh—well, I actually signed with an agent last week."

"An agent?" I echo in question.

"Yeah, a talent manager. He reached out to me and I'm going to sign with a record label for a three-record deal, which is absolutely insane," she explains.

I draw my head back in confusion. "Wait, when did this happen?"

She looks down at the ground and murmurs, "Last week when I had my appointment, I met with Kyle."

"Kyle?"

"My new agent."

"And you've already signed a contract with him?" I ask.

She nods, refusing to make eye contact with me as she wrings her hands together.

Standing up, I walk over to her and cup her face in my hands. "Will you please look at me, baby?"

She does as I ask, and when her tear-filled mahogany eyes meet mine, it's like a shot to the chest.

"Why are you sad about this? Shouldn't you be happy?"

Tae's head shoots back as her brows knit in confusion. "You're not angry?"

"I mean, I'm a bit hurt you felt like you couldn't come to me with this. But I could never be angry with you for chasing your dreams. This is what you want, right? To write and record your own music?"

She blinks slowly as she stares into my eyes, almost as if she's searching for the lie. "It is, but I never imagined it would happen like this and so soon."

"You're beyond talented, Tae. Any record label would be lucky as hell to sign you early. Anyone who'd pass you up is an idiot," I assure her.

"Well, there's also the fact that I won't be going to Boston in a week. They want me in Nashville."

"Oh, well—" I pause to scratch the back of my head. "Do you think you'll have to miss the first week of classes or is it just for a few days during freshmen orientation and move-in week?"

Avoiding eye contact again, she stares into the corner where my guitar is splayed across my desk. "No, J. They want me to move there."

I feel like I've been struck. Taking a step back, I ask, "What are you trying to say right now?"

Tae worries her quivering lips together before she whispers, "I'm saying that it's a once-in-a-lifetime opportunity that I can't possibly pass up, Jackson."

Swallowing past the emotion clogging my throat, I choke out, "Okay. Okay, so we have to do the long distance thing earlier than we had planned. That's okay. It's not like we won't see each other. You can come to visit me in season, and whenever I have a break, I'll come see you in Nashville or back home."

"You'd seriously consider trying to make long distance work your freshman year in college?" she asks in a skeptical tone that has me rearing back.

"If that's what it takes to make your dreams come true, I'll do it for you, Tae. Is it ideal that it's happening right away before we've had a chance to experience any bit of college together? I mean, no. But you're right, it's not an opportunity you can pass up. And you seem to have made up your mind."

Tae takes a deep breath. "You're right. I have." Wringing her hands together again before fisting them tightly, she finally looks up at me, and when her eyes connect with mine, my heart sinks.

No, don't do this. I want to scream it, shout it until she decides against what she's about to say.

Her voice trembles as she continues. "I've made up my mind that it's going to be too hard, Jax. You and I both know this won't work out the way we're hoping. Instead of letting us burn out from the distance, I think we should make the conscious choice now to let things go. That way we can part ways as friends instead of winding up hating each other when the distance becomes too much. Before you resent me for not making it to one of your games because I've got to record or have a gig. Before I get my hopes up that you'll be there for a milestone only for our schedules not to align."

I grip my chest and rub my sternum as if that will stop the hurt consuming me right now. "How can you say that? We-we made vows." She looks down again, breaking eye contact with me. "And you're giving up without even trying. That's not what I meant when I *vowed* to love you through good times and bad, Taevin. Jesus, you won't even look at me right now. Why are you really doing this?"

She shoots her gaze up and locks it on mine. "You want me to look at you while I break us? Fine. Take a step back from everything and take off your rose-colored glasses when it comes to me. I was never going to be your forever, Jackson." She shrugs and lets out a halfhearted laugh. "I'm just me, and you're *you*. You're a big, beautiful presence that I'd only be holding back. You're going to be someone's everything someday, and I'm going to be sorry for the rest of my life that it wasn't me."

I think I might actually be dying with how badly my chest hurts.

"Why don't you just shoot me straight, Tae?" I grit out the question.

Her brows wrinkle in confusion. "I am."

"No, you're not. You're acting like you're making this decision on my behalf, but you're not. This is all in your best interest. You're looking over the fence and considering whether or not the grass is greener on the other side. You're moving onto bigger, better things without me. Everything we've talked about, all of our hopes and dreams for the future. You're going to do them, you're just choosing to do them without me at your side." Shaking my head, I let out my own despondent laugh.

"There's really nothing I can do to change your mind? Nothing I can say to stop you from breaking us?" I question, still hopeful she'll change her mind and come rushing back into my arms.

She shakes her head and clears her throat as tears steadily stream down her face. "No. But I think one day you'll look back and realize that I did you a favor. It isn't fair to hold you back from your dreams. Neither of us should have to sacrifice our future for the other," she argues.

Taking a step back, I bring my hands up in exasperation. "See that's where you're wrong. I've never once asked you to sacrifice anything for me. *You* applied to Berklee before I ever mentioned Harvard. *You* chose to hide signing an agent and a record deal from me. And it's *you* who's choosing to give up—to break what we have—without even trying."

Taevin hiccups a gasp, bracing her hands on her stomach.

Dropping my hands to my sides, I look into her eyes. "Oh, and there's one more thing. You're so wrong. Because I'm never getting over you, baby. There will never be another for me."

Letting out a strangled sob, Tae takes off toward my bathroom before I hear her stomach wretching. Running in to join her, I gather her hair in my hand and rub soothing circles on her back as she continues to heave into the toilet.

When her stomach finally settles, she peeks up at me from where her head is resting against her arm. "You'll forever be my greatest loss, Jackson Wilson," she murmurs, completely withdrawn and devoid of emotion.

"I don't have to be," I point out in a tone matching her own.

"It's beyond that. If it were simply up to what I want, this wouldn't be happening," she whispers as her eyes swell with tears. When a stray one escapes, I swipe it away with my thumb.

"I'll never love again. I mean that. So if you ever change your mind, if circumstances change, there's no reality that exists where I wouldn't drop everything to be with you."

She hiccups. "Stop, please. You're making this even harder."

Brushing stray strands of hair behind her ear, I hold the embrace for a moment longer than I should. "Maybe that's the difference between us. Because wherever you go, my love would—*will*—follow. You're just not willing to let me yet, and I'll accept that, for now at least. But make no mistake, Taevin, I will always hold on to what we could be—what I hope our future will be someday, when you're ready."

She shuffles to her feet at that. "I should go."

Don't. Stay. Look at me before you walk away, baby, I silently plead as the love of my life walks out of my life with my bleeding, shattered heart in her hands.

Pain I've never experienced envelopes me, burning me alive as the distance between us grows.

Taevin doesn't look back, not even a glance over her shoulder.

After a sleepless night, I'm delaying my departure to Boston, refusing to leave until I've talked to her in the light of day. Hoping dawn has brought Taevin clarity and she's changed her mind.

I pound and pound on her front door until finally her father answers it. When he opens the door, his face is crestfallen and I can't stomach the words I know are likely going to come out of his mouth.

"Taev isn't here, Jackson. She left for Nashville earlier this morning."

My head rears back as his words sink in. "What do you mean she left?"

Her father runs his fingers through is black hair. "She has a meeting with a record label this afternoon, and no matter how much I tried to talk her out of it, she said she wasn't a minor anymore and she could choose what's best for her. I don't know what's gotten into her."

Clasping my hands together above my head, I look up at the sky and let out a sigh of defeat.

"I'm sorry, son. I figured she'd leave me one day for greener pastures, but I just want you to know I can tell she really loves you."

"Yeah, just not enough, I guess."

Not wanting to break in front of her father, I turn and storm off to my truck, slamming the door shut with frustration before slamming my fist against the steering wheel.

"Fuck!"

I'm still screaming internally hours later as I settle into my new dorm room at Harvard. A milestone I was once excited for is now one I wholeheartedly resent because I know deep in my heart that if it weren't for me being here, I'd still have the woman I love in my arms.

31

Taevin

Now

After living in Nashville for the past decade, I nearly forgot how cold early October days here can get, especially when the weather is dreary like it is today.

Tugging the sleeves of my cardigan down over my hands, I snuggle further under the fuzzy blanket Ryan sent me and try to absorb as much heat from the fireplace beside the chair I'm curled up in as I finish the last few chapters of my book.

My phone vibrates with a message and I unlock it to find I've got a string of messages. Kenna, Dakota, Alexa, and Scarlett added Walker and I to their bookclub, which meant we were also added to their group chat text thread. Not only is the group name funny as hell, but the content shared back and forth is hilarious bordering on slightly unhinged. Like now, for example, as I read through and catch up on my missed texts with them, I can't stop the laughter.

The Smutty Stickhandlers:

Kenna:

Alright, babes. Are we still on for bookclub this week?

Dakota:

Saturday afternoon, right?

Scarlett:

Yes! Gemma and her friend Eva said they'd babysit the kiddos for us again at our place if that works?

Kenna:

That's amazing! Thank you!

Dakota:

I know we're going to talk about the book on Saturday, but I just need to say the angst in this one had me in a chokehold.

Alexa:

Oh my gosh, me too! I read it in the span of one red-eye from CA to NY this week.

Kenna:

OMG, same!

Scarlett:

I'm obsessed. I've only got a few chapters left.

Me:

I'm planning to finish the book today as well!

Alexa:

Tae! How are you feeling?

I smile at Alexa's message, the two of us have become fast friends in the past few weeks. I can't help but feel foolish that I ever felt threatened by her friendship with Jax.

Me:

I'm feeling much better today.

And I am. Today is day four after my second round of chemo, which seems to be when the nausea subsides and I'm mostly just exhausted. The fatigue is unlike anything I've experienced before. But hopefully by the time book club rolls around on Saturday, I'll be feeling even better.

Adjusting the cool capping device on my head, I snuggle deeper into my blanket as I fight off the chill the device causes. The cool capping was recommended to me by the cancer center I'm receiving treatment at, and the nurses told me that it's supposed to help minimize the hair loss from chemotherapy. Just as I move to pick my book back up, my phone buzzes again.

Kenna:

Okay, now I'm jealous and officially craving Chinese food.

Dakota:

Considering the two of us will be having a sleepover with the kids tonight, I'll pick up Chinese on the way over, Kenna.

Kenna:

drooling emoji God, you're the best!

Alexa:

I wish I wasn't away on a work trip so I could join you ladies!

Me:

You'll be back on Saturday for bookclub though, right?

Alexa:

Wouldn't miss it for even an exclusive interview with Brody Meyer!

Dakota:

I'm pretty sure he'd rather get kicked in the face by a steer than do an exclusive interview.

Alexa:

gasp not his beautiful face, anywhere but there!

Kenna:

Tae and Walker, if you didn't already know this, Brody Meyer aka the quarterback for the Voyagers, is also Dakota's older brother, who just so happens to be Alexa's dream interviewee and she most definitely has the hots for him.

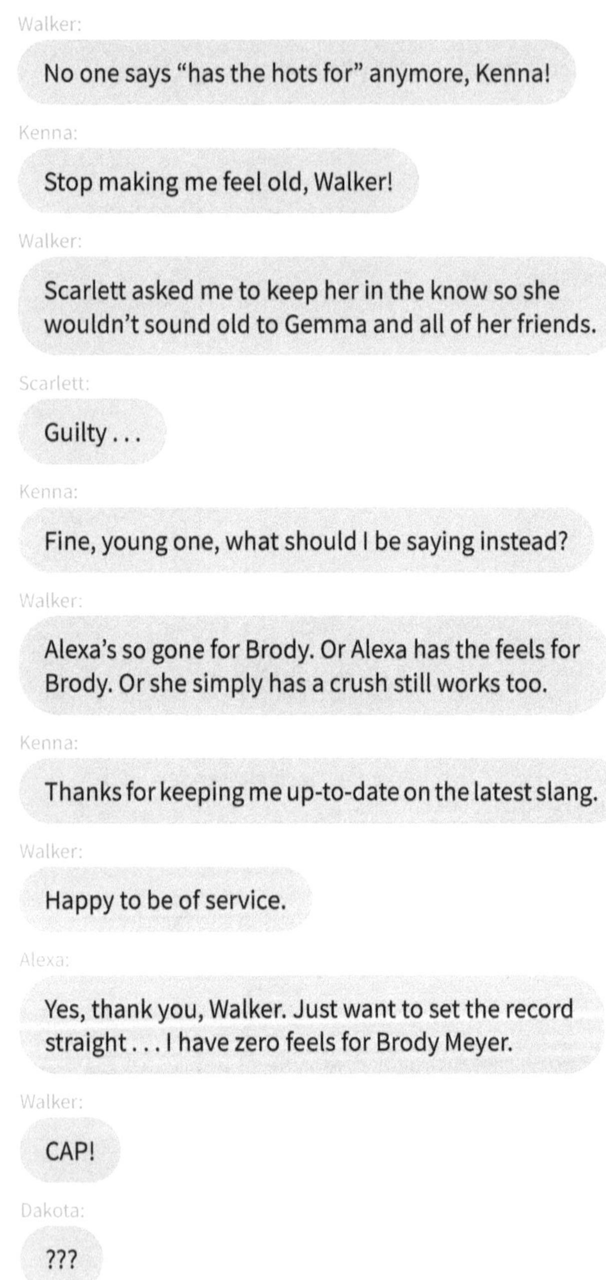

Walker:
No one says "has the hots for" anymore, Kenna!
Kenna:
Stop making me feel old, Walker!
Walker:
Scarlett asked me to keep her in the know so she wouldn't sound old to Gemma and all of her friends.
Scarlett:
Guilty . . .
Kenna:
Fine, young one, what should I be saying instead?
Walker:
Alexa's so gone for Brody. Or Alexa has the feels for Brody. Or she simply has a crush still works too.
Kenna:
Thanks for keeping me up-to-date on the latest slang.
Walker:
Happy to be of service.
Alexa:
Yes, thank you, Walker. Just want to set the record straight . . . I have zero feels for Brody Meyer.
Walker:
CAP!
Dakota:
???

Scarlett:

Oh! I know this one! That means: LIES!

Walker:

You've been paying attention, Scar!

Kenna:

You've been called out, Lex!

Me:

Wait, didn't you do a sideline interview with Brody last Thanksgiving that went viral?

Dakota:

Do you mean the one where my brother basically told her to kick rocks until after the game?

I wince as I think back to the interview.

Me:

Yep, that's the one.

Alexa:

He also told me "you're welcome" the next time he saw me at Dakota and Carson's house.

Me:

Why would you thank him for that?

Alexa:

Because apparently the quarterback's diva tendencies gave the network quite the boost in viewership.

Walker:

Dakota, you should see if he'd come on Lex's podcast!

Alexa:

That's a hard pass.

Dakota:

I don't know . . . it could be kinda fun!

Kenna:

Yeah, all of the building tension between the two of you might come to a boiling point while you're recording the episode!

Scarlett:

10/10 recommend workplace romance trope. Not that I'd know from experience or anything.

Me:

Also 10/10 recommend recording booth spicy time.

Walker:

GROSS.

Scarlett:

Oops, my bad!

Me:

Sorry, not sorry!

Kenna:

Don't be sorry, Tae! You've got a decade of spicy time to make up for!

Walker:

Definitely didn't mean you should be sorry for it. More power to you sisters! But you are doing these recommended actions with my brothers so . . . GROSS.

Me:

Touché. See you tonight, Dubs!

Shaking my head at their antics, I close out of the text thread and it's only then that I realize I have missed texts from Jackson.

Bear:

I miss you already! Does that make me pathetic?

Bear:

Carson just watched me text you that over my shoulder and said I am indeed pathetic. You don't think I'm pathetic, do you baby?

Bear:

Alright, I'm having full blown Tae withdrawals. My playlist keeps shuffling to either songs by you or songs we used to sing together.

Bear:

We just landed! I love you!

Me:

And I love you, my adorably pathetic husband.

Bear:

I love when you call me that.

Me:

Pathetic?

Bear:

Well, no, not that. Your husband.

Me:

I know.

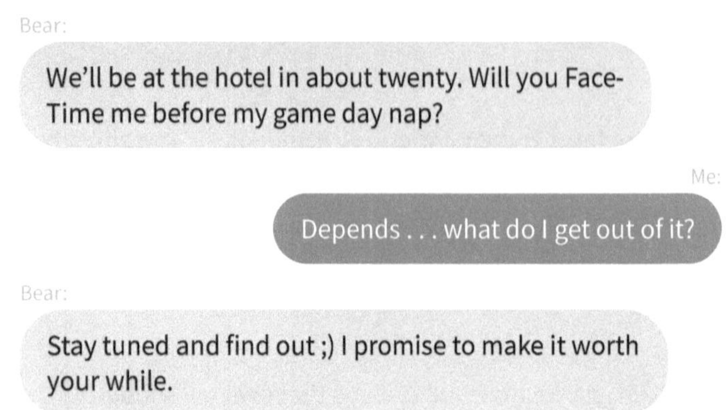

I miss him something fierce and it's only been a matter of hours. I'm officially just as pathetic as Carson said Jax is. But I'm not sure either of us can help it; we're in the nauseatingly, infectiously in love honeymoon stage of our second act.

Over the past few weeks since I started chemo, our bond has strengthened and we've grown closer in ways I'd never imagined. My walls are finally coming down and I'm allowing his help while reminding myself that it's okay to lean on someone I love. Jackson has been my rock through all of this and I honestly don't know what I'd do without him.

Setting down my phone, I pick up my paperback copy of *When I Come Back* by Alise Monroe, our book club pick of the month, and allow myself to get lost within the pages of this second chance love story.

I'm so absorbed in the story I don't realize how much time has passed until I receive a FaceTime call from Jax. Swiping to accept, I give him a shy smile in greeting.

He shoots me a crooked grin when his gaze locks on mine. "Hey, T. We just got settled into our rooms."

Oh, he's settled alright. On the other side of the screen sits a shirtless Jax with his back propped up against a wall of pillows and the headboard of his bed. His broad chest stretches as he curls one arm behind his head.

I could spend hours tracing the lines of his biceps that twitch each time he situates himself to get comfortable.

When he quirks a brow at me, I realize I've been silently ogling him instead of greeting him back. Clearing my throat, I murmur, "Hi. How was the flight?"

"It was good. How's it going holding down the fort by yourself?"

I have to bite my lip from blurting out how much I miss him. Instead, I go with, "Good, though I think we should discuss getting a pet to keep me company while you're on the road."

Jax's eyebrows lift in surprise and he sits forward. "Yeah? What kinda pet are we talking about?"

"I've always wanted a cat."

He chuckles at that. "I know. But I feel like you're the kinda gal who wouldn't stop at just one cat so before you know it you'd turn into the crazy cat lady and we'd have four or five of them."

"You're right. I would so do that. Besides, if memory serves, you're allergic."

"Yup, probably my biggest flaw."

I chuckle at that.

"Is Walker still planning on coming over tonight to watch the game with you?" he asks.

I stretch my arms wide and stifle back a yawn.

"Yeah, she's going to bring Chinese food over for dinner. I haven't really had much of an appetite lately, but I've never been one to turn down a takeout container of chicken fried rice."

"Dubs knows everyone's favorites. She has the uncanny ability to remember the smallest details about everyone."

"She does," I agree, biting my lip in hesitation before I decide to ask him something that's been on my mind lately. "Have you noticed anything different about your sister?"

"What do you mean?"

"I don't know. It just seems like she's . . . lonely. Even when we're hanging out together, I catch her staring off into the distance with this forlorn expression. I can't quite put my finger on it, but I feel like she's been sad ever since she moved here and I wasn't sure if you knew anything."

"I mean, she did decide to abruptly quit her dance career and move home to attend college as a twenty-one-year-old freshman. I'm sure she's having a harder time making new friends and transitioning into a new routine when she's had the same one for nearly four years."

My eyes widen as I process what he's just said. "Wait, she was only seventeen when she moved to LA?"

He nods his head. "Crazy, right? I was so shocked my parents let her move out there on her own while she was still a minor. But she got a once in a lifetime opportunity with a ballet company out there and my mom didn't have the heart to tell her no."

"I'm still having a hard time separating her now as a grown woman from the shy, horse-loving eleven-year-old she was when we started dating."

Jax smiles fondly before tossing himself back on his pillows.

"So, where is everyone? Who's your roommate?"

"Carson is pretty much my permanent roommate by now. Which is good for me because he doesn't snore and he can take a hint—kinda like right now."

"Is that so? What does that mean?" I humor him by asking, though I have a pretty good idea of where he's going with this.

"It means Carse went to Griff's room to play some video games. He picked up on the fact that I was going to call you and wanted a little privacy." His voice is lower now, raspier than it was only moments ago.

"And why would you need privacy?" I ask, standing up and letting the blankets that were covering me fall to the floor as I trek across the cool floors to our bedroom.

I tuck myself beneath the covers just as Jax lets out a pained groan, and I startle from the noise.

"What?" I question, searching the screen for any sign of danger or injury.

"You're wearing my jersey when I'm not there to witness you in it?"

I look down as realization sinks in. I'm wearing his black and lime green Wolverines jersey, and he's right, while it's not the first time I've worn it—quite the opposite, in fact—it is the first time he's seen me wearing his name and number.

Deciding I don't care if he thinks I sound needy, I admit, "I miss you and wearing it made me feel closer to you. Well, that, and I sprayed some of your cologne on this and my pillowcase before you left so they'd smell like you."

"That's honestly one of the cutest things I've ever heard."

I should've known Jax would think my neediness for him would be cute.

"Yeah, except whenever I smell your cologne I get incredibly turned on, which poses a real problem considering you're thousands of miles away right now."

I shift to my side, propping my phone up on an extra pillow and stare at him through my hooded eyes.

Jax smirks at me, making his dimple pop, and I'm suddenly uncomfortably turned on. "I mean, I don't need to be there with you to give you an orgasm, Tae."

"Yeah?"

"Yeah," he rasps.

"And how are you gonna do that?"

"Well, for starters, you're going to take off my jersey and show me those perky tits of yours that have starred in every fantasy I've had since I was eighteen years old."

I do as he says, lifting his jersey above my head before moving my phone to the nightstand and adjusting it so he can get a better view of me. "Now what?" I question, feeling somewhat shy all of a sudden.

"Now you drag the fabric over your nipples to give them just a tease of friction."

Again, I comply, eager to see where he goes with this. When his jersey does exactly as he said it would, I bite my lip until I feel a sting of pain.

"Lie back and continue dragging the fabric lower, over your stomach and stop just before you get to your clit. Do you still have panties on?"

"I wasn't wearing any," I say, feeling breathless from how tightly wound I am already.

"Fuck, T," Jax groans, tilting his chin up to the ceiling.

"Are you touching yourself?" I ask him.

"Yeah, baby, I am."

This is hands down one of the hottest moments of my life. I've never done anything like this—it has me feeling a bit melancholy thinking about all the missed opportunities we had to make each other feel this way when we should've been together instead of apart all those years.

As if he can sense my mood taking a turn, Jax interrupts my intrusive thoughts when he says, "I want you to touch yourself too, Tae. Tweak your nipple but move my jersey lower so it skims just over your clit."

I do as he says and let out a moan of approval.

"You're fucking perfect, you know that?"

My cheeks heat from his compliment. When my eyes connect with his, my stomach pulls taut from having his lust filled gaze locked on me.

His voice is graveled when he says, "Now bunch up my jersey so it's resting just beside you and then hover above it on your knees."

"What?" The shock of what he's asked pulls me from my lust spiral.

"Trust me?" he asks.

"Of course."

"Then do as I say and I promise I'll make you come."

I hesitate a moment before bunching up the fabric and then move to straddle it, hovering just above it like he said to.

"Sit back on your heels but don't let your pussy touch the fabric, not yet." Again, I follow his every word because at this point I'm beyond desperate to come. "Cup your breasts in each hand and knead them just like I do when I want to drive you crazy out of your mind with lust."

"I think you've already accomplished that. I'm desperate at this point. Please tell me how you're going to make me come."

Jax chuckles. "Patience was never one of your virtues. You wanna come, T?"

"Yes," I hiss, annoyed that he called me out for my impatience.

"Lower your hips and rock them against the fabric but don't let go of your breasts. In fact, alternate between kneading one and tweaking your other nipple."

I do exactly what he's requested of me, and I'm so wound up that when I rock my hips over his jersey, my clit throbs from the friction.

"Fuck, baby. Look at you following my every command. God, you look so beautiful I can barely take it." Jax props his phone on the hotel nightstand, giving me the perfect view of his rippling abs and his waist where he's currently working his sweatpants further down his thighs so I can get a full show.

When he wraps his large hand around his rock hard length, I nearly combust right then and there. I'm not sure I've ever been this needy or this turned on in my life.

The combination of seeing him like this, on the brink of losing control, and the reflection of myself in the corner of the screen, looking desperate to come at his command, is something I can't wait to repeat over and over again while he's on the road.

"Keep rocking your hips and pinch your nipples while you do so."

I thought I'd feel self-conscious being on display for him like this, letting him see my scars and all of my flaws, but I couldn't feel more coveted—he's looking at me like I'm the very thing sustaining his life while also being the only person who can bring him to his knees.

"You look so sexy fucking my jersey."

His words wrap around me like a vice, bringing me to the precipice. Lust floods my core as Jax pumps his hand up and down his shaft while his other desperately fists the blanket. I match his pace, working my hips to the same rhythm as him.

"You gonna come for me, Bear?"

"Yes! I'm so close, baby."

"Me too," I moan, my clit pulsating with each pass against the fabric.

"Together?" he grits the question through his clenched teeth.

"Yes!" I scream, throwing my body forward as my muscles lock and I begin to convulse through the first waves of my orgasm.

"Fuck, T!" he groans, and it's the sexiest thing I've ever heard.

I continue to ride out my orgasm, wishing like hell it was Jax beneath me instead of his jersey. Imagining it's his skin against mine and his cologne mixed with the scent of his sweat instead of a spray on his pillow clouding the room.

Fighting to catch my breath, I begin to come down from the high only he can give me when he makes me come. Even from thousands of miles away, through a phone, he commands my body in the way only he's ever been able to.

"I thought I wasn't superstitious, but I think that may need to be my new pregame routine for road games," he pants, letting out a sigh of contentment.

"Consider it done. We've got years' worth of road games to make up for."

"Lucky for us, I don't plan on retiring anytime soon, my love," he retorts, instantly putting me at ease.

Throwing myself facedown on our bed, I blindly reach for my phone. Grasping it, I turn my head slightly, only peeking at him with one eye. "You better go score me a goal, Jaxy."

"Only one? Easy."

"And an apple."

"You're so fucking cute when you use hockey slang. One goal and an assist coming right up."

"If you manage to pull it off, then I'll be waiting in our bed in only your jersey when you get home," I tell him.

"No need to give me additional motivation, but I'll take it. I'm pretty sure I'll never get the image of you fucking my jersey outta my head, but I've always fantasized what it'd look like taking you from behind while my name and number are splayed across your back." He looks pained as he squeezes his eyes shut. "Shit, now I'm going to have to take my pregame nap with a boner."

"I think I'll join you for that pregame nap. I'll need all the rest I can get before Walker gets here."

"Okay, get some sleep. Have fun with Dubs tonight. I love you."

"I love you too. Good luck tonight."

"Thanks, baby."

I blow him a kiss before he smacks a kiss on his screen and accidentally hangs up with his lips. Chuckling, I roll out of bed to use the restroom and wash up.

Pulling on a pair of my comfiest sweatpants, I sift through my hangers and settle on the limited edition retro Wolverines jersey with number twelve on the back. Then, I make my way back to the bed and snuggle up to Jax's pillow, imagining it's him I've got nestled beside me as I drift into a peaceful sleep.

I've just completed building a nest of blankets and pillows on the sofa in the living room when Kyle calls me. Accepting the call, I put him on speaker so I can finish setting things up for when Walker gets here any minute.

"Hey, Kyle."

"Oh, so you do know how to answer your phone. Good, I was getting worried that maybe you'd lost it," he says in greeting.

"Clearly not lost. What's up?"

That question apparently earns me a scoff. "What's *up* is that my biggest artist isn't creating anything at the moment except for speculation and negative media buzz."

"Kyle," I say his name in warning. "You are one of only a handful of people aside from the label who knows why I am not creating anything right now."

He hums dismissively. "Look, you're the one who gallivanted back to Minnesota to live with your estranged husband. And you've even got a studio inside his house. You'd think that would inspire you to at least write and record some things while you're taking your time off."

I fluff—more like karate punch—the pillow in front of me to get some of my frustration out. "I'm going to cut you off right there. Are you missing the point of why I'm taking time off right now? I have cancer,

Kyle. And you already know that. Forgive me if I can barely function through the nausea and exhaustion, let alone try to create anything worth recording while I've got extreme brain fog."

He lets out a deep sigh on the other end of the phone. "You're right. I'm sorry. It's just been really difficult to dodge every news outlet's questions on your whereabouts and why you've taken time away when you're supposed to be recording your album. The timing thankfully worked out to where the label hadn't announced and scheduled the tour you were supposed to have next summer."

"So what's this really about?" I question him, grabbing my phone and doing my best not to stomp into the kitchen to finish prepping the snacks.

"I need you to make an appearance. Well, actually, I need you to perform for the Country Gives Back Concert happening in Nashville the week before Thanksgiving."

I scoff, because is he for real right now? "I'm not traveling to Nashville while I'm in the middle of treatments."

"The label was adamant that their artists be among the performers."

Even though he can't see me, I throw my hands up in frustration. "I believe I am exempt from that list during my leave."

"Unfortunately not when it comes to this performance. Can't your medical team in Minnesota connect with the one you had here in Nashville if there's anything that comes up?"

What the fuck is his deal?

"Why are you acting this way?" I ask, hurt and confusion lacing my tone.

"What way is that?"

"So pushy and persistent? I don't get it."

"It's not like you had a baby and you're on maternity leave or anything that the label has listed in your contract."

I rear back as if I've been hit. Is he serious right now?

"That was below the belt," I choke out, fighting back tears.

Kyle sighs again. "This is why I hate communicating over the phone. You know we communicate best in person. Things have a way of getting misunderstood like this."

"Maybe you'd have an argument if we were texting. But you said that and now you can't take it back."

"What I meant was the label would be more understanding if you were taking a maternity leave to heal and bond with a baby, but unfortunately your current circumstances are different."

"Yeah, because instead of healing from giving birth, I'm healing from a hysterectomy and receiving chemotherapy. And instead of taking care of a baby, I'm taking care of myself. How could you even ask me to perform during this time? And by November, I might look even more unrecognizable than I already do," I point out, my voice quivering with a mix of hurt and anger.

"Even more reason to get a performance in so your fans don't think the worst."

My hands are shaking so badly I have to grip onto the counter to steady myself. "I'm not sure why you're not hearing what I'm saying . . . I don't give a fuck what my fans or the label, or anyone else thinks for that matter. I am fighting for my *life*, Kyle. I thought you of all people would understand that."

He sighs on the other end. "I know *you*. And that is why I *know* you don't want all of the little girls who've looked up to you for years now to be disappointed in you thinking you're hiding out in some rehab center in the Bahamas. Do the performance, give back to the community who gave you your career, and then you can get back on a private jet to Minnesota in no time."

I don't respond at first. I'm honestly too pissed off to find words right now. He's right, he does know me far too well, which is how he knew just the right thing to say to manipulate me into doing the performance.

"When did you say the concert was again?"

"Saturday, November 18th. It's the weekend before Thanksgiving."

I keep him on speaker so I can scroll through my calendar app, and that's when I notice Jackson will be on an away trip. He actually has a game in Nashville that Friday before they head home for a home game on Monday. Maybe he could try to get out of traveling home with the team and stay an extra night with me. It's a long shot, but it's worth the ask. I'm just about to add the concert to my calendar when I realize the timing of events.

"I've got a round of chemo that Tuesday. So far I haven't been feeling well for the four to five days following treatments. There's a very real possibility I will be too tired or sick to perform, but as of right now you can tell the label I'll do it. One song. I refuse to do anything more. And it'll be a song of my choosing. I want full creative control if I'm going to agree to this."

I can hear the smugness seeping through the line when Kyle says, "I can work with that. I'll give them a call now. See, I knew you'd come around. Next time don't make me have to work so hard for it." He chuckles as if what he's said is funny, but like most things when it comes to Kyle lately, I get this funny feeling deep in the pit of my gut.

"Right. Well I'll let you get to it."

Before I can hang up, he pleads with me. "You know I'm just looking out for your best interests, right?"

I bite back the snarky retort he's rightfully earned himself tonight and instead say, "Sure. Bye, Kyle."

I don't give him a chance to say his goodbyes before I end the call. Something feels off, and if I'm being honest with myself, it has for awhile now. I can't quite put my finger on it, but I'm also too exhausted to try to contemplate it much farther right now.

Lying down on the glorious bed of blankets, I let out a deep sigh and debate whether or not to take another cat nap before Walker gets here. With all the unease that has slithered up my spine, this little bestie date night really could not have come at a better time.

Breaking News

Celebrity birthdays – Taevin Gray October 12th

Taevin Gray is twenty-nine, divine, and thriving . . . or is she?

By LARA BRADLEY

Taevin Gray hasn't been spotted in Nashville in months, so where in the world is she?

The country music star turns 29 today, and is rumored to have checked back into an exclusive rehabilitation facility somewhere in the Dominican Republic for substance abuse.

No one has seen the country music star since her August performance at The Summer Stampede in Texas.

While we'd love to wish her a happy birthday, we haven't seen her near Broadway Street in quite some time.

So if not rehab, then where in the world is she?

Country Know Now has reached out to Gray's reps for comment, but have not yet heard back.

To stay up to date on all the latest country celebrity news, subscribe below.

32

Jackson

Now

Settling back into the bed beside Taevin, I pull the covers over me and slide my arm around her waist.

The late morning sunlight filters through a crack in the curtains and I'm paralyzed by my captivation for my sleeping wife. And it's not even because she's the most gorgeous woman to have ever walked the planet. Beyond her looks and god-given talent, she's a genuinely good person who is beautiful inside and out.

I've been doing my research, trying to get caught up in all things Tae since we'd parted ways. She amazes me with everything she's managed to build—she's more than just a singer and songwriter. In only ten years in the industry, she's become a household name and crossed several genres with her music.

A few weeks ago, we were in the studio and she was showing me how to use some of the equipment so we could mess around with testing out the sound quality. Getting to watch Tae in her element was unlike anything I've ever seen before. She's become a far better guitar player than I ever was, in fact she showed me a thing or two, which turned me on far more than it should've. There's just something so innately sexy watching her come alive behind a piano or with a guitar in her hands.

Beyond her talent, I'm amazed at how much she's flourished in our time apart despite living under the spotlight and now knowing the loss she was healing from. You never know how people will manage having that much fame and fortune—some people let it get to their heads and they think they're *holier than thou*. Not Taevin. Not only has she started a foundation to provide financial assistance to young women battling cancer like her mother did, and now she has the same fate, but she also sponsors several college scholarships for teens who've lost a parent to cancer. Beyond that, she is generous to her team, band, producers, and fans.

Pride like I've never felt swells in my chest, and the fact that I get to call this enigmatic woman mine is beyond comprehension. It's not lost on me that I'm the most fortunate man alive.

Today is Tae's birthday and I'd give anything to be able to spend the entire day with her uninterrupted, but unfortunately I have practice this afternoon. Thankfully the girls planned their bookclub meet-up during the same time, so I don't feel quite as guilty leaving her.

I've just put the finishing touches on a surprise set up in the kitchen with a few decorations, her gifts, and a small breakfast spread for the two of us. But knowing how tired she's been, I don't want to wake her up. Instead, I hold her close and preoccupy myself with counting the number of breaths she takes and studying the details of her tattoos.

I'm so absorbed in memorizing each line etched across her skin, I don't notice her stir awake at first.

She rolls onto her back and smiles up at me. Pitched up onto my one elbow, I cup her face and bring her in for a slow kiss that starts out innocent but turns carnal pretty quickly.

I break the kiss, getting lost in her coffee-colored eyes. "Happy twenty-ninth birthday, baby."

A radiant smile eclipses her face. "Thank you!"

"This is the first birthday of yours I get to spend with you. Isn't that crazy?"

"It is. Especially because I remember your birthday we spent together like it was yesterday."

"Is that so? If I remember correctly, I believe it began a little something like this," I muse, tugging her waist to bring her closer. Chest to chest, we kiss again. I'm not sure anything beats a lazy morning makeout session with the person you love. Our tongues swirl sensually until we're both panting for air and I'm thoroughly worked up.

"I made breakfast. Do you want to eat in bed or in the kitchen?" I ask breathlessly.

"Mmm. What do you prefer?" she asks, her eyes hazy with lust.

I smile down at her and bite town on my bottom lip to stop myself from kissing her again before she's eaten her birthday breakfast. "Doesn't matter. It's your birthday, love."

Tucking a stray piece of her hair behind her ear, every muscle in my body locks in place when I pull my hand back and see several strands of Taevin's raven hair tangled between my fingers.

Her brows pinch in confusion. "What is it?"

I make a fist and do my best to hide the evidence before she can see it but I'm unfortunately not quick enough because Tae catches sight of them out of the corner of her eye. She startles and shoots out of bed to flee into the bathroom, and that's when I see her white pillowcase littered with several long, black locks.

Flying out of bed, I hurry after her but stop dead in my tracks when I find her sitting on her vanity bench in our bathroom with her head in her hands as muffled sobs wrack her body. Inching closer, I see another clump of her hair on the vanity table in front of her.

Without hesitation, I straddle the little space left of the bench seat and pull her into my lap, running my hands up and down her spine to try to comfort her.

Ideas of what to say race through my brain, but I can't seem to land on anything worth saying to her when she breaks the silence. "I knew this was more than just a possibility. I mean, I've noticed increased hair loss for the past week or so just when showering or brushing my hair. But I still held out hope that maybe the cool capping would prolong it."

I bury my head in her neck and breathe her in, attempting to not only comfort her but also calm my racing heart. "I'm so sorry, T."

"It's not even so much that I'm losing my hair as it is the fact that cancer has stolen so much from me already." Her voice breaks and my chest cracks right down the center at the despair evident in what she's just said. I wish for nothing more than to make this better—to be able to turn back the clock and eradicate the very first cancer cell in her body before it ever started multiplying.

"I already look in the mirror and hardly recognize my reflection," she adds.

Tae has lost a lot of weight from the treatments combined with her nausea and lack of appetite. I've found myself up late at night staring at the ceiling as I hold her withering body in my arms, questioning why this is happening. Why her? Why now when she's so young? Why curse her with the same fate her mother had? I then find myself feeling immense guilt and anxiously wondering if my dwindling faith has made God mad and this is my punishment for my sins.

I rub my hands up and down her back in an attempt to soothe her. "You're the most beautiful person I've ever met—inside and out. Right now, nothing and no one else matters outside of you getting better. I can't imagine how hard this is for you, but as far as the fans are concerned or the label, their opinions don't matter in the grand scheme of things."

Tae pulls back just enough to wipe the tears from her cheeks. "Yeah, you're right. I think Kyle just got in my head even more when he demanded I do that performance next month."

"Wait, what?" I question, taken off guard by what she just said.

Tae starts to wring her hands together so I clasp them in mine and rub my thumbs along the backs of her knuckles. She searches my eyes, for what, I'm not sure. I give her a nod of encouragement, hoping it'll help spur her on.

"Kyle called me right before Walker came over to watch your game the other day. He said the label was demanding I be a part of their Country Gives Back Concert happening in Nashville the week before Thanksgiving. Apparently almost all of the other big country artists from the label are performing."

I bite my cheek to stop myself from telling her what I've come to think of Kyle after spending more time together and hearing more and more stories of what he's said over the past several months. The guy seems like a manipulative, controlling asshole. Shocking to no one, I don't like him at all.

Instead of telling her how I really feel, I roll my lips together as I mull over how to react to this. "How many songs do they expect you to perform?"

She bites her lip in contemplation. "I told Kyle I'd only perform one song of my choosing."

My brows pinch in confusion. "This concert is such a big deal that they'd have you fly to Nashville while receiving cancer treatments just for one song?"

"Apparently so. The label is one of the main sponsors who has helped put this concert together, and my participation is strongly advised."

"When is the concert?"

"It's actually the day after your game in Nashville. Saturday, November 18th. Do you think maybe you could ask Scar if you could stay back instead of flying with the team to MN?"

I take a moment to think of logistics then let out a curse when I realize that Saturday is when Scar had planned for our team to have our mom's weekend where the players bring their moms on an away trip.

"Shit, I'll double check with Scar, but I'm pretty sure that's the mom's trip. I believe we'll still be in Nashville, but the itinerary has us scheduled for dinner and then a concert at the Grand Ole Opry."

"I love the Opry," Tae sighs wistfully, a brief reprieve from the anxiety that comes roaring back. Her face crumbles, her bottom lip quivering. "What if I'm completely unrecognizable by then?"

I kiss her forehead again. "Have you considered sharing your story? Telling your fans about your diagnosis? It might alleviate some of your anxiety around keeping it a secret."

"I've mulled it over hundreds of times—questioning whether keeping it under wraps is the right thing to do. I just don't want the pitying looks everywhere I go."

My brows pinch. "Is that how you feel about me and our friends here?"

She shakes her head. "No. I swear I don't. But I've learned to be okay with being vulnerable around you, and your friends have made me feel so welcomed and loved, I wouldn't imagine keeping my diagnosis a secret from them. They're not only here for me, but most importantly, they're your biggest support system. I know I'm not the only one affected by all this."

Wrapping my arms tighter around her, I wish my love could heal her right here and now. "Don't worry about me, baby."

"I do. I always will. But because of your friends and family, and the love they've consistently shown us both, I know I don't have to worry about you as much." Tears fill her eyes, and the quivering of her chin just about kills me.

"You keep calling them my friends and family, but they're ours. In fact, I'm starting to feel like they love you more than me. And I'm oddly okay with it because who wouldn't love you? You're perfect."

She scoffs. "I'm far from perfect. *Our* friends are though."

"That's my girl." I place a chaste kiss on her cheek. "Come to the kitchen with me, I've got a little birthday surprise for you."

"Okay. Give me a minute?" she asks, and I reluctantly let her go.

"Yeah, of course. I'll be out in the kitchen when you're ready," I tell her as I make my way out of the bathroom. Shutting the door behind me, I make quick work of gathering the stray stands from her pillowcase, wishing I could erase not only this memory but this next phase of her battle.

My girl is strong and fierce—I just wish she didn't have to be at times like these.

Minutes later, after I've rearranged her presents for the third time, Taevin comes to a stop as she rounds the corner into the kitchen.

"What's all this?"

Pointing to the gift bags on the counter, I tell her, "I've got a decade's worth of birthdays to make up for."

Tae's eyes widen. "Jax," she breathes, a hint of shock in her tone.

Erasing the distance between us, I wrap my arms around her waist and tug her into my chest, placing a whisper of a kiss on her forehead. "Happy birthday, T. I'm so bummed I can't get out of practice today, but I've made it my mission to be sure you still have the best day. Starting with breakfast and presents."

I spin her around so she's facing the kitchen island that's littered with heart-shaped pancakes, berries and toppings, and eight gift bags of various sizes.

Tae's hands come around mine, squeezing them as she wraps my arms around her tighter. "You didn't have to do all of this. I told you I'm sort of weird about my birthday."

"Pretty sure that's the Libra in you, baby. Which is why it's a good thing you're married to a Cancer—we balance each other out perfectly." Walking her closer to the presents, I point to the largest gift wrapped in black wrapping paper. "Okay, open this one first," I tell her.

She listens, wasting no time ripping into the paper and revealing a box with a mobile puzzle table. Lately, Tae's become obsessed with doing puzzles while she recovers from her chemo treatments.

"I thought this way you could do puzzles in any room in the house, so that way if you're not feeling the best, I can just carry this into the bedroom or living room," I explain before pointing to a black gift bag. "Open this one next."

"It's perfect. Thank you!" Tossing the black tissue paper aside, Tae pulls out a black wooden box with a black and white photo I took from backstage of her performing at The Summer Stampede.

"What's this?" she asks on a gasp.

With one arm around her waist, I bring the other on top of hers, helping her slide the top of the box to the side to reveal puzzle pieces. "I snuck this picture of you, knowing I needed to capture that memory forever. Then, when you took a liking to puzzles, I found a company that makes custom puzzles and had them make a thousand piece puzzle out of it."

"It looks like it'll be a tough one," she points out, an electric smile on her face, assuring me she's up for the challenge.

"I'm sure you'll get it done in no time. You've been flying through all of them no problem."

Turning to face me, she wraps her arms around my neck and brings me in for a kiss. Once she pulls away, she whispers, "This was so thoughtful. Thank you, thank you, thank you." She punctuates each expression of gratitude with a kiss on my cheek.

"You're welcome. But you're not done yet. Here, take a seat and I'll get you a plate of food while you open the next one," I suggest, pulling out a barstool for her as I set another present in front of her.

This one is just a basket filled with her favorite bath salts, bubbles, oils, a new rose-scented candle, and a book of black-stemmed matches.

Filling up her plate with pancakes, bacon I stored away in the oven to keep warm, and fruit, I set the plate in front of her before grabbing us each a cup of coffee.

As I set the mug in front of her, she picks it up and laughs. "I'm so sexy even life gets hard?" she questions, reading the white lettering out loud before turning the black mug toward me.

"Saw it and thought of you," I muse, smiling as I take a sip of my coffee.

Her smile only grows. "That's actually perfect."

Taking the seat beside her, I hand her another gift bag. "Here, open this one. I had it specially made."

Tae pulls out a lime green Wolverines jersey with my number on the back, but above the number reads MRS. WILSON. Waggling my eyebrows I tell her, "Thought after the last road trip you might need a new one."

She chuckles, shaking her head. "You just want to have me wear this while you take me from behind so you can admire the title across my back."

"Am I that obvious?"

"Very. But I love it nonetheless." She hugs the jersey to her chest and leans in to kiss me.

"Good." I reach for the last two presents on the table, handing her the larger of the two first.

"Jax. This is seriously too much."

"Nonsense. A present for each year we were apart, though two of them will have to wait until later."

"You're spoiling me rotten."

"And I've never met someone more deserving. Now open this one before I lose my nerve over it." Truth is, I'm nervous as hell for her to open this one. Vulnerability floods my system as she carefully opens the paper, exposing a leatherbound notebook filled with lyrics and sonnets I've written for her since we first started dating at eighteen.

"Some pages are filled with song lyrics, some with notes to you, or texts I wish I could've sent during our time apart," I explain to her, pointing to each entry she flips through that's dated throughout the past almost-eleven years.

Taevin closes the book just as tears drip from her cheeks and land on the front cover.

"This is the most precious gift I've ever been given. You still wrote all this time?"

I nod, rubbing the back of my neck, hesitating how much I want to admit. "There were times I couldn't bear to write anything, and then there were others where I'd fill up multiple pages in a matter of hours. Since you moved in, I finally got to the last page of this notebook and started on a new one."

She closes her eyes as her chin quivers. "I can't wait to read every word."

"Maybe one day we could record one of the songs together just for us," I suggest.

Taevin opens her eyes and turns to me. "And then can we have recording booth sexy time again?"

I nod before pulling her into my lap. "Literally anytime you want," I tell her and then kiss her senseless.

I get so lost in the kiss, I almost forget the last present she needs to open. Pulling back, I grab the small box from behind her and place it in her hands.

"What's this?" she asks, opening the box. "Oh my gosh, I loved this picture." Tae holds up a keychain with a photobooth picture of the two of us from the fair when she first performed and the words "drive safe, I love you" beneath the photo.

"I think you're gonna love what the key attached to the chain is for more." Standing from my barstool, I grab hold of her around her waist and carry her out the front door where a matte black Mercedes G-Wagon sits in the driveway with a large red bow.

"Jackson! No! You did not need to get me a vehicle!" she squeals, while contradicting her words as she leaps out of my arms and runs to the front of the SUV and lays her arms on the hood like she's giving it a big hug.

"I couldn't help it. I wanted you to have something safe to drive in the snow, and the dealership was just taking this beauty off the semi truck. Couldn't let her go home to someone else."

"Can I name her?" she asks, clapping her hands together in excitement.

Nodding my head, I chuckle at her reaction. "You must."

"Gigi," she responds without hesitation.

"Do you wanna take Gigi for a spin?" I ask her, taking the actual key fob out of my sweatpants pocket and tossing it to her.

"Oh my gosh, yes! Let me get some clothes and shoes on and we'll go." She rushes past me into the house, a giddy squeal leaving her as she does the most adorable dance-celebration I've ever seen.

I'm praying some of the excitement from the gifts, along with the surprise I still have in store for her, will distract her from the emotional morning she's already had. My girl deserves to have the best birthday possible, and I'm making it my mission to give it to her.

Minutes later, I'm rounding the vehicle to the passenger side, when I turn and tell her, "I just realized this will be the first time I ride in a car with you driving since you've had your license."

She guffaws, pausing outside the driver side. "You sat in the passenger seat plenty of times while giving me lessons."

A cocky smirk spreads across my face. "Yeah, but you weren't a licensed driver at the time." I get in while she does the same, both of us fastening our seat belts before I place my hand on her thigh and give it a gentle squeeze. "I promise I'll be on my best passenger princess behavior."

Tae presses down on the ignition and runs her hands over the steering wheel enthusiastically. "You might want to keep your hands to yourself if you don't want me to crash. I need to focus. I'm not sure if I told you this or not yet, but when I was in Nashville, I didn't drive much, if ever."

As she puts Gigi in drive and begins down the gravel driveway, I take my hand off her thigh and turn to face her. "Are you sure you're still up to having the girls over here for bookclub? I'm sure they wouldn't mind at all if you wanted to move it back to Scar and Benny's house."

Tae looks both ways before turning out of the driveway. "No, it's fine. The kids will all be at Scar's house with Gemma and her friend." She pauses, chancing a quick glance at me with a sexy little smirk spread across her lips. "I think considering the books we read aren't exactly kid-friendly, we should probably keep it at our place."

"Have I ever told you how much I love that you read smut?" I ask, waggling my brows to try to get a laugh out of her. It seems to do the trick, thank god, because I don't think I could leave her for practice without seeing her smile and hearing her laughter at least a few more times.

"Only about every time you benefit from me reading a spicy scene," she quips.

Looking at the time on her vehicle's display, I toss my head back against the headrest and grumble, "As much as I'd love to stay with you all day, I unfortunately need to get to practice. We'd better head back."

"No problem," Tae says, turning on her blinker before she whips the car around in the direction we'd come.

She's silent for a few minutes, seemingly lost in thought as she bites her bottom lip. Once she parks, she looks over and gives me a soft smile. "Thank you for making this the best birthday morning. Despite the emotional start, it really has been better than all of the past ten birthdays combined."

Hope flares in my chest that her words are sincere and I can try to erase some of the pain she felt earlier today. I know that's not likely—that I can't just eradicate the fact that she's losing her hair—but it doesn't stop me from wishing it all the same.

I smile back at her. "I haven't even given you the surprise I'm most excited about yet," I admit.

Tae leans over the center console and brings me in for a kiss that's over far too soon. "I love you. Have a good practice and then get your sweet ass home so I can thank you in kind for all of the birthday love you've showered upon me."

Regret and guilt churn in my stomach, making a destructive concoction that has me itching to call Coach to tell him I won't be at practice today. Even knowing I can't afford to do that on one of her "good" days, I still consider calling Scarlett to see if she'd make an exception considering the circumstances.

Minutes later, it takes everything in me to pull out of the garage and make my way to the practice facility.

I thumb a beat on my steering wheel even though there's no music playing. Narrowing my eyes at the road deep in thought, I consider my options a moment before pressing call on my sister's contact.

"Hellooo," Walker's voice rings out through my car's speakers.

"Dubs?" I say in greeting.

"What's up, Jax?"

"Can you do something for me?"

"Depends."

"Sorry, can you do something for Tae?" I amend my previous questions.

"Absolutely. What does she need?"

"Real nice . . . If I weren't so desperate for your help I'd probably point out the fact that you're a little shit sometimes."

"Ah, but you see, you just said that out loud. You're lucky I love your wife so much, or I wouldn't even consider helping you with how you treat me sometimes."

"Right. Anyway, as you know, it's Tae's birthday today, and I was wondering if you'd be able to help me make it a great day for her."

"Obviously I'd do anything to help make her day special. What'd you have in mind?"

"I need your help picking up her last two birthday presents. I got her ten gifts, one for each year we were apart, but I've only given her eight so far."

"Oh my gosh! That's so cute!" Walker squeals. "Who knew I had two big brothers who were such simps? The apple fell the farthest it could from the tree."

Fuck yeah it did.

"Listen. One of the presents is just picking up her favorite cake from the bakery that'll be on your way to my house when you come over for book club. The other one will be a little trickier for you to hide until I get home from practice."

"How tricky are we talking?"

"A puppy."

"What?!"

"Well, more of an adolescent dog. It's a rescue and he's about six months old."

"Shut up. Are you for real right now?"

Instead of answering her squeals of shock, I continue on. "He's so fucking cute. Tae said she wanted a cat for a pet while I was gone, so I went to the rescue center looking to see if they had any hypoallergenic ones, but they didn't. As I was walking out, the cutest corgi was playing in a pen out front. The little guy just stole my heart."

"Oh, it's a he? What's his name?" Walker asks.

"Connor the Corgi. I mean, that's what his name was at the center. If Tae wants to change it, I'm up for whatever she wants."

"Stop! That's so freaking perfect. How exactly do you expect me to keep my nephew a secret from her?"

"Right. Okay, so I coordinated with the owner of the center to have him dropped off at my condo in the city at noon. Think you could swing by there and then put him in the detached garage until I get home? I have the heat on and I set up a kennel in there with some food and water and toys. Hopefully by the time I get home, he'll only have to be out there for two hours."

"Jax, she's gonna lose her mind."

"Here's hoping she loves the little guy as much as I already do."

"She will. I'm sure of it."

After I give her the details on how to get into my condo, I hang up and mull over whether or not I should just let Walker move in there now that she's back in Minnesota. I'm still upset she gave up her dreams of dancing professionally to go back to school. Bennett on the other hand is ecstatic she's choosing an education over living by herself in California. I guess I liked the idea of her being away from our father's overbearing toxicity so she could focus on her passions and dreams free from his influence. But after she assured me that going to college to get a degree was the right move for her, I had to put my own insecurities and hopes for her aside to support her.

And one of the best ways I could do that is provide her a place to live so she doesn't need to stay under our father's roof. I make a mental note to discuss it further with Taevin tomorrow to see what she thinks. The condo is close to Abbott University, which is where Walker is now attending classes. This could be my way of still offering her a place of independence and reprieve without being too overbearing. Besides, it's not like my whipped ass will be needing it anymore.

33

Taevin

Now

The door to the house from the garage opens and slams shut. "Happy birthday, you sexy little thing!" is shouted from the mudroom before a blur of curly blonde hair comes around the corner.

"So, I'm not sure how to ask this of you, but I need you to do me a favor," I blurt the moment I see Walker.

She sets down the oversized white box she's carrying on the kitchen island. "Okay . . . what kind of favor?"

I take a deep breath to try to gain the courage to ask her this. "I need you to shave my head." My hand shoots up to cover my mouth like even I'm unable to believe I've just come right out and asked that of her.

Closing my eyes, I try to quell the tears welling in my eyes. "My hair has been falling out slowly—little bits here and there—but this morning when I woke up, there were large clumps of my black hair on my pillowcase." I pause, squeezing my eyes shut like that'll help erase the image from this morning. "And now, no matter what I do, I can't seem to unsee it, or the look on your brother's face when he discovered it."

I'm not sure I'll ever be able to get the look of Jackson's eyes widening in concern out of my mind. Another moment that could've been beautiful was stolen from us and tainted because of my cancer.

I try to compose myself as my chin quivers and my eyes sting with tears. "I just need it gone. Today. And I was wondering if maybe you, and the girls if they're comfortable, could help me with that? I've never really had a group of friends who supported me, especially not to the extent that you all have since I was diagnosed. And I figured if there was anyone I'd want to do this for me—to see me at my most vulnerable—it'd be you all."

I stop my ramblings and fidget with my hands as I await her response.

Walker stares back at me wide-eyed for a moment before she blinks out of it and clears her throat. "Of course I'll do it, T. I would never want you to go through that alone. Do you want to wait until Jax gets back?"

A lone tear slides down my cheek and I quickly wipe it away. Shaking my head, I fidget and look down at my hands. "No. I've thought about this quite a bit today since he left earlier for practice. I think maybe I'd like each of you to take a turn cutting some locks with the buzzer. That way, maybe I won't feel so alone? I don't know." I shrug my shoulders, shifting my weight from side to side. "But what I do know is I'd like to do it before Jackson gets home. He's already had to be my rock and hold me through every hard moment I've gone through in the last four months. I want to do this with my newfound friends by my side."

Walker closes the distance between us and wraps me in her arms. The moment my cheek connects with her fuzzy knit sweater, I lose all semblance of control. She rocks me in her arms as she whispers, "It's all going to be okay. I'm right here—I'll always be here for you Tae."

And suddenly I'm filled with bone-deep guilt as her words settle over me. She was just a kid when I left Jackson and moved to Nashville, but Walker and I had a connection that was the closest thing I've ever had to a sister. I believe wholeheartedly that she'll always be here for me; I just wish I could've done the same for her over the past decade.

I missed so many of her milestones, her successes, her highest highs and lowest lows, times when she could've used a sister to lean on all because I feared her father would ruin her brother's future as well as my own.

From what Jackson has shared with me, Walker hasn't had it easy the last five years. Her life may have looked picturesque on social media—living in LA by herself at seventeen as a professional dancer and model—but appearances can be deceiving.

"I missed you so much, Walker. I'm so sorry I wasn't here," I croak, stepping out of her arms to wipe my cheeks with the sleeves of my sweater.

"Shh," she hushes me, rubbing a hand up and down my arm. "None of that. I missed you too, but you're here now, and that's all that matters."

Our moment of regretful reminiscence is interrupted when McKenna, Dakota, Alexa, and Scarlett walk in the front door and hang up their jackets and purses.

"It's too damn cold for mid-October!" Alexa complains, shimmying her shoulders in a shiver. "Oh, thank fuck. You've got a fire going!"

"Hey y'all!" Dakota greets us, setting down a large bowl and two bags of tortilla chips.

"Hey!" Walker tells her, stepping forward to give them each hugs before they step to me and pull me in for a hug.

Aside from Ryan, I haven't had a lot of female friendships—or any other friendships for that matter. Over the years, I've been burned quite a bit by people who pretended to be my friend but ultimately weren't genuine. I quickly learned that fame and fortune aren't all that it's cracked up to be when it comes to making authentic, lasting relationships. However, this group is different. I knew that from the moment I met them. Hell, before that if I'm being honest with the way Jax talked about them.

"Hope y'all are hungry, I made a double batch of my mama's cowboy caviar recipe," Dakota tells us, opening the lid to the tupperware bowl.

My mouth waters, and for the first time in too many weeks, something actually sounds appealing enough to risk the nausea that's plagued me.

Walker opens a bag of chips and brings a heaping scoop to her mouth.

"Mmm," she moans in delight. "This is so good. I need the recipe," she demands, bringing her hand up to cover her mouth.

"I'll send it in the group chat when I get home. It's pretty straightforward but my mama adds just a touch of honey to offset the acidity of the lime and vinegar," Dakota explains.

Walker snaps her fingers and points to Dakota. "That's totally it. This is by far the best I've had."

"Let's grab something to eat, and then I want to ask a favor of you ladies before we get caught up in our book discussions," I tell them, setting a stack of rattling plates on the kitchen island. I shake my hands in an attempt to rid them of the trembling.

Kenna doesn't miss a beat, closing the space between us when she takes me in. "Are you okay? You're shaking. Do you need to sit down?"

I sigh, sick of the constant frustration I feel toward my body at all times. "I'm fine. Just a little rattled." Mulling over how I want to ask them, I shift my weight from side to side as nerves take over before finally taking a deep breath and looking each of them over. "I have a favor to ask, and if you're not comfortable, I totally get it."

"Anything," Scarlett says without hesitation.

"Yeah," both Dakota and Alexa agree.

"Whatever you need," Kenna adds, rubbing her hand up and down my arm.

My knee-jerk reaction is to wince at their willingness. If I'm being honest, I'm not used to people unknowingly agreeing to do something for me without there being something beneficial in it for them.

"You might not be so agreeable when you realize what I'm asking of you."

"They'll be on board," Walker encourages.

My stomach tightens before I decide to just go for it. "I wanted to know if you'd be willing to buzz my hair for me. It's been falling out slowly—I thought maybe the cool-capping was helping delay the inevitable, and I suppose it was for a while—but this morning my pillowcase was nearly covered in hair and I've come to the decision that I just want it to be over and done with. I know this may be a lot to ask of you as my new friends, hell, I wouldn't blame you if you think this is awkward as fu—"

I'm cut off from my rambling when the group of women closes in on me in a group hug.

I stiffen in shock, momentarily stunned by their kindness, before I absorb their embrace and allow myself to let go of the lid I was doing my best to keep on my emotions.

"We may be newfound friends, but we love the hell out of you, Tae," Scarlett tells me, wrapping me in another warm hug when the rest of the group takes a step back.

"Thank you," I manage to get out through the emotion clogging my throat.

We all grab something to eat and make small talk about our initial thoughts on our book of the month. Once we've all finished, we file into my bathroom that Jax and I now share while Walker grabs a hair trimmer from somewhere on his side of the vanity.

My hands shake uncontrollably as I lower myself onto the bench in front of the wood-framed mirror.

This moment feels monumental but not at all as scary as it could be, and that's entirely due to these women surrounding me. The way they've all shown up for not only me, but Jackson too, is something I'll be eternally grateful for.

Clearing the emotion swelling my throat, I ask, "I'm not sure if this is weird of me to ask, but could we maybe take a picture of the group of us before my hair is cut?"

"For sure! Here," Walker says as she props her phone up on the counter and the girls start to huddle in.

With the timer set, Walker rushes to join the girls, who now have me wrapped in their arms. I smile and look up at the phone with bleary eyes as the numbers count down until it captures a snapshot of a group of women holding me up when I feel anything but steady.

After the picture is done, they hold me in a group hug before pulling away one by one until only Walker remains glued to my side. "Are you ready?" she asks, and I nod my head.

The buzzing of the clippers fills the space and echoes off the tiled walls. Walker's eyes meet mine in the reflection of the mirror, and when I give her another nod of encouragement, she closes her eyes briefly and takes a deep breath before opening them again. A single tear escapes and trails down her cheek as she lines the clippers up at the front of my part and then slowly drags them down my part to the back of my head.

I close my eyes as silent tears pour out of me.

"I'll go next," Kenna says and then I feel her step up beside me. She places a hand on my shoulder as she works the buzzer over my scalp.

My shoulders shake from the quiet sobs as Dakota switches places with Kenna and whispers, "We've got you."

When I open my eyes again, I look down to find locks of my raven hair strewn on the floor. The sight merges with the one from this morning and I can't find it in me to meet my reflection in the mirror. Not yet.

Bringing my foot up on the bench, I wrap my arms around my knee and hug it to my chest.

Scarlett steps up and grabs the clippers from Dakota. She gives my shoulder a squeeze and tells me, "You're beautiful inside and out, Taevin. Don't ever forget that."

After she's done, she hands the clippers off to Alexa, who reaches her hand out and clasps it in mine. "I'm so happy fate brought you and Jax back together. And I'm thankful you came into my life. You've got this, Tae."

Once she turns the clippers off, I bring my shaky hand to my head and am met with a faintly fuzzy scalp. Running my fingers over the buzzed strands feels foreign, and when I lift my eyes to the mirror, I don't recognize the reflection staring back at me.

The girl in the mirror looks terrified of the battle ahead of her. But when I see the group of women surrounding her, I know she won't be fighting alone.

Their presence blankets my fear in peace and security.

What would I have done if I had to do this alone? If Bennett hadn't hired me to perform at their wedding and I hadn't run into Jackson again at that exact time? A vision of me alone in my Nashville penthouse as I woke up this morning to find a pillowcase full of my hair makes my chest cave in.

I can't fathom having to go through this alone. And thankfully Jax made sure I wouldn't have to.

"You're going to be okay," Walker whispers, wrapping me in her arms just as the security system beeps notifying us that the front door has opened.

We walk out to the main living area to find Jackson, Bennett, Carson, and Griffin in their Wolverines knit stocking hats taking off their shoes and hanging up their coats.

When Jackson's eyes fall on me, he halts as he takes in the stark change. After a moment's pause, he closes the distance between us and pulls me into his chest.

"I love you so fucking much, T," he rasps and then places a kiss on my temple.

"I love you too," I reply just as he takes a small step back.

My lips turn down in a frown until I realize he's pulled away to take off his hat. I'm stunned silent and my stomach swarms with butterflies at the sight before me.

"Jax," I finally gasp, stepping forward and dragging my fingers across his freshly buzzed hair. "How did you—"

Before I can finish my question, he cuts in. "Walker texted me. I'm glad they were here with you, but me and the guys wanted you to know we're also here for you." Just then, Bennett, Carson and Griffin take off their hats and I see their haircuts match mine.

I bring my hand to cover my mouth as I shake my head in disbelief.

"Jax! You guys didn't have to do this."

"We know. But we wanted to show you you'll never be alone in this fight," Jax explains, tugging me against his chest again.

Moments later, the guys surround the two of us as they wrap us into a group hug.

"You've got this, Tae," Carson murmurs as he squeezes both mine and Jax's shoulders.

I've never felt more supported, and though I first wondered if I would be alone in this fight, I'm happy to say I've now got my answer. These friends I've gained through Jax have become a second family I never knew I needed.

"I really hate to break up this moment, but um, Jax, I think Tae's last birthday surprise is needing to be revealed, if you know what I mean

. . ." Walker says, wringing her hands from where she's sitting at the kitchen island.

"Shit, you're right. I'll be right back," he replies, placing a quick kiss on my forehead then turning to get his boots on and heading outside.

I hardly have time to guess what he's got up his sleeve before he's walking back inside a few minutes later with what looks like a freaking puppy in his arms.

"Is that what I think it is?" I ask, closing the distance between us.

Jax is beaming with joy. "Meet our son, Connor the Corgi."

My eyes widen and my jaw drops. "Shut. Up."

"Happy birthday, baby." Jax pulls me into his side and I melt against him as I shower the cutest dog I've ever laid eyes on with kisses.

"Welcome home, sweet boy," I coo, praying like hell that one day in the future we'll be saying the same thing to a baby or child.

34

Taevin

Then

Life hasn't slowed down for me for a moment since I moved to Nashville nearly six weeks ago.

Kyle wasn't kidding when he said the label he was in talks with was highly interested in me. The first day I flew out here, I met with them and they signed me on the spot. I had told Kyle I wanted to think about it and look things over with my dad, but he insisted it was one of the best deals he'd ever seen for a debut artist and I shouldn't risk insulting the label executives who were willing to take a risk on me.

Between the writing and recording sessions, as well as small gigs Kyle's booked for me around different bars in Nashville, I haven't had much time to think, let alone wallow in self-pity for what I've done.

I walked out on Jackson six weeks ago—on the vows I'd promised him—and yet he's still made every attempt to contact me daily throughout that time. His calls, texts, FaceTime requests, voicemails, DMs, and even emails have all gone unanswered, and yet he remains persistent.

My phone rings again, and my stomach sinks just like it does every time it rings lately. Flipping my phone over, I peek through one squinted eye, scared that if I see his name on my screen again, I just might crack this time and answer.

Instead, Ryan's name and picture are splayed across the screen. Swiping, I accept her call.

"Ry! I miss you," I greet her, emotion coating my throat.

"Taev! Thank god you answered. I feel like it's been forever since we've talked."

I chuckle at that. "We just talked last night, you needy brat."

"Exactly! Wayyyyy too long. I miss hanging out with you everyday."

"Me too," I choke out as tears sting my eyes, threatening to spill down my cheeks. Because, god, do I miss her.

"Want to have a FaceTime movie date tonight? We could do a *Twilight* marathon."

"I don't know, Ry. I'm not really in the mood. I think I'm over-working myself because I'm not feeling the best. I'm exhausted, and if anything else I'm nauseous."

Ryan cackles on the other end of the phone. "God, you're not pregnant are you?"

I hesitate for a moment, just long enough for Ryan to pick up on the fact that I'm not laughing along with her.

"Tae? I didn't hear you tell me there's no chance in hell, so I've got to ask . . . is there any way you could be pregnant?"

"No. No, of course not. I haven't been with anyone else."

"Yeah, I kind of figured considering you're still married and all that. But, I mean, when was your last period?"

Yeah, so I spilled the beans and told Ryan that Jax and I got married. Let's just say she was shellshocked for all of a minute before she accepted it far too quickly than I would've if the roles were reversed.

"I don't know. The end of August I think?"

"You think. Hmm, well do you track it on an app or anything?"

"Here, let me check. I think I texted Jackson asking him to get me tampons. I'll just search my messages for that."

Time seems to move at a snail's pace as I wait for the search in my texts to load.

"Shit! No, that can't be right. I had to have had it since then. There's no way."

"What? When was it?" Panic matching my own laces Ryan's tone.

My stomach sinks and my world comes to a halt as I stare down at the screen. "According to this, my last period was at the beginning of July."

"Holy shit!"

"Stop it, you're not helping!" I shout at her.

"Taevin, that was like almost three months ago! You've missed three periods and you didn't notice?" Ry's on the edge of hysteria at this point.

"I've been avoiding dealing with a broken heart and more than a little busy trying to record my first album," I grumble, pleading my defense.

"You've got to take a test. Do you want me to fly down there?"

If I were able to laugh right now, I'd snort at her absurdity. Instead, tears well in my eyes from her sincere friendship that hasn't dwindled at all since we've become long distance. It has me wondering what other relationships I could've held onto.

Clearing past the emotion swelling my throat, I respond, "No. I can take one. I'm supposed to be flying to Boston to hang out with you next weekend anyways. I'll just wait to see if I get my period before then, and if I don't, we can get one while I'm there."

There's a pause on the other end of the line. "Taev, I don't think it's a good idea to wait. I mean, shouldn't you be seeing a doctor soon?"

"I'm sure I'll be fine to wait a few more days to find out. Besides, I'm probably just so stressed with the move and recording and the breakup that my cycle has been affected. I'll get it any day now, I'm sure of it."

Though even as I say it, doubt weighs heavily in my mind when I think of all the times Jax and I had unprotected sex since we decided to forgo wearing condoms after the Fourth of July weekend.

Dear god, please please please let me get my period.

I did not get my period.

Shocking, I know.

Especially considering the five positive pregnancy tests littering the floor surrounding Ryan and I in her dorm suite's bathroom. Thank god it's private. I can't even imagine taking one of these in the communal bathrooms down the hall.

The reality of my current situation is so far outside the realm of things I drew up in my mind when I allowed myself to fantasize about all the things I'd do in Boston.

Instead of walking down the cobblestone streets of Beacon Hill hand-in-hand with Jax as the fall leaves littered the streets and gaslit lamps dimly illuminated our path, I'm hyperventilating on tiled flooring, praying with everything in me that I haven't just ruined everything.

Thoughts of all the ways this pregnancy could destroy not only my future, but Jax's as well have nausea churning deep in my stomach.

Ryan rubs my back, quelling some of my anxiety. "Are you gonna tell him?" Her voice is unsure like she debated whether or not to ask me.

With trembling hands, I pick up one of the pieces of plastic that has forever altered the trajectory of my life. As much as I'd love to desperately cling to the carefree and in love version of myself I was only a few months ago, I can no longer do that. My life is not solely my own anymore, and in turn, Jackson's is also about to change. I realize that, I really do, but it doesn't mean I'm not terrified of what his father will do in retaliation once he hears about what I've done.

"I have to." Swallowing past the tears, anxiety, and fear clogging my throat, I shift to face her. "Regardless of where the two of us stand right now, he deserves to know we're going to have a baby."

"Don't you think he deserves to know about his father blackmailing you into breaking his heart too?"

Yeah, so there wasn't a way for me to hide the real reason for my abrupt change in my future from Ryan. She knows me far too well and saw how broken I was after leaving Jax for her to believe the story that I chose a possible record deal over him. Ry didn't even have to press much before the truth came spilling out about Jax's dad and his blackmail disguised as an ultimatum.

I shake my head. "No, he can't."

Ryan grabs my one hand in hers. "Taev, come on, be sensible about this. He's your husband and about to be the father of your child, he needs to know what his father is capable of. There's no way Jax will let you walk out of his life while carrying his baby."

"I should probably, like, confirm I'm really pregnant first before I blow up our whole lives for nothing," I tell her, grabbing my phone off the bathroom vanity.

She snorts out a scoff. "I mean, I doubt you're unlucky enough to receive five faulty pregnancy tests that all happen to be a false positive. But I know there's a Planned Parenthood a few blocks down. We can go together if you want and see if they'll do a pregnancy test at the clinic."

"Do they do walk-ins like that?"

Ryan shrugs. "Not sure, but we can go see." She stands up and offers me her hands. "Come on, let's go before they close."

After we grab our jackets and make our way out of her dormitory, we walk hand in hand toward the clinic. As we walk down the street, I can't help but fall in love with October in Boston. The weather hasn't turned yet in Nashville, we're still having seventy-degree days without the need for a sweater. The brisk breeze is one I welcome as I hug my jacket around me a little tighter.

I can tell Ryan's been silently mulling over something since we left her dorm, so I finally prompt, "Out with it."

She rolls her lips together in hesitation. "I wasn't going to suggest this because I didn't want you to feel ambushed but Harvard has their first exhibition game tonight." Chancing a glance at me, she looks sheepish. "It's actually one of the reasons I suggested you come this weekend. They play at home versus Emery University."

I look down at my feet as we wait at a crosswalk. "I'm not sure he'd want me there, Ry."

"I'm pretty sure if the number of missed calls from him and unreturned texts is anything to go off of, he'd definitely want you there." Ryan pulls me in, wrapping her arm around my shoulder. "Just think about it, okay? I may or may not have got us two tickets in case you wanted to go . . . so we're covered on that front."

She doesn't even flinch as I bat at her arm.

Shaking my head, I breathe in a deep sigh. "After I get through this appointment I'll contemplate whether or not I want to face him tonight. It's only Friday. I've got until Sunday evening before my flight back to Nashville."

With one quick nod, she drops the subject and instead grips my hand in hers, squeezing it to let me know she's here for me. And I lean into her strength and support, praying I can channel some of it to get me through this.

The sound of a whirring heartbeat echoing off the walls only hours ago is now replaced by the chants and cheers of the Harvard student section as I watch the love of my life skate to center ice to start the game.

Across the faceoff circle from Jackson is a player with a familiar last name splayed across his shoulders.

TURNER.

Griffin plays for Emery University, and though I watched him a few times on the ice this summer playing in pickup games against Jax and Carson, I hardly recognized him when he skated by our seats earlier during warmups. He looked so broken.

His little sister Katie was killed last month in a drunk driving accident that almost claimed Kenna's life too.

I wasn't able to make it back for the funeral because Kyle scheduled my first gig in Nashville.

But I should've gone. I should've turned down the gig. It would've been the right thing to do, especially considering how emotional I was.

Even though I didn't know Katie for that long, it didn't matter. She accepted me as a part of their friend group without question and with open arms. She was kind, caring, smart, beautiful, funny as hell, and *young* with a full life ahead of her that was stolen in the blink of an eye.

Tears well in my eyes as regret churns in my stomach.

I should've been there. For Kenna. For Griffin. For Carson. But most importantly, for Jax.

Jackson reaches his gloved hand across the red line to give Griffin knucks but Griff just shakes his head once and crouches down to get ready to take the faceoff. Jax's shoulders fall in defeat before he mirrors Griff's position.

The puck is dropped and Griffin wins the faceoff back to one of his defensemen.

From what Jax told me this summer, Harvard's team is young with mostly freshmen and sophomores making up the roster aside from their junior goalie, Enzo Calvetti.

Just as I think of the name, it's announced over the roar of the crowd as Calvetti makes a glove save off of an Emery winger's shot on goal.

"Not today, asshole!" Ryan shouts, causing a few Harvard fans around us to cheer and high five her.

Shaking my head, I bring my gloved hand to cover my laugh.

I have the best friend in the world.

She knows just how to ease my mind and quell my anxious thoughts that were riddling me only moments ago.

I decide right here and now to make a vow to myself. For the next few hours, I won't think about all of the ways my life is about to irrevocably change in the coming months. Instead, I'm going to watch the man I married live out his dream of playing college hockey for the next three periods before I turn his world upside down.

I'm going to pretend his dad didn't blackmail me into breaking both of our hearts, that I didn't accept a record deal that thwarted our plans for college together in Boston. Instead, I'll imagine I did move into my dorm at Berklee and I'm here supporting Jackson.

One truth still remains: I'm still his, and no matter what happens, I always will be.

The game is closer than I thought it'd be considering I overheard a few guys in front of us talking about how much older Emery's team was than ours and that they had planned to leave after the first or second period because they were sure it'd be a blow out.

Instead, Harvard managed to hold them to a tie with only a goal apiece.

Apparently there are a few parties where it's likely players from both teams will be in attendance considering how close the universities are in proximity to each other.

Ryan does some digging on social media and finds a party where some of the Harvard players are going.

Feeling unsure of myself, I wring my hands together as we walk into the foyer of a Harvard frat house. The loud music makes it hard to hear anything Ryan is trying to tell me, so she leans in and yells, "Give me your hand so we don't lose track of each other!"

I place my hand in hers as she works her way through the crowded entryway and living room areas toward the large kitchen at the back of the house. An oversized island is littered with liquor bottles and mixers that I gloss over without a thought as I search for Jax in the sea of people.

A guy with jet black hair that looks as if he's just showered reaches across me for a bottle of Diet Coke to mix into his cup.

"Pardon my reach," he murmurs, giving us an easygoing grin.

He looks vaguely familiar, though I can't place where I've seen him.

The guy catches me staring when he turns to face me and he must misinterpret my puzzled look for intrigue because he says, "Were you ladies at the game tonight?"

Ryan answers, "We were."

"Yeah? Nice. Who were you cheering for, Harvard or Emery?"

"Harvard. My girl here is actually hoping to find Jackson Wilson. Do you happen to know if he's at this party?" Ryan asks, looping her arm through mine and blinking innocently at the guy.

"Wilson? What is a gorgeous girl like yourself doing wasting your time with a rookie?" he asks, raising my hackles. *Who is this guy?*

"She's his girlfriend," Ryan tells him, thankfully not telling him that I'm his wife.

"Ah, so you're the girl who broke the rookie's heart." He pauses to look me up and down while taking a sip of his drink. "You know what, I think I just might know where Wilson is. Come with me," he suggests.

"Who are you?" I question, finally finding my voice.

"Enzo Calvetti. And from what I hear, you're Taevin Gray." Enzo holds his hand out and I hesitate for a moment before shaking it.

"Nice to meet you. You had a good game tonight."

He clenches his jaw before mustering a curt, "Thanks."

I nod. "So . . . Jax?"

"Right. Follow me." Enzo nods behind him and we follow him toward the back of the house into a large den that has five couches surrounding a pool table. There looks to be about a dozen guys all with Harvard hockey sweatshirts or stocking hats on. They're either sitting together on the couches or playing pool.

Off in the corner there's also a group of girls talking to a few guys.

"Oh shit," Enzo murmurs at the same time my eyes land on my husband for the first time in over six weeks.

As if in slow motion, I watch as a girl sits down on his lap, wraps her arms around his neck, and leans in for a kiss.

My heart sinks to my stomach and my mouth becomes watery from the nausea threatening to take over. I cover my mouth and run from the room in search of the nearest bathroom.

Ryan hooks her arm around my elbow and guides me to a sliding door that brings us out to the side of the house. I'm throwing up into the bushes before I've even taken three steps.

"Motherfucker!" Ryan seethes while simultaneously holding my hair and rubbing soothing circles on my back.

Pain ricochets from my chest to my stomach but the pain in my abdomen is different from the heartbreak I'm experiencing.

A stabbing pain has nausea rolling through me again and sweat dotting my brow.

"Something's wrong," I gasp through the heaves wracking my body.

"Unfortunately I think he's just an asshole," Ryan counters, misunderstanding what I'm trying to tell her.

"No—" I breathe. "Something is wrong." Just as the words leave my lips, my pants soak with a gush of liquid.

I bring my hand between my legs and even in the dim lighting from the nearby outdoor light I can make out the blood covering the pads of my fingers.

In disbelief, I frantically swipe my other hand through my legs and it comes up covered.

Blood. There's so much blood. It's soaked through my pants. I fall to the ground and drop my head into my hands as sobs wrack my body with an unyielding force as the likely reality of my situation hits me.

"Oh my gosh! Tae, we need to go to the hospital. That's a lot of blood."

"I can't, Ry. Not yet. He doesn't know. Jackson doesn't even know."

I can hardly breathe as tears stream down my cheeks. Ryan uses all of her strength to get me to my feet before guiding me toward the street where an Uber is waiting.

"Please take us to the nearest hospital!" she shouts to the driver.

"Are you Angela? It says you're going to Shake Shack—" he starts, but Ryan cuts him off.

"I'll give you a hundred bucks cash if you just bring us to a fucking hospital!"

"This better not mess up my driver's score," he mumbles as he puts the car in drive.

It's been two days since I heard my baby's heartbeat for the first and last time.

Cervical incompetence. That's what caused me to miscarry the baby I only got to know about for a matter of hours.

How can God be so cruel?

Why should I even believe He's real when so much has been stolen from me?

My mother. My marriage. My baby.

"Do you want a cup of tea?" my dad asks, startling me from my thoughts.

I pull the sleeves of my sweater over my hands and ball them into fists. "No thank you."

"Taev—" he starts but hesitates, rubbing the back of his head. "I know I'm probably the last person you want to talk about this with considering everything you've just gone through, but are you sure this is what you want?"

Tears well in my eyes for what has to be the hundredth time today, and I sniffle before nodding my head. "I'm sure, Dad. I need to move on from this."

He sighs. "I understand that, honey. But don't you think you should try to talk to Jackson before you blindside him like this?"

My bone-deep agony is temporarily replaced by anger as I stare at my dad. "Are you seriously trying to defend him right now? I just miscarried our baby after watching my husband kiss another woman."

My dad crosses his arms and looks down at the floor, unwilling to meet my eyes that I'm sure are full of fury. How can he defend someone he hardly even liked? Especially after I unexpectedly came home this morning and told him that not only had I eloped behind his back, but I also managed to get myself pregnant at eighteen.

"I'm not defending or excusing his actions, Taevin. I'm simply trying to do my job as your father and make sure you've fully thought this through. I don't want you to make a rash decision when you're hurt and angry. You exchanged vows. Filing for an annulment would mean on paper that your marriage never happened."

"That's exactly what I want. Besides, Jackson broke those vows."

"Didn't you break them first when you left?" he counters, and my stomach sinks. But there's no sense in telling my dad the reason for my leaving now. Not when Senator Wilson went so far as threatening my father's position at the church too.

Regardless of who broke whose heart first, this is what is for the best.

"I want an annulment, Dad. And I came here to ask for your help. If you can't do that, then I'll do it on my own from my apartment in Nashville," I snap back at him.

My dad puts his hands up in surrender. "Alright. If you're sure, I'll help you. Just give me a day to have the paperwork drawn up. Then you can sign it before you fly back to Nashville and the lawyer will send it to him."

"Thank you," I murmur just as my phone rings.

Kyle's name flashes across the screen and before I answer, I look up at my dad. "I've got to take this, I'll be right back," I tell him before walking up the stairs to my room and answering the call.

"Hey Kyle," I greet.

"Taevin! There you are, I've tried calling for hours now. How are you doing?"

"I'm okay. I just got settled at my dad's house in Minnesota. I'll probably be here for another day or two before I fly back to Nashville."

"But you've got the studio booked for a recording session tomorrow afternoon."

"I won't be there, Kyle," I tell him, barely restrained frustration lacing my tone.

"You can't throw away your entire future because of a bad breakup, Taevin."

As much as I want to snap at him for assuming he knows what happened or what's best for me after only knowing me for two months, I swallow down my angry retort and take a deep breath.

"It wasn't just a bad breakup. I, um, I actually was pregnant."

"Pregnant?!" he echoes back in disbelief.

"Yeah, and I unfortunately miscarried when I was visiting my friend in Boston. That's why I'm home."

"Are you—" he starts but huffs out a breath. "Do you need—" he cuts himself off again, sighing. "What can I do?"

"Nothing. There's nothing you can do. I just needed to be home for a few days."

Kyle clears his throat. "I understand. And I'm sorry to hear about your miscarriage."

"Um, thanks," I mumble, swallowing past the swell of emotion.

There's a long pause on the other end of the line before Kyle lets out a heavy sigh. "Maybe it wasn't meant to be, Taevin. Maybe this was God's way of telling you you're truly not meant to be with Jackson."

I rear my head back. "How could that be? The only real reason we're not together right now is because his father is terrible. I'm fairly certain he's the devil disguised as a senator."

"Isn't that the case with most politicians?"

His blasé tone grinds on my last thread of patience. Did he just really imply that my miscarriage was God's attempt to break Jax and I up for good?

When I don't respond after nearly a minute, Kyle apologizes. "Look, I'm sorry. That didn't come out right. What I should've suggested was that you should take a few days and then when you're ready, come back to Nashville and pour your heart into new music. Maybe then something good can come from this."

I couldn't possibly write about my miscarriage.

Instead of telling Kyle that, I decide to end this phone call as quickly as possible before I say something that will likely ruin the only thing I have going for me right now.

"Yeah, maybe," I placate him with a lie. "I'm going to try to take a nap. It's been a long few days and I'm still in quite a bit of pain."

"Of course. I'll let you go so you can rest up."

After mustering a quick goodbye, I hang up and toss my phone onto my bed before crawling under the covers and wishing there was something that could ease this pain and the heartbreak threatening to consume me.

I'd do anything to numb the ache so I never have to feel this way again.

35

Taevin

Now

The fire crackles and I watch with fascination as the embers dance in the air before turning to ash. Curling my legs beneath me, I burrow my body further into Jackson's side.

This last round of chemo hit me the hardest of any of them. The combination of the nausea, weakness, and exhaustion have me feeling like I'm withering away to nothing.

A chill seeps beneath the fuzzy blanket Jax draped over me when he put another log on the fire.

"You still cold, baby?" he asks, covering my one frigid hand with his warm one.

"Yeah, I can't seem to get warm no matter how many layers I put on and no matter how many fuzzy blankets and fires you make me."

"Would some hot cocoa help?"

A soft smile curves the corners of my mouth. "I'm pretty sure hot cocoa cures everything."

"Well, in that case, hold tight," he tells me, lifting off the couch. I pout at the loss of his warmth and bring the blanket up to my chin and do my best to fend off the chills that have replaced his body warmth.

From his spot in front of the fireplace, Connor's head shoots up and he tilts it to the side in the most adorable way.

"It's okay, boy. Daddy's just getting Mommy some hot chocolate. I'm sorry, but you can't have any."

Connor takes that as his cue to go in search of Jax, and I laugh as he waddles into the kitchen.

A few minutes later, Jackson walks back into the living room with two steaming mugs and a puppy trailing behind him with a brand new toy in his mouth. I shoot a look at Jax, and he just shrugs with a bright smile on his face because we both know he can't help himself when it comes to spoiling our little guy.

Once he hands me one of the mugs, I nearly moan from how good the warm ceramic feels against my freezing fingers. After I'm situated back under Jax's arm, I bring the mug up to my face and breathe in the mixture of chocolate, cinnamon, and cream.

"You make the best hot chocolate," I declare, sighing in contentment.

"Facts," he agrees with a chuckle.

We sit there in comfortable silence as we watch the flames dance, only the sounds of the crackling fire filling the room until I sit forward to set my mug down on the coffee table and shift my frail body so my head is in his lap. I love laying like this with him so I can gaze into his gorgeous sea glass eyes. I get lost in them for a few moments before mine begin to water and I whisper, "How will you remember me?"

Jax's head rears back at my question. "What do you mean? I'm not going to have to remember you, Tae. You're here"—he places his one hand over his heart and cups my face with his other—"you're *right here.* And you're always going to be here."

Emotion swells behind my eyelids as I close them in an attempt to hide how little faith I have in what he's just said. Because what if I'm not? What if I don't get to grow old with him? What if I don't get to see if our two embryos will become our beautiful babies? What if his arms wrapped around me aren't the first thing I feel in the morning and the last before I fall asleep?

Since my last treatment, I'm the most physically drained I've been since my diagnosis. No amount of rest could prepare me for the toll the chemo would take on my body. The exhaustion paralyzes me, chaining me to my bed for most of the day.

Shaking my head, tears stream down my cheeks as I open them and admit, "I don't think I've got this. I'm so scared of leaving you, J, but my body is failing me—failing *us*. My cancer is the biggest thief of all because I think it's going to steal a life with you from me."

"It's not—" he starts, but I cut him off.

"Promise me something?"

"I don't like when you do this," he tells me, wiping at my tears with his thumb so lovingly it causes the tears to fall faster as his own eyes water.

"Promise me you'll remember me carefree and wild. Promise me you won't remember me like this"—a choked sob escapes my lips—"never like this."

Jax looks at me with a mix of devotion and desperation as tears trail down his cheeks. "I'll remember you with rain-soaked hair as we ran wild and free through the field behind my house. I'll remember you with sun-kissed skin and ice cream in hand on the day you married me. I'll remember you in neon lights and beneath a blanket of stars. I'll remember you on the ice singing and watching me play. I'll remember you on stage at your first solo sold-out show. I'll remember every damn moment spent with you, and I'll do it with you beside me because there's not a chance in hell I'm letting you leave me again, Taevin. I refuse to sit here and think about what our life could've been when you'll be beside me as we discover all of what our love could be—what it *will* be."

Tears spill more rapidly down my cheeks now, blurring my vision so I can barely see his face breaking.

"I think it's time you promise me something," he rasps, tears spilling down his face.

"Anything," I whisper between hiccups.

"Promise me eternity together. Because when you go, I go, baby. Whether it's here or heaven, I'll never not be by your side."

I shake my head furiously. "Don't you dare say that."

"Then don't you dare talk about leaving me." His voice is shaky but stern.

My chin quivers with a mixture of frustration and fear. "If cancer takes me, you can't let it take you too. Please don't say things like that. I promise I'll never willingly leave you, so long as you promise to keep living for the both of us if I can't be here with you."

I try to turn in his arms to give him a hug but a sharp, stabbing pain has me grabbing my stomach and curling in on myself. "Ouch!"

"T! What's wrong?" Jax questions, looking me over frantically.

Breathing through the pain, I grit out, "I'm not sure. I had a sharp pain in my stomach, but it's dulling a bit now."

Jax lifts me in his arms. "Let's go to the bedroom and lie down."

Out of the corner of my eye I catch sight of softly glowing lights just outside the front windows.

"What's that?" I ask.

"We can go look later if you're feeling better or tomorrow morning," he tells me, starting for our bedroom.

"The pain is already feeling better. It's done that a few times today and each time my stomach has felt better a few minutes later." I wiggle in his arms so he'll put me down. "Come show me."

Grabbing his hand in mine, I lead us to the front door where we put on our shoes and coats before going outside.

"Jax! What's all this?" I ask, my gasp causing a cloud of cold to expel in front of me.

"You always said you wanted the house to look like a tree farm at Christmas. I know it's only the second week of November, but you mentioned the other day that you like to at least put up the tree before Thanksgiving so you can admire the lights longer. So I had the guys help set these up while we were inside. I bought more so we can have one in every room like you've always wanted. Though we don't have enough decorations for them all. I thought I'd leave that up to you."

I shake my head in disbelief. "You remembered."

"Of course I did."

Of course he did. I'm not sure why I'm even surprised at this point. He's told me countless times he remembers everything, and this is the perfect example.

"J! I love them. I can't tell you how excited I am to spend our first Christmas together." Glancing over my shoulder, I watch as his face lights up with a detonating grin that I'm sure matches mine.

"I'm happy you're happy, baby."

With my arms thrown out to the side, I spin in a slow circle until I'm facing him. "Maybe we'll make a theme for each room. Wouldn't that be fun?"

"I love that idea." He moves to stand in front of me, grabbing my hands in his. "Are you cold? Want to go inside?" Bringing my hands to his mouth, he breathes warm air onto them.

"I want to admire them for a few more minutes," I tell him, looking around in wonderment.

"In that case, I've got something else for you," he starts, dropping to his knee in front of me.

Reaching into his jacket pocket, he reveals a black velvet box. "I believe this belongs to you, my love." When he cracks it open, my wedding ring from when I was eighteen is revealed, nestled between the cushions of the fabric.

"I honestly don't know why it took me this long to take this out of the safe. It belongs on your finger, always has. And even if you're not ready for all that it stands for, I'd love it if you'd still consider wearing it."

My breath comes out stuttered as I struggle to breathe through the tears of joy clogging my throat. "I want everything it stands for, Jackson. Will you put it on me, please?"

He does as I ask, and when he slides the ring into place, nothing has ever felt so right.

"Now that I have it back, I'm never taking it off."

"Swear on it," he says, bringing my hand to his lips and placing a kiss over my ring.

"I swear," I whisper.

Jax stands to his full height, lifting me up and spinning me around. The first snow fall of the season blankets our shoulders in thick flakes, and it feels like we're on the set of a Christmas movie.

"Oh my goodness!" I squeal, holding my hand out in an attempt to catch one of the cottony flakes.

Out of the corner of my eye, I catch sight of three SUVs turning into our long driveway. As they approach, Jax sets me back on my feet and curses. "Shit, I completely forgot. I can tell them to leave."

My brows knit in confusion. "Who? What's going on?"

Jax tugs at my knit hat covering my head and then pulls me against his chest, attempting to wrap me in his warmth. With my face pressed against his chest, he explains, "This is our only weekend off before Thanksgiving so the group decided to bring Friendsgiving to us in case you weren't feeling up to leaving the house. But I can tell them we just want a quiet night in. I know you're exhausted, and if I'm being honest, I don't want to share you with anyone."

I run my hand along his chest, loving the way my ring looks back on my finger. "I'm not sure how much energy I have to host, but it would be nice to see everyone."

"Are you sure?" he asks, his voice laced with worry. "You were just telling me how exhausted you were. And your stomach."

"Yeah, I'm sure. I have no clue what we're going to eat though. Maybe we can order some pizzas?"

Jax pulls me impossibly closer against his warm chest when I let out another shiver. "The ladies have been cooking all afternoon while the guys came over to set up the trees. Let's get you inside by the fire and then I'll help them carry everything in."

Once I'm settled into my favorite chair by the fire with my reheated cup of hot cocoa, Jax helps everyone inside. I feel bad that I'm not feeling up to greeting everyone the way I'd like, but after they hang up their jackets and take off their shoes, they make their way toward me and I don't even try to bite back my tired smile.

"Hey, girlie! How are you feeling?" Kenna asks, bending down to give me a hug.

"At the moment? Cold. But also extremely grateful for you all coming over here and preparing everything," I tell her.

Scarlett steps up next and bends to embrace me. "It's our pleasure. We're just glad you're able to be here and that we found a day that worked for everyone's schedules."

With that, Walker comes bouncing over with a reserved Gemma by her side. Her shyness is something Scar and Bennett told me is really only around me. Jax has said she's a little firecracker around everyone else, so I've made it my mission to get her to loosen up around me.

"Hey, sis. I can't wait to spend the night with you while the boys are away next week," Walker says, sitting on the arm of my chair and squeezing me to her chest.

"I'm looking forward to one of your breakfast smoothies. I've tried and failed multiple times attempting to recreate the one you made me last week," I admit, wincing when I think of how badly the last one turned out.

The door opens again, and when I look to see who else is joining us, I'm surprised as hell to see Enzo Calvetti in our home. I mean, Jackson told me that the two of them hashed out their differences about a week ago after they lost one of their games, but I didn't think their reconciliation meant he'd be joining us for Friendsgiving.

When I feel Walker stiffen beside me, I look up at her and see I'm not the only one shocked to see Calvetti.

"What's he doing here?" she whisper-hisses.

I shrug my shoulders. "I'm just as surprised as you are."

"I highly doubt that," she mutters.

Biting the inside of my cheek so I don't laugh, I murmur, "I guess he and Jax must've kissed and made up."

Enzo looks over the room and when his gaze lands on Walker, he puts his hands in his pockets and lifts his chin at her.

"Oh, fuck no! Is he for real?" Walker stands abruptly and storms into the kitchen.

While I'm not entirely up to speed on what's happening there, I do know the two of them were both on *Ballroom Battles*, the competition show Walker was a professional dancer for this spring and Enzo was her celebrity partner. They made it to the finals and were the runner-ups, but there was heavy speculation that the two were doing the tango on and offstage, if you know what I mean.

At one of our sleepovers while the guys were on the road, I asked Walker about it, and she brushed it off, saying her agent told her to lean into the speculation for more votes. What she didn't realize is the two of them sold it maybe a little too well . . . So much so that her brothers were apparently ready to hop on a plane to LA to confront Enzo about his ten-year age gap with their "baby sister."

Whatever did or didn't happen is none of my business unless Walker wants to confide in me, and I've reminded her that I'm here for her if and when she needs me. Last week she mentioned she's been seeing someone new, so I guess we shall see.

I'm pulled from my thoughts when Gemma shyly waves at me.

"Hey, Gems! It's so good to see you."

"Hey, Taevin. You too!"

Jax mentioned Bennett has been giving Gemma guitar lessons for the past year and that she was a talented songwriter, though she kept it under wraps. I don't want to overstep, but I think she'd get a kick out of seeing the home studio Jax built for me so I wave her closer and murmur, "I hear you like to play the piano and guitar. Can I show you something?"

Her cheeks heat but she nods her head in reply. I lift from my chair, albeit slow as hell, and hold my hand out for her.

She helps me down the stairs into the basement, and when I turn the lights on in the music studio, Gemma lets out a gasp that makes me internally squeal in delight.

I trudge along, showing her around the space and pointing out different equipment, loving the opportunity to take her under my wing, even if only for a moment. I'm suddenly the most creatively energized I've been in months, and I'd love nothing more than to hole up in the studio with her for hours.

"If you have some time during your winter break next month, we could record something if you're up for it."

"Oh my gosh, are you serious?!" Gemma squeals. I don't even try to stop the smile that mirrors hers.

"Absolutely," I assure her.

"I'd seriously love that," she replies, and I clap in excitement at the prospect of working with her.

Once we get back upstairs, it's as if the main level has been transformed. A second table has appeared out of nowhere and is set with dinnerware matching our dining room set. The entire kitchen island is overflowing with food and appetizers, complete with a turkey cooked to perfection in the center.

I gasp. "You guys, this is amazing!"

Jax rounds the table he was setting and pulls me into his arms. "Scar had the idea to host a Friendsgiving last season and we decided to make it a tradition."

Scar chimes in, "This year we wanted to bring it to you so you didn't have to worry about traveling. This way, if you get tired you can lay down in your own bed."

"You're so sweet. Thank you for including me." I can't help but look around the kitchen and living room, taking in all of our friends—and Enzo Calvetti—together under our roof.

The doorbell rings again, and Gunner shouts, "Can I get it, Cap?"

"Sure, Champ," Bennett replies, shifting to see who's at the door.

In walks Alexa with two huge men I'm not sure I've met yet.

Jax guides me toward them and introduces us. "Hey guys. I'm pretty sure she needs no introduction, but this is my wife, Taevin Gray. Taevin, this is Nathan Connelly, he's the major pain in my ass I've told you about," Jax says, gesturing to the younger one, who mouths *fuck you* to him before holding his hand out for me to shake.

I do, and Nathan says, "Pleasure to meet you. I'm, unfortunately, one of your husband's teammates. And, let's be honest, if anyone's a pain in the other's ass, it's definitely you."

"Aw, thanks for talking me up in front of my girl, Nathaniel." Jax flutters his eyelashes like he's flattered before a mask of indifference takes over. "Now take it back or you're on dish duty."

Connelly shakes his head. "Sorry, Jaxy."

The two do some weird bro-slap-hug thing before Nathan saunters off to stand beside Gemma at the fireplace. Even from here I can see her cheeks heat the moment she sees him.

Interesting.

Turning my attention back to the entryway, I watch as Jax gives Alexa a hug before he slaps the other guy on the shoulder and then, wearing one of the biggest smiles I think I've ever seen on him, he introduces us. "Tae, *this* is Brody Meyer. He's the—"

He's cut off when Alexa chides in a mocking tone, "*The quarterback of the Voyagers, one of the greatest of all time.* Yeah, yeah, we all know." She rolls her eyes before a salacious smile slowly spreads across her face. "I'm pretty sure you've seen him referenced as Dakota's douche canoe big brother in our group chat."

I snap my fingers together, playing along. "Ah, that's where I know him from. He's Mr. Too Cool for Interviews, right?"

Brody barks out a husky chuckle, causing the smile lines around his mouth and eyes to wrinkle in a way I'm not sure has ever been so wildly attractive. He looks like Scott Eastwood, ruggedly handsome and a little dangerous. All of that paired with his six-and-a-half-feet frame is definitely the reason why Alexa is doing a horrible job of hiding the eye-fucking she's giving him right now.

When he meets her eyes, her ogling quickly turns into a scowl.

Oh, the tension! I'm sensing an enemies-to-lovers plot, and I'm here for it.

"It's a pleasure to meet you, Miss Gray. Or should I say Mrs. Wilson?" Brody asks.

The question causes me to laugh because up until now, even all those years ago when we were first married, we never discussed whether or not I'd change my last name.

And while I've built my career being Taevin Gray, I can't imagine starting a family with Jackson and not sharing a last name.

Jax cuts in, moving to wrap me in his arms once more. "We'll have to wait and see."

A snort comes from the front door, followed by a voice I know all too well. "Jackson Gray. That'd be a great stripper name."

My heart nearly explodes out of my chest when I catch a glimpse of Ryan's pink hair as she walks through the front door and shuts it behind her.

I fly out of Jax's arms and into hers. "What are you doing here?" I ask, unable to believe she's really here.

"Heard there was going to be a house full of hot athletes," Ryan says as if her reasoning weren't obvious.

"Mostly married," Jax admonishes.

"I'm kidding, hockey boy. I'm actually here because your monthly bag of dicks should be arriving today, according to my confirmation email."

"Oh my god, his *what*? Please don't tell me I heard you wrong," Alexa squeals, overjoyed by this new development.

"You heard me right," Ryan assures, winking at Alexa once I've stepped out of her arms.

Keeping a hold on my shoulders, Ryan openly looks me over, detailing all of the ways I've changed since she last saw me. I can't imagine what she must be thinking. "In all seriousness, your hubby flew me out here so I could go to your next chemo session with you since he'll be on the road."

My eyes water from his thoughtful gesture, and without my permission those pesky songbirds take flight once again. Before I even realize what I'm doing, I'm moving back across the entryway into his arms. Right where I belong.

As I look around the space, a sense of ease I haven't felt in far too long sinks in. This feels right. Being here, in our home, surrounded by our friends who have become our chosen family is everything I never knew I needed.

36

Taevin

Now

I've never had to battle stage fright, it's just not something I've ever had to deal with. Being on stage has always felt like a second home to me, a place that fills my cup and soothes my soul.

Tonight that feeling of nostalgia has been robbed from me.

Nothing feels right.

Every little thing down to the last detail feels off.

For starters, I shouldn't even be performing in front of a live audience while secretly battling cancer and going through chemotherapy.

Then there's the fact that I'm wearing a wig that is supposed to be an exact replica of my pre-cancer hairstyle, long, inky black waves that come down to just above my waist.

But that wig won't grow back my eyebrows. My makeup artist, Elsie, had to draw them back in, and while it might not be obvious to others, I can't stop staring at the difference. Nor will it magically make my once-long eyelashes suddenly reappear. I've never had to wear fake eyelashes, but with the sparse amount I have left, Elsie suggested I add that to my makeup routine for tonight's performance so I'll look somewhat like my normal self. Well, she didn't say that, Elsie would never, but I sure as hell don't look like myself.

Throughout treatments, I've not only lost nearly every hair on my body and scalp, but I've also lost nearly twenty pounds I didn't have to lose in the first place. I'm a shell of the woman I once was.

And what Kyle doesn't understand, what he refused to listen to me on, was that this performance won't curb the media's interest, it'll only fuel their assumptions that I was in a rehab facility.

I look like I'm clearly unwell. But it's not like the media will assume it's because I have cancer. No, they're going to spin every headline to make it look like I'm an addict spiraling out of control.

And even though I know the truth, as do the people closest to me, it's the young girls and women who look up to me that I'm most upset about. The news stories ultimately don't affect me, but the way I'm perceived by those little girls who idolize me, girls like Cadence and Gemma, yeah, that's the shitty part that keeps me up at night.

I stand from the chair in my dressing room and bend over the vanity table to take a closer look in the mirror. Adjusting my wig ever so slightly, I sigh in defeat at the reflection staring back at me before grabbing my signature deep berry lipstain and coating my lips with it.

My armor for the night.

If I try to look like my old self, maybe I'll start feeling some semblance of the woman I once was before cancer robbed nearly everything from her.

There's a quick knock before my dressing room door opens and Kyle steps inside with a far too enthusiastic smile on his face.

"There's my superstar! God, I think this is the longest we've gone without seeing each other since we first met."

That is oddly surprising, even though it shouldn't be. I guess I hadn't realized how deeply he'd been ingrained in my life. The past several months of distance between the two of us has been good for me. I haven't been constantly badgered for more songs or berated for what

I chose to wear. In short, I guess I hadn't realized how badly things had spiraled between us until I got away from Kyle on a daily basis.

"Sure, come right in I guess," I murmur under my breath, unfortunately not quiet enough for Kyle not to overhear.

"Oh, come on. It's not like I haven't pretty much seen it all over the years."

Well, that's . . . unsettling. *No*, he hasn't pretty much seen it all. At least, not that I can recall.

The unsettled feeling mixes with the already churning doubt I've been feeling about Kyle more and more as of late.

Now that we've had time apart, the small things I used to think he did to be protective or were just part of him "doing his job," I'm seeing them through a different lens. Instead of looking out for me, I'm pretty sure he was just trying to control my every move. They say hindsight is 20/20, and things are definitely coming into focus that were a blur early on in my career.

My first record deal, for one—the label had full creative control over my first three albums, and I was expected to produce and release them at an unreasonable speed. Especially considering the fact that I was touring for eleven months at a time with only two months off between, in which time I was expected to be writing, recording, and performing smaller gigs.

And behind the scenes, Kyle was my puppeteer pulling the strings and stretching me in all directions. I was a candle burning at both ends until this diagnosis forced me to slow down.

Now that I have, everything I thought about my career and aspirations has changed.

I've decided that if and when I win this fight, I'm going to live my life differently. My priorities have shifted, and I want nothing more than to soak in my time on this earth with those I love most.

Jackson. Ryan. My father, who I've thankfully reconnected with. My newfound friends. And hopefully one day, a family of our own.

"Well, I would appreciate it if you knocked moving forward," I inform Kyle, my tone firm as I narrow my gaze on him to make sure what I've said sinks in.

Apparently I hit my mark because Kyle's hands shoot up in surrender. "Knock. Got it."

He moves across the small space until he's standing beside me. "Can I have a hug, or is that too much to ask for?"

I roll my eyes at the condescending edge to his question, and cross my arms in silent reply.

"What's gotten into you, Taevin? I'm worried about you," Kyle says, now sounding genuinely concerned.

"Oh, really? That's rich. You're all of a sudden worried about me? Yet, when I was recovering from a major surgery and then had several chemotherapy sessions, where were you? Where was your concern then? And now, here I am having to perform for a live audience while still receiving treatment after you forced my hand."

I'm so pissed at him right now my body quakes with anger and I have to ball my hands into fists to keep him from noticing.

He rears back as if he's been slapped. Good. I'm glad to see that what I've said has affected him. I hope he realizes what he's done by forcing me to be here.

"Taevin, you should know this decision was out of my hands. As for giving you space while you had surgery and began treatments, I thought that was what you wanted. You ran off to Minnesota with your *estranged husband*, dismissing both Braidy and myself. Excuse me for misunderstanding what it is you wanted from me."

I scoff and shake my head. "Is that your backwards way of apologizing?"

"Did it sound like an apology?" he retorts in a harsh tone he's never used toward me.

"No, it didn't," I grit out.

"Good, because it wasn't one. Now, I'll leave you to get ready to go on stage. Hopefully everything goes off without a hitch since you missed your sound check earlier. Honestly, Taevin"—he shakes his head—"I'm not sure what's gotten into you but you need to get it together. I shouldn't need to remind you how important tonight's performance is to the label."

Without giving me a chance to rebuttal, he turns and leaves the dressing room.

Uncrossing my arms, I attempt to shake out the anger and nerves. I turn around and place my hands on the edge of the vanity counter. Looking up at my reflection, I take one final deep breath before giving myself a pep talk.

"You can do this. It's one song. Get it together then go out on stage and shine."

With one final check of my wig, I adjust my necklaces and give myself a once over. I'm wearing a black dress with a black, long-sleeve overlay that has rhinestones adorning the mesh fabric. It's not the same dress Jax picked out for the Summer Stampede, since that one was too big on me now, but it's close enough.

Even though he can't be here with me tonight, I wanted to feel him here with me. I'm thankful Walker was able to join me, though I'm regretting sending her to her seats so she could watch the other performers. She would've been the perfect shield from Kyle.

What the hell has gotten into him? I hardly recognize him anymore.

Suddenly, a sharp pain in my stomach has me doubling over to grab the counter.

Shit. Shit. Shit.

What am I going to do if this happens while I'm on stage?

It won't. It's one song. You'll be fine.

I try and fail to quiet the doubts swirling in my mind. Because what if I won't be fine? What if I'm breaking my promise to Jackson?

I'm just so fucking exhausted.

My body already feels like it's gone ten rounds in a boxing ring. Every chemo session has left me so weak and tired, most days it's hard for me to even get out of bed and move after.

I can feel my fight dwindling, though I would never dare admit that out loud.

A pounding on my dressing room door echoes off the walls and then a stagehand shouts, "You're on in ten."

That leaves me just enough time to get my in-ear monitors set and find Sterling. As much as I'd love to play my guitar myself tonight for my acoustic version of "Amazing Grace," I just don't have it in me.

Gripping the counter with all the strength I can muster, I breathe through the pain as I walk out the door that leads me toward the stage.

Just as I've finished placing my in-ear monitors, I'm announced by the host.

"And now, Nashville, help me in welcoming one of my favorite artists onstage—Taevin Gray!"

Cheers erupt, but just as I make my way onto the stage, I look back to see if Sterling is beside me and find he's still backstage. When I give him a *what the hell are you doing* look, he just shakes his head and points behind me.

I turn slowly, and then from the opposite corner of the stage, Jackson emerges from the shadows. My heart hiccups in my chest at the sight of him in his white T-shirt and denim pants that mold to his thick thighs.

How is he here?

"Jax!" I rush out once he's finally close enough, falling into his outstretched arms and then soaking in the warmth of his body against mine. When I step back, I stare up into his eyes. "What are you doing here? I thought you had a team dinner tonight."

"I did. But when I mentioned to Scar that you were performing for the first time since before your surgery, she not only insisted I come to perform with you, she purchased the last suite available for the team and any of the moms who made the trip to join her and Bennett. Gemma is up there freaking out as we speak."

"You should've told me. I would've let her join me on stage!"

Jax shakes his head but grins nonetheless. "There's no way she would've if you had. She has extreme stage fright."

"I did for the first time tonight too, until I saw you. Wait—did you say Scar insisted you perform *with* me?"

He shoots me a wink and that's when I see the leather strap across his chest and his trusty old acoustic guitar I've always loved. "Apparently Walker has been conspiring with Sterling. He sent me the song you're performing, and Walker somehow snuck my guitar case into her luggage."

"What?" I squeal in disbelief, unable to believe he's really here, about to perform with me.

Onstage . . . oh, shit! We're on stage!

My eyes widen and Jax grabs my hand after reading my expression, leading me to the two stools with mic stands set up in front of them.

The crowd cheers as we make our way to the front of the stage. Once we're seated, a single spotlight illuminates us in the otherwise moody lighting.

Jax leans over and murmurs into my ear, "This is incredible."

As I look out into the crowd of thousands of country music fans, a sense of home washes over me. Licking my lips, I adjust the microphone and take a deep breath.

"Good evening, Nashville," I greet the crowd, my voice still a bit unsteady at first. "I'm so happy to be back here performing in my favorite city."

Looking out over the crowd, I take a moment to soak it all in. Just when I think I'm done scanning the crowd, my focus is stolen by a little girl propped on her dad's shoulders holding a sign that reads "I'VE MISSED YOU, TAEVIN! WELCOME HOME."

Welcome home. The phrase squeezes my heart. Four months ago, Nashville was unquestionably my home. Now, however, that isn't true. Because as I look beside me and find Jackson perched on a stool with his guitar slung across his lap, I see not only my future, but my home.

Warmth floods my chest as my throat tightens with emotion. I take a deep breath before uttering words I had no intention of saying tonight. "There's a sign that says you've missed me, and I've missed you too. I know there has been a lot of speculation about where I've been the past several months. The unfortunate truth is: I have cancer." Shocked gasps ring out through the stadium. I lick my lips and then take a deep breath before continuing. "And while I'm fortunate to receive the best care, I'm only realizing just now that I don't need to battle this in secret anymore." Tears swell in my eyes, causing my vision to blur, but I don't take my gaze off the little girl.

"Tonight is the first time I've shared my diagnosis publically. And I was supposed to play 'Amazing Grace,' but what would y'all say if instead I play a new original I've been working on that's been near and dear to my heart these past several months?"

The crowd erupts with cheers of encouragement.

"Alright, this one's still a work in progress, but it's called 'Revival,' and it's about my journey back to my favorite person who just so happens to be sitting beside me tonight, my husband, Jackson Wilson!"

When I look over at Jax, he's beaming with pride and has the biggest grin I've ever seen. Thankfully, this isn't the first time he's heard this song. After Friendsgiving, I felt inspired to produce a melody to accompany the lyrics I'd been working on. Jax had been in the home studio with me for hours before he had to leave for his away trip.

I give him a sheepish shrug to which he smiles even brighter in reply.

He strums the opening chords and I begin singing the opening lyrics.

"Black and blue, I'm counting bruises. How much more can I stand to lose? Tired eyes and heart of doubting that I will make it through. Here we are now, secrets unveiling. Stitching up the broken parts, every whisper calms my cold heart. Will this be a new start? "

When the chorus hits, Jax harmonizes with me and I sing with a smile on my face, not taking my gaze off his.

"When I'm breaking, hurting, time unfolding, you make me feel brand new. You're my revival through pain and trial, built me a new cathedral wall. I might be fragile, but you have a soft soul, baby, I only sing for you. 'Cause you're my revival."

Jax surprises me by adding a new riff between the chorus and second verse, and I sing solo with a smile on my face.

"Every storm, nights are heavy. Scars remind me where I've been. In your arms, I feel steady. I found my strength again. When the silence lingers, you lace our fingers, reminding me of what's true."

And when it comes time for the bridge, we both stand from our stools and sing into one microphone while staring into each other's eyes. Longing, love, and adoration fuel me to get through the remainder of the song as we sing in perfect harmony.

"You're my revival, my place of survival. Your arms are the home I never lost. I might be fragile, but you make me feel whole again. Make me sing again, my muse. You're my revival. Yeah, you're my revival."

The crowd erupts in cheers so loud I can't make out what Jax is saying until he slings the guitar behind him and pulls my back to his chest, wrapping me in his arms. He leans down and murmurs into my ear, "You're incredible! I'm so fucking proud of you."

I'm buzzing from the adrenaline high performing with him has given me. I grab hold of the microphone stand in both hands and with my voice shaky from sheer exhaustion, I thank the crowd. "Thank you so much for having us tonight, Nashville! I've missed y'all so much!"

Jackson keeps an arm slung over shoulder as we make our way off the stage. I lean into him and don't even try to hide the way I'm breathing him in.

God, he's everything.

Once we're in my dressing room, I use all of the energy I have left to throw myself into his arms.

"Jax—thank you! You were amazing out there."

He rubs his hands up and down my back, making me burrow further into his embrace. "Literally anytime, baby. Just say the word and I'm there."

I pull back just enough so I can look up at him. "I didn't even have to tonight—you just knew I needed you."

The bashful smile he sends my way is my favorite. He clears his throat. "That was my favorite performance of yours you've ever done, and not just because I was on stage to join you."

"Mine too. But it's definitely because you were with me. I couldn't have done it without you."

"You could've."

"I never want to have to," I whisper my admission. And it's true. Performing without him beside me might never be possible again now that I know how magical it feels with him next to me.

Jackson

I'm just about to pull my wife in for a kiss when the dressing room door flies open.

My shoulders tense as I spin my head around only to come face to face with Kyle Blackwood. And instead of the ease I should feel around Tae's manager, I'm even more on guard.

"Do you always barge in without warning?" I practically snarl the question.

Kyle's face scrunches up in disgust. "Didn't realize you were in here."

I don't even try to hide my disdain for him or my hands that are fisted at my sides now. "Thank your lucky stars I am. Because if Taevin were to be in here alone, and, I don't know, changing, you wouldn't be walking out of here."

"Is that a threat?" Kyle laughs, shutting the door behind him. My hackles rise when I see the look on his face.

"Kyle? What are you doing?" Taevin asks, but he ignores her.

Staring solely at me, his gaze narrows. "You shouldn't threaten me."

I scoff, crossing my arms at my chest. "And why's that?"

His eyes drop to where my biceps are threatening to break free from my T-shirt.

He lets out another laugh. "All those years ago, you just let her walk out of your life without putting up any kind of fight." He raises his arm to gesture at Taevin without so much as looking at her once again. I don't dare take my eyes off of him though.

Shaking his head, he continues. "See, that's the problem with rich boys like you who grew up with a silver spoon in your mouth; you don't appreciate a rare thing when it's right in front of you. Taevin has the kind talent that only comes around once in a generation. No one in the music industry is as talented as her or as gifted lyrically when it comes to songwriting. I knew it the moment I saw the videos of her performing. Thanks for that, by the way, I hear if it weren't for you, she wouldn't have gotten on that stage at the fair all those summers ago."

I feel as though I'll be sick knowing I'm the reason he's been put in her life.

Kyle begins pacing the small space, making him look truly unhinged. "What I didn't realize at the time was that she was married to you. And when I learned she was pregnant with your—" He pauses to shake his head and let out a scoff before continuing. "Thankfully fate intervened and took care of the little bastard so I didn't have to." He lets out a chuckle that causes the hairs on the back of my neck to rise.

Motherfucker.

I want nothing more than to punch that look right off his face.

"I had to play my hand right—bide my time and become ingrained in her life. But in the end it didn't matter, she came running to you anyway. Ten years!" he shouts, pointing to Taevin and finally turning his focus on her. "Ten fucking years of putting up with your shit day in and day out. Of quietly cleaning up your messes and dealing with the heartache he left you with. And what did I get in return for loving you so selflessly for over a decade? Betrayal. Deceit. Cheating, lying, and scheming all so you could take one look at *him* and fall right back into his bed."

Wanting to fuck with him and honestly so over his monologue, *because what the fuck is happening right now?* I interrupt. "Poetic isn't it? Our love story is one for the ages."

"It's fucking pathetic is what it is. And I won't stand for it." In a turn I didn't see coming, Kyle lunges for me.

"What are you doing, Kyle? Stop! Someone help!" Taevin screams.

Before I can do a thing, the dressing room door flies open and in a blur, Braidy has Kyle tackled to the ground.

I pull Taevin into my arms, and do my best to shield her from any potential fall out from their wrestling match. Thankfully, Braidy manages to restrain Kyle just as two security guards rush into the hallway.

As they take Kyle away, I lower us down onto the dressing room couch and pull a crying Tae into my lap. Rubbing my hand up and down her back, I try to console her as sobs continue to wrack her body.

I'm not sure how much time passes before there's a soft knock on the door and Bennett calls out, "J, are you and Taevin in there?"

"Yeah, come in," I answer, breathing out a sigh of relief to have him here.

Bennett opens the door and both he and Scarlett step in. "You good? We saw security handing over Kyle to the police."

I stand with an unsteady Taevin, bracing my hand on her waist to keep her from toppling over.

Clutching her stomach, she staggers as she tries to keep her balance.

"T, baby, what's happening? Are you okay?"

She looks lightheaded, I think just before she falls forward into my arms. As I hold her, she squints her eyes and writhes in pain.

Before she can form any sort of answer, her eyes fall shut and her body goes limp in my arms.

420

37

Jackson

Now

I'm living in the horror story version of Groundhog Day.

Instead of reliving the exact same day over and over again, I keep living in a moment where my beautiful wife is lying in a hospital bed as I sit beside her devastatingly helpless.

After Taevin collapsed in my arms, I screamed for Bennett to call 9-1-1.

We got her in an ambulance that sped us to the nearest hospital where they told me she had an ovarian torsion that required emergency surgery.

They just came out to the waiting room to tell me Taevin is now alert but refusing to undergo surgery until she can speak to me.

I'm brought back to her small triage room where a nurse stands beside her entering Tae's vitals into the computer.

"There she is," I say, mustering all the bravery I can. The sight of her body being swallowed up in yet another hospital bed, only this time a shell of what it once was, is heartbreaking.

I go to her bedside and take her hand in mine. Looking up at me with watery eyes, she whispers, "I'm not sure how much longer I can do this, J. My body has failed me so many times, and it's doing it again. If I don't make it through surgery—"

A choked sob escapes me and I cut her off. "No, don't say that, baby. You and I both know you're the strongest person to ever exist. So please don't talk like that; I won't hear it."

She shakes her head as tears stream down her face. "You've given me so much to fight for. I love you for that and so much more."

I take a moment to take her in. She looks so tired—beyond exhausted. It's killing me to see the defeat in her eyes. Leaning down, I grasp her face in my hands and bring my forehead to hers.

Closing my eyes, I plead with her. "Not like this, Tae."

A soft whimper leaves her lips. "Okay," she murmurs, pulling her head back just slightly to look into my eyes. She brings a hand to my face and wipes my tears. I bring my lips to hers in the gentlest kiss I've ever given her. It's my plea for her to keep fighting, to make it through surgery and back into my arms.

We break away when a nurse comes back into the room and informs us it's time for them to take her into surgery.

Before she leaves the room, Tae takes a deep breath and sets her shoulders. With a look of determination she squeezes my hand and says, "I'll see you soon."

High heels click against the linoleum floor before the sound halts just outside the hospital's surgical waiting room. There's murmured conversation, but I don't pick up on any of it. I can't focus my energy on anything other than willing Taevin to make it out of surgery.

She's got to be okay.

Raking my hands through my hair for the dozenth time, I perch my elbows on my knees and hang my head in my hands.

A large hand comes to rest on my shoulder, the warmth seeping through my shirt and quelling some of the anxiety churning in my stomach.

"I brought you some toiletries and a change of clothes," Bennett says, setting a duffel bag down in front of me.

"Thanks," I mutter, keeping my gaze fixed on the ground. If I look at my big brother right now, I know I'll lose it.

And I can't do that.

I need to be strong for her.

There was a time I wasn't there for her—when I wasn't her calm in the storm—but it'll be a cold day in hell before that happens again.

I know I haven't been the most devout Christian my entire life, but I have an insane urge to drop to my knees and beg God to keep her safe.

To let her stay to fight another day.

To let me keep her.

I'm willing to be selfish right now because I fucking need her, plain and simple. Without Taevin, well, I can't even fathom it.

I'd be lost without her.

Looking up at the ceiling, I blink to keep the tears welling in my eyes from falling.

Bennett takes a seat beside me and wraps his arm around my shoulders, embracing me in a way that makes the dam of my emotions break. "Have faith she's going to be okay, Jax. You've got to keep your head up—stay positive," he encourages, but it's not what I want to hear right now because he can't promise that anymore than I can.

I shake my head, lowering my gaze on my hands. "Every setback she's had, every hurdle she's had to overcome has tested my faith to the point of depletion. Hard to have faith when I'm not sure I've got any left."

Scarlett walks over and takes the seat on my other side, grabbing one of my hands in hers. "Taevin has been nothing but valiant in this battle.

Even if you've lost your faith in everything else, don't lose it in her. She's a fighter." Scar squeezes my hand in hers. "And so are you."

I lift my gaze to Scarlett and her eyes search mine. For what, I'm not sure. But as a sense of determination washes over me, she gives me a reassuring nod.

Bennett pulls me against him. "We're here for you, Jackson. Here for Taevin. And we're not going anywhere."

Taking a deep breath, I let his words sink in, and as they do, my shoulders ease as some of the anxiety and fear bleed off me.

I'm not sure how long we sit like that, with my brother holding me steady as his wife tries to distract me by showing me pictures of my niece and nephew, but eventually I succumb to impatience.

Clenching my jaw, I grit out, "What the hell is taking so long?"

My heel anxiously taps on the cold hospital floor as I watch the hands on the clock move in what seems like slow motion. The doc estimated one to two hours for the procedure and in just two more ticks of the big hand on that damn clock, it will have been three. I run a hand through my hair and let out a long huff of air, casting my eyes to the ceiling.

The double doors that lead back to the OR swing open and I snap my gaze down at the sound to see Taevin's surgeon emerging. My stomach churns and I fight back the nausea as he finishes toweling off his hands and speaks to a nurse in hushed tones. The second his eyes meet mine, my head drops into my hands.

Breaking News

Taevin Gray's shocking onstage confession

Here's what we know so far about Taevin Gray's cancer diagnosis.

By LARA BRADLEY

Taevin Gray, 29, took to the stage last night for the Country Gives Back Concert in Nashville. She was set to perform "Amazing Grace" but instead debuted an original called "Revival."

Before she sang her new song with her husband Jackson Wilson, she shocked fans when she revealed she's been quietly battling uterine cancer for several months.

The beloved country music star was then taken by ambulance to a hospital in Nashville where she underwent surgery only hours after performing. It is unclear at this time what the surgery was for, though it is being reported that the surgery was emergent.

Details of her prognosis and current status are still unknown at this time.

Country Know Now has reached out to Gray's reps for comment, but have not yet heard back.

To stay up to date on all the latest country celebrity news, subscribe below.

38

Taevin

Now

"**G**ood morning, Taevin." Dr. Prescott smiles at me from the door of my treatment room before turning to Jackson and Ryan on either side of me and greeting them as well.

"How have you been feeling?" Dr. Prescott asks.

"I've been feeling much better each day since the surgery in Nashville. I'm hoping that if I get nausea from this round of chemo, it'll be milder than the last one though; that was a rough few days."

She nods in understanding before looking down at the tablet in her hands. "Well, I not only wanted to come by to check on how you were feeling, but I'm happy to inform you that today will be your last chemotherapy session. After today's treatment, you'll get to ring the bell."

Jackson's hand reaches for mine at the same as a gasp leaves Ryan.

To say I'm shocked by her words is an understatement. "Wait, what?"

With a soft smile, she explains, "After reviewing your labs from your visit last week, as well as your bloodwork from this morning, we're confident that you won't be needing additional treatment at this time. We'll get the rest of the results back from your scans in about a week, and we will discuss the next steps of your care plan once those results are in. Do you have any questions for me?"

I'm somewhat stunned at this turn of events, so much that it takes me a moment to process my thoughts. "Yes." I hesitate, wondering if she's going to think I'm a weirdo for asking her this, but ultimately decide to say fuck it and just go for it. "Can I hug you?" I ask, standing from my treatment chair, wobbling slightly until Jackson shoots to his feet and rights me.

After giving Dr. Prescott the biggest hug I can muster, Jax helps me back into my chair. For the remainder of my treatment, we play Cribbage and Sequence, two games that have quickly become my favorite ways to pass time during chemo.

And once my final treatment is complete, Jax and Ryan help me stand and walk me out into the hallway where nurses and doctors have crowded around the renowned bell.

"I'm so glad I'm here to witness this," Jax tells me, a contagious smile lighting up his face as he guides me toward it.

"Me too!" Ryan agrees, clapping in excitement.

I turn to give her a hug, and while we're still embracing, I murmur, "I'm so happy you were able to fly in for this, Ry. I can't believe we get to spend Christmas together."

"And another two weeks after that," she adds.

I smile at her. "I can't even remember the last time we had two whole weeks together. After my surgery doesn't count because I was barely a functioning human being."

She rubs my back and gives me a big squeeze. "Well, if it weren't for your hockey boy, I wouldn't have been able to convince my asshole boss to let me off. But as soon as the almighty winger from the Minnesota Wolverines called in a favor and gifted him tickets on the glass to their upcoming game in Boston, my work responsibilities were suddenly delegated to other team members and my time off was approved."

I turn to look at a sheepish Jackson. "I didn't know you did that."

"It's not a big deal—" he starts, but I cut him off.

"You're right. It's a huge deal. You knew that it'd mean everything to me to have Ry here, and you made it happen. Thank you so much."

"And the best husband of the year award goes to—" Ryan does a drumroll against her thighs. "Mr. Hockey Boy himself, Jackson Wilson!"

"I don't know if I like the sound of that."

"Why? I think it's a cute nickname."

"I was referring to my last name. Maybe I'll take a page out of Bennett's book and take your last name."

My eyes widen. "Are you serious? I love your name."

Jax takes my hand in his and brings it to his lips, placing a kiss on the back of it before running his thumb over my wedding ring. "Yeah, but you've built your entire career around yours. We're a family, we should have the same last name."

"If you're serious, why don't we just hyphenate our last names? We could do Wilson-Gray," I suggest, still unable to detect if he's fucking with me or not.

"How about you ring this bell and then we discuss our last names after we celebrate?" he counters, a soft smile he reserves just for me lighting up his face. My stomach swoops, and I've learned by now that I couldn't stop the songbirds from taking flight even if I tried.

Stepping forward, I don't hesitate at all as I grab the rope hanging from the bell. Pride, relief, and hope combine to spur me on as I ring it with all my might. As chimes echo off the walls of the hallway, I'm unable to keep the tears from streaming down my cheeks. The only sound I hear over the ringing is my husband's cheering.

Looking back over my shoulder, I shoot him a watery smile before turning and crashing into him. With his arms wrapped around me, I feel safe and secure and, above all, optimistic.

Jackson has been my rock through this journey and getting to share this moment together means the world to me. I take his face in my hands and give him a far more chaste kiss than I'd like, hoping that it conveys all of my gratitude and love for what he's done for me.

"Ready to go home, baby?"

I pull back to look into those sea glass eyes that have held me captive since the very beginning. "There's no place I'd rather be."

"Good. I was hoping you'd say that."

I once thought not all stories have their happily ever after, and while there has been beauty in the breakdown, I'm looking forward to what our future holds with Jackson by my side.

Not every love story is eternal but I damn sure pray ours is.

Epilogue

JACKSON

Six Months Later

Two more minutes stand between our team and winning game seven of the Stanley Cup finals.

Two shifts before we find out if we'll hoist the cup over our heads or suffer one of the most devastating losses in sports imaginable.

Sweat drips down my face as I fight to catch my breath on the bench after another strenuous shift.

Playoffs are an entirely different beast in comparison to regular season. It's almost as if we're playing two entirely different games.

The intensity. The physicality. The pressure. The desperation.

Exhaustion beyond what your mind can comprehend while pushing your body to the very brink of deterioration.

The purest form of adrenaline pumps through my blood as I glance up at the jumbotron to see there's just under a minute left.

If we keep our one goal lead for one more minute—

Before I can finish that thought, Coach calls for our line to hit the ice for the defensive zone faceoff. The line before us iced the puck to clear the zone, and now my line—me, Carson, and Griffin—will have to give it our all to be sure we come out on top.

Before I line up at the hashmarks, I look up at the time remaining on the clock: fifty-two seconds.

Tapping Calvetti's goalie pads with my stick, I give him a nod before getting into position.

I'd love nothing more than to kick Boston's asses.

Across from me is Boston's Nicolai Orlov, a former teammate of Griff's from Emery University. He's a tall, burly fucker who happens to be one of the most physical enforcers to play in the NHL over the past decade. *Lucky me.*

The ref blows his whistle and Griff wins the draw back to Bennett who chips the puck just over Boston's defenseman's head. Carson wins the chase to the puck and possesses it through the neutral zone.

I skate like hell to try to keep pace with him so we have a two-on-one rush.

The moment the defenseman pivots toward Carson, I scream for the puck, hoping like hell he hears me over the roar of the crowd.

Carsey sauces the puck across the ice to me, and after two more strides, I shoot the puck low into the empty net.

The goal horn blasts as the arena erupts with cheers from our home crowd.

I look up at the clock.

Forty-one seconds.

We've fucking got this.

There she is.

My beautiful bride.

God, she's everything.

Taevin's waiting to get on the ice with Scarlett, Gemma, McKenna, Cadence, and Dakota. She's got her back turned to me, and I smile when I see she's wearing the custom playoff jacket Scarlett designed for all of the players' significant others.

This year's jackets are all black lettermans with lime green patches sewn onto the sleeves as well as the front. The back of the jackets display the players' last names with the numbers on the sleeves. WILSON-GRAY has never looked better than it does when it's splayed across her back. And you guessed it, number *twelve* is on her sleeve.

My wife is stunning no matter what, but when she's proudly claiming me in front of a stadium of tens of thousands of fans, I can't take my eyes off her. Tae's raven hair has grown several inches in the last few months into what she's deemed a pixie cut? Not sure what the hell that is, but it suits her nonetheless.

This is the first season I've played with her by my side, and I've made it known that she's my lucky charm.

I'd say it's undeniable at this point.

After what feels like an eternity, Taevin turns to face me. When her beautiful brown eyes finally connect with mine, I skate to the zamboni door where our families have gathered.

"There's my Stanley Cup Champ!" Tae says, beaming with pride.

That's right.

Stanley Cup Champ is the second best title I've ever held.

I don't waste a second as I lift her into my arms, step back onto the ice, and spin her around until she's squealing for me to stop. Halting my movements, I smile down at her and she cradles my face in her hands. "You did it, you guys really did it!"

Shooting her one of the cockiest smirks I can muster up, I taunt, "Did you ever have any doubts?"

She shakes her head and rolls her eyes. "Couldn't go two seconds without turning into the cocky boy I met at eighteen."

"Hey, you not only fell in love with that cocky son of a bitch, you married him. So I musta done something right."

"Yeah, yeah. So, are you gonna kiss me or not?" she asks, and before a smile can even pull at her lips, my mouth is on hers.

With adrenaline still pumping through my veins, I remind myself to hold back. We're still in public, after all.

We're interrupted when a camera crew shuffles across the ice toward us with Alexa following closely behind.

"Mind if I get a quick interview, you two?" Alexa asks.

Setting Tae on her feet, I tuck her into my side so she won't slip on the ice.

"We don't mind at all," Tae tells her, stepping out of my hold to give her a quick hug.

Not wanting to chance Tae's terrible balance, I wrap my arm over her shoulders again.

"Alright, Carter, count us down," Alexa tells the cameraman before tapping in an ear piece.

"Three . . . two . . . one . . ."

"Thanks, Dylan. I may be biased, but I'm here with two of my favorite people on the ice tonight, Jackson and Taevin Wilson-Gray." Alexa turns to face the two of us and asks, "Jackson, your team just won the Stanley Cup for the first time in franchise history, what does this moment mean to you?"

"Well, Lex, I'm not sure I have the words right now to properly express what this means to me and my teammates. We had a heartbreaking loss last season in the playoffs, and I think that had us coming into this season with a bit of a chip on our shoulders. We worked together, trained harder, and pushed ourselves to the brink so we could be here to experience this moment."

I look down at Taevin and smile. "This season will always be my favorite for so many reasons. Obviously winning the Cup is something I've dreamed of since I was a little kid, but this season is also the first one with my wife by my side. I've been telling her she's my lucky charm for years, do you think it's time she sides with me?"

Taevin buries her head against my chest until she realizes I'm still wearing my equipment and Alexa laughs before saying, "I'd think you're valid in that statement, all things considered. I noticed your peach suit as you walked into the arena tonight. What inspired the bold fashion choice?" Alexa asks, shooting a wink at Taevin.

I adjust the Stanley Cup Champs hat I'm wearing to try to calm my rising emotions. "My wife. At the beginning of this season, Tae fought like hell to beat cancer. She inspires me everyday far beyond my fashion choices, but June happens to be uterine cancer awareness month and the official color is peach. You might have noticed my teammates wearing peach ribbons on their suit jackets as they walked in today too."

"What does it mean to have your teammates' support through this difficult time for your family?" Alexa turns the microphone back toward me.

Shuffling on my feet, I blow out a deep breath and consider my answer. "My teammates are an extension of my family. I'll never forget the lengths they went to to support my wife and I over the past year. Without the understanding and support from the Wolverines organization, my teammates, and the fans, I'm not sure I'd be on the ice tonight to hoist the cup over my head."

"What a great way to bring awareness to uterine cancer. Taevin, how proud are you of your husband?" Alexa asks, holding the mic out in front of her.

Taevin looks up at me with stars in her eyes. "I've never been more proud to watch someone achieve their dreams. This moment for him is something I've wished and prayed for since I first watched him on the ice at a high school playoff game. His love for the game made me a lifelong fan."

I go behind her and wrap my arms around her shoulders. "Ah, she's being modest. It wasn't my love for the game that made her a fan, it was watching me stretch my hip flexors on the ice in warmups."

Tae's cheeks heat with the most adorable blush, and I don't waste a second giving her a chaste kiss on her cheek.

"One final question. Now that you've won the Stanley Cup, what are your plans this summer?"

I point to Taevin. "I'm planning on being her biggest fan at the two shows she's performing this summer. Other than that, we'll be spending as much of the offseason at the lake."

"Good answer. Thank you both for your time. I'll let you get back to celebrating!" Alexa smiles as she turns to face the camera again. "Alright, Dylan, back to you in the studio."

I lift Taevin into my arms bridal style again and skate us toward where my brother and sister are standing near my mom. I pass by Kenna, Dakota, and Scarlett who are staring at us and smiling like they're starstruck.

"Why are they looking at us like that?"

"Like what?" she asks.

"Like they've got hearts shooting out of their eyes or something."

"Oh—" She chuckles. "Probably because I told them we were considering starting to look into surrogates and adoption."

I look down at her, wearing the dopiest smile. "So does that mean what I think it means?"

She wraps her arms around my neck, running her fingers through the hair fanning out of my hat. "It means that I'm definitely ready to start adding to our family. I know that however and whenever that happens is out of our control, but I want to fill our house with sounds of little feet padding across the floors, fits of laughter, and squeals of joy. I want everything in this life with you, Mr. Wilson-Gray."

I'm about to pull her in for a kiss when something snags my attention from the corner of my eye. A blur of curly, platinum blonde hair whirs by until my baby sister throws herself into the arms of Enzo Calvetti. He spins her around briefly until her lips crash against his.

What. The. Fuck.

Extended Epilogue

TAEVIN

Two Years Later

Salt air floats through the open french doors of our overwater bungalow, accompanied by the calming soundtrack of the ocean lapping against the wooden stilts of our suite.

Smiling to myself, I relax further into the mattress. Two weeks here in Fiji will never be enough, but knowing what's ahead for us, I'm excited to get home. What we had originally planned as the honeymoon we never had, turned into our babymoon when we got the news six months ago that our surrogate was pregnant with not one, but two babies. Both embryos implanted and now, by some miracle, we're going to have twins.

I stretch in bed, noticing how gloriously sore my muscles are after yesterday's snorkeling session and last night's extracurricular activities. Rolling over, I'm surprised to find the other side of the large canopy bed empty.

The early light of dawn peaking through the sheer white curtains billowing in the ocean's morning breeze is the first thing I notice when I sit up. Before I have to go in search of him, my husband opens the bathroom door and steps out in nothing but a plush, white towel wrapped deliciously low around his waist.

"Good morning," I greet him, my voice gravelly with sleep.

Jax smiles, but when I drop the sheet that was covering my breasts, he throws his head back and lets out a deep groan that has heat pooling in my core.

"Come lie down with me, Bear," I say, patting the spot beside me.

He steps forward then hesitates. "Aren't you sore from last night? We got a little . . . carried away."

Oh, we did, and in the best of ways. In fact, I hope like hell he'll be up for a repeat. Last night before dinner, Jax handed me a pair of vibrating panties that he used to tease me with all through dinner, edging me until I was on the brink of tears. When we got back to our bungalow, he fucked me senseless against every surface.

"I'm not sore, and I'd love to get carried away with you again. I actually was thinking maybe we could—" I cut myself off, unsure if I want to go there or not.

"Could what, baby?" he asks, lying on the bed beside me.

I roll over onto my side to face him, propping my head up on my fist to mirror his positioning. "Try something new," I say. Vague, I know.

"What do you have in mind?

Biting my lip, I decide to go for it. "I've always wanted to be . . . double penetrated."

His eyebrows raise to his hairline. "Tae . . . I'm not sorry when I say I'll never share you."

My cheeks heat with embarrassment before I bury my head in the pillow. "Oh my god, that's not what I meant!" I squeal, though it's muffled.

"Okay, what *did* you mean?" he questions, brushing my hair back from my face.

"I-I brought a toy. A dildo. The one you love to have me use when you're on the road. I mean, I know you've used it on me before, it's just—"

"We've never used it together like that," he finishes for me.

I let out a sigh. "Yeah, and I just thought with this being our babymoon and all—"

Jax's chest rumbles with laughter, the sound is one of my favorite things. "Tae, you never need to feel shy or embarrassed to ask me for something you want. I'll always give you anything you desire."

Aiming a shy smile his way, I reach my arm around his neck and pull him in for a kiss. It quickly turns from slow and sensual to hungry and desperate, and in no time he's rolled me on top of him so I'm straddling his now naked waist.

"Ride me, T." He punctuates his request by thrusting his hips up against mine so my pussy glides along his length in the best way.

I *tsk*. "Is that any way to ask your wife?"

"Please, *baby*. Take control. Ride me," he pleads, and I'm nothing if not generous.

Sitting up on my knees, I grab his cock, giving him a firm stroke before lining him up at my entrance and slowly lowering myself. I ease him inside me, inch by inch, and when I'm full in the best way, I begin teasing him, moving my hips in slow, methodical circles instead of riding him the way I know he craves.

Deciding I'll give him a show, I trail my hands up and down my body, starting by combing my fingers through my shoulder-length hair, then gliding them from my collarbones to my chest. I take my time, alternating between tweaking my nipples and cupping my breasts.

"Where's your toy?" Jax asks just as he grips my hips and thrusts up hard.

"I put them in the drawer in the bedside table," I tell him breathlessly.

"*Them?*"

"I couldn't decide which one I wanted to bring, so I brought two and some lube."

He bites down on his bottom lip before a sexy smirk stretches across his face. "Vacay Tae is naughty. I love it."

Lifting myself off him, I crawl over to the bedside table, open the drawer, and debate which one to use: the purple dildo that he's seen before or the new one I ordered before the trip, it's called the rabbit and has a clit and G-spot stimulator. Ultimately, I grab the rabbit and the small bottle of lube and turn to Jax.

Kneeling beside him, I ask, "So how should we do this?"

He chuckles. "It was your fantasy. You tell me. What do you want?"

"I want to use this clit stimulator so . . ."

He quirks his brow before another slow, salacious smirk appears. "Want me to fuck your ass, T?"

I bite the inside of my cheek, feeling coy about admitting it aloud. "Yes," I murmur.

Jax moves from the bed and stands off the side, facing me. "Come here."

Doing as he says, I move until I'm kneeling on the very edge of the bed.

"Turn around and get on your hands and knees. Head down, ass up," he rasps the command.

Setting the lube and toy down, I turn and eagerly comply.

I close my eyes and listen to him open the bottle of lube and squirt it on what I'm assuming is the toy because shortly after I hear the vibration turn on, and then the silicone tip is circling my entrance.

"Look at you, doing exactly as I say," Jax muses. "You look so fucking good on your hands and knees for me, baby."

He pushes the tip of the toy inside me, and the vibration feels so good, but when he gets it fully seated in me and readjusts the clit stimulator so it's in the perfect spot, I nearly jump off the bed from the sensation.

"Does it feel good?"

"Mmm," I moan in response.

"Do you want me to make you feel even better?"

"Yes!"

"Good girl," he hums, the praise sending shivers down my spine.

He keeps the toy in place and I hear the bottle of lube opened and squeezed again.

I look back at Jax as he strokes himself before lining himself up. Hesitating, he looks at me. "You're sure?"

I lick my lips and nod. "Absolutely."

He nods in reply, but adds, "If it's too much, tell me. I-I don't want to hurt you."

I know this is a first for both of us—we've talked about it before—and that little fact only makes me want this more. I want one of his firsts and every single last.

We both take a breath in unison as he nudges his tip against my tight hole, and when he pushes past the barrier, I feel a slight sting of pain.

Gripping the sheets, I breathe deeply and try to relax my muscles, which is harder than I thought it would be considering I'm on the precipice of an orgasm from the toy's stimulation.

"You good?" he asks, halting his movements.

"I'm good. Can you keep moving?"

"Yeah," he answers before pulling his hips back and then slowly thrusting forward another inch. The sting subsides, and instead I feel incredibly . . . full.

"God, your ass is fucking perfect," he groans, gripping my cheeks in his hands. "So tight," he murmurs.

Each time he presses his hips forward, it drives the toy deliciously deeper.

"Oh, fuck. Jax!" I call out, the sensations from the fullness and vibrations combine in the best way, and my blood spikes feverish with white hot pleasure.

"Are you close?" he asks, and when I look back I see he's clenching his teeth, telling me he's on the brink of his climax too.

When he throws his head back in pleasure, the sight drives me wild and arousal like I've never felt rushes through my veins. My pussy clenches the toy as my legs begin to shake and quiver.

"Jackson!" I scream, unable to hold it in as I'm brought to the very pinnacle of rapture. Jackson joins me in ecstasy with his own release, and when I feel him come inside me, bone-deep satisfaction settles throughout my body.

When he pulls out of me and takes the toy out and turns it off, I face plant into the mattress.

"That was . . ." I start, but have a difficult time coming up with words to describe what *that* was.

Jackson lets out a low chuckle. "It was," he agrees. "I'm going to go get you a washcloth."

I lift my shaky hand up before dropping it back on the bedding. "I'll be right here."

Once I'm cleaned up, I move back under the covers because I honestly don't feel like I have full functioning of my legs yet.

My phone rings as an unfamiliar number is displayed across the screen. Knowing we're waiting on several calls, I reach over to pick it up from the bedside table, fumbling the device as I try to answer.

"Hello?"

"Good morning, is this Taevin?"

"This is she. Who am I speaking with?"

"Oh, excellent! Apologies, this is Marsha with the Happy Homes Adoption Agency."

"Of course! I'm sorry, Marsha. My caller ID didn't recognize this number."

I turn the phone on speaker and look over at Jackson, motioning for him to come here.

"No worries, dear. I'm just so excited to let you know that you've been matched!"

My body has contradicting reactions to this news we've been waiting on for well over a year now because what does she mean we've matched?

Looking at Jax, I see he's wearing the same wide-eyed look of shock as I'm sure I am.

I clear my throat. "Really? Oh my goodness, this is wonderful. Do you have any information on the child?"

"Children, actually. They're siblings."

I'm momentarily stunned silent. "Siblings?" I squeak out in question.

"Yes, two boys. They're ten and six years old."

Jax reaches out and clasps our hands together, giving me a squeeze. When I meet his gaze, no words are necessary. I simply nod. We don't know a single thing about these boys; we don't know their faces, their likes, their dislikes, their fears, their dreams. But Jackson's eyes say exactly what my heart is screaming: we've been waiting for this—for them.

We both turn to look back at the phone and together we say, "When can we meet them?"

"Ensnared Hearts"

Lyrics by Alyssa Brigiotta

Pinch me, tell me am I still breathing
I can see, but is it clouded feelings?
Kiss my hand
And I go home
I'll walk blindly to the unknown
Daddy doesn't love a story
Written in the stars
I've got a list of secrets
No one knows are ours
It's a sin, and you're redemption
Strength and beauty tangled tight
Hold me now, pain and protection
Lose myself in seaglass eyes
My heart won't be contained,
I'm yours in every way
Ensnared hearts, you and me
Pull me free, but baby, keep your hold on me
Butterflies, just like a wildfire
In your bench seat, I'm new to this desire
Press me against your reckless ways
I can't breathe knowin' you feel the same
Honey, I'm a pastor's daughter,
Breaking rules tonight

Every first, it feels forbidden,
But I feel so alive
It's a sin, but it feels like heaven,
Strength and beauty holding tight
Love me now, no need for questions,
Lose myself in sea glass eyes
My heart will find its way,
I'm not afraid to stay
Ensnared hearts, you and me
Pull me free, but baby keep your hold on me
Ensnared hearts, you and me
You're the one who sets me free

"Revival"

Lyrics by Alyssa Brigiotta

Black and blue, I'm counting bruises.
How much more can I stand to lose?
Tired eyes, and heart of doubting
That I will make it through
Here we are, now secrets unveiling
Stitching up the broken parts
Every whisper calms my cold heart
Will this be a new start?
When I'm breaking, hurting
Time unfolding
You make me feel brand new
You're my revival
Through pain and trial
Built me a new cathedral wall
I might be fragile
But you have a soft soul
Baby, I only sing for you
'Cause you're my revival
Every storm, nights are heavy
Scars remind me where I've been
In your arms, I feel steady
I found my strength again
When the silence lingers
You lace our fingers

Remind me of what's true
You're my revival
Through pain and trial
Built me a new cathedral wall
I might be fragile
But you have a soft soul
Baby, I only sing for you
'Cause you're my revival
You're my revival,
My place of survival,
Your arms are the home I never lost.
I might be fragile,
But you make me whole again
Make me sing again
My muse,
You're my revival
You're my revival
You're my revival

Also by Grayce Rian

The Off Ice Series
What It Was
(Griffin & McKenna's story)
What It Should Be
(Carson & Dakota's story)
What It Must Be
(Bennett & Scarlett's story)
What It Could Be
(Jackson & Taevin's story)
What It Can't Be
(Enzo & Walker's story)
TBA
(Gemma's story)

Acknowledgements

First and foremost—I'm going to change things up and acknowledge the fact that I almost didn't finish this book. It was the hardest thing I've ever written, and arguably will ever write. But I did the damn thing after months of darkness, publishing this book and bringing it to light is the greatest reward. I couldn't have done it without the hours of voice notes and endless encouragement from Sam, Ginsa, Hannah, and Ciara.

Thank you to you, my dear reader. As an indie author, my dreams wouldn't be a reality without your support!

To my husband and forever best friend: thank you for loving me each and every day. Your unyielding support means the world to me.

To our three children: you have changed me in inexplicable ways, all for the better. I will never be able to express how much and how fiercely I love the three of you.

To my parents and two big sisters: I love you all immensely. Thank you for allowing me space to grow, for your unwavering support, and fostering my creativity growing up!

I have to thank my amazing in-laws. One of the biggest bonuses to marrying my husband was gaining the large, loud, and loving family I married into. Thank you so much for your support and love!

I want to give the biggest thanks to my incredible editor Ciara, aka my most compatible musical bestie. I can't wait to work together on so many projects to come!

To my book designer, Kateryna: wow, your creativity amazes me! You were such a joy to work with and your enthusiasm for this project had me so much more excited. I cannot wait to work on the rest of the covers in this series together!

To Alyssa, the lyricist I commissioned for "Ensnared Hearts" and "Revival": Thank you so much for contributing your creative genius to help bring Taevin's story to life! Working with you was so great and getting to see your creative process was awe-inspiring.

Samantha: Becoming friends with you has been one of the best surprises on this indie journey. Thank you for being a critique partner and for all of our plot brainstorming sessions!

Hannah: You're the best friend I never saw coming! Thank you for being an alpha reader, for sharing your creativity, for your spreadsheet skills, and all your words of wisdom. I cannot wait to hug you again hopefully so soon!

Ginsa: Stop it right now! I cannot wait for what we have in store together. I want to shout it from the rooftops! ILY so big!

Brit: Holy moly! I am so glad to have met you through Hannah. Thank you not only for the amazing content you've created for my socials, but also for the friendship and late night chats! I feel like we could talk for hours on end without running out of things to say!

Sariah & Chels: Thanks for listening to my unhinged plotting session on the way back from Tennessee. That trip was so much fun & I hope we do one again soon! Also… Sariah is to thank for the extended epilogue spicy scene in this book.

Payton: Thank you for being a sensitivity scene reader for me and helping me with some of my content notes!

To my betas Michele, Em & Molly: I couldn't have shaped this book into what it was without your input and feedback! Thank you for your patience with me on this crazy writing experience of mine.

To my ARC & Street Teams: Thank you so much for your never ending support and for your love of my books. Your excitement for my releases, creative edits, and amazing posts fuel me to keep typing and creating!

About the Author

Grayce Rian is a contemporary romance author living in Wisconsin. *What It Could Be* is the fourth interconnected standalone novel in the Off Ice series.

Grayce's stories perfectly combine spice, angst, and sweetness to make readers swoon. When she's not writing about your new, favorite book boyfriend, you can find her with her high school sweetheart, chauffeuring their three kids to every activity imaginable, or with her nose buried in a book.

Grayce fell in love with reading and writing at a young age and pursued the creative outlet as a minor in college. She contributes a lot of her creativity and passion for reading to her mother, and Grayce now shares the same love for fictional escapes with her three children.

www.ingramcontent.com/pod-product-compliance
Lightning Source LLC
Chambersburg PA
CBHW061040310726

48969CB00004B/1029